# HIS MAJESTY'S SHIP

# HIS MAJESTY'S SHIP

BY

ALARIC BOND

Fireship Press
*www.FireshipPress.com*

*Fireship Press*
*www.FireshipPress.com*

ISBN-13:.978-1-61179-283-6 Paperback
ISBN-10:.978-1-61179-284-3   Ebook

Second Edition


BISAC Subject Headings:
FIC014000FICTION / Historical
FIC032000FICTION / War & Military

Cover Art Christine Horner




*Address all correspondence to:*
Fireship Press, LLC
P.O. Box 68412
Tucson, AZ.85737
USA
*Or visit our website at:*
www.FireshipPress.com

2.0

TO TIM

iii

| NAME | PRINCIPLE CHARACTERS |
|------|---------------------|
| HMS *Vigilant* | |
| Shepherd | Captain |
| Dyson | First Lieutenant |
| Rogers | Second Lieutenant |
| Tait | Third Lieutenant |
| Gregory | Fourth Lieutenant |
| Timothy | Fifth Lieutenant |
| Humble | Sailing Master |
| Carling | Captain of Marines |
| Bate | Marine Sergeant |
| Jackson | Marine Corporal |
| Rooke | Master's Mate |
| King, Pite, Hayes, Mintey, Mason, Nash, Davis, Roberts | Midshipmen |
| Bryant | Chaplain |
| Wilson | Surgeon |
| Morrison | Purser |
| Critchley | Master at Arms |
| Johnston | Boatswain |
| Clarke | Boatswain's mate |
| Rooke | Master's mate |

| NAME | PRINCIPLE CHARACTERS |
|---|---|
| Smith | Carpenter |
| Donaldson | Gunner |
| Rollston | Cooper |
| Lindsay | Captain's clerk |
| Skirrow | Loblolly boy |
| Flint, Simpson, Jenkins, O'Connor, Barnard, Lewis, Crehan, Copley, Pamplin, Baldwin, Kelly, Dreaper, Kapitan, George, Robson | Seamen |
| Matthew, Jameson, Jake, Diggins | Boys |
| *Lozere* | |
| Lafluer | *contre-amiral* |
| Duboir | *Captaine de vaisseau* |
| *Savarez* | |
| Rouault | *Captaine de vaisseau* |
| Also | |
| Jake | A retired seaman |
| Mackenzie | Schoolmaster and smuggler |
| Katherine | Shepherd's wife |
| Anna | Shepherd's sister in law |

# PART ONE
## AT ANCHOR

# CHAPTER ONE

"I'll miss you, Rosie."

She stopped folding the clothes and looked at him doubtfully.

"Go on, in a couple of days this ship'll be at sea. You'll have enough to do without thinkin' of me."

"Mebbe you're right." Jenkins sat back against the smooth oak knee that marked the limit of their small space on the crowded deck and fiddled aimlessly with his tobacco box. It was made of tin, with a horse's head embossed on the lid. It was also empty. He'd had the box more than ten years yet had never really looked at the decoration before.

"I could be around when you gets back." The lower gundeck was filled with a constant clatter of conversation, even so, her soft words found their mark.

"You won't know when that'll be."

"I won't, but I could look out."

"You'll be wi' someone else, most like." Strange how he couldn't say, "another man."

"Might be, then again..."

That was one of the things he always forgot about women. Men teased, but with women there was a sexual edge that definitely raised the stakes. He felt a lump growing in his throat. The ship was being cleared of doxies; within half an

1

hour they'd all be single men again. Single men, after six weeks of marriage; the longest time Jenkins had ever been with one woman. *Vigilant* had been in commission for almost as long as they had been at war; he'd grown used to both, and didn't suppose the coming trip would hold any surprises. There had been many other doxies in his past, but none he'd missed, and he had thought it would be exactly the same.with Rosie.

"We had a good time, Clem."

"Didn't get no shore leave."

"Didn't expect none. 'Sides, costs less staying on board."

"No privacy."

She met his eye and smiled. "We done all right."

The voice of Clarke, one of the boatswain's mates, cut through their intimacy. "Come on, come on, you got to be off afore the next bell." He walked through the crowded gundeck, the knotted rope's end of his starter swinging in gentle parody of a censer. Without stopping, the petty officer swooped down on a piece of discarded female underwear and swung it aloft, before it was roughly snatched from him with a squeal and some uncouth laughter. Then his eyes travelled to the quiet couple by the knee and for a moment he almost paused. The coarse smile softened, and, looking away, he moved on with a maturity and understanding that would have surprised many.

"They don't seem a bad bunch," said Rosie.

"No, reckon we're all right. Captain's a seaman, at least."

"Make a difference, does it?"

Jenkins nodded.

"Well, that's me finished." She stood up from her bag, and brushed her hands together, her dark hair hardly touching the low deckhead.

"You're going then?" It was an odd question for a seasoned campaigner to ask and again their eyes met; this time it was the woman who broke the spell.

"I have to, 'less I grows a beard and signs on."

Together they made their way to the entry port and joined the crowd of men and women who waited there. For most of the time they were silent; then, as her turn came, he suddenly spoke out.

"I don't know how to find you, I mean, where you live, an' all."

Without speaking she pressed a small bone brooch into his hand.

"Ask at The Crown, see Mrs Powell, she'll know where I'm about." Then she kissed him once, and was gone.

The noise of the ship slowly broke into his thoughts, and he was roughly pushed aside by a couple of drunken women who shouted and stank with equal force. Turning away he looked briefly at the brooch before placing it in his tobacco box and making his way back to the area of deck that had been their home. Rightly his quarters were further forward, but that space had been taken by others, and the small patch of gundeck next to the knee had accommodated them well enough. With the ship working up he'd have to return to his proper berth, and Jenkins slowly began to gather his few possessions together.

"She gone, then?"

He looked up at Clarke, the boatswain's mate, searching his face for some glimpse of humour, and finding none.

"Aye, she's gone," he said.

"Never mind, there'll be others."

Turning, Clarke caught the spectacular rump of a large woman with his starter. The sound of the laughter passed over Jenkins.

"Aye, maybe there will," he said.

*****

The sun was low in the sky, and the spring afternoon air had cooled considerably. Shutters were starting to appear over the

Portsmouth shops, and a raw breeze sliced through the narrow streets and alleyways. The elderly master's mate was on his way to a warm fire, and he stopped reluctantly when a boy approached him.

"Which ship are you looking for?" he asked, the impatience evident in his voice.

"A f-frigate," the lad stammered slightly and appeared awkward. He added a mumbled "sir" as an afterthought.

The warrant officer considered the boy, or perhaps youth was a better description. Slightly below average height, although still with a bit of growing to do, and dark, serious eyes. The man put him at fourteen; clean, reasonably fit, and, if he was planning on joining the Navy,.quite possibly mad.

"What's her name?"

At this the boy faltered, and the officer half expected him to run.

"I...I'm not sure, I don't know, sir. I was jus' lookin' for a frigate."

So, his assessment had been remarkably close. "You're looking to join a ship?" he asked, more gently.

"Yes, sir."

"*Royal* Navy?"

The lad nodded.

"I see," the old man said, and he did; all too clearly. But it was too cold to stand about. "Walk with me and tell me about yourself. An' don't call me sir, I was never that sort of an officer."

The two of them strolled easily, once the youth's initial shyness had worn off. The man learned about the small house in Leatherhead where the boy had grown up, and the old sailor who worked as the town's carpenter and unofficial naval recruitment officer, or so it appeared. The boy's father was a schoolmaster, and the idea of his eldest son joining the Navy sounded very much against his wishes.

"But he knows you're here?" the man asked, pausing to look the lad straight in the face.

"He knows," the dark brown eyes looked black in the shadowed light. "He would have sent me as first class volunteer, but it didn't work out."

The old man nodded. It was the fastest way to the quarterdeck for anyone not associated with the Navy, but it needed money, or the right connections. Captains could grow rich on the considerations of wealthy parents eager to be rid of troublesome offspring, and in a world where much depended on influence, finding a berth for the younger son of a lord would do most officers nothing but good. It was doubtful if a simple school teacher would find anyone willing to give away such a valuable position.

They reached the harbour wall as the lad came to the end of his story. There was a pause as the warrant officer considered him.

"What did you say your name was?"

"M-Matthew J-Jameson."

"So how did you get here?" he asked, for something to say.

"I w-walked," Matthew replied simply.

It must be over sixty miles from Leatherhead: three days—two at a push, and yet the youth seemed happy to stroll with him, no limps or complaints. The man eyed him carefully; clearly this was more than a dream-struck boy. He pulled his watch from his pocket.

"All right, my lad. It's gone six; if we stay here much longer you could end up in the Navy, likes it or not."

They turned from the sea and began to retrace their steps as the officer continued.

"I can't promise you a frigate, in fact I can't promise you nothin'. You'd be better off trying for a collier and learn to sail without His Britannic Majesty's discipline, but I can tell you're set, and it'd be wrong of me to put you off."

Matthew's step had picked up and he was almost skipping as he continued.

"Keep yourself clean, obey orders, and never let your mates down. Other than that, you've got to trust to luck. Oh, and you'll have to try and speak more clearly."

"It's a s-s-stammer. M-my f-father said it would g-go in time."

"Belike it will, but lose it—if you want to get on and give orders."

They stopped outside a whitewashed building where an ensign flew from a jack rigged over the door. Matthew had noticed it when they passed by earlier, but had been too intent on his story to give it thought.

"You're certain?" the officer asked, and received a nod in return. "All right, this here's the Rondey; go inside an' they'll look after you."

Matthew viewed the place with a moment's hesitation, before moving forward. The man stopped him.

"Take care of yourself," he held out his hand almost harshly. Matthew took it, feeling the same well-remembered roughness as of the village carpenter's.

"Th-thank you." He opened his mouth to say more, then closed it, feeling suddenly foolish. He pushed the door open in front of him and disappeared into the darkness beyond.

For a moment the elderly officer stood and looked after him. His seafaring days were over, and he was not sorry. This lad would find a navy different from the one he had joined thirty-seven years ago. Probably a better one, but certainly no less tough. For all his belief that it was not dreams that led him, the boy was in for a shock. If he lasted out he might carve a career for himself. He might find the life to his liking, and even prosper. He could get himself noticed, encouraged and promoted, only to finally be sent ashore when he had no more to give. And then he would find there was little for him to do, little that anyone asked of him, except maybe to send another kid off in his wake.

The wind was suddenly icily cold. The old man shivered, drew his watch coat about him, and set off for the boarding house that was his home.

*****

It was a mere pile of books, but they transformed HMS *Vigilant* from a purposeless hulk to a commissioned ship of war —and all were all currently heaped in front of her captain. At thirty-eight Shepherd was no stranger to the position. In the fourteen years that he had held post captain rank, *Vigilant* was the fourth ship he had commanded, and the first to be classed as a line-of-battle ship, albeit, as a sixty-four, the smallest of the type.

He had been in command for almost two years, having commissioned her back in 'ninety-three, just after the French declared war. Together they had sailed with Hood at Toulon, and later met Howe's fleet coming home after the drawn-out action that ended on the first of June. Those had been satisfying times, but for the last seven weeks *Vigilant* had been penned up at Spithead, and the next cruise, following a bunch of worn out merchants down to St. Helena, looked like being about as exciting.

At that moment, however, Shepherd had other matters on his mind, matters that ambushed him on occasions like this and kept him from his proper work. In all his time, never had the urge to break away from land been so great. For a moment he gazed into the distance, before bringing himself back to the problems in hand with an effort that was very nearly physical.

He must think about the crew; they had been idle for too long. The wedding garland had been hoisted after eight days, but even the novelty of women on board had done little to ease men who were used to the activity and strain of life at sea. Three had deserted in the first few days, and even after one was caught, dragged back, and punished in front of the entire crew, there had been a steady wastage of one or two a week ever since. And it was always the better seamen who deserted, the ones who would be readily accepted on board a merchant ship and paid handsomely for their risk. The consequence was that he was over twenty topmen down, and almost equally lacking in ordinary seamen. There would be the usual offerings from the press, and the local assizes might produce some landsmen, but it took a long time to train real sailors. Of course, a spell at sea would knock a few of them into shape, and a decent cruise to the South Atlantic was better for training hands than beating about on some God forsaken blockade.

Shepherd's mind, dwelling on the intake, naturally moved on to the new lieutenant. Curtis had been taken ill with tubercular consumption and transferred to the hospital at Haslar, where he seemed destined to stay for some while. In his place they had been given an enigma by the name of Rogers. Shepherd was naturally cautious about unknown officers. In a relatively small world the usual reason for a man to be anonymous was fast and silent promotion, frequently bought by means of interest, favours or outright bribery. There were few other ways to progress without having creating something of a name or reputation.

Unfortunately the practice was becoming far too common. Shepherd knew of more than one captain to have made post before the age of eighteen, and more than a few who openly boasted about being allowed to compile sea time before taking a commission while still in their cradles. Tricks like that might work in the army, but when at sea, where a ship and every life on board could so easily depend on the judgement of one man, it was downright foolhardy.

The call from the sentry outside the door interrupted his thoughts, and Shepherd was annoyed to realise that for the last five minutes he had been doing little other than staring into space. At his curt word the door opened and Dyson, his first lieutenant, entered.

"Message from ordinance, sir. They'll be ready to load at noon."

Dyson was a solemn man, several years older than his captain. Shepherd had retained serious reservations when Dyson was appointed as there had been a number of rumours circulating about him and his methods. It seemed that Dyson was known for being rather a cold fish, with a taste for discipline that bordered on the unhealthy. However his references had been good, and so far Shepherd had been pleasantly surprised by the efficiency of his second in command. He was able to carry out most tasks without the feverish activity exhibited by some executive officers, and Shepherd was quick to appreciate that discipline in a ship-of-the-line was more important and harder to enforce than in the frigates he had been accustomed to.

"Very good. Have you alerted the master?"

"Yes, sir." Dyson's face bore no expression.

It was the duty of the sailing master and his assistants to supervise the loading of any stores. Taking on shot and powder would affect the ship's trim and alter her sailing abilities.

"I was wondering if we should send the starboard watch to dinner early, sir. That would give us the entire afternoon to see it finished"

"Can you do it in the time?"

"Yes, sir." Dyson was reassuringly positive.

"Very good, make the arrangements." As Dyson turned to go Shepherd noticed a mark just behind his right ear. It was a hint of soap, and it stood out quite plainly. Clearly the lieutenant had shaved in the dark that morning, and missed the lather. More importantly, no officer or servant had bothered, or dared, to advise him of the fact. It was a small point, but one worth remembering.

9

# HIS MAJESTY'S SHIP

*****

"*Vigilant*." The lieutenant spat the name out, before settling himself into the stern of the lugger. Unseen by him, the three-man crew busied themselves with loading his belongings and casting off. They had carried too many bad-tempered young officers to be surprised at one more. The wind might be cold but it was excellent for the short passage to Spithead, and the small craft fairly shot through the dark, crusted waves.

It was a damn bad show, being posted to a ship-of-the-line, a damn bad show. The least he had hoped for was first luff of a frigate, although really he was ready for command, and promotion. He was aware of the strings his father had pulled to get him this posting; well, he would just have to pull a few more, and harder.

The lugger drew near to a sixty-four, and for the first time Rogers looked on his new ship. Small, when judged against the average British liner, and lacking in power: twenty-four pounders rather than the normal thirty-twos. It would also be a good deal more crowded than a frigate and less likely to be despatched on the sort of cruise that won promotion and prize money. Of course a lot depended on the captain; Shepherd had been known as a frigate man in the American war; maybe he would breathe a bit of life into the old barge.

A heavily laden wherry was pulling away from the larboard side; the cackles of laughter and shouted farewells identified it as carrying doxies. So, the ship had been under the wedding garland. That would mean a lax, and probably unhealthy crew, with countless little stores of sailor's joy hidden about the place. Hardly an inspiring start.

The midshipman of the watch hailed Rogers' boat as it passed under the counter and approached the starboard main chains. One of the boatmen looked at Rogers for confirmation, before bellowing "Aye, Aye!" in reply: the accepted signal that a commissioned officer was on board. The boat bumped once against the side before hooking on. Rogers stood, fumbling in his pockets for coins, and clambered up the slippery battens to the entry port. A tall, fair-haired lieutenant was there to meet him. Rogers accepted the hand guardedly and gave his name to the younger man.

"I'm Tait," he was told in return. "Welcome aboard."

Rogers eyed Tait evenly. "Been with the ship long?"

"Nearly two years," Tait replied. "I passed my board in 'ninety and was commissioned in March 'ninety-one." The man looked in his early twenties, a good five years younger and yet only a few weeks junior to him.

Rogers smiled for the first time. "February, same year," he said, with ill-concealed satisfaction.

Tait took the information in good heart. "In that case you'll be number two."

That sounded like a fresh set of officers; it was better than it could have been, and Rogers began to perk up slightly.

"Is the captain aboard?"

"In his quarters. Doesn't like to be interrupted, though. First Lieutenant's in the wardroom. Maybe you should report to him there?"

"When do we sail?" Rogers studiously ignored the advice.

"Ship's currently being cleared of wives, we're taking shot and powder tomorrow, with the last of the water the day after. Most of the convoy's been ready to leave for ages, but we've been waiting on two more John Company ships joining us. They won't be here 'till the morrow"

"Convoy?"

"Yes, we're acting as senior escort. Slow as far as St. Helena, then straight back with the next home bound."

Tait had one of those open, honest faces that pleased Rogers. He'd be a useful junior: eager for the boring jobs and satisfying to boss about. That, and the almost independent command they would enjoy as a senior escort, placed him in a decidedly better frame of mind.

Rogers nodded at the younger man. "I have a few things to discuss with the First Lieutenant. Have my dunnage brought aboard and sent below, will you?"

He strode past Tait and made his way to the wardroom without waiting for a reply.

*****

"Two more days of Peter Warren victuals," said the old man, to no one in particular. "Then we're back to salt beef and pork, with pease puddin' twice a week, an' suet on Sundays." He smiled to himself as his mates began dropping the meat into the boiling coppers. "That fresh stuff jus' ain't got the quality or the flavour; t'aint natural."

The stained meat sack was almost empty. Three more would be needed to feed the men; that was two less than yesterday, when the women were being fed as well. The fact that the doxies were all but gone pleased the cook almost as much as the prospect of salt beef; he didn't care for the company of women.

The empty sack was tossed aside. It fell against the range with an ominous clatter.

The cook looked up. "That empty, Tom?"

The man pursed his lips. "Seemed like it."

The cook retrieved the sack and held it upside down. A horseshoe fell out onto the brick flooring of the galley deck with a loud metallic ring.

"Well, bless me!" said his mate, bending over it.

"They says it were beef!" said another.

The cook pulled a wry face, "'S what you come to expect from fresh. They don't check it like preserved." He glanced up. "Stick it on the deckhead, with the others."

Tom looked up to the beam just above his head, where five horseshoes already hung in a line.

*****

Tait remembered the traditional toast of the day as he moved his seat back and stood at the crowded wardroom table.

"Gentlemen, I give you, sweethearts and wives."

"And may they never meet," added an anonymous voice.

The officers drained their glasses, before all eyes turned to Dyson, who dabbed at his lips with a linen cloth.

"I think this would be a good time to formally introduce our new fellow officer," he said, conscious of their attention. "Please welcome Anthony Rogers, who will be second lieutenant of *Vigilant*."

Rogers sat at the far end of the wardroom table. He rose, a trifle unsteadily, or so Tait thought, although the emotion of the moment may have been partly to blame. In the few hours that he had been on board Tait had not acquired a good opinion of Rogers, and now, as he slurred his way through his reply, he studied him more carefully and liked him less.

Certainly you could not criticize his dress. To officers used to the relaxed regulations of a ship under the wedding garland, Rogers fairly dazzled in excellence. His uniform, and Tait guessed from the vast amount of dunnage that it was one of many, was tailored to the highest order, with bullion buttons and silk stockings. His sword was also fine quality, boasting a five ball hilt and what appeared to be some sort of crest set into the grip. When snuff was offered, Rogers produced his own from a gold and tortoiseshell box, and his hair was heavily powdered, a common enough sight in the wardroom of a flagship, but never before seen aboard *Vigilant*.

Rogers sat down to a polite tapping of glasses from the other officers, and there was a break in the general babble of conversation; Carling, the captain of marines, had asked Rogers a question, and Tait broke off from his study of the new man to hear his reply.

"My father? Quite possibly; he was fifteen years with the Guards before he went into politics."

"He is a member of parliament then?" Dyson this time, asking in his casual manner that Tait had learnt was anything but.

Rogers winced. "God no, sir. The Lords!"

There was general laughter from the table, and Tait switched his attention momentarily to Dyson, who absorbed the reply without any visible reaction.

"No, despite being a soldier at heart, my father takes an interest in matters naval. In fact he regularly lunches with Sir Andrew at the Admiralty."

His father's position, together with the casual mention of the Comptroller of the Navy by his first name, was enough to stir every officer present. In a world where promotion was dependent on acquaintances and connections as much as personal achievement, any man who had the ear of government instantly became important in himself. Tait watched as most of the others preened themselves in Rogers' presence, each taking care, as the conversation progressed, to show him deference and courtesy. Only Dyson and the elderly Gregory remained unimpressed. From what Tait knew about the first lieutenant, it was clear that any promotion and position he had achieved had been won entirely on merit. Very much the same could be said about Gregory, who had started his shipboard life as an ordinary seaman. Now as a lieutenant, and elevated to commissioned officer status, he had lost none of the common sense essential on the lower deck, where frauds, cheats or liars are quickly identified and exiled.

From the head of the table Dyson tapped his fruit knife against his glass, and the conversation ceased.

"Gentlemen, this has been a pleasant evening, but I am sure you will all wish to get some sleep before tomorrow."

Stewards appeared unbidden from the pantry, and as a body the men rose from the table. In the crowded conditions of a ship-of-the-line, even the officers were cramped for space, and most had to walk just a few short steps before they were in the little penned off cubicles that were their cabins. Tait found his and closed the light door behind him, before loosening his stock. Rogers had the cabin next to his, and through the thin deal wall he heard the man belch loudly. He pulled a face to himself and began to undress. Rogers was clearly ahead of him, and as Tait drew back the blanket and blew out his dip, he heard rich, generous snores begin. He swung himself into his cot and stared up at the deckhead. The forthcoming cruise should not last long; they might even be back within three or four months. But long or short, Tait felt with that particular companion on board it was certainly not going to be easy.

# CHAPTER TWO

THE night aboard the receiving ship had been a hard one. With morning Matthew eased his stiff body into a sitting position, being careful to avoid the Irishman on his right who was sleeping fitfully. The place was airless and still quite dark, although enough light now penetrated the grating to allow him to examine his surroundings. He ran his fingers through his hair, feeling grubby and uncomfortable. His mouth tasted as if he had been sucking copper coins and he had a pain in his neck from lying awkwardly. The sleeping man snorted and gave a slight moan. Matthew looked at him, noticing that the shallow wound on his temple had ceased to bleed and that a bruise was now plainly visible along his forehead.

Matthew had been brought to the receiving ship late the previous night, after spending the evening in the Rondey, or *rendezvous*; the base used by the impressment men. He had been reasonably well treated, even to the point of being given hot food, and his first ship's biscuit. The latter had been a surprise to him, as Jake, the old carpenter, had regaled him with stories of biscuits riddled with weevils, or "bargemen" as he had called them. Matthew had tapped the biscuit tentatively, but only managed to dislodge a few dusty crumbs. It was hard to the touch but soon softened in the stew, and the actual taste was quite pleasant after the strangely flavoured meat of the meal.

The first press had gone out shortly before he ate and returned within half an hour. He soon noticed a pattern to the evening's activities. The separate gangs were obviously working close by, and to a recognised plan. They seldom returned with more than one man, who was unceremoniously dumped in his room, which he came to realise was actually a cell. By the end of the evening Matthew had twelve companions, all wearing the short jacket and slop shirts of seaman, all holding up their trousers, from which the belt had been removed, and all there unwillingly. Three, he learned, were from the same ship, which had arrived that afternoon after a two year round trip to New South Wales. Of all the prisoners these were the most vocal, although most of what they had to say was lost on Matthew, who was as innocent of sailor's jargon as he was their profanities.

His companions had learned of his enlistment with a mixture of scorn and pity. One, the wounded Irishman who now slept next to him, actually tried to persuade him to change his mind, to say he was younger, the son of a gentleman, under indentures, anything to avoid the path he had chosen.

The light increased as the grating was removed, a ladder appeared, and a young officer, splendid in crisp, clean uniform, descended into their lair. With him he brought a draught of fresh air, and the contrast made Matthew realise how stuffy and oppressive the atmosphere in the hold had become. Around him men began to rise, clearly knowing what was to come. The officer produced a sheaf of papers and began to read out names. At the school in Leatherhead Matthew's father would begin each day by reading out the nineteen names of his pupils. This register was very much the same, with the relevant men answering when called. Matthew replied to his own name, and before long the officer finished. He then shuffled his papers and appeared to begin again, although this time the list was shorter. The men replied more readily on the second reading, and as the officer ended with the words "...are here in fault," a low sigh seemed to travel about the crowded hold.

Those chosen stood up and climbed the ladder to freedom. The others watched, there were no words of envy or banter from either side; apart from that involuntary sigh, the free men left in silence.

"Those remaining will be transferred to a line-of-battle ship due to depart shortly. Any who have been of service before may retain their record; they will mention this to the rating board. They will also be given the choice to volunteer, and benefit from the bounty. Ten guineas is allowed every able man, eight for ordinary and six for landsmen. Boys will receive one guinea. False claims of ability will result in the forfeiture of all bounty."

A murmur spread amongst the prisoners, and Matthew could tell it was generally favourable. Some, he guessed, might refuse the bounty out of pride, although the majority would take the money. The officer retreated up the ladder and two seamen descended, carrying large wooden buckets of water.

"Clean yersel's up, lads!" one shouted, a toothless grin on his face. "Gotta make you look nice for the King!" There was no response from the crowd; the fight had been knocked out of them, and they were resigned to their fate.

"Better do as he says," the Irishman muttered. "Else they'll only to do it for yer. An' you can kiss goodbye to them curly locks!"

Matthew joined the ragged queue next to the buckets, although when it came to his turn the water was quite stale. Despite this he threw a handful over his face, then collected some of the bread that had been tossed down to them.

"Right, then," a voice came from above. "Let's have a look at you in daylight!"

The ladder came down almost in front of Matthew, and he climbed up, finding himself on a gundeck.

Heavy, blackened guns resting on wooden carriages sat at regular intervals along each side, their muzzles secured above the closed ports in front of them. They were much larger than he had expected, bigger in fact than any weapon he had ever seen. He wandered over to one as the rest came up from below, and placed his hand on the cold iron cascabel cautiously.

"Armstrong pattern," said a seaman nearby, who was peeling an onion with his clasp knife. "Old stuff, but good enough for us." He bit into the onion as if it had been an apple.

Matthew blinked at him. "It's b-big," he said, instantly feeling foolish. The seaman gave him a good-natured grin.

"Na, only a tiddler. Twelve pounder. Accurate though." He took another bite and spoke though the mouthful. "You with that lot?"

Matthew nodded.

"You'll be going to *Vigilant*. Good ship, an' a fair captain."

Matthew opened his mouth to speak, but felt the stammer building and knew he would be unable to add to the conversation.

"Better get 'n line, or you'll start off bad."

Looking round he saw the men had formed up and were about to climb an open staircase to the deck above. Hastily he joined the end of the queue, avoiding the eye of the officer who was counting them. The sailor grinned at him again and gave a small wave of his onion as Matthew clambered up to the next deck.

They lined the waist in the spring sunshine, the fresh air and light emphasizing their bedraggled state. A large boat hung from tackle at the front and middle mast—fore and main, Matthew hurriedly told himself. Guided by two men the boat swung above their heads and was transferred to further pulleys set at the yardarms. The boat was then lowered, and the men clambered awkwardly aboard. Matthew found himself once more next to the Irishman with the head wound.

"You should've spoken to y'r man," his companion told him. "Said you'd been mistaken, that way you might've got away with the first lot."

Matthew wanted to tell him that it was not that easy, that he had volunteered, and the idea of backing out now was abhorrent to him. Whether it was the shock of his surroundings, the dreadful night in the hold, or just plain nerves, he did not know, but again he found the words hard to find.

"You can do like me an' try it on with the rating board; they might take pity on you. Sometimes they're not so up to date with t'law, but it'll be a long shot."

"I'll stay," Matthew said, finally recovering the gift of speech. The man looked at him with a trace of concern on his soiled face.

"That's up to you," he said. "But it'll be a mistake you're making."

\*\*\*\*\*

"Lambs to the slaughter!" laughed Jenkins, as he watched the launch approach *Vigilant*. He and his mate were serving the starboard main backstay, and they had an excellent view of the boat and its cargo. "Most of 'em look like they went to bed a prince and woke a pauper!"

The other man paused, mallet in hand. "Mebbe you're right, and all," he grinned. Both had been pressed several times, and drew great enjoyment from watching others share their fate.

"That's Samuel Wilson," Jenkins continued, in a quieter voice. "He was with me in the old *Amazon*."

"Wonder what he'll call hisself now?" his mate, who was currently known as Simpson, pondered. Simpson had used three names previously, on account of the three times he'd jumped ship.

"Na, not Samuel. He'd be fair and square." Jenkins shook his head before continuing. "You'll not find a man like Samuel running."

Simpson considered this, aware that there might have been an insult hidden in Jenkins' words. But men such as he lived precarious lives, and he decided to let it pass. He wrapped the paper around the backstay, while Jenkins covered it with another turn of lighter line that fitted neatly into the grooves of the shroud.

"Tain't no more'n fourteen of 'em," Simpson grumbled, while Jenkins worked the line in with the serving mallet. "Hardly enough to fill two messes. An' most'll be lubbers, used to livin' in style!"

"Maybe there'll be a few warm 'uns amongst 'em," Jenkins said reflectively.

"Some'll have bounty." The two men stopped work, as the same idea occurred.

"Crown and Anchor?"

Simpson grinned, twirling the end of his red pigtail in the air meditatively, and nodded.

Betting was illegal in ships of the Royal Navy, although an innocent game of Crown and Anchor could always be spiced with a clandestine wager on the side. Jenkins and Simpson were past masters of the art, especially with raw recruits who knew nothing of the inflated value of money on board ship, and had little idea of the game.

"Couple of rounds'll soon sort the men from the muggers!" Jenkins laughed.

"And you'll be joining the muggers if you're not so very careful!" The approach of Johnston, the boatswain, had gone unnoticed by both men, so intent had they been in their planning.

"I want this stay wormed, parcelled and served by six bells," the boatswain shouted, inches from their faces. "Come on, larboard party's almost reached the 'ounds!"

Jenkins and Simpson fell to work with a will. Neither particularly minded the boatswain bawling them out, in fact of all the petty officers he was one of the most respected; the rattan cane he carried used more as a symbol of office than a scourge.

"'E gone?" asked Simpson after a while.

Jenkins nodded, and both stopped work. "Aye, for present." He looked across the deck where two men were working on the larboard forestay.

"Them's not at the hounds," he said, in a tone completely free of malice. "Them's hardly three ahead of us!"

\*\*\*\*\*

The rating committee consisted of the captain, first lieutenant and sailing master, together with the boatswain, gunner and other heads of department who would appoint the new men to their posts. They sat behind a long table set out on the upper gundeck, with a marine sentry to each side. Dyson, sitting on the captain's right, picked up the rough list sent by the impressment officer when the men were delivered.

"No Billy Pitt's men here, sir," he commented quietly. Shepherd nodded. The recent quota act brought in by Pitt's Tory government had proved a mixed blessing to the Navy. Certainly the chronic shortage of men had been eased, but the introduction of criminals, vagrants and other undesirables was starting to prove a strain on the officers responsible for training them. He placed the list back on the table, his face, as always, void of expression. There were other reasons why Dyson was wary of quota men, reasons that he had not discussed with another officer, reasons that he almost dare not contemplate.

The quota had already collected its fair share of intellectual criminals, the kind that would have normally avoided the press by claiming the status of gentleman. It only needed a few of these crooked bookkeepers or lawyers' clerks to talk to the men, point out how bad their shipmates' lot really was. With a level of pay, and conditions that had hardly changed since Cromwell, the men were ripe for rebellion. In Dyson's opinion it was only time that kept them from revolting *en masse*. When that dreadful day came it could mean the end of everything, for an outright mutiny would lay England open to invasion, and all because a parsimonious government preferred to force men to serve, rather than entice them with better wages and more reasonable conditions.

There were a total of fourteen names on the list; hardly enough to make up for the men who had run in the last few weeks, but it was all they would get. The captain nodded at Dyson, who was to preside over the board.

"All right, sergeant, let's have them up."

The men were led into the officers' presence and stood, bedraggled and in the main part bitter, glaring back at their betters.

"At the call of your name you will take one pace forward and give your age and experience," the sergeant chanted.

Dyson looked at the first name on the list.

"Richard Kelly."

Kelly stepped forward. "Thirty years old. I'm a tailor, sir, an' I ain't been to sea afore."

"Where do you work, Kelly?" Dyson's voice was quiet and studied.

"I've me own business. In Common Lane, Southsea."

"Do you own the property?" A freeholder would be exempt from service, although it would be strange if the impressment officers had not spotted his name on the role.

"That I do. I owns it, an' I pays taxes."

It was a bad start, especially as the others would be encouraged to argue if they saw the first man set free.

"Beggin' your pardon, sir." The marine sergeant stepped forward and turned to the prisoner. Placing one hand on the man's jacket, he gave a sharp pull. If Kelly really had worked as a tailor he was a poor judge of cloth, for the sleeve fell away in the marine's hand.

"Tattoos, sir," said the sergeant, pointing to Kelly's arm.

He was right; all could plainly see the colourful designs that no normal shopkeeper would dream of sporting.

"Those are sailors' tattoos, Kelly," Dyson said, simply. "If it is true that you own your own business, you will have a record we can check. If not, you may well be a deserter, and as such, liable to the penalty for desertion." Dyson let the words sink deep, noticing how the man raised his head slightly and swallowed.

"As it is, you can count yourself lucky that we are due to sail shortly." Better a healthy, able hand than one weakened by the cat. "Make sure you give me no reason to look into your past for as long as you are in this ship. Now, what skills have you?"

"Captain of the foretop, sir." Kelly said, quietly. "In a previous vessel."

"Do you wish to volunteer?"

There was a brief pause. "I do, sir."

"Very well." He looked at Shepherd for confirmation, before continuing. "You'll be rated as a topman, and I will be keeping my eye on you. Read him in, Mr Morrison."

The purser had the ship's muster book open and pressed his finger at the space for Kelly to make his mark. He would be given a number which he would keep for as long as he served aboard the ship. He would also be allocated a mess, which he could elect to change if he wished. Kelly scribbled on the spot, making himself eligible for any punishment his officers cared to set for him.

"Kieran Crehan." Dyson called the next man, and the Irishman with the head wound stepped forward.

"American citizen, sir," he said in a broad brogue.

Dyson looked at him coldly, as a murmur of laughter spread through the men and some of the officers.

"You are an American?" he said, with just a hint of incredulity.

"That I am, sir." There was no humour in Crehan's voice as he continued. "Born in Derry, but captured when serving under Admiral Hood, sir. I took the country as me own after the war ended."

It was a reasonable enough explanation, but Dyson had to continue.

"What are you doing in England?"

"Second mate of *Katharine Frances*, a merchant brig, due out at the end of the week. I came ashore on ship's business. I has papers and a protection and I'd like to have words with the American consul, if you'd be agreeable, sir."

Crehan delved into his jacket pocket and placed something small on the table. Dyson reached out and took it. It was paper, rather than parchment, although the bold heading and emblazoned arms of the Republic appeared impressive.

Dyson looked up. "This does not make you an American. Why, you can purchase these for under five pounds in any pot house, as well you know."

"It has my description there, sir."

"Height under five feet ten, and twenty-four years of age," Dyson read. "There must be more than eighty men on board this ship who could answer to that." More to the point, if this rating board gave Crehan a discharge, a far more accurate description would be provided, and that document would become a very real and valuable protection.

"You hail from Ireland: you are Irish." The small muttering that had started amongst the recruits and onlookers ceased as

Dyson spoke again. "This country has protected you for most of your life and is currently at war. What gives you the right to ignore your responsibilities and bargain a separate peace with our mutual enemy?"

"I have fought for Great Britain, sir. An' now I've a mind to stand with the Americans. An' I would like to send that message to the consul, sir."

Dyson knew it was important to keep asking questions, while deciding in his own mind what course of action to take. "Why did you not show your papers to the impressment officer?" It was an important point. The regulating captain would have soon spotted a forged protection. For a split second Crehan hesitated, and his eyes lost a little of their intensity.

"Knocked me cold, they did, sir. Was out all the time. They might even have called me name, but I wouldn't have known," he swallowed. "Only came round when they dropped us in the boat to come here."

"Really?" It was the first piece of Crehan's story that rang false. The press were known for their rough tactics, but they were also liable for a charge of murder if any man wrongly arrested subsequently died. The treatment Crehan described did not sound likely, although he had a head wound that appeared fresh. Dyson was on the point of standing him down when Crehan continued.

"You can ask any of the men, sir. They know what happened, they'll speak for me."

Dyson looked along the line and naturally picked out Matthew as the youngest.

"You there," he pointed, noticing the way the boy's face blanched two shades of white. "Is what this man says correct?"

Matthew opened his mouth to speak but, as often happened, the words would not come. This time it was not just his stammer; he simply did not know what to say.

"The child has a stammer, sir." said Crehan, there was a hint of worry in his voice that was not lost on Dyson. "Ask another man. They'll be tellin' you."

But the first lieutenant's eyes stayed fixed on Matthew. "What is your name?" he asked, quietly.

"Jameson, sir." It was barely a whisper. "M-Matthew Jameson."

"I see that you are down here as a volunteer, Jameson." Dyson continued, almost kindly.

"Yes, s-s-sir." It was no louder.

"There is a good future for any volunteer in this ship. A very good future." His eyes sought out the young man's and locked on. Then, in a tone that was almost hypnotic, he continued. "Now, is what Crehan states the truth?"

Again he opened his mouth, but no more.

"He's nought but a boy what cannot speak, so he is." This time the panic was evident in Crehan's voice. "Ask any man, sir. They'll tell you!"

"I'm asking Jameson," Dyson continued. "Does this man speak the truth?"

Matthew looked along the line of officers. Men wearing different uniforms, most of which meant nothing to him. Everyone was silent, even the normal noises of the ship seemed to have been suspended as they waited for him to speak. Crehan, in front of him, did not look round, but he knew he would be listening as hard as anyone. He opened his mouth.

"Come on, Jameson," Dyson's voice was soft, and encouraging, and his expression held their eyes together. "Come on, Jameson. Tell me. Tell me the truth."

"N-no, sir," said Matthew finally. "No. H-He's lying."

# CHAPTER THREE

HMS *Vigilant* was a third rate line-of-battle ship, the first two grades being reserved for more powerful three-deckers. She was also one of the smallest of her rate, officially carrying only sixty-four guns, rather than the seventy-four more commonly found in ships-of-the-line.

Built at the Adams Yard on Bucklers Hard, she was of the *Ardent* class, sharing the same lines as *Nassau, Agamemnon* and *Indefatigable*. Over forty acres of forest had been cleared to provide the two thousand oak trees needed for her frame, trees that had first seen life during the reign of James II. Her ironwork alone weighed more than one hundred tons, while thirty tons of copper bolts and thirty thousand treenails were used in her construction.

She was ordered in 1779 when the first American War was depleting Britain's ships, and launched in 1783 at a cost of forty thousand pounds, not counting her armament or copper sheathing. For several years she had been laid up in ordinary before finally being refitted in November 1792 and commissioned early in the following April.

Her optimum complement was six hundred officers, men and marines, and she displaced just under fourteen hundred tons. From the height of her main masthead an horizon over thirty miles wide could be swept, and her lower deck battery, although lighter than that of a seventy-four, was made up with the latest Blomefield pattern cannon that weighed nearly fifty hundredweight each: cannons that could send their twenty-four pound shot over two thousand yards and still penetrate the hull of another warship.

Fully provisioned, *Vigilant* could stay at sea for more than three months at a time; longer if fresh water was available. She was the culmination of several hundred years of design and experience, and enclosed in the 160 feet of her hull was everything necessary to conduct a war at sea.

On that morning in early May she rode easily at anchor. With the wedding garland only recently lowered, the crew had been detailed to scour the ship free of all memories of the women. Men swept the decks clear before scrubbing them with liberal amounts of vinegar and water. Lower, in the bilges, sulphurous fires were lit in cast iron braziers, the acrid fumes filling the damp ship, causing most of the crew to choke and retch in a manner considered highly beneficial to their health. Ports were opened on the lower gundeck, and fresh air and light allowed into places where both were relative strangers. The boatswain and the sailmaker supervised the laying out of the sails, each taken in rotation from their lockers and hung from the lower yards to air in the spring sunshine.

While at anchor the purser had been provisioning the ship under "Peter Warren", or petty warrant victuals, sending to the shore for fresh meat and vegetables, so as to conserve his precious store of preserved food. Now he pored over his lists, making certain he had just enough of everything to keep the ship at sea, and not an ounce more. Pursers paid a personal bond of up to twelve hundred pounds to assure the value of the goods they requisitioned. It was up to each to see that this was done as economically as possible, as any money outstanding would go straight into their pocket. They could benefit from their position in other ways: by seeing that meat was issued at fourteen ounces to the pound (officially to allow for wastage, of which there was notoriously little), and make a handsome commission from the halfpenny per man, per day, they were allowed for turnery ware. The purser also ran the only shop permitted on board, and gained from the sale of clothing and equipment, as well as small luxuries such as tobacco and raisins. Because of his somewhat capitalistic approach, most members of the crew, officers as well as men, treated the purser with caution, suspecting him of the most devilish schemes to rob them of their due, and in the main they were right.

The purser was now in front of Matthew, who was the last to be rated and read in.

"Listing you as a boy, are they?" the older man asked.

Matthew nodded.

"Speak up!" The marine sergeant was almost finished with the new recruits and had other matters to concern him. "You'll get nothing in this ship for staying quiet!"

"Y-yes, sir." His stammer must have been noticed by the rating board, although no comment had been made about it.

"Make your mark there, laddie," the purser continued, indicating a space below a column of smudges, symbols and the occasional signature. "You have the number seven hundred an' sixty-nine, Think ye can be remembering that, do ye?"

Matthew nodded, before hurriedly stammering out a confirmation.

"Who will ta'e the lad?" The purser looked to his steward, who consulted the watch bill.

"Fletcher's mess is light two men, but they already got a boy. What about Flint? He's taken Crehan."

"Aye, Flint will do nicely."

Matthew felt himself pushed away towards the large staircase that led below. The Irishman was directly in front, and as they trooped down into the depths of the ship, he turned to the boy.

"Sharing the same mess, so we are," even in the half light the man's expression was unmistakeably filled with menace. "Now isn't that a wonderful piece o' luck?"

"Mess subscription's a guinea a week, paid one month in advance." Carling, the captain of marines, had a neutral face that seldom bore more than the most rudimentary of expressions. It was blank now as he addressed Rogers, although he had already made his mind up about the new officer.

"Sounds agreeable," said Rogers, reaching into his purse and handing over four gold coins. "What, pray, do we get for our consideration?"

"The mess subscribes to additional wine and cheese, plus fresh vegetables and meat when we can get them. We have nine laying hens, a goat, a sheep and two pigs, one about to produce. We also take a copy of the *Naval Gazette*, in addition to a news sheet or paper every day we are in an English harbour."

Rogers nodded, his face equally bland. "No cow?"

"No cow." Carling did not explain that the majority of the officers found it hard to find the guinea a week which was more than half their earnings.

"I may wish to purchase a cow," Rogers said evenly. "Never could stomach the taste of goat's milk."

"That would be your choice." Carling remained impassive, although he was conscious that Rogers had nettled him in some subtle way.

"You could procure a cow for me?" The lieutenant continued. "I assume that is within your duties?"

Unreasonable anger welled up inside the marine officer. There was an intangible implication in Rogers' tone that triggered feelings of resentment and fury, and it was with effort that he was able to continue the conversation without losing his temper or striking the man.

"I administer the wardroom accounts. If you wish for a cow you should speak to the purser." His tone was final; he wanted nothing more to do with the man.

"I need additional furniture for my cabin."

The screened off area where Rogers had spent the previous night was certainly bare. Apart from a cot, and a twenty-four pounder, there was nothing.

"You can arrange that with the carpenter. Until then, make use of the wardroom store and share with anyone willing." He closed the accounts book with a snap, and stood up. Whether Rogers intended it or not, he had a damned unpleasant manner about him, and Carling had no intention of being considered as one of the willing.

*****

Flint was a young, fair-haired man with clear, dark blue eyes and a light but powerful physique. He stood up from the table where the men of his mess had clearly just finished eating, and took a step towards Matthew and Crehan. The other men, seated at forms to either side of the mess table, studied the newcomers critically. A heavy gun behind each bench, rigged with the muzzle above the closed port, made a division between messes and gave the group a degree of privacy. Flint introduced himself and shook hands with the two newcomers. His hand was as hard as any Matthew had shaken, although the grip was gentle, and without threat.

"Good to have you, lad." It was an easy smile, but genuine, and for the first time Matthew began to feel welcome. Flint turned and introduced the other members of the mess. Matthew caught no names. Crehan stood next to him, apparently more interested in his fingernails.

"We're detailed for loading work on the afternoon watch. Have you two eaten?"

They had not. The sergeant of marines had passed them on to the gunroom, where they had spent the rest of the forenoon watch, apparently forgotten until the surgeon appeared to give each of them a rudimentary prod. Throughout that time, Matthew had done all he could to stay away from Crehan, although whenever he glanced in the Irishman's direction, he found himself under scrutiny.

"No, w-we..."

"The lad's a bit light in t'head," Crehan burst in. "He has a problem wit' speakin'." Myself I've had nut'ing to eat all day."

Flint looked directly at Crehan, considering him for more than a moment, before turning to the men behind him.

"Any of you have somethin' over for a messmate?" The others looked slightly shifty, but a couple of pieces of hard cheese and a lump of boiled beef miraculously appeared and were handed over. Flint gave the two newcomers a piece of cheese each. Then, taking out his clasp knife, he placed the meat on the mess table and cut it into two chunks. He gave the slightly larger portion to Matthew, who took it almost reluctantly.

"Growing lad." He turned to Crehan. "Whereas this one could do with losin' a little!" Crehan accepted his meat in ill humour, amid laughter from the other men.

"Come on, then, let's get you kitted out." Matthew, who had bitten into the meat, wasn't certain if Flint meant for him to follow, especially as Crehan made no attempt to follow. The feeling of helplessness was starting to return when a man with a vivid red pigtail caught his eye and nodded his head in the direction Flint had taken.

He rushed after, swallowing the meat in one lump while nearly knocking into someone dressed in blue with a stiff hat and a pile of papers under the one arm. The man swore at him; Matthew hurried on, hoping he had not caused too great a breach of discipline. Flint was about to descend a staircase to a lower deck when he finally caught up.

"D'ya have any dunnage?" Flint asked him.

The word threw him for no more than a second; he guessed what Flint must be referring to. "Spare set of clothes an' a bedding roll."

"You'll need more'n that, and we'd better get you hammocks and biscuits, 'fore they all go."

"What about the other man?"

Flint snorted. "He's the type who looks after hisself."

This deck was darker and lower than all the others, and there were no ports, scuttles or guns. Matthew guessed that they were on or below the waterline. Flint walked in an assured way, nodding a greeting here and there while speeding along, his back slightly bent and head lowered, missing the beams above by a fraction of an inch. Matthew scampered along next to him, without the ease and economy of movement that his companion seemed to possess naturally.

He stopped by a panelled deal door and rapped lightly on the shutter.

"New hand to see the purser," Flint told the elderly man who appeared at the entrance.

"Let them through!" came a deep Scottish voice from within, and the steward stepped back to allow the two inside.

Morrison, the purser who had signed Matthew in that morning, sat on a stool at a small desk. To his right was a pile of ledgers, while another was laid open in front of him. About the room there were several unlabelled tubs. As his eyes became accustomed to the gloom, Matthew noticed a light dusting of flour that seemed to cover every surface. The air was thick with the smell of burning tallow, raisins, and rancid butter. Morrison viewed the pair with professional interest.

"You've found your new laddie then, Flint?"

"Aye, Mr Morrison. I'd like to kit him out."

"What will ye be wantin'?"

"Hammock, blanket, biscuits, soap, knife..."

"Steady, steady!" Morrison wagged his quill at Flint. "There's some he's 'titled to, and some he's not."

Flint grinned. "I'll go through the normal with Jack Dusty, Mr Morrison." Flint glanced back at the elderly man. "But we'd 'preciate a few specials from y'rself, sir."

Morrison smiled at Flint and got up from his stool. "You come wi' me, boy, an' I see what I can do."

Before the watch was called Matthew had two hammocks, plus biscuits, which he learnt were the hard mattresses that went inside. He also had a heavy blanket, a pillow, a brown pea jacket, two pairs of white duck trousers, two worsted caps, three shirts, and a knife. The last few items he had bought himself, using the bounty guinea and a promissory note, which Flint had helped him write out. The purser said he would destroy the note when Matthew's earnings covered it, although Flint was strangely insistent that it should be returned instead.

"We'll dump that lot in a ditty bag." They were now heading back to their mess deck, although Matthew was finding it hard to keep up, his arms overflowing with kit. "First dog watch I'll take you back to t'orlop and you can stow some in my chest."

"Th-thank you," Matthew was more grateful than he could say, and not just for the share of a sea chest.

Flint caught his eye as they climbed up the companionway. "I'm not saying it will be easy," he said, "an' I won't always help you—even if I'm able. You've found yr'self an enemy, and that kind's a nasty one, so I reckon you need a friend or two to make a balance."

The mess table had been taken up, and the men stood about. For the first time Matthew noticed the line of canvas bags hanging from the ship's side. Flint went over and collected an empty one, and Matthew piled the clothing into it. There were no hammocks about; for a moment Matthew wondered what to do with his, then, taking the initiative, he laid them in a neat pile under the bag.

A bell rang from above, and the ship was suddenly alive with piercing whistles and shouts. The bell continued to ring; measured strokes about half a second apart, until it had rung eight times. Even before it had finished Flint was gone, heading the swarm of men that made for the companionway. The deck was filled with rushing bodies and excited cries; Matthew caught sight of two men he recognised from his mess and stayed behind them as they reached the upper deck and daylight.

*****

The cockpit was also on the orlop deck, the lowest deck of the ship and, due to its lack of ventilation and proximity to the bilges, the smelliest. The berth was divided into two, and housed the midshipmen and master's mates as well as several other inferior warrant officers. At that moment the starboard berth was full. Some were eating or drinking, and a group of four played cards about a single shielded sconce. A few hammocks were filled with  resting bodies, and there was a general clatter of conversation that was a characteristic of the berth for most hours of the day.

Mr Midshipman King lay in his hammock, although he had no plans for sleep. In his hand he held a copy of Hamilton Moore's *Practical Navigator*, an essential book for any man wanting to gain a commission. He mouthed the words silently to himself as he trudged down the page. King had always found reading a slow process, although he was usually able to gather the gist of a story by missing out the odd indecipherable word. But dry prose such as this gave him few clues, and he ended each paragraph with the air of one who had completed a particularly boring task knowing full well it would have to be repeated.

The purser's dip, a source of light that added yet more to the oppressive atmosphere, guttered slightly as Pite entered the berth. King glanced down at him. Pite had the second dogwatch that ran from six until eight. He'd only just gone on duty, and even though they were at anchor, his rightful place was on deck.

"Forget something?" King asked, pleased to be distracted from his book.

"Aye, forgot to tell the bosun how to spin a yarn." At seventeen Pite was three years younger than King.

"Dressed, are you?" Pite rested his arms on King's hammock, making it tilt alarmingly. King was in shirt and second best britches, his blue jacket hung on the row of hooks on the deal wall of the berth.

"Pretty well, why d'ya ask?"

Pite shrugged. "Sumfin' about the captain wantin' to see you in his quarters." King was out of his hammock in one easy motion and reaching for his coat as his feet hit the deck.

"This had better not be one of your japes, my lad!" His hat was dusty; desperately he tried to brush the nap, but like most of King's possessions it was cheap and refused to come clean. Wordlessly Pite handed over his own hat, a far better affair, one of three bought for him by his indulgent father. King looked his thanks, pulled his jacket into shape, and headed out of the berth.

Pite watched him go somewhat wistfully, before picking up King's battered hat, stuffing it under his own arm, and making a more leisurely progress back to the quarterdeck.

*****

According to Lieutenant Timothy, Cowper's poem about the loss of the *Royal George*, still popular twelve years after the incident, was nothing but tiresome doggerel. Though short and slightly plump, Timothy was every inch a professional officer, and dedicated to the sea. He knew his own mind, could not tolerate a fool, yet found no shame in taking his poetry in sweeter, softer measures. Not for him the rambling passages of

Coleridge; cryptic and clever phrases only taxed his mind and hurt his head. But Marvell, Donne, Gray, these were men worth reading. Men of passion and intensity; tenderness, love and lust. Men he could relate to, however coarse his own character and world may have become.

The fall of the dogwatches meant that, after only two hours on duty, he now had eight in which to relax, although with the ship preparing for sea, no officer could look for recreation in the time when not working or asleep. Still, on most days Lieutenant Timothy read at least a few pages from one of his well thumbed volumes, successors to the anthology of verse that his mother had given to him when he had first joined the Navy.

His father had hoped he would follow his own trade of bookbinding, but the lure of the sea had been too strong. Besides, Timothy felt there would be more romance and excitement on foreign oceans than ever entered an airless workshop. To be a naval officer and have access to poetry was all he had ever aspired to, and he was quite content. Today he found the fragrant words a welcome contrast to the work of heaving the ship back to her real purpose. After a tiring spell of duty supervising the loading, to relax in the comfort of well remembered lines and phrases was as welcome to him as any spirit or tobacco.

At that moment the wardroom was empty, save for the snoring of some anonymous officer in a screened off cabin, and Timothy was able to place his book down flat on the table, rest his head in his hands and read in comfort, lips moving in silent sympathy with another's thoughts. His fellow officers knew nothing of this strange habit, and never would, if Timothy had anything to do with it. He had undergone untold humiliations in the gunroom and the cockpit, where his contemporaries made merry play of the fact that mere words could stir emotions deep inside him, emotions that most would never know or understand. Now, despite reaching the status of a commissioned officer and mixing with those known as gentlemen, he had no intention of allowing anyone else to share his secret.

Absent-mindedly he reached for the bread bin and selected a piece of hard tack, which he tapped on the worn table in time to the measure of the verse. That first book had been torn apart, and with it a part of James Timothy had been altered for ever. His outrage had opened a vein of anger, one that drove him to assert himself in a way he would probably never have managed otherwise. Though shorter, and certainly no stronger, he had fought the lout who had done the dreadful thing. Fought him and won, although nothing could remove the horror of his mother's last present being shredded about the warrant officers' round house like so much bumfodder. It was an image that stayed with him, and one he freely recalled whenever he felt he was turning soft and the need came for a more forceful personality to make an appearance.

"Reading, James?"

It was Tait, probably closest to him in temperament although several years younger. He walked into the wardroom, a friendly smile on his face and settled down on the chair opposite.

"Just off watch," Timothy explained smiling cautiously back, and raising the book like a small barrier between them. "I like to relax a bit if I can."

Tait nodded, he knew the feeling well, although he had never found any book particularly relaxing. Casually he leaned across and peered at the leather spine.

"*Dr. Seally's Geographical Dictionary?*" he muttered, surprised. "Hardly light reading. Planning on getting lost, are we?"

Timothy gave a neutral smile and continued to read; there were some advantages in being the son of a bookbinder.

# CHAPTER FOUR

"IT won't be half so crowded once we're clear of Spithead."
Jenkins was attaching the clews of Matthew's hammock to rings
set in the beams of the deckhead. To the young man's eyes the
knots he tied appeared rather too simple, but Jenkins had the
air of a seaman, and he decided to trust him.

"See, at the moment larboard and starboard watch is all
below, so's we has to share with 'em. You get fourteen inches to
sling y'r hammock, take more'n that, an' yer on a charge, for
stealing another man's space." He pulled the line tight. "But we
berths one and one, the two on either side o'you will most likes
be on watch, so main times you get more room." Now he had
tied both ends, and the empty hammock swung perilously.

"Then yer takes yer biscuit, yer blanket and yer pillow, stuffs
them inside, like so," he pressed the straw-filled mattress—the
'biscuit'—into place. "Gets yerself in, pull the blanket over, an'
you'll sleep tight."

Matthew paused. The other members of his mess were also
preparing their hammocks, except now all had stopped and
were silent, clearly intending to watch him. He had long ago
learned that putting off the inevitable only aggravated matters,
and with a half skip he leapt up and across the canvas,
intending to straighten himself once secured.

Of all the damnedest jokes—the hammock slipped away and
he found himself heading sideways for the deck. Desperately he
pushed a knee and a hand out and felt the jolt as they hit. He
rolled to one side, stunned, but aware of the laughter all about

him. Tears welled up behind his eyes, although he guessed that to cry would only make the mocking that much worse. Gritting his teeth, he pushed himself stiffly from the deck and drew a hand across his eyes, before looking at his messmates.

Jenkins was the worst; he had collapsed on to the deck and sat there now, laughing and pointing at Matthew, his mouth wide enough to swallow an apple. Matthew struggled to his feet. Flint was laughing as well, not quite as outrageously, but enough. Of all his so-called shipmates, only Crehan was seemingly ignoring him.

"Y-you t-t-tricked me!" Matthew clambered to his feet, and glared at Jenkins.

"Nay, lad. I've not tricked yer!" Still the humour was impairing his speech. "I'd not have to, you tricked yerself!" Another chorus of mirth erupted, and Matthew had time to study his hammock. Both ends were still firmly secured, and it appeared no different to any of the others that were being slung about him.

"I don't understand, I-I..."

Flint took a pace towards him, his face still showing signs of laughter.

"He's not done nothing, it's how you climbs aboard." Then, holding on to the canvas, he kicked his right leg up, gave a small jump and swung himself in. The hammock rocked to and fro a couple of times as Flint settled himself. He peered over the side to Matthew.

"It's a knack, one we all 'as to get when we're learnin'." The others smiled in confirmation, and Jenkins stood up.

"Aye, Flint's right enough," he said. "Time I joined, I was too small to get up into an 'ammock at all. They 'ad to lift me in, they did!"

"Still do," Simpson, the man with the red pigtail, added, "'specially when 'e's got more'n two sheets to the wind!"

The laughter came again just as it had with Matthew and the boy noticed Jenkins taking it in good heart.

"L-let me try again," he said to Flint, who immediately swung himself down from the hammock and steadied the canvas for him. Again there was the pregnant silence, although this time Matthew was more on edge, knowing that another failure would bring an even greater reaction. He kicked up suddenly, and swung in a manner he hoped approximated Flint's. The canvas stayed more or less beneath him, and despite the whole world swinging left and right, he was able to grab the edges and straighten his legs. The men were laughing again, but it had a different edge to it this time, as if they were sharing in his success. Matthew pulled the blanket over his feet and settled himself on the mattress. It was then that he discovered to his amazement that he was laughing as well.

\*\*\*\*\*

Flint slung his hammock at the end of the line, taking for himself the extra space normally only allotted to quartermasters and other junior petty officers. It would soon be the start of another voyage, another of the irregular anniversaries when he was leaving England.

He was twenty-five, and had been listed in one or another ship's books continuously for the past nine years. His father had been a sailor, and it had always been Flint's intention to follow him. And he was doing exactly that, although not in the way that either had anticipated.

Brighthelmstone, their home town in Sussex, had been under the care of the Duke of Newcastle, who proclaimed it a free port, where no impressment would be tolerated. This had protected Flint's father from the attention of the press and allowed him to work in relative safety.

He had been a fisherman; a respectable trade, although one that did not quite provide for his family. To make up the deficit he also acted as a free trader, smuggling anything that could find a ready market. It was certainly less honest than his day work, but many times more lucrative. When Flint had turned ten he was considered old enough to accompany him to work, both legitimate and illicit, and his apprenticeship began.

The first time he had seen action was with a revenue cutter. They had noticed it coming out of a squall on a dark night when they were just about to start the transfer with their French counterpart. She came down on them, the wind on her quarter, pendant flying and extended bowsprit waving an admonishing finger.

Flint, who had charge of the tiller, had been terrified, but his father leant across and briefly placed a steadying hand over his. Without a word or signal the French ship turned into the wind and set a course, close hauled, that would take her from danger, while his father ordered their boat on to the opposite tack. Flint nervously brought the rudder across; the boat settled and began to take on speed. They passed the revenue cutter, with only the night and the weather to hide them. Flint took time to glance across and recognised the Shoreham boat; he had seen her many times before, moored in the nearby harbour, and probably knew most of the men who crewed her. The thought comforted him for a moment. Then a pinpoint of light, followed by a puff of smoke that was instantly whipped away by the wind, caused him to wonder; and it was only with the shriek of passing shot that he fully understood what was about.

At that moment Flint had known true fear; he dropped the tiller, allowing the boat to fall off the wind, and scuttled for shelter. Immediately his father was at the helm and coaxing the boat back to her true course. Then he turned to his son.

"Don't min' the noise, the one you hear has gone past—noise can't hurt you." The ship was lightly crewed, and the threat from the cutter meant every available hand must be ready to tend the sheets. Flint knew he was needed and returned to the helm. His father bellowed for the men to be ready to tack, and as each went to their places, he turned back to grin at his son. It had been dark and raining, and yet Flint could see his father's expression of confidence. He was treating this contest that could so easily end their lives as no more than an entertaining diversion, deriving excitement and actual pleasure from a situation that would have finished many men. It was a lesson that had stayed with Flint ever since, and one reason why he was often considered bold, self-assured and something of a rogue.

Their boat had kept the cutter on the run for nearly an hour, tacking and jibing like a fox eluding the hound, each time with Flint manning the helm like a seasoned hand. Eventually they were able to pass over shoals that forced the deeper hulled vessel to bear away or be grounded. At the time Flint felt relieved, although another sensation was also present. Never before had life seemed so clear, so vibrant. The heaving deck beneath his feet, the squeal of the blocks, the crack of the sails as the boat tacked, all these now held more for him, and the thought of a normal life on land seemed too mundane to even consider.

In the following months he had continued to learn from his father and soon acquired a thorough grounding in the sailor's craft. Then, on the twenty-fourth of July, the men from the Shoreham press had converged on Brighthelmstone and surrounded the town. Flint and his father were at sea at the time, and knew nothing of this, or the death of the Duke of Newcastle that had occasioned it. For the ten hours that the town was besieged no man left his house, and only one stray unfortunate was captured and pressed. Disgusted by their failure, the troops were heading back along the coast road when Flint's father's boat was spotted.

Contrary to popular belief, only those acquainted with the sea may legally be pressed. Of course there were always exceptions, and the occasional mistake, which accounted for the vast number of weavers, butchers, builders and the like that filled most ships' books. But smugglers? Which of them could claim that they were not men who earned their living on the water? Besides, capture meant prison, and possibly the gallows. It was likely that then they would be given the chance to volunteer for the Navy, so why not simplify matters, and take them straight away?

The boat was beached and being relieved of her booty when the press struck. Although used to dodging five or maybe ten from the revenue service, no one was expecting the rush of forty or more disciplined men under the command of naval officers. The smugglers spread along the beach, ducking into old hiding places, and generally doing all they could to evade capture. But five were taken, and one was Flint's father.

Flint, being under age, was ignored in the mayhem. He had watched, determinedly unmoved, as his father was manacled up and led away. It was common knowledge that a man pressed for the Navy would be gone for some years, maybe a lifetime, and in truth Flint had not looked on him since.

And so he had gone from being the son of a successful fisherman and entrepreneur who provided well for his family to a boy forced to accept the charity of others. His mother had died seven years before, during the birth of his sister. Fortunately John Mackenzie, the local schoolmaster, heard of their misfortune and accepted them into his family. Only later did Flint discover why he had shown such kindness. As far as Flint had known, Mackenzie and his father were hardly on nodding terms; he had been surprised to learn of the part the Scot had played, and was continuing to play, in organising the smugglers.

Flint stayed with the family for five years, during which time he benefited from a sound education and the company of Amy, Mackenzie's daughter, who was a few months his junior. It was a relationship that was doomed to fail, for whatever plans Amy may have had for Flint, she could offer him nothing that would compete with the call of the sea and the possibility of meeting up with his father once more. Mackenzie had been adamant that Flint could not join any of the other smuggling crews, and volunteering for a merchant ship did not appeal to the young firebrand.They received one letter from his father after he had taken part in the Battle of Dominica, which some now called the Battle of the Saints, and another just before Admiral Rodney returned to England and his fleet demobilised. There had been no welcome homecoming however. Despite Mackenzie's enquires, no one could say what finally became of Flint's father. When he first offered himself at the *rendezvous* in 1786, Flint had hoped he might find out more.

"There's got to be fifty thousand in the service now, lad," the impressment officer told him. "Can't keep track of 'em all." Then Flint had taken the shilling, and made it fifty thousand and one.

And now, now he was a seasoned hand, useful, if somewhat unpredictable, a sound man in a fight, and needed for as long as he could hand reef and steer.

Flint closed his eyes and, smelling the sweat odour of clean canvas, fell quickly into a deep sleep.

\*\*\*\*\*

"Ah, King. Come in, will you?" King took three more paces towards the captain, who sat behind his desk, his back to the open stern gallery. The cabin was all but dark, only the twin candles on the captain's desk, and a distant glow of lights from Ryde, broke the evening gloom. Captain Shepherd finished his work and sat back in his chair. He smiled at King, who, feeling something was expected of him, smiled awkwardly in return.

"We'll be putting to sea on tomorrow's afternoon tide," Shepherd told him, although every man on board knew as much. "That is, if the water hoy arrives in time." King felt something more was called for from him and gave the only reply he could.

"Yes, sir."

"I wanted to have a word with you before that."

King braced himself; this could be very good, or very bad.

"The incident with the coaster, when was it—last year?"

"End of 'ninety-three, sir."

"That's right. I said at the time how impressed I was, and I do so again now. You have the makings of a good officer, and I expect to see you progress."

"Yes, sir." He was going to add something about trying to, but fortunately held his tongue at the last moment.

"When Mr Curtis left I had intended to move everyone up a place and promote you to acting lieutenant." *Had intended.* This was not going as well as it might. "However, another man has been appointed and I am sure he will do very well." Shepherd looked down at his desk. The last remark was a lie and he was ashamed of himself. The fact that it would do only harm to express his reservations about Rogers was hardly justification.

"Still, I have considered the matter, and consulted other officers." That could only mean the first lieutenant and Mr Humble, the master. "Quite a few third rates are carrying six lieutenants now, and we have decided that a further lieutenant is needed in *Vigilant*. For that reason I will rate you to the acting rank of lieutenant."

King stiffened, and swallowed hard, remembered at the last moment that it was Pite's hat that he now squashed under his arm.

"You have nothing to say?" The smile was back on the captain's face, and this time King had no hesitation in returning it.

"Thank you, sir."

Shepherd's smile faded slightly. "In giving you this advancement I wanted to be sure you deserve it."

"Sir?" King was still thinking about the promotion, but sensed that a reaction was called for.

The captain's expression grew more thoughtful. "I have the power to promote and disrate; certainly as far as acting ranks are concerned."

King was not sure what was coming next, and for a moment placed his excitement on hold.

"Let me just say that many men have been passed as commissioned officers who do not deserve the privilege. By giving you an acting rank I am protecting the service as much as anything else. Should you prove to be a competent officer," he paused for a warmer smile, "as I think you will, I shall have no hesitation in putting you forward for promotion at the next round."

"Thank you, sir."

"But if you in any way displease me, if I detect any of the practices that I personally find deplorable in a King's officer, I will not only send you back to the midshipman's' berth, but also see to it that you never get so much as a glimpse of a promotion board for as long as you remain in this ship."

King swallowed again, he understood exactly what the captain meant; in fact, viewing the matter dispassionately, he agreed with his sentiments wholeheartedly. A simple "Yes, sir" voiced all he could on the subject.

"I have one more thing to add." King was attentive. "There are many points that impress boards, but none more so than book work." It was King's turn to smile now, and he did so. The captain had often had cause to comment on his weekly journals.

"Obviously, as acting lieutenant you will be the junior, and I don't think I need spell out the important duties attached to that post?"

Indeed he did not. King would be in charge of the ship's signals. It would mean learning the code book, and all the intricate ways the Navy used to send messages. A daunting task, especially for one who found reading arduous. Still, it was promotion; there were only four commissioned ranks in the Royal Navy, and he was well on the way to the first.

Shepherd dismissed King and watched as he turned and walked from his cabin. The expression on the young man's face had been obvious, even in the half light. He thought back on the conversation; what he had said was completely true: he was impressed by King, and honestly expected him to progress. With a modicum of luck the next board would see him a lieutenant. Sheperd could even envisage a time, not so very far away, when King made commander, or even post captain. What he did not know, indeed, what he would never have guessed, was that at that moment and for many more to come, King would have willingly died for his captain.

*****

At anchor the normal watch system was slightly modified, and by nightfall most of the hands were in their hammocks. Matthew felt at rest for the first time since he had met up with the warrant officer the day before. The thought naturally followed that just four days ago he had been at home, and he quickly found something else to set his mind on. His hammock moved slightly as a man climbed in or out of his own, sending a jolt through the entire line. He himself had ventured out a few minutes before, struggling with his newly acquired skill for a much needed visit forward and returning to his own berth, miraculously without losing his way. The deck had appeared strange with all hammocks down, the closest he had come was when he had been caving as a child, and chanced upon a line of bats at rest. He remembered the time, and the smell of the tainted, airless cave. The stench on the deck was not dissimilar, except the cave had been cold and wet. The deck was warm with the combined heat of many hundred bodies, although there was still a rich dampness in the air. His berth was on the lower gundeck, close to the other members of his mess, and the pieces they would serve. There was little ventilation, but at least the ports would be opened occasionally, better than being below on the orlop, which must be truly stifling.

A few snores started, and somebody coughed. Then came the unmistakeable rumbling of a groan. He froze. The noise gathered in intensity, until he realised he was listening to not one, but many hushed voices in unison. Slowly a semblance of form appeared and the moaning grew into a song, sung deep and low. He recognised the tune as "Admiral Hosier's Ghost", one of the many that Jake had taught the kids of Leatherhead. But that had been a spirited, majestic affair; this was more like a dirge. It grew louder still, until he knew that men on either side of him were singing; there could not be a sleeping soul on the deck. Jake had regaled them with stories of jolly parties, hornpipes and music, and the comradeship of fellow sailors. Never had he mentioned the monotonous roar of penned up men; men separated from their loved ones for heaven knew how long, men tied to a service that spoke highly of adventure and wealth, while it callously killed, maimed and maddened.

From his cabin on the orlop the master at arms heard the singing and decided a prowl was in order. Setting his hat straight on his bullet head, Critchley worked his way to the lower gundeck as the song continued. He sniffed; there was a slight whiff of "sailor's joy", the illicit spirit that was his constant enemy. Men had died from the lunacy it induced, or had been invalided out, blind and stupid. He knew from the amount in the air that there was not enough about to cause real damage, however; and with the wives only just departed and the ship due to sail on the morrow, he could hardly blame them for seeking some comfort in drink.

The singing carried on, seemingly without break or repetition. He could order it to stop, indeed he would have to if an officer heard and thought fit to complain, but Critchley passed on, the song gently eating into his subconscious, bringing back times when he had been younger. Times when he too had been a normal hand, and frightened. Times that he only remembered in circumstances such as this, so ingrained in his job had he become.

As a younger man he had married, indeed had sired a child and might be a husband and father still, for all he knew. The last time he had seen his family was some thirty years back. Since then the service had taken him as its own, given him food, shelter, and his life a meaning. He was proud of his position, proud also of the life he led, although he would only admit both to himself. And he was glad to be at sea, rather than scratching out a living on land for children who didn't care and a wife who did, but only for other men.

He had no illusions on the last point. Critchley had heard too many stories of sailors' wives to have any respect for women. His own had been starting to show signs, which was probably one of the reasons he allowed himself to be sucked back into the Navy. Then there was the behaviour of the men the last few weeks; strong men, whom he'd seen endure flogging without uttering a word, crying like babies because some woman or other had gone off with another man.

The bell rang three times, and from every sentry post came the call "All's well." Critchley completed his circuit. "All's well." As senior hand, his cabin was as large as any warrant officer's, and he held the respect of every man on board. After a year or two he could expect to move from this to a proper line-of-battle ship, maybe a first rate, where the decks would always be white, and all the brassware shone like gold. And when it had to end (as Critchley was starting to see would be the case one day), there should be an honourable retirement with, if not exactly riches, at least a comfortable time ashore, and he might even be in line for a berth at Greenwich if it all got too much.

"All's well." He considered the matter for a moment as he blew out the purser's dip that was another privilege of his rank, and soberly decided that they were probably right.

# ALARIC BOND

# CHAPTER FIVE

MATTHEW awoke to the shrill sounds of a whistle, followed by a hearty roar. "Whe-e-ugh all hands on deck ho-o-y! Do you hear the news there below?" His eyes opened wide as his body slowly came to life. "Come jump up, every man, every one, every mother's son of you!"

The voice was getting nearer, but so far Matthew was certain no one else had moved. His head ached, and he had the odd taste in his mouth he had experienced the morning before.

"All right, you've had your lie in!" Another voice this time, closer and with more force. Matthew felt the man next to him stir, and waited while he clambered down to the deck. "Out or down, out or down!"

A whack cut into Matthew's hammock at about the small of his back. The blow was cushioned by the mattress, but the shock was still sufficient to start him out and on to the deck below. He stood for a moment, a faint wave of dizziness sweeping over him. All about men were climbing from their hammocks, coughing and yawning. A man in a dark uniform with a stiff hat was passing quickly amongst them, a length of knotted rope in his hand.

"Out or down, out or down, I say!" he swung the rope's end to and fro indiscriminately, hitting men in their hammocks or as they staggered to their feet until only one hammock was still occupied. The man with the rope approached it with a look close to relish on his face.

"A sharp knife, a clear conscience, and out or down is the word!" he whipped out his own knife and slashed through the clews at the head of the hammock. The man inside dropped to the deck like a stone, landing painfully on his head and shoulders with an impressive thud. Matthew watched in horror as the body rolled over, and then realised it was Jenkins, the one who had laughed so much at his own efforts the night before. It was his turn to be laughed at now, something which the other members of his mess took full advantage of, as Jenkins rose gingerly to his feet, one hand rubbing his skull.

"Come on, lad, we're for the quarterdeck first thing." Flint pushed him gently towards the companionway, and Matthew obediently began to walk, feeling vaguely guilty about leaving his hammock still hanging with all the others.

On deck it was dark, although the cold fresh sea air was welcome. Flint led his mess forward to where a pile of large flat stones had been left.

"You right, lad?" Flint enquired, as he collected a stone for himself and another for Matthew.

"Yes, I..." The pain in his head was suddenly quite acute. It had been the same yesterday, and he wondered if he were sickening for something.

Flint glanced at him. "Tell me."

"M-my head hurts," Matthew stammered, feeling foolish as Flint's look of concern changed to a grin.

"Bad case of fat head, by all likes. It's nowt to worry over."

"Aye, It'll go with the fresh air," Jenkins, who had joined them and was more than entitled to a headache, assured him. "It's what comes of sleeping with two full watches below. Told you, 'tain't half so bad at proper sea quarters."

The men had formed up into a line, facing the bulkhead that marked the stern end of the quarterdeck. One of them sprinkled handfuls of white sand onto the deck, and another followed, splashing sea water. Flint began pressing his stone into the sand and rubbing it backwards and forwards along the deck strakes in an odd polishing motion.

"We're smoothing the decks," Flint explained, "so as we don't catch no splinters when we gets about."

Matthew had heard of this daily ritual from Jake, although the old man had said nothing about starting in the middle of the night. The sand was fine but sharp, and Matthew found his stone hard to shift at first. With a little more effort it began to move, and soon he was stretching forward and back with the rest of them.

"These 'ere are holystones," Flint informed him after a while. "Past twenty years the Navy's been takin' 'em from an old church on Wight."

"Aye, an' bloody great Bibles, they are too," Jenkins added.

"All right, lads, turn about." Flint stood up and inspected their work. Though wet, the scrubbed area of deck appeared white and smooth in the half light. The men turned so that their backs were to the cabins before kneeling down and beginning again. This time they were resting on the area they had just treated, and the deck was moist and gritty with sand. Matthew felt the damp though his trouser knees, although that was soon forgotten as his belly and back muscles began to object to the punishment.

"Gets better, after a while," Flint grunted. "Do this for a couple of weeks, and ya won't know yerself."

"That's if somtin' else don't kill yer firs'," Crehan added, some way down the line.

Matthew determinedly turned his mind from the Irishman's threat, although at that moment endless mornings of this particular exercise seemed a bleak enough future.

"It's just talk, lad." The man on his immediate left was also Irish, although he spoke softly and without Crehan's unpleasant nasal twang. "An' as for the stoning, you'll not be seeing a proper sailorman with a belly now, would you?"

Matthew set himself to the work, and the line moved forward slowly, oh so slowly, while the bare deck lay before them all like an unvanquished enemy.

*****

At first light, a marine drummer appeared and mounted the poop, the highest deck and right at the stern of the ship. For two seconds he held his sticks in the air before bringing them down on his drum, beating out a rousing tattoo. In every commissioned ship at the anchorage the ceremony was performed, and soon all of Spithead vibrated with the stimulating rhythm.

Simpson broke off from his scrubbing to go below. He was the cook of Flint's mess, and it was one of his duties to collect the men's rations from the stewards' room, where the holders would be bringing them up from store. The drumming continued as Simpson explained his purpose to the marine sentry, then passed down one companionway. It would carry on until the port admiral's office took a fancy to fire a gun. The official definition of daybreak was when a grey goose could be spotted a mile off. On the sound of the gun, all ships would hoist their colours, and signals could be passed to and fro. It was the way of the ship, the way of the Navy, and on that particular morning it irritated Simpson.

Clambering down the next companionway, he joined the queue outside the stewards' room. As mess cook he was responsible for what had to be taken to the galley, and labelling it with a lead seal. Other items, such as butter, fruit and any luxury that might be going, would also be under his charge, and it would be up to him alone to distribute them to the men. This he would do fairly, as all men took turns in being the mess cook; besides, Simpson had long ago discovered that the world had a habit of getting even.

Still, it irked him, as did most things at that moment. The strict routine, the pattern for everything that the Navy seemed so fond of; all the humdrum work that had to be measured into strict timetables and regulated patterns. He made no allowances for the difficulty of organising several hundred men to do several thousand tasks on a daily basis, he just longed for a break, a chance to order his own life and set his own way of living it.

This was not a new sensation for Simpson; it was one he had experienced many times before. And now, after a period of relaxation, when the ship was not fully worked up and men could do pretty well as they pleased, the first days back to normal routine were very hard for him to bear; he felt frustrated, controlled, and longed for a way to end the monotony.

The chance came when he was heading from the galley back to his mess. Some of the lower deck ports had been opened; odd, because it was not a Saturday, and the deck had been vented only the day before. The quickening of his heart gave him the idea before he had even thought of it himself, and after stowing the day's dry provisions in the pewter containers, he stepped back and looked furtively along the deck.

A minimal number of men were about, and the only officer, a midshipman, seemed more interested in berating two hands who appeared to have spilt something on the deck outside the wardroom. They were to the stern, while Simpson's mess was amidships. Silently he stole towards the bows, trying not to attract attention or look behind as he went.

Luck was with him: he passed the manger, where the only hand was a simpleton who tended the animals. The forward ports were cut deep, so that their angle of fire almost covered the bows, and were ideal. They also sat in the lee of the manger, so that he was all but hidden from the causal glance. It was slack water, the first of the flood not being due for ten minutes. He would be passing directly under the heads, which were currently in use, but that consideration meant little to Simpson. He began to breathe deeply, both from excitement and in preparation for what was to come. He peered through the port, pulling his red pigtail tight against his head. The bulwarks were thick and the port ledges deep enough for a man to kneel on. Looking up and back he could see the forechannel where the marine sentry would be on duty. The channel jutted out by well over a foot, and he guessed that he would be shielded. But it was only a guess, a chance he would take, one of many, but worth it, if he wanted to end the dreadful monotony.

Silently he eased himself out of the port, until he was facing the side of the ship, his hands gripping the inside edge. His feet were touching the water; once he straightened his arms most of his legs would be under. A distant report of a gun echoed about the anchorage, making him start with fright and almost loose his grip. From above the drumming stopped, and he heard the whistle of the boatswain's pipes as *Vigilant* raised her colours. He smiled to himself as the tension left him. It was as good a time as any; Simpson relaxed his arms, feeling the crisp seas creep up his legs. His hands released their grip and he allowed himself to slip into the water.

This was the hardest part; a sentry on any one of the other ships at anchor might have spotted him climbing from the port. He had to gather his breath as quickly as possible; the hunt could be raised against him at any time. The water was cold and heavily tainted from the heads as he had expected. Two breaths, three, and hold; without a ripple he pressed himself under, diving down and seeking safety in the depths.

He opened his eyes, and immediately saw the single anchor cable that stretched down to the sea bed. It made an excellent guide and he swam on, hoping that he was far enough under to be invisible to the watching marine guard. On, and past the cable; now it was more difficult. He had to surface within the next few seconds, or his lungs would burst. With luck he would be under the shadow of the bowsprit, if not he could expect to be fired upon.

On his way up he expelled what was left in his lungs, so that when he finally broke into clean air he just gasped a breath, before descending once more. He carried on, not knowing what had been noticed above, only conscious of the need to put as much distance between him and the ship as he could. In an anchorage like Spithead he would have to continue this porpoise-like progress until he could be sure of swimming without detection. It only needed one man, one bright sentry on his or another ship, and the alarm would be raised. Hands from every available vessel would be drafted into finding and bringing him back. And should it happen, should he be unlucky and caught, there was little he could hope for; the Navy had a way of treating deserters, one that served not only to punish the crime but to dissuade any who might be harbouring similar ideas. But then the world had a habit of getting even; his thoughts came back to mock him as he swam on, teeth set in grim determination.

\*\*\*\*\*

Flint was aware that something was wrong when Simpson failed to return. They finished their portion of the quarterdeck just as "up hammocks" was piped, and he engineered a place next to Jenkins on his way to the lower gundeck.

"Simpson's not back from cook's duty."

Jenkins hardly moved his head, but Flint knew he had heard.

"Don't think he might be back at 'is old tricks, do yer?" he continued.

This time he got a faint grimace and a nod of the head in reply. Flint was not surprised, in fact of all in his mess, Simpson would have been the first he would have picked as a likely runner.

"Better lash up his hammock, for 'im, eh?"

That triggered a definite reaction; Jenkins was not the kind who took to doing other men's chores.

"Lash 'is 'ammock?" He looked at Flint as if he had just suggested something immoral. "You wants me to lash 'is 'ammock?"

"It's up to you; you're his mate."

Jenkins mused; the bonds of friendship had strict limitations.

"Otherwise he'll be missed," Flint continued. "You want that?"

"Daft booby should've run after'ds," Jenkins muttered, but Flint knew he could be relied on for that much at least.

*****

Breakfast was burgoo, a dish based on oatmeal, served out of a pewter tub by O'Conner, who had been detailed by Flint as the new mess cook. Matthew took his wooden bowl and held it up. As boy of the mess he had the last of everything, although the burgoo was served in generous measure and there was more than enough to fill his bowl. The other men were eating, some using wooden spoons, others their hands, a couple adding vinegar or salt to the mash after tasting. Matthew cautiously dipped a finger into the stuff and was pleasantly surprised. It was porridge, different from any he had tasted before, for the oatmeal had a certain flavour: sour, but not hopelessly so. He scooped out a handful and another after that. It wasn't what he would have chosen to eat, but at his age he wasn't fussy.

"Taste's all right wit' molasses," O'Conner, the friendly Irishman, informed him. "Otherwise a drop o'rum spices up nice." Matthew smiled; he would have liked to make small talk, but had learned that his stammer could turn light conversation into an ordeal for both parties.

"You're one man short, Flint!" The men continued to eat, but there was a noticeable wariness about the table, and all conversation ceased.

"What's that yer sayin', sir?" Flint looked up at Lieutenant Gregory as if he had been simply passing the time of day.

"You're one man short," Gregory persisted, looking down at his watch bill for confirmation.

"Two men joined us yesterday, sir." Flint did not normally like to play the fool, but a man's life was worth the indignity.

"I'm accounting for that, an' there's still one man short," Gregory cleared his throat. "Where's your divisional midshipman?"

"Mr Pite? He's not been to us yet, sir."

"I see, well, I'd better check." The divisional inspection was not for a good half hour; Simpson was unlucky that his absence had been noted that much earlier. "Answer your names as I call. Flint I know, O'Conner?"

"Sir!"

"Simpson?" The silence was emphasised by men at the other tables who, guessing that something was up, had stopped eating to listen.

"Simpson not here?"

Flint looked about. "Now that you mention it, sir..."

"Don't bull with me, man. I'm not a Hoxton newcome!" Indeed Gregory had begun on the lower deck and knew their ways, and insults, as well as any of them. He turned on his heel and headed away. For a moment there was quiet at the mess table, and then O'Conner returned to his breakfast.

"Ah, and he was a hell of a man, so he was," he said after a while. It seemed a reasonable epitaph.

"Aye," Jenkins added. "An' I'll give anyone a sip to an 'ogshead.' e's not seen no more 'ereabouts."

The men laughed, and returned to their food. Dead or deserted, it made little difference; none of them expected to see Simpson again.

# CHAPTER SIX

THE loss of another man did not trouble the captain for long, although, as with many small irritations, the annoyance lay more in that it had happened so often before. He pushed the thought to the back of his mind; there were other matters to contend with. The convoy was now fully assembled and would be ready to sail on the afternoon tide. The only problem remaining was the incompetence (he could give it no other word) of the Commodore. As senior captain, Shepherd was in overall charge of all escorts, but the convoy itself was made up of John Company ships, and commanded by one of their senior officers.

Shepherd was aware that commissions in the Honourable East India Company were greatly valued; indeed, an exact price could be placed on them, as they were frequently purchased. Such a policy should not shock him, when his own service was littered with the sons of admirals, lords and politicians who only carried the King's commission because their fathers knew someone, or something, of note. But Shepherd had trusted that such trash would be kept a long way from salt water, certainly never given the command of a fleet.

He had the Commodore's order of sailing in front of him now; the fact that a civilian should have had the gall to instruct an officer of the Royal Navy only fuelled his resentment further. The Commodore's flagship was also carrying a retinue of diplomats, bound for the Far East; doubtless these petty officials, acting on advice from their wives for all he knew, were behind some of the more extreme directions. "All ships to reef at dusk, to avoid the possibility of waking passengers, should sail need to be shortened during the night." He drew a deep sigh and allowed the paper to fall to the floor.

To sour the lemon, he could not take a straight course and send the document back, with a pointed reference to the Merchant Shipping Act which spelled out the differences between a courtesy rank in the merchant service and a King's officer. Instead he was forced to beat back and forth, countering the inept orders and proffering the normal tried and tested arrangements, which would no doubt be returned with idiotic questions and impossible alterations. In addition, everything had to be versed in prose so obsequious and sycophantic it would make a bishop sick. Shepherd gloomily predicted that the valuable hours before sailing would be wasted in sending messages to the flagship, with the only measure of progress being the falling level of ink in his bottle.

Two things that could not be changed were tides and weather. As far as the former was concerned, the first of the Solent's double high was due in three hours, and if the wind held, Shepherd was determined to sail with it. He picked up his pen and began to scratch notes. Later he would call for Lindsay, his secretary, and dictate a letter that obeyed the rules in every respect, but first he had to decide what he really wanted to say.

A shout from the marine sentry at his door and the clump of a musket butt on the deck disturbed him, but he continued to write up to the end of his sentence. Then he sat back from his work and paused for a moment, before calling for his visitor to enter.

Dyson stood in the doorway, cold and precise as ever. "Last of the water's just been taken on, sir. We're ready to sail at any time. Tide rises in..."

"Yes, I know, thank you, Mr Dyson." It was measure of the captain's impatience that he snapped at his first lieutenant. As always it gave him little pleasure and no satisfaction; Dyson appeared to absorb anger, and every other emotion, without any obvious change, just as a sponge takes in water.

"Very good, sir." He turned to go, but Shepherd asked a question, if only to make amends for his behaviour.

"Have your heard anything regarding Simpson?"

"Not from the port admiral, sir," Dyson replied. "And we've had no news from the other ships in the anchorage. All the hoys and lighters will be searched as a matter of course, but so far it looks as if Simpson got a clear passage."

*****

Dyson was right: Simpson was still very much at large. Once clear of the other anchored ships he had risen to the surface before settling to a slow, powerful breaststroke.

He had considered making straight for Gilkicker Point on the west side of the harbour and the closest piece of land. However, the area thereabouts was quite barren, and with the increased guard that patrolled to stop patients escaping from Haslar hospital, he thought it better to risk crossing the harbour and make for Southsea instead.

An early sun appeared as he swam; the light was weak, but welcome, and before long Simpson was actually enjoying himself. Unusual amongst seamen, who regard their natural element with caution, Simpson loved to swim; and the steady progress across the harbour, sun on his shoulders and red pigtail flowing behind, brought a smile to his face. Whatever he was doing, whatever risks he took, it certainly beat stoning decks and was just the break from routine he had been looking for.

A victualling lighter set out from the harbour making for the anchorage. Simpson slowed his pace, content to almost drift in the gentle swell until it had passed. The shore was growing nearer now, and he could choose his spot, avoiding the area busy with fishing boats, and the castle that looked out over the harbour. Between the two was a stretch of common, and a beach. Three small boats were pulled up there, but he could see no sign of life, and he cautiously approached the land.

A woman walked along the foreshore carrying something in a wicker basket. Simpson began to tread water until she had passed, then eased himself in with the gentle surf.

Clear of the sea he felt clumsy and vulnerable. He stepped quickly through the shallows and made for the shelter of one of the boats. The beach consisted of loose shingle and to Simpson's mind his horny feet made far too much noise as they crunched the stones. The boat was small, with one mast that was set well forward. Simpson guessed it was for shellfish or sport, and gave it little thought other than that. His clothes were more important: they would take a while to dry, and for as long as he appeared wet Simpson would be marked out as a runner. He pulled his shirt off, wrung it out, and rubbed it across his chest before ringing it once more and putting it back on. The same procedure followed for his trousers. He was still damp, but not as conspicuously so, and he took two furtive looks about him before making the quick sprint across the shingle for the common.

His feet left the smooth stones and found soft grass. He paused in the lee of the first full tree; his heart pounded inside his chest, but still luck was with him. To his left the nearest house was three hundred yards away. Someone might have seen him come up from the beach, but Simpson decided it was unlikely. The castle was very visible to his right, and there his presence might well have been spotted; it would be best to keep moving. The common spread for two or more cables before the town of Southsea began. He set out once more, cutting an erratic route that made use of all possible cover, while suppressing the urge to run, as that would make him far more noticeable from a distance. If he kept to the outskirts of the town he could head east, round the back of the castle, flank Eastney, and up towards Milton. With luck he should be passed the Hilsea Channel and on to Drayton by the end of his watch. True safety would not come until he was at least thirty miles clear of the coast, but he should be relatively secure by evening, and with *Vigilant* sailing on the afternoon tide, he only had to keep his head down for the next few hours to say goodbye to the ship and her people for ever.

He was approaching the houses now, and deliberately hunched his shoulders and slowed his rolling walk down to a shamble. There was a pay ticket sewn into his trouser waistband. Once that had dried sufficiently he'd rig himself with a long jacket and see about some victuals. Really there was nothing to this desertion lark; all it took was a bit of gumption and a clear head. He slowed his walk further and merged in with the people of the street until all differences between them and him vanished completely.

*****

Topmasts had been set up immediately after the water hoy had left. Now it was just before noon, the time of day the men yearned for. At a nod from the officer of the watch, Baldwin, the ship's fiddler, stuck his violin under his chin and struck up "Nancy Dawson". Immediately all eyes rested on the purser, who walked ahead of two of his stewards as they brought a wooden pin of rum up from the spirit room. The pin was placed next to a kid of water, and the ceremony began. Murmuring with anticipation, the senior hands from each mess queued in order. The purser's stewards emptied some water out of the deck kid, until it held roughly three times the amount of the rum they had drawn, and then tipped the contents of the pin into the water. It was naval custom that the rum must always be added to the water, never the other way. Sailors swore that it made a difference in the tasting, just as some middle aged ladies insist that tea should be added to milk. Once the ship had been at sea for six weeks, lime juice, to prevent scurvy, and sugar would be added and the concoction served up: a rich fruit cup that would take the edge off the hardest day.

Morrison consulted a list and formally authorised the issuing of spirits. Beer, at a gallon to a man, was more usual when a ship was in home waters, but Morrison had come to an agreement with Boyle from the victualling board, and there were few amongst the crew who would voice any objections. This was not the first mutually beneficial "agreement" that Morrison and the victualling clerk had come to, and both earnestly hoped it would not be the last.

Apart from the scratch of the fiddle the ceremony continued in silence, until the hands carrying the grog reached their mess, when hushed murmurs rose up from the excited men.

From the quarterdeck Mr Midshipman Pite looked down on the proceedings without any hint of condescension. At a time when concern for fellow men was confined to liberals, some of the clergy, and those with ulterior motives, Pite was careful to hide any compassion he held for the seamen. Few had joined the ship voluntarily, and none were allowed to leave unless illness, injury or enemy action made them useless to the Crown. Before that could happen they would eat preserved food and drink fetid water, while undertaking dangerous work for long hours. Discipline was customarily enforced by corporal methods of the most basic kind, and if they ever rose up to complain or object, they stood a good chance of meeting the hangman's noose. Of course life on land could be every bit as hard; but Pite was of the opinion that, if the men found solace in a gill of rum twice a day, it was probably less than they were actually due.

Lieutenant Gregory came and stood next to the midshipman, and together they watched the ceremony. Officers such as Gregory were commonly known as tarpaulins, men who had started on the lower deck, often *via* the press gang, and yet taken to the life well enough to achieve warrant, and even commission status. The odds against a common sailor rising as high as Gregory were approximately two thousand five hundred to one, which made Gregory quite an exceptional man.

"I've always thought that a bit of a waste, sir," Pite ruminated. "Throwing the rum out like that." The ceremony was almost over now, and the cooks from each mess were forming lines to the galley as two stewards carried the leftover to the side and tipped it overboard.

Gregory smiled at the lad. "Offends you, does it; seeing grog go to the deep?"

"Why don't they save it, issue it next time?"

"If they did there'd be problems; men would want to start sharing it out. 'Sides, it can't be saved; it's got water in, and rum and water only stays drinkable for a brief while."

"Is that right?"

"Why do you think it's diluted in the first place?"

"To make it weaker?"

"No, lad. Water don't make alcohol disappear, just dilutes it. What it does is stop the men from hoarding the stuff. Like I say, rum in water's not worth a light later in the day. Stops them stowing it for a Saturday night spree!"

"I never knew that, sir," said Pite.

"Neither did I, once," he smiled. "We was all born knowing nothing, but there's reasons for most things in the Navy."

Gregory walked away. He was now a lieutenant, a King's officer, with a commission drawn out on parchment to prove it. Still, the memories he carried of being a lower deck seaman were very much alive. In the wardroom he could choose from a variety of wines and refined spirits, but nothing could stop him secretly sniffing the air for the very last scent of that rum.

*****

The warmth of the drink stayed with the men as dinner was distributed. Matthew, too young for spirit issue, was conscious of a universal feeling of goodwill as they seated themselves at the mess table between the great guns. Even Crehan bore a neutral expression that was very nearly benign, while he stacked the square wooden platters that would serve as plates.

Matthew fingered one inquisitively. It was made of a dark, close-grained wood, burnished by much use. The edges were slightly raised, giving it a frame.

"Fiddles," said Jenkins, noticing Matthew's interest. "Stops the food fallin' off, an' anyone takin' too much."

Matthew looked at the fiddles again.

"When they serve slop it's got to stay inside, see? If you're found with food on the fiddle, you're gettin' more 'n your share."

"Why's it square?" Matthew asked.

Jenkins pursed his lips. "Blow'd if I knows. Easier to make, p'raps? But when you gets three servins in a day, that makes the three square meals they promises in the Rondey."

Matthew nodded. He'd eaten that morning's breakfast from a round wooden bowl, but didn't feel inclined to press the matter.

"Banyan days we gets slop," Jenkins continued. "Boiled peas, fruit duff, an' t'like—no meat. Otherwise its made meals like lobscouse: that's meat an' biscuit wi onion an' tatas, or skillygalee. T'day's straight boiled, with pickled cabbage. We got 'nother way of setting that out fair, you wait 'n see."

Matthew watched while O'Conner opened the pewter tureen on the table and began to load a platter with boiled beef. At the far end Lewis had turned away, and was staring intently at the spirketting below the nearby gunport.

"Who be this for?" O'Conner asked conversationally, holding the platter well out of Lewis's sight.

"That's Jenkins'." Lewis replied, and the platter was placed in front of Matthew's guide.

The serving continued with Lewis nominating each man in turn, until the entire mess had potions of varying size before them.

"Cooks cut the meat up into regular 'mounts," Jenkins continued with his lecture, while he examined his meat with interest. "But some's more regular 'n others."

Matthew watched cautiously while the other men ate. A few delicately cut off portions using their clasp knives, while others bit deep into the chunks and tore the flesh away with their teeth. He picked up a lump of beef, glossy with fat, and nibbled into it. The flesh was hard, but not unpleasant. A faint tang of salt gave it flavour, and he began to chew with a lad's appetite.

"Victual's good in *Vigilant*." Jenkins informed him, generously spraying Matthew with shreds of beef as he spoke. "Some ships you'd be better off scrimmin' the meat than' eatin' it." He paused to belch. "I 'member *Cambridge*, my first ship. She's guard at Plymouth Dock now, but it were a terrible hulk for victuals when I knew 'er. We used to breed rats in her cable tier, then fight the 'olders for 'em, just to keep body an' soul together."

Matthew swallowed his current mouthful dryly and paused for some moments before taking another bite.

O'Conner, an ordinary seaman of middle years, had noticed Crehan, but so far had not spoken with him beyond the normal courtesies. He had kept an eye on the stranger, however, and during dinner managed a place next to him.

"You're new then, are you?" asked O'Conner, through his food.

"To this ship, I am, yes." The broad accent was unmistakable, but O'Conner decided to sound out the man a little further.

"Volunteer?"

"For the King? No, I was persuaded."

Well over half the crew could have answered in the same way, but O'Conner had the clue he was looking for, and he continued in Gaelic, using a far softer voice.

"Are you straight?"

Crehan stopped eating for no more than a second; his eyes flashed at O'Conner, who was looking nonchalant, as if he had just been passing the time of day. To speak in Gaelic was illegal on board a King's ship, and the subject made the crime more iniquitous still.

"I am." The reply was hard to hear amongst the background noise.

"How straight?" Again there was no sign between the men that they were saying anything untoward.

"As straight as a rush." Crehan was eating heartily now, although a faint tinge of red could be noticed in his complexion. The mess table was full, but in a ship of war a lack of privacy is expected, and the two continued, confidant that no one would overhear their language in the din that sounded all about them.

"Go on then," O'Conner urged.

"In truth, in trust, in unity and liberty."

"What have you in your hand?" O'Conner could see what he had in his hand, but that was not the question.

"A green bough."

"Where did it first grow?"

"In America," Crehan muttered, adding a belch for good measure.

"And where did it bud?"

"France."

"Where are you going to plant it?"

Crehan turned and looked O'Conner in the face. "Where are *we* going to plant it?"

O'Conner nodded seriously, and the two men spoke together in no more than a whisper: "In the crown of Great Britain."

Now both were smiling, as they had a right to, for they had each found a brother.

"Are there any more on board?" Crehan, who had been a member for many years, reverted to English.

"Aye, some, I've yet to check out all the new men."

"Now somehow that doesn't surprise me, seeing how long it took you to find one in your own mess.

O'Conner's grin was bitter. "There's been a purge of late; even to be Irish is seen as a crime in some ships."

"An' do you always sound men out over dinner?" There was a hint of seriousness in Crehan's voice now.

"Where is private? 'Sides, if the man can't take a risk, he's no use to us."

No more was said, the conversation switched quickly to that of shipboard life, with no mention of Trees of Liberty, Wolfe Tone, Napper Tandy, or any of the other subjects the two latent revolutionaries would have much preferred to discuss.

*****

At just before four bells in the afternoon watch Shepherd stepped from his cabin and walked along the quarterdeck. Dyson was already waiting by the binnacle. It was the time finally agreed with the Commodore for the convoy to sail, and he could see bustle on some of the merchant ships as their crews prepared.

"*Taymar* and *Badger* have signalled their readiness, sir," Dyson said, when the captain joined him. "The flagship's flying a Peter; her sails are bent, and she's taking up the strain on her cable."

"Very good." Shepherd put the deck glass to his eye and inspected the small fleet. Sure enough, the ships appeared ready; there seemed little reason why they should not take maximum advantage of the tide. Furthermore the wind, blowing light from the shore, was fair. Shepherd wondered if his doubts about the voyage had been misplaced, certainly things were going well at the start.

"Commodore is signalling, sir." King had already taken up his duties as signal lieutenant. He fumbled through the book, while Mintey, an oldster midshipman, prompted him in a stage whisper. "C-Convoy will proceed, sir," King said, although it was clear that he had not found the right page.

"Very good, Mr King." Shepherd meant the words. The fact that the signal midshipman, until very recently the same rank and actually senior to King, had assisted him was a sign that his promotion had been accepted by the other young gentlemen. He turned to Dyson.

"I think we can begin, Mr Dyson. Would you be so kind as to make sail?" The last two words, although phrased as a question, were enough to initiate a thousand orders.

"All hands make sail!" Dyson touched his hat and issued the command, stirring up a cacophony of whistles and shouts. Topmen from the starboard watch ran to the weather shrouds and scampered up the ratlines, followed by their midshipmen, who would stay at the tops to encourage them. The marine sentries, standing guard at channels and entry ports, unfixed their bayonets as the men went aloft. The guard snapped to attention, before clumping from the posts they had manned for the last seven weeks and taking up position at the braces. Below, more marines and a few waisters were gathering at the main capstan where they would provide the motive power to raise the anchor.

"We are to take station to windward of the convoy, Mr Dyson, so allow them to forereach on us."

"Aye, sir. Topsails and forecourse on my command, Mr Johnston," Dyson called to the boatswain, as the men took their place along the yards and the afterguard went to the braces.

Below, Matthew had been herded with the other ship's boys and now stood on the lower gundeck, holding a piece of light line uncertainly.

"Nipper work's wet'n foul," the boy next to him, who looked about thirteen, informed him. "Best wear your number three's next time."

The entire conversation meant nothing to Matthew, although he understood from the boy's expression that he intended to be helpful. A heavy cable was in the process of being released from the bitts, the massive wooden frame, polished by years of use, that sat towards the bows. Five sailors pulled the cable straight and ran it alongside the lighter line that ran to the capstan. Matthew felt he had to ask a question, and automatically went through the necessary stages of gathering his words, breathing deep, and closing his eyes, before addressing the lad.

"I've n-not done this b-before," he said, opening his eyes again, to gauge the effect.

"No?" the boy did not seem surprised. "Nuthin' to it, no harder than herdin' cats." Though younger, he was years ahead of Matthew. "You got to bind the anchor cable to the messenger, that's the line goin' round the capstan." He pointed to where marines were forming up at the far end of the deck. "Messenger's a loop, see? We lash the cable to it with these nippers." He held up his length of line. "Then you follows your nipper along as the Guffies wind the capstan. When you gets to the end, you unwraps it, and run back to the beginning again."

Matthew nodded. It seemed simple enough, although he wasn't at all sure if he had the coordination. Then it occurred to him that he didn't know what knot to use when tying the anchor cable to the messenger. He opened his mouth to ask, but was interrupted by a bellowing from one of the boatswain's mates.

"Look lively there! Form a line! Crown buoy's up, let's get this cable in an' dried!"

The boys spread themselves along the double line of the anchor cable and messenger and began to strap their nippers, binding the two cables together. Matthew tried to watch what knot the others were using, but they all seemed to just wrap the line about. To be safe he tied a reef, in the way Jake had shown him.

Another squeal from the boatswain's mate's pipes and the marines, looking unusually scruffy in their working clothes, began to turn the capstan. There was a loud clapping sound that increased with speed, and before long the cable and messenger were moving along the deck at a brisk walking pace.

Soon it was Matthew's turn to untie his nipper. The others had come away as if they were only wrapped about, and as he fumbled with his knot he wondered how they could manage it so quickly.

The hitch had turned itself into a granny, and seemed impossible to undo. He began to panic, it was past the place where he should have loosened his line, and soon the messenger would be up to the drum of the capstan.

He strained at the knot, as the marching marines came closer and closer. If he didn't free it soon, he would be amongst them. Sweat broke out on his forehead as he struggled again with the knot.

"Avast there—avast!" the roar from one of the boatswain's mates came from close behind and made his feet almost leave the deck. The capstan came to a halt, and the line stopped, just as Matthew was about to collide with the outermost marine.

"Now then, what's this?" Clarke stepped forward and examined Matthew's knot. "Fair bit of knitting you have there, youngster!"

The line of boys laughed, but the marines stayed silent.

The boatswain's mate brought out a knife and cut through the knot. "Don't tie it, wrap it!" he said. He took Matthew by his ear and dragged him back to where the last nipper was about to be unleashed. Pulling the ear down, he stopped with Matthew's nose about an inch from the messenger.

"You see?" Matthew could see perfectly. The line was wrapped round, three turns and a half hitch. There were no knots.

Clarke let go of the ear and blew on his pipe. Immediately the line began to move again, and Matthew ran back to the end of the queue of waiting boys.

He knew his face was red, and he was ready for the teasing that he guessed would be inevitable. Instead the boy in front of him merely grinned, and once the line took up speed they were all too busy to think more of the incident.

In no time they had reached the area of cable that had spent the last seven weeks on the bottom of the anchorage directly beneath the heads, and Matthew began to understand what the first lad had been talking about. He was wet through and covered with green slime, but then he was not alone, and as he hurried back along the deck he noticed that they were all grinning. It was like a weird relay race, where everyone was on the same side, and each getting steadily wetter. Then they were lifting the anchor itself; the clank from the capstan pawls slowed, and the nippers needed four or five turns to hold. The massive cable seemed to groan as it was dragged along the deck lifting the seventy hundredweight of iron from the bed many fathoms below. Before long the capstan stopped, and the boys stood back from their work, panting but excited.

"Starbolins dry and stow, larbolins, cat n' fish!" yelled the boatswain's mate, as the marines removed the capstan bars, and began replacing them as deck supports. Matthew knew that he was larboard watch, but the ludicrous instruction was beyond him.

"Come on!" said the first lad, and Matthew followed as he ran for the companionway.

On the deck above another bank of marines had been turning the upper level of the capstan and were now formed up in three lines. The boys ran up to the main deck and on to the forecastle, where the dripping anchor could be seen hanging at the bows.

"Anchor's stowed at the catshead," the boy informed him, pointing to a heavy wooden beam that jutted out over the larboard bow. "Fish tackle raises the flukes to the side, an' we strap the crown," he explained.

Matthew opened his mouth to ask more, then closed it again. He watched as the others went about securing the anchor, finally helping when the line was passed about the heavy ring at the end.

The lad stood back and grinned at Matthew. "Y're lucky we'd singled up day 'for yes'day," he said. "Otherwise we'd 'ave it all to do it all over again with starboard 'ook!"

Matthew had grown used to feeling incompetent amongst men, it was almost a natural feeling; he was young after all. But now, with lads of his own age and younger, he wondered if he'd ever really settle to the work. Something of this must have shown on his face, as the boy gave him a hearty slap on the shoulder that almost produced tears.

"Next time you'll know," he told him, then grinned. "An' you'll wear som'at different!" He was right; they were both damp with slime. "Come on, let's watch the topmen!"

Matthew followed his glance up to the mast where men waited to release the sails. Topsails and forecourse, Dyson had ordered, so the mast nearest to them had a row of seamen along the two lower yards. They stood with feet resting on a thin line and their bodies bowed over the yard, while at each yardarm one sat astride looking inwards.

"Most times they make sail while the anchor's comin' up, but tide's with us an' there ain't no hurry today."

Matthew nodded, hoping his lack of speech would not be taken as unfriendly.

"They got to 'lease the yard arm ends firs', followed by the bunt," the lad continued. Matthew gathered that the bunt was the middle part of the sail, and he tucked the information away for future use. "If they does it all together the sail can fill 'fore all the gaskets are loosened. Best way to get pulled off the yard, they say."

Matthew nodded wisely, although the men's perches seemed perilous enough as it was.

Ahead, the convoy was under sail and creeping from the anchorage. It was time for *Vigilant* to tag along. A shout from the quarterdeck was quickly followed by another whistle and the sail began to be let out. Matthew and the boy watched in awe.

The sails were not the white silken stuff of stories, but dark patched canvas that smelled of mould and had a line of damp running just below the yard. The forecourse flopped down heavily until it was almost within reach of Matthew. Above, the topsail, a subtly different shade of grey, was also released, and for a moment it seemed that the wind had died. Then, with a slight rustle, followed by several loud claps, the sails began to billow with graceful ripples.

"Let go an' 'aul! Let go an' 'aul!" The yards creaked round as the afterguard at the braces hauled them into the wind. Now the sails were full and proud, the sheets tightened and the ship began to heel. It was as if a hibernating animal had finally stretched itself awake, and Matthew was transfixed.

"It's a sight an' there's no mistakin'," the lad next to him was clearly as impressed as Matthew. The deck leant slightly and the bows began to rise and fall. A faint murmur issued from the stem as it cut through the water.

"It's b-b-beautiful!" Matthew stammered, eyes fixed on the sails.

The lad grinned at him. "Aye," he said. "It s-s-certainly is!"

*****

Tait approached the captain and removed his hat. "Shore boat's making for us, sir."

Shepherd sighed. That would be from the port admiral's office. Probably nothing more than someone forgetting to sign a return, but the unexpected delay was infuriating when his mind was already at sea, especially when he had his own personal reasons to be free of the land.

"All right," Shepherd said testily. "Back mizzen tops, let's see what they want."

The lighter came alongside smartly enough and stayed for no longer than two minutes. Shepherd was about to pace the quarterdeck when he decided he would be better off seeing to the matter personally. He hurried down to the entry port where a small group had assembled. There seemed to be a great deal of talking, and someone was rattling a chain. He drew closer and the group separated as the unexpected presence of their captain was felt. Shepherd noticed one of his lieutenants and automatically addressed his question to him.

"What's going on here, Mr Timothy?" he asked, and opened his mouth to add more, when the cause of the confusion became obvious. Hands and feet were bound by chains, and the face was dirty and bruised, but there was no mistaking the red hair, and that pigtail. The port admiral must have acted quickly to get him sent back on board, probably glad to rid himself of the problem. But that problem was firmly in his hands now, and so was Simpson.

# PART TWO
## AT SEA

# CHAPTER SEVEN

VIGILANT emerged from the shelter of the Isle of Wight and met the full force of the channel. Her fabric, spoiled by many weeks at anchor, grumbled and groaned as it was forced to flex once more, while the fresh rigging stretched and sagged at the unaccustomed punishment. Johnston, the boatswain, stood in the waist, looking up at his beloved masts and shrouds and tapping his cane against his leg with annoyance.

"Take another turn on the larboard t'gallant backstay!" he bellowed to one of his mates positioned above him at the fore crosstrees. He turned to Jake, who had just brought a message and was now eager to leave. "You sees, it's important to keep all stays even an' regular," he said to the boy. "They can do it easy enough using t'lanyards that run through the hearts."

Jake nodded wisely, rolling his eyes only slightly as his better continued. "Problem is the masts are flexin'." He held his hands up to demonstrate. "That means if you tighten up at the wrong time, when they're slack, like, an' the masts springs back, you strain the housin' in the foretopmast hounds."

There was a pause that Jake felt obliged to fill. "That's bad, is it, Mr Johnson?"

The man snorted. "It's never happened in any ship I served in, and I'm damned if it's goin' to now."

83

Jake edged back as the boatswain's attention returned aloft. "Handsomely, handsomely, now," he bellowed, using the word's original meaning. Slowly and with care the slack was taken up and the shroud tightened.

"Fastening her up, are you bosun?" Gregory approached, looking up appreciatively at the rigging, while Jake grabbed his chance and departed.

"Aye, sir." Johnston touched his hat briefly. "Cordage they gave us fair stretches like wool. We've taken in about as much as we set."

Johnston trusted Gregory more than most, in fact he held a grudging respect for any commissioned man who had risen from the lower deck. However talented or educated an officer may be, none, in Johnston's view, would have the necessary understanding of a ship unless they had started out as an ordinary hand. But then captains and lieutenants might only stay for a year or so, whereas the standing officers, like Johnston, had been with *Vigilant* since her re-commissioning and would remain devoted to her until one of them was of no further use. Consequently he was inclined to be a bit of an old woman as far as the ship was concerned, jealously guarding her from danger and openly mistrusting any officer who might command her badly.

"How's she feeling?" Gregory asked, He too held a good deal of regard for the boatswain. The man knew *Vigilant* like his own child and loved her every bit as much. Johnston swayed back and forth slightly before answering.

"Trifle light in the bows, sir. Nowt to worry 'bout though. Know more when we wear."

A loud crack cut the air, and both men looked up to see part of the mizzen forestay fly forward in the wind. Immediately the boatswain let forth with a stream of orders in a voice intended to carry to every part of the ship.

Standing next to him Gregory watched for a moment before turning back and making for his rightful place on the quarterdeck. The boatswain had recently been charged with cap-a-bar; the misappropriating of government stores. The case revolved around a length of supposedly used three inch hemp that was meant to have been returned to the dockyard, but mysteriously ended up at a commercial chandler. The single black thread that identified government rope from standard mercantile was an obvious give away, and Johnston had grudgingly admitted the theft when confronted with the evidence. There was little unusual in the crime; boatswains were often nicknamed "missionaries" due to their talent for converting anything that came their way, and with his good record he would probably get off with nothing more than a reprimand.

A thief he may be, but there was no question that Johnston held the ship's interest dear; with him in charge *Vigilant* could be manoeuvred and sailed with absolute confidence. It was not something that would even be commented on publicly; no boatswain was ever commended for a shroud that held, or a spar that stayed firm, but when actions could be lost or won on a ship's ability to manoeuvre, it was important nevertheless. Gregory reached the quarterdeck ladder and clambered up. Mintey, the oldest midshipman, was sharing the watch with him. He stood next to the binnacle, with his hands clasped behind him. Gregory nodded; Mintey had failed his examination for lieutenant at least four times, and yet he was well liked by the crew and seemed perfectly competent at his work.

"Bos'un's sweatin' her up," Gregory said and gave a half smile. Then, as he went to say more, it happened.

A fiddle block, a heavy double pulley with a metal loop to one end, fell from the maintop and hit the deck almost midway between them. The action made both men freeze mid-step and it took a second or two for them to realise how near to instant death they had come. Gregory was the first to recover; looking up at the main top he drew his breath in and bellowed.

"There, in the maintop!"

The head of one of the boatswain's crew peered down at them.

"Keep hold of your tackle, you lubbers, or I'll see you all on report!" He pointed at the fiddle block, now in the hands of Mintey, who was examining it with interest.

The man knuckled his forehead and withdrew before Gregory was certain who he was.

"Trouble, Mr Gregory?"

It was the boatswain, who must have heard the block fall.

"Your mates are not too careful with the running tackle," Gregory said.

Johnston looked at the block. "Sorry about that, sir. We've had a deal of bother, an' it ain't al'ays easy to keep the traps together."

Gregory nodded. With the ship just out of harbour there was bound to be a few mishaps; it was simply fortunate that no one had been hurt.

"Shall I note it in the log?" Mintey asked. Gregory was conscious of the boatswain stiffening slightly. A mention in the log might well bring forth an official reproof, and the man was in enough trouble already.

"No, let it be," Gregory told him. He could see no need to record the matter; a block falling from a top was something to be expected, expected and dismissed without further thought. It wasn't as if anyone had done it on purpose.

*****

Critchley, the master at arms, led the small procession towards the punishment deck. Simpson dragged his way after him, flanked by corporals to either side, while two uniformed marines, their pipeclayed straps glowing in the half light, marched stiffly behind.

"Got a nice little berth," Critchley confided, glancing down at the dull metal bilboes that lay waiting for him. "Strap you up safe, 'till the cap'n decides what's to do wi' you."

Simpson said nothing as the chains were removed from his legs. His mind ran back over the day's events: the pawnbroker who had turned out to be a crimp and sold him to the impressment men. The laughter as they dragged him through the crowded streets, streets where he had only recently walked as a free man. The brief time in the Rondey, before being packaged off in the lighter. And now he was back in *Vigilant*, the ship he had written off in his mind. Back and facing punishment, twelve lashes at the least. The most? Flogging round the fleet, or, with his record, even the noose.

"Teach you to run from this man's Navy!" The face of the master at arms was fat and gloating. It hung in front of Simpson as the bilboes were clamped about his ankles.

"An' I'll be watching you," Critchley continued, while the chains were released from Simpson's wrists. "Watching you for as long as you're in this ship. *If* you survive punishment, you can say goodbye to shore leave, boat work, or anything that takes you off the board." He paused, drawing breath with satisfaction. "We're in for a long commission, laddie, an' you're gonna be around for all o' it!"

The words struck deep, and Simpson felt his anger rise up once more. Rise up until it flowed over, and took control of his body. The final smirk from the master at arms was too much: Critchley failed to see the blow that hit him and hardly felt any pain at all as his head cracked back and his body crumpled down on to the deck.

\*\*\*\*\*

The wardroom was more than eighty feet away from the punishment deck, quite a distance on a ship where six hundred souls shared a hull one hundred and sixty feet long.

Furthermore, an entire social class separated its occupants from Simpson and his problems. But despite this Tait was experiencing similar emotions to the failed deserter.

When Rogers wanted to ingratiate himself, his face took on a leering smile and pressed close to his victim. Unfortunately the occasions were increasingly frequent, and with each intrusion Tait felt the desire to squash the rich, damp mouth with his fist grow stronger. At all hours of the day the man's breath was stale, and the mixture of false *bon-homie* and genuine halitosis was sickening.

"I wonder if I could beg a small favour of you?" Tait made it a matter of personal pride not to flinch as Rogers confidently continued. "Small matter of the furniture in my cabin."

This was a new angle; Roger's favours had previously confined themselves to swapping duties or articles of toiletry— exchanges that always proved to be one-sided.

"Your furniture?"

"That's right; I understand that the carpenter is rather obliging?"

"Yes," Tait had to think for a moment. It was late evening on their first full day at sea, and cabin furniture had been the last thing on his mind. "Yes, Mr Smith. He made most of mine. He'll do yours if you ask him."

"That's exactly as I had hoped."

"Send for him, I'm sure he'll accommodate you." As an idler Smith kept predictable hours, and was able to spend most of the night peacefully asleep. Tait eagerly turned back to the table where the cheese was about to be passed. Rogers had only been on board a couple of days but already he was becoming an annoyance. Tait had noticed that a few of the other officers appeared irritated, but there were others who treated him with annoying deference, like a rich and potentially generous uncle.

"I wonder if I could ask that favour?" Still that face taunted him with its leer and proximity. "Could you speak to the carpenter for me? I am still a relatively new boy, and our cabins are so similar. He appears to have made a credible job on yours, and no doubt could be tempted to repeat your furniture in mine."

"I could have a word." It irked Tait that Rogers had seen fit to inspect his cabin, although he supposed that there was nothing so very terrible in the act. At least he wouldn't have minded if it had been anyone else. "I have the first dog watch, I'll send for him then."

Dyson at the head of the table was tapping his fruit knife on his glass. Roger's smile faded a split second before he turned to look at him, and in that flash Tait saw a different expression. It was the look of a conceited, spoilt bully who had got what he wanted, and Tait felt a wave of revulsion wash over him.

"If I could have your attention for a moment, gentlemen?"

The murmur of conversation dwindled to nothing.

"Steward?"

A face appeared at the pantry door in answer to Dyson's call.

"See that you and your staff are employed elsewhere for the next ten minutes."

The man, who had been at sea longer than any of them, disappeared without a word. In no time the small pantry was empty, and the wardroom left to commissioned and senior warrant officers alone.

"I am sorry to have to speak to you all in such a confidential way so early into the cruise, but a matter has been brought to my notice that I fear is of the utmost importance."

He had their attention now, even Rogers, his hand on his brandy, stopped in the act of bringing the glass to his lips.

"I also have to say that I am aware that Lieutenant Gregory and several others are not with us. I will be speaking with them as soon as the opportunity arises." Gregory still had the watch, and had eaten some while before.

"One of the young gentlemen has reported a Tree of Liberty on the orlop deck."

The murmurs rose, only to die swiftly as Dyson went on to say more.

"He did not seem to be aware of the significance, he simply announced that there had been chalking on a deckhead. It is fortunate that I bothered to enquire of the subject, rather than assuming the usual."

Rogers broke out with a crude snigger, although everyone else remained silent.

"Does any gentlemen present not understand the relevance of this matter?"

It was significant that, although of greatly differing backgrounds and experience, no one spoke.

"Let me say this once." Dyson had the knack of holding each man's attention as if he were speaking directly to them alone. "However romantic or wistful the Irish question may appear, the Nationalists are as much our enemy as the French. Ignoring some of their quaint revolutionary ideals, they have openly spoken of aiding a French invasion of England in their fight for an Independent Irish Nation.

"That they have support from some of our politicians can only be regretted, that they are present, and presumably active in this ship, is a matter of the deepest concern."

Tait felt the urge to scratch at his nose, but the silence was heavy, and he did not want to draw attention to himself.

"I have inspected the muster, and can report that we have fifty-four Irish amongst our people. Naturally these will have to be watched." He drew breath. "And while you are watching, please remember this: until we know better, they can be trusted no more than you would any enemy."

The murmurs rose again, and Tait managed to get in a crafty stroke of his nose while his brother officers muttered around him. Fifty-four was approximately a twelfth of the crew;

a large proportion, but by no means unusual. Tait considered the matter further. Fifty-four known Irishmen—those who had declared their nationality. What of the other foreigners, or even any English with Irish sympathies? There were pressed Americans on board; who could say where their allegiance lay? In a ship where every man's life might, and often did, depend on the next, it was a worrying way to start a voyage.

"Stay watchful, gentlemen," Dyson continued. "Notice any action that might be construed as sabotage or mutiny; any gossip that you or your young gentlemen pick up; anything that could have bearing to the matter, and report it to me with the utmost despatch." A series of nods passed about the table. Tait began to think back over small incidents that had occurred recently. None seemed to be anything other the normal frictions of shipboard life, but, in the light of Dyson's announcement, he became suspicious.

"I am confident that we can nip this matter in the bud." Dyson smiled grimly. "Maybe scratch the back of a few ringleaders; show them the British Navy will not put up with their continental ideas. Meanwhile keep your people busy; nothing breeds mutiny and rebellion as much as idle minds. I want to see individual divisions fully occupied at all times. Keep them on the move and they won't have the energy for revolt." He looked about the table, catching all eyes in one sweep before adding, "Thank you. That is all."

As he finished speaking Dyson nodded briefly before sitting back in his chair, effectively withdrawing himself from the table. Tait noticed how the other officers talked around him, none even attempting to ask an ancillary question or pass a comment to the first lieutenant, who was apparently no longer there. Tait had been commissioned for a little over four years and felt himself reasonably well versed in most of his duties, although time spent with Dyson had taught him there was more to being an officer than simply knowing one sheet from another. The man had a way about him; a subtle command of both language and men that could never be included in any training manual. Whether learnt or natural, Dyson held it in spades; diplomacy worthy of admirals, and yet certainly not wasted amongst this collection of King's officers.

If there were to be a mutiny on board *Vigilant*, England would suffer. The French would take great delight in publicising the overthrow of authority, and every British officer would find his job that much more difficult as a result. That was all in addition to the loss of a line ship, and the encouragement to the Irish rebels. Should Dyson be able to prevent such he would be doing his country as great a service as physically winning a battle, even if his actions would never be recognised. Tait took a sip from his own brandy. It was simply Dyson's job, he supposed. That he did it well meant that he should be picked out for promotion, although there were many more places for lieutenants than commanders. In the meantime Tait was fortunate in having such a worthy mentor; one he could observe from close quarters, and learn from for as long as he was able. He smiled quietly to himself. This was yet another of Dyson's responsibilities: role model to junior officers. In this he was equally effective, and just as unlikely to be rewarded.

*****

At least five post captains would be needed to hang Simpson. Shepherd sat at his desk, a closed copy of *Regulations and Instructions Regarding His Majesty's Service at Sea* in front of him. It was a long title for a big book, and most points were covered thoroughly, if not with elaboration. In the convoy he could rouse only one other post captain: Douglas of the *Taymar*. Richardson, captain of the sloop *Badger*, was only a commander in rank. More than that, they were still in home waters, where the death penalty was subject to Admiralty confirmation, and even then liable to reprieve by Royal prerogative. It would have to wait, at least until they reached St Helena, and possibly even longer.

He grunted and stood up. The only other course he could take was to put back to harbour. That would mean delaying the convoy for two days at least, probably longer. Shepherd was glad to be at sea, and eager to wash his hands of the convoy, especially its Commodore. The idea of going back when they had already made the break from land was repugnant to him, and yet so was the thought of spending the next ninety days or so with Simpson languishing in irons. He would be the object of pity and morbid curiosity; worse, he might even become the focus of a mutiny. Men of the lower deck were known for being sentimental fools, and it was by no means beyond them to take the most stupid of risks to save one of their number. Of course he had the power to hang Simpson there and then if he truly considered him a danger to crew or ship. But both points were debatable, and the Admiralty would not look kindly on a man who put another to death without going through the proper channels.

But a crime as blatant as this was not one that Shepherd was allowed to ignore, even if he wanted to. Critchley had escaped without major damage, but his authority would be diminished if the correct procedures were not followed. The twenty-second Article of War called for no lesser penalty than death. There was really no alternative other than for Simpson to remain in captivity until a court martial could be assembled. Then he would hang; there could be no doubt about that.

*****

It was odd that the lad who had befriended Matthew at the anchor cable should also be called Jake. The echo of Christian names with the old carpenter back in Leatherhead seemed to lend the boy even more knowledge and maturity. Matthew

93

followed him as he clambered down the companionway and on to the orlop deck.

"If it's only Jack Dusty we'll be all right," he whispered back at Matthew as they walked past the midshipmen's berth. Matthew nodded, although he had little idea of what Jake had in mind. The possibility that it contained some degree of felony was not lost on him, but in Jake's presence this hardly seemed to matter at all.

The purser's room was shuttered, but some light peeped through the slats. Jake looked about him, before peering through and into the room. He stepped back and nonchalantly began to shuffle away.

"No sign of Morrison," he whispered. "We're in luck."

For upwards of a minute the two lads loitered next to the carpenter's store, with Matthew trying hard to match Jake's professionally indifferent pose. Then the younger boy approached the purser's room once more.

This time his step was bold, and he rapped on the deal door with all the assurance of a lieutenant. The same elderly man who Matthew had first met the day before opened the door and stared myopically at the pair.

"Message from Mr Morrison," Jake's voice was loud and confident. "Says you're to meet him in the stewards' room."

"Stewards' room?" He shook his head uncertainly. "But I got me manifests."

Jake paused a fraction too long, and Matthew felt his body tense.

"'E said to forget about them, and meet him." Jake's voice had lost some of its assurance, although the old man still listened intently. "'E said it were important."

"I see. I got to go to the stewards' room, an' meet Mr Morrison?"

"That's right."

A faint twinkle appeared in the faded eyes. "An I suppose I jus' leaves this room wide open?"

Jake opened his mouth and considered for a moment.

"You all knows I ain't 'lowed keys, I suppose you were gonna stand in and guard the place for me?"

Matthew made ready to run, for the elderly man now had a sly grin on his face.

"Think jus' 'cos a man's old, 'e's gonna be daft an all, do 'e?" He stepped back into the room before the boys could conjure up an answer. Jake flashed a worried smile at Matthew, who had taken a pace back, and both turned to walk away. Then the door opened again and the man was back. He held two clenched fists out towards the boys.

"'Ere you are, an' don't try no tricks in future."

Jake seemed unwilling to go near the man, but Matthew sensed something in his manner and walked towards him. He held his hands cupped under one of the fists and received a warm handful of raisins. Seeing this Jake immediately came forward, hands outstretched for his share, before skipping off into the darkness of the orlop.

Matthew stayed and, looking up, he whispered his thanks. The man gave him a tired smile. "Bugger off," he said, and Matthew left.

# CHAPTER EIGHT

THE next morning was grey and filled with rain. Lieutenant Timothy, who had the watch, stood in the dubious shelter of the mizzen shrouds, hands behind back, glass tucked under one arm, and shoulders hunched to allow his hat to cover the nape of his neck. A short man, inclined to portliness, and currently covered in many layers of clothing, his stance gave him an odd, beetle-like appearance, although there were few on deck to appreciate this. It was six bells in the forenoon watch; before long the other officers and midshipmen would assemble to take their noon sights, and the new navigational day could begin. But for the moment Timothy had the quarterdeck, and the rain, pretty much to himself.

A shout from above drew his attention, and Timothy reluctantly returned to his correct position next to the binnacle.

"What do you see there?" he bellowed.

The masthead's voice was equally strong, and carried easily down to the deck. "Three ships incoming to larboard, look like merchants."

Timothy nodded. Not an unlikely sighting for the Channel, although they could be the first of a large convoy, in which case there would probably be Navy vessels as escorts.

"I saw three ships come sailing in," he said, absent-mindedly. He turned to Pite, the midshipman of the watch.

"Beg pardon, sir?"

Timothy smiled. "Never mind. Tell the captain, then pass the word for Mr King." Pite nodded, much relieved, and touched his hat before dashing off. King was new to his post, and it would do him little harm to be prepared for the exchange of recognition signals.

Within half an hour the ships were in sight from the deck, although the rain distorted their images into a vague smudge. Shepherd inspected them for several minutes before turning his glass onto the Commodore's ship. A slight smile spread across his face as he lowered the telescope and closed it with a snap. At that moment Humble, the master, appeared on the quarterdeck, sextant in hand, followed by a group of midshipmen with their quadrants. Shepherd turned to him.

"Mr Humble, There are three inbound merchant ships on the larboard quarter. I would be obliged if you would take us closer."

Humble touched his hat and, exchanging his sextant with Timothy's glass, inspected the convoy. His mind already carried all the necessary information about their present heading, wind and the set of the sails.

"Take her two points to larboard," he muttered to the helmsmen.

Timothy called the hands to the braces and *Vigilant* creaked slowly round in the light wind and drizzle.

The quarterdeck was soon alive with officers, drawn by the unexpected change of course. Tait and King exchanged a glance. It was quite conceivable that the captain had a personal reason for closing with the ships, possibly wanting to pass a message home. He may even be intending to send Simpson back, although that was less likely. They were not left to wonder for long.

"Mr Timothy, you have the watch, I believe?"

"Yes, sir!" Timothy stepped forward and touched his hat.

"We're closing with home bound ships. I propose to make up our numbers." The captain turned and caught the first lietenant's eye. "Some more people would be welcomed I am sure, Mr Dyson?"

"Indeed, sir." Dyson very nearly smiled. The possibility of extra men was more enticing than anything else the captain could have offered him.

"We'll use the launch and the long boat. Get the crews ready, and appoint a lieutenant and a midshipman to each."

Dyson touched his hat before turning to attend to his duties. Seasoned hands, trim from months at sea; just what was needed to bring *Vigilant* up to scratch.

*****

Lewis watched them go. He knew from experience that the ship would remain hove to for some while, and nothing would be required of him during that time. He had noted the noon sight, and now was fairly sure of the ship's exact position. He placed his journal safely inside his jacket and pulled out a little grey book that was always in his trouser pocket. The young gentlemen and master's mates were still puzzling over their calculations, and he guessed that any assistance from him would not be welcomed. Instead he swung himself down the quarterdeck ladder and strode along the waist towards the forecastle. Once there, in what he regarded to be his own territory, Lewis selected a convenient corner next to a knee and settled himself down to read. The thin pages of the book were almost learnt by heart now, but he read them through again, his mouth moving slightly with each word.

In battle, able seaman Lewis worked the flexible rammer on number three gun, lower battery. At twenty-four he had been at sea for nine years, the last two in *Vigilant*. During his time he'd seen action at Toulon with Hood, and had been in numerous minor scraps, before the ship was transferred to the Channel Fleet and just missed out on the Glorious First of June. Most notably he had been one of a prize crew sent to take a merchant ship back to Gibraltar, and all but recaptured by her former company, who'd had other ideas.

Besides working the rammer and his various other duties, Lewis was being trained up; in fact, he would shortly be leaving number three gun, his mess and the lower deck. It was a change he had won for himself, not with youth and strength, but an inherent thirst for knowledge and his natural affinity with numbers.

It had come about nine months back, when he was on the middle watch. At the time he had been part of the afterguard and, as the night was quiet, they had been stood down. Lewis lay on his back next to the mizzen braces, watching the stars through the shrouds. He noticed the constellation immediately next to one of the yards, and tried to see if it moved as *Vigilant* crept through the night. Of course, even without the swaying of the ship, the change would have been impossible to detect, but several nights later he found himself in the same position, and looking as before. To his disappointment the constellation lay in what seemed to be exactly the same position. Lewis felt cheated, cross that an observation so carefully taken should have let him down.

At that moment a midshipman had come on deck and began experimenting with his quadrant. Lewis watched him for a moment before crossing over and asking permission to speak. He mentioned his observations to the young man; it was King, one of the better mids, and Lewis had been lucky. Rather than scorn his ignorance, King had listened, before explaining a little about the accuracy of the instruments they used. This led to Lewis's first holding of a quadrant, and it had been a natural step for King to talk more about navigation, and finally lend him some books on the subject.

To Lewis, reading had always come easily, but he found this book difficult to follow. He had more questions, and King, recognising genuine curiosity, was patient in answering them. He then drew Lewis's interest to the attention of the sailing master, who sent for him one evening during the second dogwatch.

The interview had been formal and, as it was the first time Lewis had stood in an officer's cabin, rather stilted.

"I understand you've been asking questions about navigation?"

The master had surveyed him with a savage, almost angry stare. Lewis had stiffened, and looked straight ahead over the older man's shoulder.

"Sir, I was interested in the stars. Mr King gave me some help."

"Yes, and a copy of Norrie's *Epitome of Navigation*."

"Sir."

"Have you read it?"

"Yes, sir."

"All of it?"

"Yes, sir."

"And what have you learnt?"

"A bit. Some of it's confusing."

"Some?"

"Sir. Most of it; all at first, but I'm getting the way of things gradual."

"What learning have you?"

"Three years reading and figures, then I worked as a clerk, sir. That was before I joined a collier. I was with the RN three year, sir, in *Aratus*. Then I did two tricks in an Indiaman 'fore joining *Vigilant*."

For the first time the master's expression relaxed.

"You make it sound like you had choice in the matter." Humble had gone to the trouble of checking Lewis's entry in the muster book: he was a pressed man.

"Sir?"

"Never mind. And never mind about not understanding the book. I have officers who have been studying Norrie for twelve month an' more, and still make a tangle of it."

It was a remark that worried Lewis. He was being given a glimpse of a world where he did not belong. The fact that it had happened without his making gave no comfort, and he silently cursed King for peaching on him.

"Tell me the use of an azimuth compass." Humble's attitude had returned to that of an inquisitor.

"Taking bearings, sir."

"Bearings of what?"

"Stars, sir. 'though I seen it being used for other things."

"Quite. And a quadrant?"

Lewis swallowed. Either the master was involving him in some private joke, or King had got into trouble for lending him the book. Whatever, the only thing a lower deck man could do when an officer asked a question was answer it.

"It measures the angle of the sun, or a star." He was about to say "celestial body", but he had only read the word, and was not certain of the pronunciation. He continued rather lamely. "Or anything in the sky."

"Against what?"

"Against the horizon, sir." The last word was swallowed, as he realised he had missed it out before.

"Yes?"

"And once you know that, sir, you can work out where you are."

"How?"

"You check the almanac for the distance between the star an the pole, an' the distance 'tween the star and the earth, sir. And you draws it out."

"Show me."

And so it had gone on, with Lewis fumbling over the master's table, clumsily using the instruments he had only recently read about. In his anxiety he almost wrote down the wrong figures, but the calculations came to him automatically, as they always did. To say he found complex arithmetic easy would give entirely the wrong impression; for Lewis arithmetic was not easy, it was natural. The master watched in silence, before taking the pencil from him and checking his work.

"You have ability, I'll give you that, and clearly some enthusiasm; rare qualities in my boys."

The feeling that he was being told things that should not concern him returned.

"I can detail you for special duty. That's if you've a mind. I've already spoken to the captain, and he's willing to rate you able, if I think you're worth it. Then you can join the young gentlemen in their class. What say you?"

It was a question loaded with connotations. Certainly navigation held an interest for him, but Lewis could guess the reaction from his mess if he was promoted and began going to classes with officers. As it was they had given him a hard time over the book. And then there were the midshipmen and the master's mates; how would they take to a seaman taking lessons with them? He would be a marked man; revealed as one going up, and everyone loved to see one going up come down again.

"You needn't worry about the mids," said the master, echoing Lewis's thought. "I'll talk to them. If any give you trouble tell Mr King, and he'll tell me. Same with the men. I'll not have ability doused by bullying. Of course you'll have to keep your normal duties, unless a situation appears amongst the clerks."

Lewis looked at the master properly for the first time. Before he had always been a uniform, a rank, and a high one at that. Now he saw an elderly man, with a balding head and a slight paunch. One who had noticed a spark in him, and had decided to fan it.

"This is a hard service, Lewis, and I'll not deceive you, or make promises. But a man can make something of himself, if he's a mind; you only have to look to Lieutenant Gregory for that. You may as well try as not." He smiled for the first time, and Lewis found that he was smiling in return.

In fact he found the classes surprisingly easy, and even discovered himself fighting down frustration when his betters took forever solving a simple calculation, or asked the same questions time and time again. As his knowledge increased he grew more confident, and proud of his abilities. The men in his mess appeared to sense this and took it philosophically, accepting that on occasions he would read, rather than share their company. There seemed to be no hard feelings, in fact Lewis noticed a certain hauteur in their manner when dealing with others; after all, one of their own was cleverer than most, and getting on.

Now he continued his duties with the secret promise that the master was to put him forward as a prospective volunteer first class. The captain would have to approve him, of course, but it was the first stage to becoming a petty officer, and the chance to put theory into practice. He could expect the change at any time.during the course of this cruise. It might even be today, although Lewis was in no great hurry. Whenever the chance came, he'd be ready.

*****

The steady rain, together with a quiet time in middle watch, meant that the heads were unusually empty, a fact that had prompted Matthew, still touched with the self-consciousness of youth, to pay a visit. The novelty of being on a ship under sail, and the absence of Flint, made him feel slightly more vulnerable, a sensation suddenly heightened by the appearance of Crehan as the lad was about to leave.

The Irishman placed a restraining hand against the boy's chest and smiled. Matthew twisted to one side and tried to pass by, but he was fairly trapped.

"Not so fast, my young friend, not so fast." A chill ran through the boy's body, and he felt dreadfully alone. "We have a few things to get straight, you an' me."

Matthew opened his mouth, but no words came.

"Trouble with the speakin', is it?" Crehan sneered. "But you were ready enough to talk to the ratin' board, weren't yer? Ready enough to set me in this ship, an' stop me chance of freedom."

"I'm s-sorry." the words stumbled out at last. "I d-didn't m-mean nothing by it."

"Nothin'? Didn't mean nothin', he says. Yet you put me in this lousy King's ship, an' now I'll be lucky to ever see me home again."

Matthew opened his mouth once more, but this time it wasn't the stammer that stopped him; he simply did not know what to say.

Crehan pushed him roughly onto the larboard chest. Matthew looked around desperately for help. The forecastle lookout could only be yards away, but there was no sign of him, not a man to be seen anywhere, and he dare not make a sound.

At the end of the row of heads stood a kid half filled with chamber lye, which was used by some of the older men when washing out clothes. Crehan's eyes flashed to the tub and Matthew saw an idea strike. Then came the heaven-sent sound of approaching footsteps.

"What's about?"

It was Critchley, the master at arms. Matthew felt relief flow through him at the sight of the swollen face and the lip that Simpson had so recently split. As a warrant officer, Critchley had use of the private roundhouses that stood to either side of the men's facilities. Something must have aroused his suspicions to bring him here, a fact that was not lost on Matthew, or Crehan.

"I said, what's about?" Critchley was certainly suspicious, and Crehan suddenly realised that he had placed himself in danger of the noose.

"Nothing, Mr Critchley. Just come to ease m'self, so I have."

Critchley turned to Matthew.

"Out of here, lad," he said, enforcing the order with a backward wave of his thumb. "I'll deal with this."

For a moment the Irishman caught his eye, then Matthew stood up from the head and gratefully hurried away, vaguely aware that his rescue was only temporary.

*****

The boat's crew held more pressed men than volunteers, but Tait knew from experience that any trouble they might give would be through over-enthusiasm. There was a fervour latent in the heart of every conscript that rose up whenever an opportunity came to see another share his fate. This became useful when the Navy needed more men, although, as a reflection on human nature, it was disappointing.

The first merchant ship was holding its course and had not shortened sail. Tait studied it as Midshipman Hayes wriggled uncomfortably next to him in the stern sheets of the long boat. She was three masted, of about four hundred tons, with a full, rounded hull that made it roll sickeningly even in the light wind. Her paintwork was blistered and peeling, giving the impression of tropical service, and Tait wondered briefly what exotic diseases might come with the men they were intending to seize.

The coxswain had taken them past the ship, then skilfully turned on to a converging course. Hayes looked at Tait, who nodded briefly.

"The ship ahoy! Heave to, in the name of the King!" When shouted in Hayes's youthful tenor the words carried little of their potential, although every master understood the meaning, and what they were about. The ship luffed up into the wind and came to a shaky halt, her sails flapping heavily in the drizzle.

"Take her in," Tait muttered, and the coxswain closed the distance, aiming for a point slightly ahead of the main chains.

"Oars!"

They were almost alongside and well within reach of the two boathooks that stretched out for the ship. Tait stood up and glanced at Hayes, before bracing himself and leaping as soon as the longboat touched the hull.

Pulling himself up over the side, Tait looked about. The deck was surprisingly empty apart from a stocky man with a deep tan who stood next to a boy at the wheel.

"Navy, is it?" he enquired, as Tait approached, with Hayes and most of the others following up behind him. He was no more than twenty-three or so, and his voice was tinged with that faint flat drawl, common among men who travel regularly to the Americas. His clothes also marked him out; the course cotton trousers being held up with a wide snakeskin belt, and a leather jacket, almost black from the rain, covered his collarless shirt.

"Lieutenant Richard Tait, sir, His Britannic Majesty's Ship, *Vigilant*." Tait touched his hat. "What vessel is this?"

"*Skimington Castle*, fifty-nine days out from Boston, carrying grain and resin."

"You are her master?"

"Samuel West, an' my people are all American, or protected."

It was an answer that Tait had heard a dozen times before and one that would make little difference to the outcome.

"You sail under the protection of the British flag, sir; I wish to inspect your crew."

So routine had the procedure become that Tait was taken unawares as the master flipped a small pistol from his belt and held it straight out, pointing directly at his face.

"That you will not," he said with elaborate unconcern.

The muzzle of the gun held a hypnotic attraction for Tait. An audible hiss erupted from the men behind him, and he sensed that any attempt to overpower West would end in his own immediate death.

"Now you will leave my deck, and return to your ship," the man wetted his lips with his tongue, "and nothing more will be said of the matter."

Tait drew breath before answering. "If I leave this ship it will be to order mine to board yours." His heart was pounding, but the lieutenant's voice sounded cool and composed—not unlike Dyson's, although this was not the moment for comparisons.

—"Like I say, my people are protected. A man could get in a deal of trouble if he weren't mindful."

West was probably right. Simply taking a few hands off a home bound ship was one thing; boarding by force and seizing the vessel was far more public and altogether different.

"I wish to inspect your crew," Tait said, returning to his original tack. "If you refuse you will be charged with..." He hesitated, suddenly uncertain of the offence, and it was then that a flash of movement caught his eye. West must have noticed this, for he half turned, and made to cry out just as Flint swung his fist and sent him spinning across the deck, to land against the combing of the hold.

Tait reached down and picked up the pistol, closing the hammer on the frizen with a shaking hand. The crowd behind him broke out in cat-calls and laughter as West clambered groggily to his knees.

"That was well done, Flint." The noise from the men covered the crack in Tait's voice.

Flint grinned and rubbed his knuckles. "I was the last to leave the boat, sir. Gathered somethin' was up, so I made me way 'long to the stern, and came over be'ind 'im."

His cheerful confidence was like a tonic, and the effect stayed with them as the crew were rounded up and inspected. They left with nine prime hands, none of whom had volunteered. American or not, they were being taken back to a ship where men who were experts at their craft would meld them into the cosmopolitan mass that was her crew. In time most would have no real country; they would belong to *Vigilant*. Some might even learn to love her as much as any clod of soil, and she in turn would give them a home as well as a community tighter and more protective than many found on land.

Tait took his position in the sternsheets, looking about him, and wondering at the casualness with which he had left the boat so very recently. Something dug into his stomach as he sat down. It was the master's pistol, still in his belt and all but forgotten. He took it out and inspected it once again.

"Interesting souvenir," Hayes commented.

"You'll pardon me, sir," Flint was pulling stroke oar, and had also seen the pistol, "but I reckon's it won't be loaded."

Tait looked up. "No? Why is that?"

"Wouldn't be no point. The only time they'd need to be armed is on the West Coast. There's pirates about that'll take a ship with nothin' more than a rowing boat, given the chance. But no master'll have a loaded pistol comin' up Channel." Flint flashed his teeth in a smile. "Otherwise I wouldn't 'ave jumped 'im."

*****

In the launch Rogers had collected twelve men: five from the second merchant and seven from the third. It had been his intention to allow his junior to call on the last ship, but Tait had spent so long with the first that Rogers had been forced to put himself out. The consequence was that he now felt he had been taken advantage of. In addition he would doubtless be late for wardroom dinner, and was almost soaked to the skin from the rain; all capital offences in Rogers' eyes. He sat in the sternsheets brewing curses, so that the noise of a shot ringing out across the water made him physically jump. This was compounded by the chorus of laughter that rose from Tait's boat, mirrored by grins from his own crew, and the lieutenant began to boil. Tait, it was clear, was making a fool of him: leaving his senior to do the work, while he gambolled like a child, then holding him to ridicule in front of his own men. A lesson might be in order; something to show his junior just what kind of man he was dealing with. He glared at the hands as they rowed him back to *Vigilant*, while his mind selected a suitable way of evening the score and asserting his proper position. Tait would be sorry, he would make absolutely certain of that.

# CHAPTER NINE

WHATEVER ideas Dyson might have had about keeping the men busy were in total accord with the heavens. On the fourth day of the voyage, when *Vigilant* and her convoy were about to leave the Channel and enter the Atlantic proper, the weather started to deteriorate. Mr Humble noticed the first signs as the pressure reading on his glass began to fall. He came out on deck and sniffed the air.

"Somethin' in the wind, master?" Lieutenant Timothy had the watch and was as concerned about the weather as Humble.

The master shook his head. "Gonna blow a storm 'fore long," he said. Both men looked up to the sky. It was late into the first dog watch and the light was going fast, but still the mackerel clouds were unmistakable.

"Stratocumulus," Timothy said, enjoying the word. The various names for cloud formations had been part of his preparation; for him they held a poetic ring. The master nodded, conscious that of late he had been inclined to forget one or two of the newfangled terms. He guessed that old age was to blame, and consoled himself with the knowledge that he was a born sailor and would always be able to recognise a dangerous sky.

"Be on us afore dawn," he grumbled.

There was another matter to take into consideration; *Vigilant* was sailing with a draft of fresh men: about one in fifteen were new to the ship, and a good proportion of those landsmen. Ships had left Portsmouth with far worse crews, but at least two weeks at sea would normally be needed to polish up the old hands and start off the new. A storm this early was a serious matter, and would certainly put a strain on the capable.

"I'll mention it to the captain," Humble said. Timothy nodded; the captain would have to know. He would also have to worry about the convoy. Timothy had no idea how well the merchants were crewed, but their station keeping had been appalling since Spithead. They might survive a squall without separating, but a full blown gale would be a different proposition. Something caught his eye and he switched back to a more immediate problem without effort.

"You there; stand still!" Two youngsters were gambolling on the foretop. Hearing Timothy's voice they froze like the guilty children they were. "Behave that way an' you'll be the first to leave this ship!" Skylarking may be approved of on still, quiet evenings, but not when a storm was brewing.

The youngsters sank from sight as the master went below, and Timothy began to pace the weather side of the quarterdeck. At a turn he paused and took time to stare out at the sea. The water was iron grey, with just a hint of opacity at the borders of each wave. It moved with an inner power that was quite beyond his comprehension, and yet its presence thrilled him in an inexpressible way.

—"Watch your luff," he growled, and the helmsmen allowed the ship to fall off a little while Timothy's eyes returned to the sea and the magical spectacle that was being played out before him. Occasionally the wind scraped a line of crystal white that contrasted with the grey and died almost as soon as it had been created. The heave of the deck made him a part of it all, and he felt humble in the presence of such force and majesty. Yes, the captain would have a lot to think about, and as far as Lieutenant Timothy was concerned, he was welcome.

*****

"That man would spot a bedbug on a royal!" Jake complained. The foretop was usually a safe place to jolly: almost out of sight of the quarterdeck, especially when the main course was set. That was one reason for choosing it when taking Matthew on his first trip aloft.

"You'd better get movin'," Pamplin, a senior topmen, told them.

"Aye," said Copley, Pamplin's particular friend. Both men were off duty and had chosen the foretop as a quiet place to be together. "That beamy 'un's a shark. If e's got 'is eye on you, it'll be the worse for the rest of us."

Jake turned to Matthew. "Come on, Matt, take you to the crosstrees?"

Matthew grinned and nodded. He seemed quite at home aloft, with none of the stupid giddiness that some had when their feet left the deck. The boys made for the shrouds.

"'Member why we takes the weather side?" Jake began.

"I-I know," Matthew stammered. "Th-that w-way the weight goes down an' the w-wind blows you against the shrouds, n-not off them."

Jake grinned, "'S right. An' if *I* go, mind you shout, m-m-man overboard!"

They began to climb. The shrouds were narrower and closer together now, and the wind, which was gaining strength, certainly held them hard against the lines. Matthew and Jake ascended quickly, their bodies knocking together as the shrouds converged. The soles of Matthew's feet hurt from the unaccustomed harshness of the ratlines, but he was enjoying himself and determined not to let Jake pass him without a fight. In fact he pulled slightly ahead, and was the first to reach the futtock shrouds and the precarious safety of the crosstrees. He looked down at Jake complacently as he touched the smooth wooden frame.

"I see, a visitor, is it?"

The voice cut deep into Matthew's soul, and all thoughts of the game were dismissed. He looked up apprehensively. It was Crehan.

"So come on up, let me show you about." Crehan, stationed as lookout at the foretopgallant masthead, had heard the boys climbing and was ready to meet them on the topmast crosstrees. He held his hand out to Matthew, who paused uncertainly. Surely there was little Crehan could do to him here? Whatever resentment the man held, it could not extend to wishing him dead. Unaware, Jake nudged good naturedly from below, as Matthew warily extended his hand to the man.

"That's the spirit." Crehan grip was hard and painful; as soon as he had Matthew's arm in his hand, he seemed to take over, pulling the boy up and away from the safety of the shrouds.

"Let's get you nice an' safe, shall we?" He was supporting Matthew's entire weight now, and for the first time the boy felt conscious of the height, and of the deck circling steadily beneath them.

"Jus' plant y'r here." He laughed, holding Matthew above the crosstrees so that his feet were inches from the supports. Matthew looked into his eyes and knew the simple pleasure within. Crehan was treating him with the same callous disregard a child might have for an insect.

"L..l-let me down," he said, his voice breaking.

"Let you down, is it?" Crehan laughed, and swung the lad so that his body swayed sideways like the pendulum of a clock.

"You 'eard, let him down!" Jake was now on the futtock shrouds and level with the crosstrees, but could do little to help his friend. "Let 'im down, or I'll report you!"

Something struck a chord, and Crehan looked down at Jake, his face reddening.

"Oh, report me, would, you? Seems you've found a friend here, right enough; real peas in a pod, you two are!"

Matthew was still dangling and could feel Crehan's grip slip slightly.

"I'm goin'!" he shrieked. Crehan turned back to him, his pleasure renewed.

"You'll go when I says you will."

Matthew felt the grip slacken again, and shouted out. The Irishman's face turned to meet his as he realised he had misjudged. He went to pull Matthew in: the boy brushed the firm wood of the crosstrees with his foot, but it was only a fleeting touch. Crehan's grip slipped on his arm as he reached out with his other hand. For several seconds the Irishman struggled to pull Matthew up onto the perch, and had almost succeeded when a sudden blast of wind caught and spun him. The boy shouted and raised his hand to Crehan, who stretched out for him. Then Matthew fell.

It happened almost slowly. A flash of Jake's concerned face, followed by the topsail billowing out beside him. Pamplin shouting from the foretop as he passed, close enough to almost catch. He banched against the forecourse yard, fought for a grip, and hung crookedly for a split second, before falling once more. Falling, but still conscious, and still fighting.

Then he was amongst the massive forecourse, the wind blasting him into the belly of the sail. His body scraped against the canvas; the coarse material burned against his fingers as he battled for a hold. He spun sideways, and caught a glance at the quarterdeck and poop. Everything appeared normal, as if nothing had happened. Only he was behaving strangely in his private, exposed, battle. The sail tried to swallow him; he grappled with it and almost held, but the force that dragged him down was stronger.

There was sudden brightness and a loud noise close to his head that made him start. The pain flowed like a thrill down his back. Then nothing was beneath him. He struck out and gasped, body flailing in the empty, open air; fighting the pull that sucked him lower. Anger welled up inside, and he gave out one single robust yell before closing his eyes. The sea below was deep and flowing but, when he finally hit the crested surface, it felt as soft as granite.

*****

*Vigilant* now rode heavy waves, and the unaccustomed motion, combined with the long spell at anchor, brought out feelings of seasickness in even the most seasoned of her people. Dyson, sitting in the only private space available at that time, the chartroom next to the captain's quarters, was experiencing distinct feelings of unease as he interviewed King in the cramped and stuffy office.

"And you have no idea what they were doing aloft?"

King shook his head. "I was off watch, sir, as indeed they were. Diggins is quite experienced; he could have been taking Jameson up to show him the ropes."

Dyson nodded. King's conjecture fitted exactly with the young lad's statement. Skylarking, the unofficial climbing of the shrouds, was allowed only when conditions were good. It was still common, however, at all times, and, in Dyson's view, probably a better way for landsmen to learn than being harried up by some bullying boatswain's mate with a starter.

"What about Crehan? Were you conscious of friction between the two?"

King paused for a moment. "There was the incident at the rating board, sir."

"I am aware of that, but since then?"

Dyson was looking at him intently, watching every change of expression as King thought through the events of the last few days. "Yes, there was something else. Mr Critchley caught them together in the heads."

"I see." Dyson withdrew his pen from his coat pocket and tapped it on the desk thoughtfully. "They were alone, I take it."

"Yes, sir. Mr Critchley said he thought Crehan was plaguing the boy."

"Do you think Crehan has a liking?" Although illegal, consenting homosexuality was tolerated on some ships, but there were few officers who would not intervene when a boy was involved.

"No, sir. No, I think it more resentment."

Dyson considered the pen nib for a second before continuing. "And do you think it was wise for Crehan to be rated at foremast lookout?" He was clearly referring to the recent wardroom conversation, and King thought carefully before replying.

"With hindsight, possibly not, sir," he swallowed. "But he is a trained hand, and I would judge him better at the fore than the skyscraper."

It was a good point. The main lookout, being several feet higher than the fore, swept a wider horizon. In daylight the fore was really only there as a failsafe.

"The other boy, Diggins. Have you spoken to him?"

"No, sir, I was attending to Jameson. But Mr Pite met him on the foretop. He says Crehan dropped Jameson on purpose."

Dyson's eyebrows rose fractionally. "Dropped?" Diggins had said exactly that to him, but only after he had been given time to consider the matter.

"Yes, sir. He said Crehan held him away from the crosstrees, and deliberately dropped him."

"He couldn't have been in the process of helping him up when he lost his grip?"

King shook his head. "I know that's what Crehan said, sir, but Diggins is certain. An' there were others on the foretop at the time; Pamplin and Copley, they say the same."

Dyson closed his eyes for a moment; he knew all about Pamplin and Copley. The break from conversation served to remind them both of the weather and, in Dyson's case, his stomach. The chart room creaked and groaned with annoying regularity, and the wind rushed through the shrouds with a high pitched and frantic scream. *Vigilant* was already running under topsails alone; preventer stays had been rigged and it was likely that a reef would be needed before long. Meanwhile, the convoy could be holding together, or tearing off on different courses and individual speeds; no one could say which. Dyson swallowed as a wave of nausea swept over him; there really wasn't time to talk about one man's fate.

"Very well, we have enough to occupy us for now. Keep Crehan under close arrest, and look to your division. I expect a report from the surgeon directly; I will inform you when I know anything more."

"Thank you, sir," King stood up awkwardly in the small, heaving cabin. "Do you think this was an act of sabotage?" It was a question that had been on his mind for a while.

"No I don't." The first lieutenant placed the statements and notes into a folder and returned the pen to his pocket. "This was far too obvious, and totally out of keeping with anything the United Irishmen might have in mind. Look for tainted drinking water in the wardroom; a rolling round shot when it's only you on deck, false reports and ridiculous signals that make fools of officers; that's more their line. Nothing so direct and personal as endangering lives. It would not serve their purpose." He allowed King a grudging half-smile. "Right now I would guess that Crehan is not a particularly popular person. If he was involved with any Nationalist ideals, his actions will not have served the cause well."

\*\*\*\*\*

Tait threw off his pea-jacket and hung it on the rack outside the wardroom to dry. It was the end of the second dog watch; he had eight hours to himself before taking the morning watch which ran from four till eight. It was a duty he usually shared with Dyson, and Tait wanted to get as much sleep as possible, as the first lieutenant was an exacting man to work with. He drew his fingers through his damp fair hair, twitched his neck cloth and brushed his coat into a semblance of order before entering the wardroom. This was, after all, a place where gentlemen lived, and the fact that he had been on deck in the very teeth of a gale was no excuse to be casual about his appearance.

The elderly steward stepped out of the pantry as he entered. Tait shook his head; he had no use for food or drink, all he needed was the chance to fall into his cot and let someone else take charge for a spell. The storm had been growing steadily; it would be a restless night, with the strong possibility that he would be called before his watch began. The only other occupants of the wardroom, Timothy and Gregory, had spread the green baize cloth over the table and were playing cards. Timothy had been trying to teach the intricacies of whist to the older man, and the table was laid with four hands face up, while Timothy patiently explained the order of play. Tait acknowledged them both, before opening the screen door of his cabin, and retreating inside.

He appeared again almost immediately, his face full of bluster and indignation.

"Has anyone been in here?" he asked. Timothy looked up.

"Mr Dyson has just left, and Mr Morrison. Neither went near your cabin though."

His look stirred their interest, and all thoughts of cards were put aside as they rose up from the table and followed him into the tiny room.

"Well bless me!" Gregory explained. This was far more interesting than guarding an ace or attempting a finesse. "Looks like you've been taken rotten!"

Tait's possessions were piled neatly in the middle of the deck. His furniture had all but disappeared; only the cot, now bereft of its embroidered cover, swung from the deckhead.

"Someone's squirreled your stuff," Timothy said unnecessarily.

"Damn right!" Tait's eyes were filled with anger. "Bloody Rogers!"

"Rogers?" Timothy could not see the connection.

"Somebody call?" The voice came from the wardroom, Rogers must have entered while they were examining Tait's cabin. Tait pushed past the others to get at him.

"What the deuce do you think you're at?"

Rogers had dined well earlier, and now had the look of a satisfied cat. He lent on the bulkhead, bracing himself against the heel of the ship.

"My dear Tait, pray do not excite yourself!"

"Excite myself?" he drew breath. "Curse you, for the stuffed up, conceited prig that you are!"

Timothy knew that Rogers was considered influential, and was junior enough to bite his tongue; while Gregory, who had no such inhibitions, grinned openly.

"I do not accept an address like that from anyone." There was a formal edge to Rogers' voice now, as if he was reciting from a prepared speech. "I advise you to moderate your language, or I shall be forced to request a meeting!"

The mention of a duel raised the stakes along with Tait's blood pressure. He opened his mouth to reply, but it was Gregory, with his solid reasoning, who was first to speak.

"I think Mr Tait is referring to his furniture, or rather the lack of it." Gregory's older voice, uncultured but authoritative, brought a semblance of order, despite the fact that he was junior to all bar Timothy.

"Mr Tait volunteered his furniture to me only the evening before last." Rogers turned to Gregory as a child might an adult. "I have merely taken him up on the offer."

"I'll be damned if I did!"

"And what about the carpenter?" Rogers continued. "Did you not ask him to make you a fresh set of furniture yesterday afternoon?"

"Yes, but for you, and at your request, damn it!"

Rogers smiled an ingratiating smile that was totally wasted. "Well surely, once the carpenter has completed his task, all will be well?"

"All will be well? All will be well?" Tait was very nearly breathless. "I fail to see how that will come about when rogues like you walk the deck!"

Roger's look grew cold and concentrated. "I have warned you about your language, Mr Tait. Now you have called me a rogue in front of other gentlemen. For that I must seek satisfaction!"

The atmosphere, already tense with anger and the enormity of the occasion, was amplified by a change in sound. The groaning of the ship's timbers took precedence as *Vigilant* rode out a sudden increase in the gale. For a moment all attention was turned to the weather, and it was only when a lull came that the conversation resumed. It was Gregory who finally broke the impasse.

"Both of you should be aware that it is a court martial offence for King's officers to challenge, or take any part in a duel while on active service."

Rogers' anger, together with his eyes, fell on Gregory.

"I know of no rules that prevent us from settling this matter like gentlemen!"

"Then you are ignorant of King's Regulations, Mr Rogers. An' before you try the same trick on me, I am speakin' the truth." It was Rogers' turn to be lost for words as Gregory continued. "It is also against regulations, and common law for that matter, for a fellow's possessions to be taken or moved without his allowance. I suggest you ask your man to return Mr Tait's furniture to his quarters."

"Damned Sea Lawyer!" Rogers glared at Gregory. "Damned peasant dressed up as a gentleman!"

"You should watch your language, Mr Rogers," Gregory twinkled. "That's another offence you've just committed!"

It was more than he could stand, and Rogers stormed out of the wardroom, slamming the door behind him.

Timothy let out a long held breath. "He's supposed to be pretty influential, y'know?"

"I don't care if he knows Farmer George personally." Gregory allowed himself a brief smile. "Now, Mr Timothy and I were exploring the intricacies of whist; perhaps, if Mr Tait would join us, I could teach you both another game. The Colonials call it poker; I learned it while stationed in New York back in 'eighty-one. A trifle less complex, but enjoyable nevertheless."

It was when they were starting their second hand that Rogers' servant entered, and together with a wardroom steward, returned Tait's furniture to its proper place.

# CHAPTER TEN

BY midnight the storm was at its worst. The wind blew across their larboard quarter with such force and energy that it ceased to be simply moving air, becoming instead something solid in the minds of the men who had to fight it. Spray mixed with the rain and scoured their skin, tormenting their throats with a thirst that could never be satisfied, despite the water that constantly attacked every sense in their bodies.

Shepherd had been summoned from his cabin for the third time in three hours and now stood by the binnacle, leaning into the gale at such an angle that he appeared on the very brink of falling over. He wiped the salt from his eyes as he tried to penetrate the deep black night.

"Still under full reefs?" he bellowed at Humble, who stood no more than a yard away.

"Aye, sir," came the reply. "An' all safe. But I'd like permission to heave to. We've been lucky; she can't take this punishment forever."

Shepherd caught his balance as *Vigilant* heeled into a particularly deep wave that drenched a group of topmen sheltering by the break of the forecastle. Humble was right, they had been lucky. But the men on deck were all seasoned hands, and it was luck that came from preparation, training and not a little skill. He wondered if the merchant ships with their laden hulls and meagre crews would have met with such fortune and survived for as long before giving in.

The traverse board banged incessantly against the binnacle, trying to disrupt his thoughts in its bid for freedom. To heave to meant losing what control they had; *Vigilant* would be at the whim of wind and wave. They might drift for days without the chance of a solar sighting; the idea went against all Shepherd's instincts, both as captain and seaman.

"What of the convoy?" he asked, with little hope.

The master held his hands wide in an attitude of despair. The storm had increased as darkness fell, and the convoy disappeared into the gloom. Shepherd had ordered sail reduced early, knowing the Indiamen's habit of snuggling down when the weather was bad. That was over six hours ago. Now, even if the merchants' lights were as bright as Eddystone, he doubted that they could have been made through the darkness. It was highly likely that, whether she hove to or not, *Vigilant* would find an empty horizon come morning.

"Yes, let her go, Mr Humble."

Gregory, who had just taken the watch, bellowed the order. Boatswain's mates appeared and piped impudently against the screaming wind. The afterguard mainly consisted of marines and landsmen; they staggered to their positions at the braces, while Humble and Gregory organised the coordination of wheel and yards, so that *Vigilant* could shelter in relative safety and ride out the storm.

From his refuge by the larboard bulwalk, Flint heard the order and drew a sigh of relief. He had been on deck since before nightfall, his sodden clothes preventing him from taking refuge below for even half an hour's rest. Four times he had gone aloft, first to take in the forecourse, then to reef topsails each time the wind increased.

The hull reeled unexpectedly as she turned, before beginning a sickening roll while the braces came round and took the pressure off the masts and shrouds. Almost immediately *Vigilant* dipped, allowing the sea to wash over her deck, but her lack of resistance drew the force from the oncoming waves and she soon settled into a regular motion.

She had ceased to fight, although it was not defeat, merely a temporary truce.

The bell rang twice; one o'clock in the morning. Flint was officially off duty for the next three hours, and it was almost worth going below, providing he had a set of dry clothes, and the energy to change into them. To "turn in wet and come up steaming" was the alternative, an idea that held little appeal. Instead he dropped down into the waist and clambered under the shelter of the weather gangway. Beyond him he could make out the vague forms of Crehan and Simpson, both still manacled in the bilboes that would not be removed until their punishment was decided upon. They too would be wet and cold, but Flint, usually a compassionate soul, spared them no thought; he was weary, horribly so, and needed sleep. He tugged his sodden jacket about his shoulders and tucked his face into the lee of the bulwark. By pulling his cap down and resting his head upon his arm he could keep relatively warm while the gangway and his back would keep out all but the worst of the weather. The position could never be considered comfortable, but his needs were met for the moment. Before long Flint had adjusted to the motion as *Vigilant* wallowed in the heavy sea, and soon he too gave in, allowing sleep to wash over and carry him under.

\*\*\*\*\*

The midshipmen's berth was damp and stuffy. Pite hung his oilskins outside and ducked under the narrow entrance. His eyes were already accustomed to the gloom, and yet it still took several seconds to make out Hayes, Mintey and Roberts seated round the mess table.

He picked up a stool that had fallen over and joined them. The remains of supper lay on the table; Pite helped himself to biscuit and accepted a tumbler of wine from Hayes.

"What's it like up?" Roberts asked, his eyes round in the doubtful light from a single sconce. Pite remembered that this was Roberts' first proper blow, and decided not to tease the boy.

"Been through the worst, I reckon," he said confidently. "We'll see it quieter by dawn."

Roberts nodded, although he still had a strained look on his face.

"What of the convoy?" Mintey this time; at thirty-seven he was old for a midshipman, and more experienced than many of the lieutenants.

"Convoy's on the Atlantic," Pite answered. "Other than that I couldn't say."

"Is the ship sound?" Roberts again.

Mintey snorted, "If twern't, Mr Roberts," he banged on the spirketting that lined hull of the ship, barely feet away from each of them, "we'd all know 'bout it!"

The other two laughed, and even Roberts allowed a faint smile. It was not unheard of for a plank to spring in weather such as this, and when one could go, two might easily follow. The British Navy had lost more vessels to foundering than enemy action, and better set up ships than *Vigilant* had gone to the bottom in heavy weather.

"Is there any meat to go with this biscuit?" Pite asked as he cleaned a fork by stabbing it through a piece of the canvas that covered the table. Hayes shook his head.

"Nothin' cooked. One of the boatswain's mates reckons there's.a rat's nest in the cable tier, but we'd never be 'lowed a fire."

Pite put the fork down and stood up, keeping his head bent to miss the low deckhead.

"Better turn in, then," he said, and at that moment they all heard the crack.

It was loud and sharp, like a pistol shot. No one spoke; the noise of rushing water that followed said everything necessary.

"We've sprung!" Roberts shrieked hysterically. The berth was cleared in seconds and outside, in the gloom of the orlop, it was obvious that others had heard the sound.

Morrison, the purser, staggered towards them in a long white night shirt. He singled out Hayes. "Get up there, laddie, and warn the quarterdeck!"

Hayes was gone, and a few idlers, not wanting to be trapped below the waterline in a sinking ship, went with him.

Pite caught sight of Smith, the carpenter, who came striding from the stern, a large lanthorn in his hands.

"Where was the sound?" he demanded. The noise of the incoming water had almost died now, presumably due to the hole being underwater; it did not look well.

"Further forward," Pite said, pointing towards the main hanging magazine.

Smith nodded. "You, there," he said, indicating Roberts. "The main chain pump is in use already, take two of my mates and get the second manned and active." The difference in rank and lack of courtesy went unnoticed by all. If a plank had started there was no one on board more important than the carpenter.

"Forward, you say?" Smith was lightly built, although he had a loud voice and an air of confidence that made him appear larger.

"I think so," Pite replied.

The carpenter considered this. "More likely to be right at the bows or stern, but we'd better take a look." He turned to one of his mates. "Sound the well and report to me. I'll be in the middle hold with Mr Pite."

Pite swallowed. He would rather have been detailed for Roberts' duties and only thought he knew where the sound had come from.

They drew back the gratings on the middle hold and stared into the black void beneath. In the noise of the storm it was impossible to know exactly what was going on. Two men appeared with ladders which were lowered into the opening.

Smith looked hard at Pite. "If we're leakin', barrels may be afloat. Keep your eyes about you!"

Pite nodded and accepted a lanthorn from one of the bystanders. There was no time to wait for a lieutenant: it had to be done now, and Pite resigned himself to the fact that it had to be done by him.

Together the two men clambered over the combings and down into the hold. The light was bad; Pite raised his lanthorn and could just make out a line of barrels lying on their sides: the first bank of several rows. The sound of water had stopped, and as he walked he felt the shingle that covered the hold through the soles of his boots. He reached down reluctantly and verified the small stones were wet. Wet, but not actually awash. So what had caused the sound?

"Seems solid enough here," Smith shouted, from his side of the hold. "Belike we'd best look for'ad."

Pite heard the carpenter's words, but was strangely reluctant to leave. Now in the hold he was even more certain that it held the source of the sound. He felt his way over to the far side, next to the hull, and shone his lanthorn on the shingle. Again, just the faintest tinge of moisture from the bilges; exactly what would be expected of a ship in a storm.

"Come on, lad!" Smith shouted. "We've to check number one!"

He was quite right, time was vital, but something about the look of the shingle caught Pite's eye. There seemed to be a lot more, quite a pile in fact and of a different size and colour. He bent down, collected a piece in his fingers, and held it up to the light. His tense expression relaxed as he knelt and picked up a complete handful.

"Mr Smith, over here!"

The carpenter came quickly, staring anxiously over his lanthorn. "What is it? What you got?"

Pite said nothing, instead he released his grip and allowed what has been covering the hold to fall from his fingers and rattle back onto the pile with a sound like falling rain.

\*\*\*\*\*

"You're wantin' to see the kid?" the surgeon asked him.

Jake nodded. "If that's 'lowd, sir."

"Aye. Everyone else 'as, so one more won't make no difference." He called to Skirrow, one of his loblolly boys, a wasted looking man with a squint. "Take him to see Jameson. Not long, mind, you got them draughts to grind."

Skirrow led Jake to the side of the sick bay where a cot was secured to the deck.

"Ain't supposed to put head wounds in 'ammocks," he explained blithely. "Mind, the thrashin' about he's had over last day an' night, I don' sees it makes no difference. You awake, Jameson?"

Matthew sat up carefully in the bunk.

"Hey, you stay lyin'," Skirrow cautioned him, and watched until Matthew lowered himself back into his bed. "I'll leave you to talk but will know if you've been muckin' 'bout. He's in our care, y'know."

Skirrow shuffled off and Jake settled himself down on the deck next to the cot.

"How's it with you, then?"

Matthew shrugged. "Not bad."

"We thought you was a gonner as soon as you fell an' the cutter's crew reckoned there was nothing left alive when they picked you up."

"Right, I was lucky."

"Lucky? I'll say!" Jake quickly moderated his voice to a level more suited to the visiting of the sick. "I've heard of men fallin' off the poop ladder and not survivin'! What dja do, anyhow?"

"Couple of ribs are bruised an' I banged me head. Other than that, they say I'm sound."

"I borrowed you an apple," Jake said, returning to more important matters. "Surgeon doesn't know, otherwise he'd probably 'ave taken it off me." Jake held out a rather withered specimen.

"Thanks, but I'm gettin' good food here."

"Yeah?"

"Yeah. Raisins, soft cheese, lobscouse, b-bit of chocolate last night. An' soup."

"I'd 'eard you do all right in sickers. Didn't know it were that good. Mind if I hang on to the apple then?"

"No, you keep it."

Jake returned the fruit to his pocket and looked around, as if searching for things to talk about.

"When you back to duties?"

"Can't say. Surgeon wants to check out me head firs'. Says it can still give trouble, headaches an' the like. I got to stay out of 'ammocks an' not go aloft for a while."

"'Specially when Crehan's about, right?"

Both boys laughed, then Jake grew more serious.

"They say he could end up goin' roun' the fleet."

"How's that?"

"Punishment. Man gets rowed from ship t' ship, an flogged at each one. They can give over an 'undred lashes, some say nearer a thousand—that's if 'e don't 'ang!"

"Hang?"

"Right. Not the sort of thing they want; people pushin' others off tops."

Matthew closed his eyes for a moment, and saw the look on the Irishman's face when he knew he was going to fall. "Wasn't really 'is fault. He didn't mean me to fall. He was jus' trying to frighten."

"Makes no difference; man fools about aloft, he gets punished. It's not for you, it's for the res' of us, an' to put others off doin' the same."

That made sense. He also saw that it would be the end to the worry about Crehan; whatever happened now, there was no way the Irishman could continue a feud that had become so public.

"I'd better leave you to caulk." Jake stood up. "Don' stay there too long. No pay in sick bay, an' t'purser will dock money for the treatment when you're ripe!"

Matthew wasn't sure if Jake was serious, but wanted to get back, pay or not. The fall had changed a lot of things; he almost seemed a different person. It was as if those few seconds of panic had frightened the boy from him. He felt more grown up, and the stammer that had plagued him ever since he could remember had all but vanished. He didn't know what had caused the change, but  it seemed that there were so many things out there waiting for him, and he had no time to waste getting back.

And there was another reason. Now he was definitely part of *Vigilant*. There couldn't be anyone on board who didn't know about the boy who'd fallen from the foretopmast. Most, it seemed, had been to visit him, including two officers other than Mr King and the chaplain. Today he'd seen most of his mess at discreet intervals, and now Jake. It was still little more than a week from the time he was walking from Leatherhead to Portsmouth and yet already there were people who cared about him. In some cases he might be no more than a macabre source of interest, but nevertheless the contrast was strong.

"Right, I'll be off, then."

"Thanks for comin'," he grinned "An' the apple."

"Do you get onions?" Jake asked.

"No, not had any onions." Matthew said seriously

Jake assumed the manner of a worldly benefactor, "I'll bring you one then," he said, and left.

*****

"You're a God-damned fool if ever there was one," O'Conner informed him. Crehan looked straight ahead, as if the words had not been spoken. His feet were secured by rings stapled to the deck, although his hands were free, and currently engaged in picking oakum. Simpson was similarly employed next to him, his presence, together with that of the marine sentry who stood at ease behind them both, made O'Conner choose his words with care.

"You could have killed the kid; you know that, don't yer?"

"He knows," Simpson replied after a pause. "He knows 'cause I, an' every jack aboard this ship, 'as told him."

"No man will converse with the prisoners," the marine spoke in a dull monotone as if reciting from a book.

O'Conner nodded, "I've no wish to talk with this one," he said, and withdrew.

*****

Crehan had been tried under Group Three of the Articles of War, which covered crimes against the fellow man and his rights. His offence could easily warrant the death penalty; for this, however, a court martial was needed, and Shepherd disliked the idea of two men on the punishment deck awaiting possible execution. Besides, in principle Crehan had committed a crime against every man in the ship, and he felt an immediate and public punishment was called for.

"Twelve lashes is the maximum I can order officially," Shepherd said, when Crehan had been removed from their presence. Dyson nodded. They both knew this, and of the various ways that punishments could be extended.

"Or you could flog him to death; there's more than just cause. The crew would be behind you."

Shepherd closed his eyes briefly, remembering the scared look on Crehan's face as he admitted to dropping the boy "in a fit of carelessness." Whatever the truth of the matter, it was clear that Crehan regretted the incident deeply. The position of captain of a ship-of-the-line had more than its share of unpleasant aspects, and Shepherd found imposing discipline one of the more distasteful.

"If it came to it I could hang him, but I feel a flogging is enough, especially as the boy seems willing to forgive." That was certainly true. Jameson, brought into his presence before they had seen Crehan, seemed almost as frightened of the impending punishment as the Irishman.

"The boy is lucky to be able to," Dyson's voice was like ice. Shepherd guessed his first lieutenant would have found little trouble selecting a punishment were the choice left to him.

He snapped to a decision. The passage so far had not been bad; they had ridden out the storm without significant loss. There had been the scare, when most of the orlop thought a plank had started. Apparently the noise of whole dried peas flowing out of a crushed barrel had sounded like the seas rushing in, but apart from a few bruised egos, no harm had been done. And they had been fortunate with the convoy; already they had rounded up most of the scattered ships, and he had no wish to insult the good luck that had come his way with a show of spite.

"No, a flogging will do. Make it seventy-two."

Seventy-two lashes; certainly not enough to kill Crehan, but he could still be left crippled, in mind, if not in body. The sight would also be sufficient to convince most of the crew that he had been properly dealt with.

Dyson nodded, betraying little of his opposition to what he considered extreme leniency. There were some crimes that merited compassion, even in a heart as cold as the first lieutenant's. But Crehan had wilfully endangered another man, worse, a boy who had barely been in the ship a couple of weeks and Dyson felt nothing but contempt for the creature.

The captain spoke again. "You can trump up the charge?"

"Aye, sir." By accusing Crehan of a series of offences, real or imagined, he could be awarded twelve lashes for each. Thus the letter of the law was seen to be obeyed, while Shepherd imposed a heavier punishment than was officially allowed. "Shall we tell him his fate?"

Shepherd sighed. "Yes, have him brought back."

\*\*\*\*\*

"Poetry, Timothy?"

Rogers reached over the lieutenant's shoulder, and plucked the leather-bound book out of reach of his sudden, desperate, grasp.

"I had no idea we had men of words aboard!"

The wardroom was reasonably full, as the midday meal was due in less than half an hour.

"I'll have that back, if you please!" It was hard to keep the panic from his voice, although Timothy had been in such situations often enough to realise that a cool demeanour is essential if matters are not to escalate.

"Fond of the odd rhyme miself, as it happens," Rogers continued. He closed his eyes, and was still for a second, before breaking out in a loud voice. "Sarah was a sailors' pet, she worked the local hard." Timothy ached to grab his book back while Rogers declared the crude doggerel to the room. A few, notably those who had had little experience of Rogers, guffawed, while Wilson, the surgeon, cackled without reserve.

Some, however, remained silent; Carling, Tait and Gregory coldly so.

When he had finished, Rogers opened his eyes once more and turned his attention back to the book, leafing through the pages. "Can't say there's anything here I know, certainly nothin' as good as that!" He closed the book to look at the title, and Timothy's heart dropped into his boots.

"Here's a rum thing an all: Hamilton Moore's *Practical Navigator*, yet the whole thing's filled with rhymes and ditties!" He thrust the book under the noses of those seated at the table, flipping through the pages to prove his point. "I'd take more care when I bought my books were I you, Mr Timothy!"

Timothy said nothing; his eyes were lowered, and his face betrayed his shame.

"But I forget, you're of that ilk, are you not?" Three of the wardroom stewards were standing by the pantry watching the scene: Rogers' voice was uncommonly loud.

"My father is a bookbinder," Timothy admitted, wondering how such a discreditable thing should be so widely known.

"Then I can only think he is a very bad workman!" Rogers chortled, this time to total silence.

"No man here need be ashamed of his station, nor his history," Carling spoke with calm assurance. "Myself, I come from farming stock, and am proud of it."

Rogers' face took on a look of absolute delight. "Farming stock, Mr Carling? Why does that not surprise me? And pray tell, exactly which field did you grow up in?"

"That'll do, Mr Rogers!" Gregory this time, although only a breath before Tait.

"Ah, Mr Gregory—you do prefer to be addressed in that manner I understand, although I dare say another form was used afore the mast!"

"You really are a deeply unpleasant man." Carling had contained his fury and now looked at Rogers in cold anger.

"Gentleman, Mr Carling, gentleman. Unpleasant I may be, to your unrefined eyes, but a gentleman I undoubtedly am; that is incontestable."

Something of the hostile atmosphere must have become apparent as his eyes swept about the other officers. "And another thing," he tossed the book disdainfully in front of Timothy and continued in a tone that was both clinical and menacing. "I am senior to all here present—every man jack of you—and likely to remain so for as long as we are in the service. I could buy and sell any in this ship, and its about time I was shown a bit more respect."

*****

Matthew was to be present when Crehan was flogged. All formal punishments were witnessed by the entire crew. The publicity acting both as a deterrent to others and an attempt to ensure that the officers were not taking undue liberties with the men. The helmsmen, watch keeping officers and masthead lookouts were the only exclusions, but even they would have an excellent view of the proceedings. And as Matthew had already been allowed up for a day, he really couldn't avoid it, however detestable the idea was to him.

"You could look on it as the end of the incident," the chaplain said, as he led him up from the sick bay into the sunlight of the waist. "When this has ended, so will any argument between you and Mr Crehan."

Matthew eyed him doubtfully. The chaplain looked very young for his job, and there was something about him, and the way he spoke, that did not ring true.

"Mr Skirrow will look after you. The sight is not pleasant, I understand."

Matthew allowed himself to be propped against a gun carriage almost opposite the grating, which had been raised from over the main hatch and rigged vertically at the break of the quarterdeck. Behind it a detachment of marines were lined up, bayonets fixed and muskets loaded.

Dyson and King were on watch. The boatswain formally approached and knuckled his forehead. Dyson nodded, and the boatswain turned away and signalled to his mates. The squeal of their pipes filled the ship, and slowly the men began to appear, talking quietly amongst themselves as they formed into their divisions. Matthew could see Flint and the rest of his mess standing on the opposite side under the gangway. Flint gave him a quick toothy smile, and raised one reassuring thumb. Of all the men who had paid Matthew a visit, only Flint had been allowed into his confidence and understood how he felt about the business.

Then the captain appeared on the quarterdeck, along with the rest of the officers. All wore swords, and serious expressions; none spoke.

Skirrow, next to him, fidgeted slightly. "I 'eard they've made a couple of south paws 'onnery bosun's mates." Matthew looked at him enquiringly, and he explained. "Bosun's mates does the floggin'. They change 'em every twelve lashes, so they need six. If three of 'em are left 'anders, Crehan'll 'ave a nice checked shirt at the end of it."

Matthew had little time to take in Skirrow's words, as the marine drummer began to beat out the Rogue's March, and Crehan appeared on deck, an armed marine to either side of him.

The last time Matthew had seen the Irishman was on the fore crosstrees, six days ago. Since then he seemed to have aged ten years; even the colour of his skin looked washed out and faded. For a moment his gaze swept over Matthew, but there was little chance of catching his eye, as his stare was blank and empty. A growl, possibly belligerent, possibly sympathetic, emanated from the men as he was brought to the grating. A marine removed Crehan's shirt and secured his hands to the top two corners of the grating. A boatswain's mate tied a leather apron backwards about his waist, so that the scarred hide draped down over his buttocks. Another boatswain's mate stepped forward, with a bright red canvas bundle in his hand. More murmuring spread through the crowd as the cat was removed from its bag, and the knotted strands of rope flopped down towards the deck.

"Half a fathom of log line," Skirrow informed him. "You'd think it was made of wire, the mess it makes!"

The drummer stopped, and for a moment there was an eerie silence. The captain read the charges in a low but powerful voice and the air hung heavy as time was suspended. Then Matthew looked away and the punishment began.

# CHAPTER ELEVEN

THE day after Crehan's punishment was a Sunday. By then the wind had dropped completely, the clouds all but disappeared, and a welcome sun shone down on the small convoy that drifted untidily across the smooth sea. On the previous day the decks had been stoned twice, once in the morning, and again in the late afternoon, to reduce work for the official day of rest. The hands were roused half an hour earlier than other days and jostled with each other over the shaving kids, running razors over necks and faces with nothing but their own hands and experience as a guide. Then it was clean shirts, white duck trousers and best blue jackets. The bell had been rung for divine service and the common pendant raised to the mizzen peak.

Bryant, the chaplain, watched them surreptitiously as he laid the union flag over a pair of upturned casks at the break of the quarterdeck. Bryant knew himself to be unpopular, and was sorry, although it seemed that any move he made to rectify the situation was doomed to rebound. On earlier voyages he had tried to empathise with the men, come down to their level and share their lot, but what could a man brought up in a bishop's palace share with another whose idea of refinement was raw spirit and a freshly toasted rat? But the efforts made on his part had merely robbed him of the dignity his office held, and Bryant knew that the next few weeks were not going to be easy.

Strangely it was precisely that knowledge that had made him stay on as chaplain, when he could so easily have resigned during his recent leave. He had decided to go ashore as soon as the wedding garland was hoisted, knowing the scenes of debauchery and sin that normally followed would be too much for him. The time with his father had been a test in itself and it had been hard to turn from the luxury of a home where he was loved and respected, to one where he could expect to be taunted, tripped or affronted at any moment. Some chaplains could carry themselves well with seamen, could earn their respect, and even be taken into their confidence. Bryant was not one of those, and he had long ago resigned himself to the fact, along with the abuse that seemed to go hand in hand with his calling. His only consolation lay in the knowledge that, if he was truly serious in his vocation, there were few more needy places for him and the Lord's word than a ship of war at sea.

And so he had returned to *Vigilant*, knowing that to do otherwise would be to deny his faith—the faith that led him as strongly and effectively as any press-gang. There may have been little empathy between Bryant and the general hands, but he had far more understanding of their plight than they would ever credit and, of all the men on board, Bryant felt he must certainly be the most miserable.

"Fine weather for it, padre," Gregory informed him as the hands fell in to their divisions and waited patiently for the service to begin. Bryant smiled cautiously at the lieutenant, never certain if he were being teased, or merely tolerated. Dyson appeared next, and gave him a nod of acknowledgement, followed by Carling, the captain of marines, and the other lieutenants. A few junior officers then emerged, taking a moment or two in deciding their rightful place on the quarterdeck, for there was little to tell which was the leeward side on such a still day.

Shepherd was last of all, and he strode up to the chaplain's primitive altar with such assurance that Bryant felt strangely jealous. He returned the captain's nod and turned to start the service; this was his time now, the time when he had charge over the ship, the men, and their souls. *And God help them all,* he thought as he began.

The marine band made a credible start to the hymn, and Bryant boldly led the singing, his voice often wavering several keys away from the musicians. Eventually it was done, and he began his short sermon. This was based on one he had given at the start of the previous voyage, and broadly similar to that used on the onset of the commission before that. It covered the leaving of home, with more than a mention of the duty every man owed to his country. In a time when wars were paid for by the rich, but fought by the poor, Bryant took care to keep the irony from creeping into his voice. Then he went on to describe the adventure that lay before them. That they, like the ship, were on a voyage, one that would take them through the rest of their life. He looked down at the bored faces, still and silent due only to the discipline they were under, and realised what a waste of time it all was.

The captain was also watching his crew while Bryant's sermon droned on. The men were hardly paying attention, but there was nothing new in that: seamen and conventional religion were hardly bedfellows. Many held a strong faith, but few accepted the conformity of organised denomination, while others satisfied any such need with aphorisms and superstition. The men appeared impatient; there were signs of shuffling and whispers; nothing anyone could identify and punish, but quite possibly the first symptoms of disruption. The first suggestion of a rebellion that might end with the loss of his ship, and possibly even his life. Sunday afternoons were traditionally declared a holiday, a make and mend period when the decks would become filled with men immersed in a dozen different tasks, from tattooing to scrimshaw. In a ship where some were new and untrained, the first lieutenant had also organised a series of drills and exercises for the following morning that should start to knock them into shape. Looking at the hands now, Shepherd longed to bring it into effect that very afternoon, but felt that it was not the time. In a world where men were mainly valued for their muscle power, it was easy to consider them as nothing more than beasts of burden. He looked along the faces, the young and old, tough and sensitive; these were people, many of whom had recently been wrenched from their homes. The next few days would give them ample time for training, but to rush things now might just encourage the restlessness he had already noticed.

The sermon finished adequately enough, and after leading them through The Lord's Prayer, Bryant left the stage to more competent players.

Shepherd stepped forward and cleared his throat. This was an opportunity to address the crew, but he resisted the temptation. Perhaps in a week or so, when they had properly shaken down, would be a better time. He opened his copy of *King's Regulations*, as important to him as any Bible was to Bryant. It was no accident that the divine service ended with the reading of the Articles of War, and Shepherd did so now with due reverence and clarity. These were the rules that bound each hand to him, the ship, and the Navy. And these were the laws each would be tried by, should they fail in any of their duties. The silence that greeted him was respectful and complete. It was their world that he spoke of, and the rules held a greater relevance than any supposed kingdom in the sky. After the reading the service ended abruptly, and the hands fell out, to mingle socially while the purser and his stewards issued the morning grog. Once this was down, they had a meal of pork and pease pudding to look forward to, followed by the afternoon's holiday of "make and mend."

Jenkins, who had endured the time as well as any, fell in with O'Conner while the preparations for grog were made.

"That were a waste of time," he muttered.

O'Conner looked at him cautiously; to openly criticize the divine service was not encouraged. "Why would you be saying that, then?"

"Blasted chaplain rumbles on about loving your fellow man," Jenkins pulled a sour face. "Then the captain chimes in and says you'll get hanged if they catch you."

*****

The coffee was hot, sweet, and very strong, just the way he liked it. Shepherd sipped appreciatively; it was his first enjoyable drink of the voyage: the new steward had taken that long to correctly interpret his wishes. He sipped again, and pushed his chair back from his desk. He was part way though a letter to his wife. The writing might well be a futile affair, as pure chance would dictate if they ran across a homeward bound transport on the way to St Helena; and as they were expecting to come straight back, there would be no point in transferring post on their arrival. Still, the exercise was good for reminding him of his home, even if it roused feelings that were hardly to be expected of a husband separated from his wife.

He had married early, as a midshipman, when he had been stationed in a frigate based at New York. His wife was the daughter of an army captain posted to America who liked the country enough to return when he resigned his commission. Despite inevitable friction during the American War, Shepherd supposed he was as happily married as any sailor had a right to expect. That was until the beginning of 'ninety-two, when Anna's father died, and her sister decided to visit England to stay with them.

Sisters they were, although Katharine was nine years younger, and the twenty years that they had been apart, living different lives under different conditions, had created two very diverse people. Anna was not one for airs and graces, but she knew her rôle in society, and had never let him down as the captain's lady. Katharine was far more down to earth. Her face was unfashionably tanned, and she had a direct way of speaking that initially amused Shepherd, although he had been alarmed to notice other feelings begin stir.

Since the summer of 'ninety-two she had stayed with them in their house near Reigate. Shepherd had already been on half pay for two years, and yet they were moderately well off, due in no small part to the estate of Anna's father. This was one of the main reasons why Katharine could move in and stay almost indefinitely. Besides, it would hardly have done for an unmarried lady to set up house on her own, so what reason could he have had for objecting to her presence? And as the summer wore on he found that any latent protest melted completely in the warmth of her company.

They had taken to walking together, the two of them (Anna never cared for being out of doors), as well his dogs, and any house guest who happened to be staying. Shepherd, taking a landsman's delight in the Surrey countryside, would have been happy to wander for days, were it not more seemly for a professional man to waste his time in other ways. But the presence of a foreign relative gave him full licence to show off his county, and who could be.more respectable to escort than the sister of his wife?

After the walks it seemed only natural for Katharine to accompany him on his regular trips to London. While Shepherd reminded the Admiralty of his existence, she would tour the Bond Street shops and meet up with him in the evening. He remembered their conversations with almost as much pleasure as the silent rides back to Reigate in his carriage.

With a twinge of guilt Shepherd replaced his cup and picked up his pen afresh. He re-read his last sentence and went to add more. His phrasing was careful; he knew Anna saved all his letters, and was sentimental enough to read them again if ever she was missing him. He also guessed that fresh correspondence would be greeted with great delight and read several times over, before inevitably being passed on for Katharine to enjoy as well.

"I wanted to show you this, sir." Pite proffered the serving mallet to the first lieutenant.

"Yes?" Dyson felt the interrogative might have been unneces-sarily sharp, and continued in a softer tone. "What of it, Mr Pite?"

"Mr Rollston, the Cooper, found it in the middle hold, sir. He an' Mr Morrison were trying to salvage some of the provisions. This was by the cask that had sprung, sir."

Dyson weighed the heavy tool in his hand thoughtfully. "And you think someone used it to start the barrel?"

"Yes, sir."

He was probably right. There were marine sentries posted at all sensitive points in the ship, from the spirit room to the gratings, both for security and to discourage the lazy from urinating into the bilges. But the middle hold carried mainly victuals of low appeal and did not warrant a guard.

"Yet there was no one else in the hold when you investigated?" It would have been impossible to start the cask and then escape without notice. The orlop had been filled with men seconds after the barrel was broken.

"No, sir. Just me and Mr Smith. But then I wasn't looking for anyone. Whoever did this could have hidden himself away until we'd gone."

Yes, there would have been no need for a rapid exit. And with the ship in the middle of a storm, no one would have commented on one empty hammock when the normal occupant might well have chosen to stay on deck. The only deadline would have been to be back for divisions, and that would have presented little problem.

"So, it seems our Irish friends are up to their tricks." He sighed. Not for the first time Dyson felt wearied by the problem.

Secretly he was not without sympathy for the United Irishmen and their plight; morally, in fact, he felt their cause was just. But any atrocities that had been committed under British occupation would pale into insignificance once the French took control. And take control they would, despite numerous assurances to the contrary. So far they had overrun Spain and Holland on the grounds of spreading republicanism while most of Europe waited to see where the stain was to spread next. And to live under French occupation would be to accept a regime far more unjust, tyrannical, and oppressive than any it replaced.

"Very well," he said. "Thank you for this. There is little we can do at the moment, however." He paused, and allowed the boy a dry smile. "Let's hope the forthcoming exercises sap a little energy from our revolutionary companions."

*****

The next day Matthew was passed fit by the surgeon and allowed back to general duties. An exercise with the great guns was scheduled, and he approached his station a little tentatively, suddenly unsure of the reaction he could expect from the other men. Flint was the first to greet him.

"Good to see you back, lad." He grinned and laid a fatherly hand on Matthew's shoulder. "Sure you're ready?"

"I'm ready." It was true; he felt fine. The rest of the men also seemed pleased to see him, and Matthew felt more settled than at any time since joining the ship.

"Larboard battery, prepare for broadsides!" Lieutenant Timothy gave the order that most had been expecting.

"Know what you have to do?" Lewis asked.

Matthew nodded. To a lad the ship's armament was one of the more attractive and easily understood aspects of the ship, and Jake had already briefed him on his duties at some depth.

"Get at it then!"

"Load with round shot, maximum elevation!" It was Pite this time, the young midshipman controlled the forward half of the lower battery.

Matthew started his run almost as soon as Pite began to speak, and came to a halt at the mouth of the main hatch. Apart from the occasional change, when first or second reduction was called for, the powder charge remained constant. Let others worry about bar or canister, round or grape shot, his duty was to supply the powder, and that was what his mind was set upon.

He stood at the mouth of the main companionway between the lower gundeck and the main magazine. Glancing down, he saw Mintey, the oldster midshipman, with two lads either side of him. It was their responsibility to pass the charges up, and his to stuff a cartridge into one of the cork and canvass carriers that hung from above. Once sealed, it would be slung over his shoulder while he raced it back to Flint's gun. Below, in the main and forward magazines, the gunners' mates would have the flannel cartridges ready when they were needed. The standard British rate of a broadside every three minutes meant that just over seventy charges (counting the carronades) had to be sent up in that time, should both batteries be in use. With each charge weighing roughly a third of the shot, over a hundredweight of explosive would be moved from one deck to another for each minute the ship was in action.

But today there was no danger. The charges Matthew carried were made up of nothing more volatile than silver sand and wadding. Gun drill was mainly for the men, those who would manhandle the two-and-a-half tons of iron into the right position to hit the enemy, and to go on doing so long enough and fast enough to secure victory.

Flint, with his steady eye and nerve, was the captain of number three gun. It was up to him to see that every man did his work, delivering a safely loaded weapon that could be primed, sighted and fired. Jenkins assisted him in this; however, as the designated topman, he could be called up in the unlikely event that the captain altered the sail pattern during an engagement. Lewis worked the flexible rammer and was also responsible for clearing any wounded out of the way, while O'Conner looked after the loading of powder and shot; a responsible job, and one that depended on Lewis's care with the sponge, for if he were to ram a charge on to a burning ember that Lewis had missed, O'Conner would be the first to know it.

The actual manhandling of the gun was done by all, with assistance from five members of another mess who worked quietly and well under the charge of Copley, a heavily built former weaver.

"Stand to your guns!" Timothy blew a silver whistle just as Matthew was poised to catch the first charge. The exercise continued without words, apart from the occasional muttered oath when one man was clumsy, or not as fast as his fellows. Matthew ran with each charge, dodging past the other guns and men in a way that soon became fluid and automatic. Quarter gunners supervised the distribution of the charges, ensuring that each gun was fed almost simultaneously. In action the cartridge would then be stripped of its casing and laid seam down into the feeder, before being slid into the nine feet of waiting barrel. The gun captain would feel for the flannel package with a small length of wire placed down the touchhole, shouting "Home!" when he had made contact. For the exercise an empty feeder was inserted, and the actions mimed.

"Shot your guns!"

At Flint's gun a twenty-four pound round shot was offered to the barrel and immediately withdrawn, before Lewis went through the pantomime of ramming it tight.

The port was opened and the gun hauled into the firing position. It would be fired using a device similar to that found on muskets. Flint had been checking the operation of this while the gun was being made ready. In action, should the flint or mechanism break, he would use the slow match burning in a bucket to his right. He primed the pan using a mixture of fine powder and spirits of wine from his priming horn, then pulled the hammer on the gunlock back to half cock.

The elevation sights were on the side of the cascabel, where they could be measured against a mark on the carriage. Most experienced gun captains were used to their gun and ignored these, preferring to set elevation when sighting down the long tapered barrel. It was this taper that caused the belief held by many that a shot rose on firing. Men easily forgot that their sighting line, along the barrel, was at an angle several degrees off that of the bore.

In this exercise maximum elevation had been called for. Lewis and Jenkins raised the breach of the gun with their crows of iron wedged against the carriage. The quoin, a wooden wedge which could be moved in and out to elevate or depress the barrel, was whipped away in one easy motion and the breach allowed to rest on the wooden bed of the carriage. Quoins were inclined to fly out during firing, so there were three replacements hanging from a deck beam above.

The hammer was pulled back to full cock as soon as the gun captain was happy with his sighting, and his raised hand signalled the gun as ready.

"Fire!" Timothy's words coincided with the captain of number one gun standing to one side and slamming his right fist, which held the trigger line, into his left palm and shouting "One!" The hammer clicked forward, making a small explosion in the pan as the priming powder ignited.

The same procedure followed a fraction of a second later with number two, followed by Flint at number three, and on up the battery. To fire a complete broadside at the same instant would eventually damage the fabric of the ship, but a ripple fire ensured that the force was staggered evenly along the hull.

"Serve your vents!" The touchholes were closed on the imaginary blast of hot escaping gas, while Copley led his team in moving the gun back against the breaching lines. This was one part of the exercise that was harder than the real thing; in action the gun would be hurled inboard by the recoil and left ready for reloading.

Lewis made to swab out with the other end of his flexible rammer that held a sheepskin wad which would be soaked in sea water, while Matthew and the other squealers brought further charges, and the procedure began once more.

At fifteen minutes to midday Timothy blew his silver whistle for the last time and ordered the guns to be secured. The men were exhausted, but went to collect their spirits in good heart. Timothy, making his way up to the wardroom, fell in with Tait.

"Lose any limbs, did you?" the latter grinned.

Timothy shook his head. "Some of the new men are a bit raw, but a few more drills will see 'em right. Give me a week, and I'll have them up to scratch."

"A week?" his friend pulled a worried face. "We'd better tell the captain; he'll have to keep us out of trouble till then."

\*\*\*\*\*

For the next few days the wind stayed low, barely giving steerage way. Each morning the sun shone anew, making the deck steam, and while the rest of the convoy wallowed in the welcome sunshine, the men of *Vigilant* set to work. Topmasts were put up and taken down, while sails were set, reefed, and changed. The boatswain took advantage of the time to replace some of the cordage that had proved weak during the recent storm, and there were team races, watch against watch and division against division, covering everything from moving guns to shifting stores. The watch bill was rewritten a hundred times, the men being sorted as fresh talents or weaknesses were discovered. All hands were summoned at any hour, and armed boarding parties called for with a moment's notice. Signals were hoisted that confused and annoyed other ships in the convoy, and boats launched and raced, both under sail and oar. *Vigilant* was taken under tow, manoeuvred, and in one glorious exercise, all but abandoned. The marine NCOs gave instruction in edged weapons and small arms fire, with further competitions between messes as to who could sink a pottery bottle left floating half a cable from the ship. The men took turns to fire in volleys, and the water bubbled about the vessel until one lucky hit smashed it, to everyone's claim and satisfaction.

And all the time the constant practice with the great guns. Men were moved from the twenty-four pounders, up to the twelve pounders, on to the carronades and back again. Positions on the gun were changed. Warrant officers and midshipmen were lent their own piece, and took pride in handling it as well as any regular crew. One exercise, a brainwave of Gregory's, involved gun crews practising blindfold, to simulate the conditions that could be expected in a night action or when the smoke of the lower deck sat like an impenetrable fog. At first the men crashed into each other, cursing and swearing, and one gun captain broke a finger in his gunlock, but eventually their skill increased, and they became proud in consequence.

In fact, after the initial reluctance, the men took to the exercises well. For some it was the first time they had found a purpose in life, and the learning of new skills and abilities did much to boost their confidence. Others, the seasoned hands, found that they were excelling in certain tasks, and delighted in the chance to shine before their peers almost as much as the minor promotions that often followed. The captain took the opportunity to watch his officers under pressure, to see how they behaved when they were called upon to think, rather than simply obey or interpret orders. By the following Sunday he felt he had welded an efficient force from the raw material given to him. The men seemed happier and even good humoured, while most of the officers went about their business with more control and efficiency.

Divine service the following week was a far more spirited affair, so much so that even Bryant, an interested spectator to what had been going on, drew fresh vigour from the bellowing of the hymn and the benign tolerance that now met his stumbling sermon. The captain also felt more content in himself, and watching the crew that was now one to be proud of, had little hesitation in ordering the end of the intensive exercises and an extra ration of beer for that night.

\*\*\*\*\*

Matthew was now truly a part of Flint's mess, and he enjoyed the evening more than any other he could remember. Supper had been cleared away, and the men took to yarning during the dog watches. Beer was passed along the table, as each in turn vied to tell a more outrageous story than the last. There was laughter, and teasing, and insults and tattle-tale.

Lewis, who had drunk less than all, bar Matthew, had just finished telling them about some adventure, real or imagined, and the others were showing symptoms of wanting to sing, when, as if to a secret signal, there was silence and all turned to see the seaman that now stood at the head of their table.

"Was it us you'd be wantin'?" O'Conner's voice was completely neutral as he spoke to the man.

Crehan nodded his head once. He was wearing a blue chequered shirt, unbuttoned down the front, and a grubby bandage could be seen about his chest.

"You're intendin' to come back to the mess?" Flint asked him.

"If you'll have me."

Membership of every mess depended on the agreement of all. Crehan might as easily be cast out, forced to mess alone or with the "pariah-dogs": others who had been rejected by their peers.

"I'd take a vote," Flint turned to Matthew. "But I think it really depends on one."

Now all were looking his way, although the boy's eyes stayed fixed on the table in front of him.

"I'll do you no harm, lad." Crehan said, "an' I'm sorry, truly, for the trouble."

Matthew nodded briefly, and was relieved when it was taken as a signal.

Crehan went to lower himself on to one of the mess benches when a raised finger stopped him. He looked into Flint's eyes and saw real meaning.

"You will do him no harm," Flint said, his words low but clear. 'Cause you'll have us all watchin', day an' night."

"'Sright." Jenkins this time, his stare strangely harsh, even in the murky gloom of the gundeck. "Lay a finger on the boy, an' I'll take yon 'part, piece by piece."

Crehan looked along the row of faces. Lewis was nodding, and looking no less firm. "Goes for me 'n' all."

"Goes for every man in this ship." O'Conner this time, wearing an expression devoid of warmth or camaraderie. "I'll finish you me self, an' they'll be others to do it if I don't."

Crehan nodded again, and sat down on the bench. From behind the next gun a voice broke out in a soft rendering of *"Spanish Ladies"* one of the songs Jake the carpenter had taught Matthew a hundred years ago. Other voices joined, until the entire deck was together in song. Matthew felt a warm glow inside. His eyes grew hot and he knew that unreasonable tears were close by. The air was thick with the smell of beer and strong men as, cautiously at first, he opened his mouth and began to sing also.

# PART THREE
# IN ACTION

# CHAPTER TWELVE

THEY sighted the enemy ships at first light, a yell from the masthead being the signal that their lives were to change beyond all measure. Initially Shepherd and the rest of his officers assumed them to be British, a small squadron despatched from the Channel Fleet, or maybe some of Smith's ships that kept guard over Northern France. The former was the more likely, as the topgallants appeared to be those of large vessels; but even then Shepherd was concerned, and a prickling feeling down the back of his neck began to grow with his suspicions.

The wind was light and from the North East, blowing offshore from the Brest peninsula a hundred and twenty miles over the horizon. It gave the strange ships the windward advantage and added importance to the hope that they would eventually turn out to be British. The number also suggested they were a friendly force; one or two enemy ships could conceivably have slipped out of the Brest blockade during the recent storm; four was unlikely, although by no means impossible: Admiral Howe did not enforce the tight blockade that Shepherd, and other younger men, advocated. Shepherd had been with Howe as a lieutenant in America, and later captained his first frigate under his command. He knew him to be a capable, indeed, an exceptional officer, but there was no doubt that, at nigh on seventy, he was getting old for his post.

It was two bells in the forenoon watch: nine o'clock, when the sails could first be seen from the deck. Shepherd and his officers studied them through their glasses. The topgallants and topsails were barely distinguished through the haze, although the unspoken impression was that they appeared white. Most British vessels on active service would have been at sea for some while, and the canvas of their sails dulled to a dirty grey brown. The French however, had endured almost two years of blockade, with the majority of their ships not at sea one day in a hundred. Consequently their sails and rigging were normally fresh from the dockyard, and four with white sails was as clear an indication of nationality as any ensign. The small cluster of officers that gathered on the weather side of the poop exchanged knowing looks. Judging by the speed of the convoy, the force should overhaul them by mid afternoon; there would be little chance of slipping silently away with darkness.

"What do you see there?" Shepherd's voice carried up to the masthead lookout perched high on the main topgallant yard.

"No change, sir. Keepin' the same course."

"What size are they?" The entire ship was silent with expectation.

"Difficult to say for sure. Two look to be frigates, and two liners, one of them might be somethin' bigger. Wait—I can see colours!

It was torture.

"Them's French, sir. Sure of it!"

*Vigilant* was keeping station two miles to the rear of the convoy. Immediately Shepherd roared out orders that sent men skimming up the ratlines to let out more sail. Adding topgallants, jibs and staysails to the forecourse and topsails would increase her speed considerably; they would be up to the convoy within the hour. He looked across to the merchantmen, who were showing a mixture of sails, as would be expected when different ships keep speed with one another. None were closer than three cables from their neighbour; they sailed in two rough columns that straggled over a mile of ocean. Shepherd surveyed them with a mild disdain; it was as tight a formation as they had managed since the voyage began; heaven only knew what would happen once they realised there was an enemy bearing down on them.

"Signal to *Badger*, repeat to *Taymar*; Enemy squadron in sight to windward."

King scratched out the signal in his note book and called for one of the midshipman, conscious that this was the first time since being promoted that he had been under real pressure. A minute later the flags soared up the halyards and were.acknowledged by the sloop that kept station on the larboard side of the convoy. The message was repeated to the invisible frigate, and within seven minutes the two escorts were also aware of the danger. Shepherd took a turn back and forward along the quarterdeck, pausing as a quartermaster and master's mate returned from the poop with a dripping log line.

"What speed?" he asked, as the master's mate began to chalk on to the traverse board.

"Five and a touch, sir."

Five knots; they could maintain that only until they caught up with the convoy. Then they would have to slow to three, while the French bore down on them unhindered.

Scattering the convoy may even be the better option. If the wind held, some of the copper-bottomed merchants would make five, even six knots. At that rate and handled smartly they should reach safety, as the French would find it hard to take them all. The flagship was potentially fast, even if her efforts to date had not been impressive. Spurred on by the threat of capture, *Vigilant* and the other warships might lead her and her precious human cargo to safety. Some of the remaining merchants might also avoid capture, and there would be the bonus that the British Navy might be notified that a powerful squadron was loose on the Atlantic: one of the escaping ships might well meet up with a friendly force and alert them to the menace.

However, to do that meant leaving the slower merchants behind without support. As senior captain Shepherd was aware that his actions must be justified to all, not just his superiors. The owners would naturally complain, and it was not inconceivable that public opinion would rise up against him. With the habit of victory established early in the war, the mob would not look happily on one who ran from his responsibilities, and that was ignoring what the Admiralty made of it. The intelligent few might see his action as the sensible solution, but they were likely to be outnumbered by those who thought him a coward. Even if he kept his command, there was little chance he would ever be given charge of a convoy again. The alternative was to keep the merchants together, and try to scare the French away. He would have considerably less than a third of their fire power, and some ships would be lost before they were even close enough to use their light guns. It was a shame he had none of the bigger Indiamen amongst his charges; some had a passable resemblance to line-of-battle ships and, boldly commanded, might even frighten the French away without a shot being fired.

The thoughts raced through his mind as he paced the deck. Sending *Taymar* and *Badger* with the flagship and the other, faster, ships would leave them a measure of protection, and there was a good chance the French would continue after the slower, safer, targets even if there was a minor line ship to contend with. He would also then have the chance to engage the squadron, delaying it to ensure the escape of the faster ships, albeit at the sacrifice of his own command. His actions would allow the flagship, and her diplomats, to go free, and also reduce the area within which the French moved, making their eventual capture that much more likely. He glanced again at the convoy, apparently sailing in innocence and unaware that they were waiting for one man, him, to make up his mind.

He finally turned to Tait, the officer of the watch, who was standing by the binnacle.

"Mr Tait, have a cutter cleared away and made ready to launch. I want to send a message to the Commodore."

"Aye, sir," Tait touched his hat and was shouting out the orders as Shepherd stepped back to his quarters under the poop.

"Pass the word for my clerk," he said to the marine standing sentry at his door.

His cabin was spacious and tidy, although the furnishings could only be described as functional. Shepherd saw no reason in spending money on items that would have a limited life. Even if they saw no action, conditions at sea were not the best for fine furniture. The heavy wooden articles the carpenter had produced did their duty as well as fine Hepplewhite or Sheraton and would almost certainly last longer. Especially if, as Shepherd anticipated, they would be roughly stashed in the hold before long as the ship cleared for action.

Lindsay, his clerk, slipped into the cabin unobtrusively and seated himself at the desk where so very recently his captain had been writing letters home.

"To Sir Thomas Davies, Commodore commanding the Honourable East India Company ship, *Pegasus*. Sir," Shepherd paused while he framed the words that would divide the convoy, sending some to safety and leaving others, including himself, to likely ruin. Lindsay waited, his nib poised just above the ink pot.

"I regret to inform you that a powerful French squadron has been sighted to windward..."

\*\*\*\*\*

On deck the spring sunshine was showing its first real hint of warmth as Tait stood with Gregory.

"What do you think he'll do?" Tait was third lieutenant, after Rogers and Dyson, although he had long grown used to asking his supposed junior for opinions and advice. The experience stored up in Gregory's stocky, almost stout, frame was always worth tapping.

Gregory stuck out his chin. "Not many choices. The obvious is to scatter, that way some'll make it through and we get to report the squadron-. Otherwise, head inshore. Make as much of a chase as we can and hope to sight some of Black Dick's ships. The captain might have other ideas, mind; he's a one for surprises."

Tait stroked his top lip as he gazed at the enemy sails that held a morbid fascination for him. The topsails were still only just visible; clearly the increase in speed had kept the French at roughly the same distance, although whenever a lucky wave lifted *Vigilant*, he caught a glimpse of their courses.

"We'll be up with the convoy 'fore long." Gregory broke into his thoughts with a gentle hint. As officer of the watch it was Tait's duty to inform the captain of any notable occurrence. The flagship was well within striking distance now; it was time to shorten sail, unless they intended to pass through the untidy fleet of merchantmen. Tait hesitated; Shepherd was aware of the situation and would be bound to return to the deck shortly. The cutter hung ready from its davits, and next to it stood the crew. With the wind as it was there would be no trouble in sailing the small boat down to *Pegasus*, and picking it up afterwards would be just as easy.

Then he heard the captain approach.

"Have this taken to the Commodore," he said, passing a letter to Tait. "Give it to a reliable midshipman, and tell him not to get into conversation."

The paper was light, and sealed with no more than a wafer. The lieutenant guessed it held the briefest of instructions; it was Shepherd's habit to be concise. Tait exchanged glances with Gregory and knew that the job of manoeuvring *Vigilant* could be left to him, as he left the quarterdeck.

"Back mizzen tops, take in t'gallants and jibs!" Gregory called, while Tait made his way to the poop. Another flurry of men sped up the ratlines, while a group of afterguard hauled the mizzen braces back. *Vigilant* staggered and checked in the apparent mishandling, then began a choppy roll as she lost speed.

"Bring her round." The last order was spoken by Gregory to the quartermaster. The large double wheel spun in a blur of spokes, and *Vigilant* came to a brief halt.

The blocks squealed as the cutter was lowered onto the water while Pite made himself comfortable in the stern. Once clear of the ship, the small crew raised the twin masts and set the lug sails, so that the boat was bearing down upon the merchant ship before *Vigilant* had even come back to the wind.

"Signal the Commodore: stand by to accept a boat," Shepherd said, without emotion.

King glanced back at his captain, knowing his penchant for irony. Anyone who missed a two masted cutter flying down towards them under sail would be stupid as well as blind. Still, protocol might be involved, and he ordered the hoist.

Shepherd watched the cutter dancing over the waves. As Tait had anticipated, the orders left no room for argument. They also contained none of the politeness expected of a captain in the Royal Navy proffering advice to a superior in an associated service. Let them make of it what they might, within hours he and his ship would be in action, whereas the well paid civilians remained free. It would be a freedom paid for by the men of his ship, and he would no more submit, advise, or request the Commodore's cooperation than decline to fight in the first place. Besides, only an idiot would go against his plan, and despite all the evidence to the contrary, Shepherd could not believe the Commodore to be quite that much of a fool.

The cutter stayed hooked on to the flagship's main chains for less than two minutes; exactly the time Shepherd had allowed for young Pite to clamber aboard, explain himself and hand the despatch to an officer. He watched the young midshipman recklessly skip over the main shrouds and swing down from the chains, landing almost exactly in his allotted space at the sternsheets of the boat. Immediately the cutter turned away from *Pegasus* and set course for a point approximately three cables ahead of *Vigilant*'s present position, to be there waiting when the line-of-battle ship reached her. A glance back at the enemy confirmed the lookout's report. Now that they had slowed the enemy had gained on them. The hulls were in plain sight from the deck, and Shepherd thought he could distinguish the individual colour schemes as they bore down.

"One's a three-decker," Tait whispered excitedly to Gregory. The older man nodded.

"Ninety-eight, I reckon."

"Signal *Badger*, repeat to *Taymar*." The captain was addressing King, although he had the ear of every officer on deck. "Convoy will divide. Accompany flag and eleven ships heading Rochefort Blockade at best possible speed."

King scratched at his pad once more.

"How many hoists?" Shepherd asked. King licked his pencil.

"Four, no, three; I can do it in three, sir."

"Very good. As soon as they acknowledge, make the size and bearing of the enemy." He turned to the officer of the watch. "Mr Tait, please pass the word for the other lieutenants and the master to join me in my quarters. You have the deck, I believe?"

"Yes, sir."

Shepherd's tense expression relaxed for the first time since the French were spotted.

"Worry not, Mr Tait; we will keep you in ignorance for as brief a time as possible."

*****

Mr Rollston, the cooper, was less than five foot tall, although what he lacked in height was made up for in his bulk, which was princely and generous. Standing in his workshop on the orlop with his knuckles resting on his hips, he seemed almost square, filling the distance between bulwarks as easily as that up to the deckhead.

"S'more than makin' barrels," he said pompously, when Matthew, Jake, and three other boys were sent down to him. "You got to know about wood, how it works, and how to use it. You got to understand 'bout the way liquid settles, how powder transports, an' when to use a copper or an iron band." He paused to roll his eyes about in his bounteous face. "They say they're gonna 'ave a battle today." Now he tossed his head dismissively towards the upper decks. "Reckon on there being a bit of fightin'—well that's as maybe. But I'll tell you this: none of them," he paused once more for effect, "none of them would even be here today if it weren't for coopers, and the barrels we makes."

Jake and Matthew exchanged glances in the gloom. When King had hurriedly detailed them to accompany Mr Rollston for a watch they had been somewhat disappointed. With the enemy in sight and a fight in prospect, four hours with the cooper seemed about the worst station possible. But Mr Rollston was not what they had expected, and now it seemed likely that the time might pass faster that they had originally thought.

*****

Light from the large stern windows cast strong shadows over the assembled group as Shepherd's glance swept over each man in turn. The majority of his officers had served with him for the entire commission, and in the main he felt he could depend on them. In turn, he had proved himself to be a reliable captain, if at times somewhat unpredictable. He smiled grimly to himself; this would be one of those occasions. And as for knowing his officers, the next few hours would tell him more than he had learnt in the last two years. It was one thing to sail with a fleet in eager anticipation of action and victory, quite another to face odds that made capture and prison the most likely outcome.

"You all understand the situation, and that I have been in contact with the Commodore. Some of you also know of the signal recently sent to the other escorts. For those who do not: briefly, we will be staying with five merchant ships who cannot make sufficient speed. They are *Jenny Rose, Orcadese, Hampshire Lass, Hever Castle*, and *Duke of Kent*. The rest, those that can show a fair turn of speed, will make for the blockading squadron off Rochefort, in company with the other two escorts. It is possible that the enemy will try to take them, as well as the slower members of the convoy, and it is up to us to see that they do not." He cleared his throat, his mouth was unusually dry.

"It is not widely known, but the flagship is carrying British consular staff bound for the Far East; it was made very clear to me that they should not be allowed to fall into French hands, and I feel this to be the best course to take to see that it does not happen." At that moment his mind stupidly wandered; on the cabinet to one side he could actually see an invitation delivered by boat the previous evening, inviting him and some of his officers to dinner in the flagship that night He felt a mild sensation of relief that he would not now have to attend. With an effort he brought himself back to the matter in hand. "If we are fortunate *Taymar* will make contact with other British ships that can come to our aid." There was a brief pause. "In which case, it is even more important that we detain the French for as long as we can, possibly even until nightfall."

A general murmur spread about the room. These men were professional officers and knew the chances of help being found and arriving in time. Similarly, stretching out such a simple scenario as they were now presented with to last until dark would take some memorable manoeuvres.

"That is all. I shall delay clearing for action until after dinner, so the people will have hot food inside them. Are there any questions?"

Rogers raised his hand.

"The French, sir. Are they from Brest?"

The fact that Rogers should ask an unnecessary and unanswer-able question fulfilled all Shepherd's expectations of him.

"Possibly, in fact it seems most likely. Either that or L'Orient. They could have dodged the blockade in the storm a week or so back."

Any ship which had cleared harbour would have headed south, even if they had planned to cross the Atlantic. It was just unfortunate that they had come upon the convoy, and doubly so that Shepherd had not sufficient force to meet them.

Further murmurs spread throughout the room, and Shepherd thought he sensed a tone of derision. It was generally held that Lord Howe, or Black Dick, as he was known, was not keeping a tight enough grip on things in the Channel Fleet.

"My Lord Howe, as you know, is not currently at sea; Admiral Bridport has charge until he returns. I think we all realise that both hold similar views when it comes to enforcing a tight blockade." At sixty-eight, Bridport was very much in the Howe mould and a less spirited man than his brother, Samuel Hood, whom Shepherd knew well and respected greatly, although for many reasons it would not do to say as much in public. "Besides, if the squadron has come from Brest, it could be to our advantage." There was silence, as he held their attention. "It would mean the enemy had only been at sea for few days. I think you all know the state of the French Navy; two days is not long enough to produce sailors." It was a small point, but a valid one. French ships were well regarded for their fine lines, but the men sent to sail in them were certainly inferior. In addition the revolution that had sprung up only a few years before had seen the departure of many skilled officers who also happened to be nobility, and even the *Corps d'Artillerie de la Marine*, the French system of seamen gunners that proved successful in previous wars, had been abolished in the general drive against *élitism*. However Shepherd knew that if all four ships were entirely manned by seasick soldiers it could not discount the advantage that fire power and sheer numbers would give them.

"If there is nothing else, we will dismiss." The tone of his voice forbade further questions, and the group broke up in silence.

"Mr Timothy."

"Sir?" Timothy turned and faced his captain.

"Be so good as to acquaint Mr Tait with the situation."

"Sir!"

Timothy and Tait were friends; it would do no harm to discipline for the junior to inform his senior. Besides, the captain had made a promise to Tait; remembering and honouring such things was the mark of a good officer.

# CHAPTER THIRTEEN

ON the quarterdeck Captain Shepherd and Lieutenant Dyson stood in silence. As he had expected, the Commodore had readily accepted Shepherd's directions, and even now the East India Company contingent, complete with diplomats, wives and attendants, were pulling ahead of their slower counterparts and making an easterly heading which should lead them to the French coast at Rochefort and, ironically, safety. The British blockading squadron stationed there would provide escorts to take them as far as Gibraltar.

Shepherd did not know who would be in charge, possibly Harvey, who had set out a few weeks before. Fresh forces could then be sent to look for the enemy squadron and the remains of the convoy. With the wind as it was the faster ships should be out of sight by the time the French squadron reached *Vigilant* and her charges, and it would be up to him to see that they remained so. Shepherd stared at the enemy again. They were holding their original course, which meant that they had not registered the convoy splitting, or they were content with snapping up his ship and the stragglers. It was strange how he felt a measure of relief in knowing that a battle squadron was making straight for him.

It was four bells in the forenoon watch: ten o'clock. Dinner would be served at twelve, which meant they would have ample time to clear for action and beat to quarters by one thirty; about an hour before Shepherd predicted they would be in range of the enemy. The wind had been holding at the same strength and direction for over fifty minutes, although the ship had started a shallow, choppy roll, which meant that there was an increase due, or a change hereabouts. Either would alter his estimations; a strengthening wind would affect the enemy first, allowing them an increase in speed; whereas a localised squall might slow him down, giving them the same advantage. On the other hand, if the squall were big enough, a storm like the one they had recently passed through, it might make matters very different. Shepherd's estimation of the quality of French seamanship was based on fact. Both England and France relied heavily on pressed men to crew their ships, and both were reasonably adept at turning such recruits into competent hands. But to do this needed sea-going experience, and here the French Navy, spending much time in harbour, was at a definite disadvantage. Added to this, the English press had access to men who knew the sea. These were usually from merchant ships, often taken from homeward bound convoys. They might not be trained fighters but their seagoing experience placed them far above the average landsman. The French merchant force was far smaller, and its men less experienced. Shepherd was reasonably sure that *Vigilant* would fare better in foul weather than any Frenchman fresh out of port.

"They're keeping together, sir" said Dyson, echoing Shepherd's earlier thoughts. "It appears they don't intend taking the others."

Shepherd nodded; that was good, although it did make their own capture more likely.

"When I was a midshipman, the French held me for two years." Dyson continued, almost absent-mindedly.

The captain turned to look at his first lieutenant. It was rare for Dyson to volunteer any information about himself. Shepherd supposed the impending action had loosened his tongue.

"I was not aware of that," he said, hoping to coax more. "How was it?"

Dyson's face was blank. "Frustrating," he said. It was about the only emotion Shepherd had heard him admit to.

The captain smiled. "You have my word, I will try to avoid it a second time."

Dyson was nettled. He moved across to the binnacle and picked up the traverse board to hide his anger, before realising that the remark was meant as light. After all, a joke proffered by a captain did not have to be riotously funny. He glanced at the traverse board, the rough slate that kept record of the ship's last few hours before being copied out into the log. For the hundredth time he reminded himself that he was completely without social skills; in a perfect world he would not be allowed in company with others.

"What speed, Mr Dyson?" asked the captain.

"We're currently averaging three and a half knots, sir."

Both men looked up to the sails; the wind had increased slightly and there was plenty of power available, if only they were allowed to use it.

"What do you think she'd do?" The captain had sensed that he had hurt Dyson's feelings, and was trying to make amends, however unintentional his offence.

"Probably double that, sir, if we were on our own."

Shepherd nodded. If they were on their own they may well avoid the French altogether. As a sixty-four *Vigilant* was different from the normal ship-of-the-line. Captains either swore at them or prayed for them, and Shepherd was one of the latter. He believed, indeed, had proved on occasions that *Vigilant* could match or outsail most of her larger cousins. Of course her broadside was that much lighter; the thirty-two pound gun of the seventy-four was undoubtedly a far superior weapon, albeit one that took longer to load. But in the captain's eyes rapid fire from twenty-four pounders made up for the weight of slower, heavier, broadsides.

That extra weight would also make the enemy's line ships less handy, even taking into account the sleek designs of French built vessels. If *Vigilant* had been alone he could probably play a pretty game, possibly to the extent of luring them into the guns of the Channel Fleet, provided they were stupid enough.

"And the French, what speed?"

"Reckon they'll be making seven, sir, maybe more." That was over doing things a little, although Shepherd did not contradict his junior. He would not have expected them to see anything past six, which meant they were being overhauled at roughly three nautical miles an hour.

The motion was increasing; both men could feel the ship as she butted into the deeper swell. There was no sign of a squall on the horizon, although the outline of the pursuing ships was a little less distinct, despite the lessening distance between them. Shepherd sniffed the breeze, which was dry and lifeless; the storm, if there was to be one, would not be from that angle.

"I think we might give our merchant friends some exercise," he said, smiling at Dyson.

"Yes, sir?"

"Let's start by getting them to show more canvas, and then set them into a "V" formation: *en echelon*."

Dyson felt that something more was called for from him, that this was one of the occasions when he should discuss matters with his captain. "They'll be less easy to control then, sir. At least when they are in a tight body we can signal to them as one."

"Yes, but spreading them now will use what wind there is to the greatest advantage. They are bound to scatter when the French close, and with luck the enemy will also divide. Ideally I'd like the enemy separated as much as possible. I'd wager *Vigilant* is faster in stays than any of their line ships; what say we run amuck between them before they account for us?"

Dyson nodded, pleased with the prospect of selling his ship dear. "We may give them a few surprises, sir."

The captain continued in a quieter voice. "In a ship to ship I feel we could take at least one Frenchman with us, but it would all be over in an hour. I intend to damage three or possibly all four. The action will take longer, with a butcher's bill to match, and we probably won't actually destroy a ship."

"There's a chance that help will come through."

Shepherd smiled. "We'll have to string it out a long time for that, but at least Admiral Howe will know where to look, and the French won't be so able to run. If we can keep them away from the Commodore's ship for now, then damage them enough to slow at least some of them down, I will be more than happy."

It made sense; taking one out of action while leaving the others relatively unharmed would reduce the enemy's strength, but the rest would be free to take the merchants and continue to their destination without delay. If Shepherd's plan was successful the entire force would remain intact, but slowed to the extent that their eventual destruction became more likely. However, both men were aware how the Admiralty, and other officers, might interpret their actions. No one would expect much with the odds as they were, but to go down without taking a single ship with them might be judged disappointing; little value would be placed on partially disabling more of the enemy's vessels, even if they were captured later. Some would understand their motives, but others, and the British press and public come to that, would be quick to damn their sacrifice— and some would call them cowards.

\*\*\*\*\*

Throughout the ship men began to prepare for battle, spreading stories and opinions about the French ships as they went. The surgeon and his assistants started to move instruments and supplies from the sick berth down to the midshipmen's quarters on the orlop. A methodical man, who knew a little medicine and a lot of surgery, Wilson laid out and inspected his tools at leisure, while his loblolly boys checked needles and horsehair, gags, turpentine, and tow needed for the inevitable operations. An empty barrel was procured for the "legs and wings" that the surgeon would discard, and canvas piled in readiness to cover the decks when the order was given to clear for action. In addition, bandages and tourniquets were parcelled up to be left at strategic points throughout the ship, where they could be used for first aid. A good supply of rum was also raised and brought down to the makeshift operating theatre. This would be needed when the work was hottest, to calm the waiting injured and, all too frequently, Wilson and his helpers.

On the main deck, just under the forecastle, the cook watched as his mates stoked up the galley fire, while stewards emptied the day's meat rations out of the steep tub and checked their lead tags. In a gesture of rash generosity he laid out several pots of slush: the fat skimmed from the boiling coppers of meat, which was normally sold to the men to spread on their biscuit. The cook was a veteran of the First Battle of Finisterre, and knew well how easily the men's mouths would dry, even without the smoke and fumes of action. He also authorised an extra ration of one lemon per man. There were no oranges, or any other soft fruit to issue, but a dessert of slush-covered biscuits might make the men more comfortable for a time, and the bite of a lemon would clear a fighting man's mouth. He might be losing money on the slush, but he was reasonably certain of being around to make it up later. The cook would see out the action in the grand magazine, ironically a place of relative safety. If death should meet him there he would not go alone.

*****

The carpenter and his crew piled wooden bungs, nails and lead sheets in the wings, the narrow corridors that ran along the side of the ship, level with the waterline. The gunner checked his supply of cartridges, and watched while his mates set to sewing more. The boatswain rousted out the spare cable, ropes and line that would be needed to keep the ship under command, trying to anticipate the master, who would be bound to call for a brace or shroud to be replaced or reinforced before action. The work was carried out with few words of command; the men fell to their tasks naturally before the call to clear for action took them to the next state of readiness.

But one man had nothing to do, and no one, apparently, had need of him. His station in action would be with the wounded, where he would make the men as comfortable as possible, both physically and spiritually, while trying not to get in anyone's way. In the dubious privacy of his tiny cabin he clenched the Bible his father had given to him, staring at the well thumbed pages with only the vaguest pretence of reading, while inwardly he trembled.

The Reverend William Bryant knew his duty, and it was a hard one. At best he was accepted by the officers, at worst he was despised by the men. Men who begrudged him their groat – the four pence a month they had to contribute towards his wages. Men who openly mocked him, taunted him, and ridiculed his faith, while the God-fearing amongst them despised the weakness that accepted the abuse.

He had thought it was faith that kept him sane through the last few months, and faith that prevented him from resigning during their recent stay at Portsmouth. In the half light Bryant decided that if he had, even his father would have understood and arranged a safe little parish for him within his own diocese. In his cramped cabin Bryant had time to consider this, and, almost for the first time, his life and the mess he had made of it.

He knew that to be proud was sinful, but when pride was removed from his faith, there was very little left.

*****

"Of course, they might not fight." It was a bold statement, and instantly the other officers gave Gregory, fourth in seniority but more experienced than any other lieutenant present, their entire attention.

"Not fight?" asked Rogers. "Why the devil shouldn't they?"

Gregory closed his journal and sat back in his chair. The wardroom was unusually crowded, and he felt the need to stretch his legs.

"We don't know where they're heading. It could be the Med., it could be America, or the 'Indies for that matter. And we don't know what they intend to do. If their senior officer has orders to meet up with another squadron, he's not going to be thanked for wasting time plundering a convoy."

The others digested this for a moment before Carling, the captain of marines, spoke.

"But if they were bound for America or the 'Indies, wouldn't they be halfway across the Atlantic by now?"

Rogers snorted into his wine with disdain and was about to speak, but Gregory, calmly shaking his head, got in first.

"South to twenty degrees, that's the usual way. Past the Canaries, then pick up the Westerlies and let them carry you across. There they can shelter to wait for others; the French have used that trick afore to assemble a fleet. That is if there aren't other ships already awaitin' them."

Rogers felt unreasonably annoyed by the older man's confidence, and as his anger grew he became scathing, the next stage before denouncement and straightforward abuse. "You're not trying to tell me," he said, reaching for the black bottle once more, "that a squadron of warships is going to sight a poorly protected convoy and just pass it by?"

Gregory eyed him coolly, noticing the amount of wine that had missed his glass and now lay in a pool on the wardroom table. "Stranger things have occurred, and we must not close our minds to any possibilities. The other factor is our captain; he may choose not to close with them."

"Shepherd will fight," answered Tait, who had just come off watch. There was an edge to his voice that was not lost on Gregory; the young man held no affection for Rogers. "Why else would he have split the convoy?"

"Right!" Carling now took up the baton. "A man who wanted to avoid action would have scattered them at the first sight."

Rogers was clutching at his glass, as if frightened that someone might take it from him. "Much good it will do," he said drinking deep and apparently oblivious to the contemptuous looks from his brother officers.

Gregory cleared his throat and stood up. "Well, we shall know everything in time. If you will excuse me, I have duties to attend to."

He walked from the table and left the wardroom. Taking his lead the others soon dispersed, until only Rogers and King were left.

"You'll join me?" Rogers held the bottle up to the younger man.

"Thank you, no." King always felt awkward when refusing to take wine with Rogers. In a hard drinking age the second lieutenant was by no means unusual. Even among officers of commission status it was customary to down more than half a bottle of spirits, or two bottles of wine in a day – occasionally both. King's stomach reeled at the thought of drinking in the morning, especially when he would need all his wits about him that afternoon. He told himself he was a fool, that he had at least an hour before he need assemble his division and a glass now might help him rest until then. But King had a long memory, and knew from experience just how he would feel when he rose from that rest.

"It's always the same before a battle. I mean, when you know you're going to have one." King allowed Rogers' words to flow over him as he helped himself to a piece of hard, pink Suffolk cheese. An idea was forming in his mind, one that might turn out to be a young man's fancy, not worth the time spent thinking, but King was intent on reasoning it out to the end.

"They get carried away remembering all they have to do, thinking of anything but what is actually bothering them." Rogers stopped, waiting for King to ask the invited question. There was silence; it was an absurd notion, yet King felt it worth writing down, and maybe even taking to Dyson or the captain.

Rogers looked up to see his junior munching through his meal, clearly unconcerned about anything he might have to say, and for a moment he wanted to start an argument. He opened his mouth to begin, when the effort suddenly appeared much too great. Instead he raised his glass once more and drank.

# CHAPTER FOURTEEN

CAPTAINE *de vaisseau* Jean Louis Duboir stood on the quarter-deck of his command, the ninety-eight gun *Lozere*, studying the British through his glass. Like his ship, Duboir was subtly different from his British counterpart, although he shared with them a thorough understanding of the sea, and the men who sailed it.

Until a few years ago Duboir had been a rich man, with a good house and a profitable business. Starting as an apprentice, he had risen quickly to become, at nineteen, one of the youngest masters in the French merchant marine. From there, seeking further excitement, he had pooled his money into a half share of a small trading brig and paid off his partner, then leased a second ship by the time he was twenty-four. The revolution, which Duboir felt had been too long in coming, hardly affected him at first; he was of humble birth and his wealth, which was by now considerable, had been earned through hard work and provided employment for many. The subsequent changes in government, both local and central, proved more of a problem, and his finances were soon hit by rising taxes as well as the necessity to grease palms, which had become the only way of continuing to trade. When war with Britain was declared it signalled the end, and his struggling business foundered under the certainty of imminent blockade.

He did consider fitting out his one remaining ship for use as a privateer. Fortunes were to be made and he could have prospered, even employing a master to sail her, while he stayed and protected his property against any fresh laws the local council might decide upon. *La guerre de course* was an option Duboir could take; but he was a merchant seaman, and others of his kind would be his victims. Despite any unfairness in his own fortunes, he refused to lower himself to the status of a commercial cannibal. Then fate had taken an ironic step, and he had found himself an officer in a fighting navy whether he liked it or not.

Duboir had seen this as nothing more than another challenge, and one that he was quite ready to meet. If he must fight at sea, then he would do it well. The lack of experienced officers meant that he had been appointed to the French Navy at his present rank without going through the usual stages of *aspirant, enseigne de vaisseau* and *lieutenant*. He had spent three months at the Naval Academy and been given nominal command of *Lozere*, a rare ninety-eight gun ship, shortly afterwards.

In the following year much changed and the revolution began to be seen in a different and more sinister light. At Christmas, Herbert, the diseased and obscene journalist, presided over the Feast of Reason in Notre Dame where a whore was elevated at the high altar amid Rabelaisian rites. Meanwhile in the prisons men and women, increasingly there due to the whim of some sadistic Party member, were fed on offal served in troughs, or sent chained like so much cattle, to run in droves through the city streets.

The menace had grown and with it the terror, until two to three thousand heads were falling every month to the Lottery of the Holy Guillotine. At Nantes five hundred children had been slain, while their mothers were given the choice between prostitution or death. Five thousand more followed at Arras, and Duboir feared there were other, greater atrocities committed elsewhere that he had not chanced to hear about.

Throughout this time he had stayed patiently by his new command, burying his head in his books, learning all he could about a new craft, while his mind blanked out the successive rumours of a terror that he assured himself he would be incapable of halting. There had been no time for sea trials, even without the powerful blockading force that hovered just over the horizon; the chaos that had replaced naval infrastructure meant that he had barely enough consumable supplies to equip his ship without risking any on training.

In fact this was his first chance to take *Lozere* to sea, and already he had found woeful inadequacies in her rig and fabric; the crew had also caused him to worry. A few were trained hands, and others, though new to their business, had learnt much even during their time in harbour. But there were also those who could spend a life on the ocean and still never have the resilience and understanding necessary to become true sailors. The balance were more dangerous still: political animals that seemed to infiltrate every rank, sent to ensure that, however far they may be from France, no one would abandon the ideals of their new republic.

He was considering just this last point when *contre-amiral* Lafluer appeared from his quarters, and Duboir felt foolishly guilty in case the man, whose eyes seemed to bore deep inside him, had indeed been able to read his thoughts.

"The enemy fleet is dividing," Lafluer commented as he joined Duboir. "You did not think it necessary to inform me?"

The guilt increased, even though there was still no basis for it. "I sent a message as soon as it was obvious." He turned, but Dumas, the *aspirant* he had instructed, was nowhere to be seen.

"It is of no matter." Lafluer waved his hand at Duboir's explanation as if it was a lie he was prepared to tolerate. "We will take what is left; there is not the time to look for more."

Duboir swallowed; Lafluer was the product of the revolution. A dry little man, old before his time, who would never have progressed past his former rank of *Lieutenant* were it not for his political opinions (which Duboir considered bordering on the insane) and the woeful lack of experienced officers without.aristocratic pedigree.

"You wish us to clear for action?" The fact that he was only in nominal command of the ship and had to request direction upset Duboir further, although he sought to hide this, as he did with all the other humiliations of his present position.

"No," Lafluer graced him with a tight smile, "there is no need. The enemy will run; some are even doing so already. We will close with the battleship, and she will strike or go also. The merchants can be collected and taken with us to meet with Canard. The ships may be of value even if their cargos turn out to be worthless."

Duboir again had to fight against his natural instincts. His knowledge of the British Navy did not suggest that a warship would flee, however outnumbered she might be. And the callous use of merchants, to be seized on the chance that their hulls may be of use, upset his trader's instincts. France had been under blockade for two years, and although she could last much longer, forever if need be, the trouble to send these cargoes home must surely be worth taking.

"How long before we are in range?"

Duboir pursed his lips and shrugged. "Two, maybe three hours. Less if these conditions hold." He too had noticed the changes in the weather; in the last few minutes the wind had increased considerably.

Lafluer nodded. "Call me if there are any developments." He turned, then stopped and stared Duboir straight in the eye. "See to it yourself, Captain. I want no more excuses."

Duboir took up his glass once more and set it on the escaping ships to hide the resentment that burned deep inside him. They were clearly the faster, more valuable vessels, and he felt that, given the opportunity, he could have collected some, if not all, and still have had the time and sea room to turn back for the others. They were being efficiently handled, their sails taking full advantage of the wind; before long they would be effectively out of his reach. Then they would continue their journey in relative safety. And there would be others; journeys on open oceans protected by a force of ships that was becoming the envy of the world.

He shrugged once more, shut his glass with a snap, and took a turn or two across the deck. With all the wretchedness and discomfort associated with serving a man like Lafluer, it was an effort for him to quell a slight and quite unreasonable feeling of envy.

*****

Whenever King stood for long in the presence of his captain he became unusually aware of his elbows. Even with his arms straight by his sides, as they were now, they contrived to stick out, proud of his body. He stretched his limbs in an effort to make them straighter still and was immediately conscious that he was fidgeting, a habit known to annoy his captain, and one it would be foolish to indulge in at that moment.

Shepherd looked up from the paper on which King had outlined his ideas.

"You seem to regard merchant vessels as expendable, Mr King."

King remained silent, there would be more, he knew it.

"That is ignoring our own people, and the danger they will be in."

"The ship is a drogher; she's been falling behind since Spithead, sir; I think the risk is worth taking." Shepherd said nothing, although he did read through the idea once more: a positive sign and one that gave King hope.

"The French did nothing when the convoy divided, what makes you think they will react when one ship makes a run for it?"

That was a hard one; King drew a deep breath. "Sir, at the time the convoy split they could not be sure of our true strength. For all they knew several other liners could have gone off with the other merchants. Now they can assess our force and see five merchants and us." He struggled slightly; what he wanted to say was the French would feel the British ships were as good as captured, but this could be construed as defeatist talk.

The captain nodded, apparently content with the explanation, and King was struck, not for the first time, at the similarity between their two minds.

"Who would you detail for this expedition?"

"Myself, sir," he swallowed. "I had hoped to lead it. And no more than ten men, from my division if possible, and the marines of course." That was an important point; part of the plan called for discipline and fire power, attributes that the marines possessed in full measure, and something that would come as a devastating shock to the enemy. "Twelve marines, and a corporal to command them."

"That's roughly five percent of my crew; worse, as you want fighting men, and almost a quarter of the marine complement."

Shepherd tapped his finger on his lips as he thought, then looked up and fixed King with his clear blue eyes.

"And how will you reorganise the watch bill, without leaving men short?"

King was prepared for this. "I could take men equally from each watch, sir. A couple of topmen would be handy, but I could even do without them. Or I could take landsmen if it came to it."

Shepherd smiled. "You are certainly determined, Mr King." Then his face straightened. "But you are also my signals officer, and I will be depending on you in the next few hours."

It was hard to argue in the face of a compliment.

"The midshipmen are trained up, sir. All have been in signals longer than me—and I hope to be coming back."

"We will still be sacrificing a merchant ship, and her cargo."

That was inevitable. King fought hard to suppress his frustration.

"Sir, at the rate the *Hampshire Lass* is falling behind, they'll snap her up in a couple of hours. This way we will rescue her crew, divert one, maybe two of the French frigates, and at the very least see they do not benefit from the ship, or what she carries."

There were numerous precedents where vessels had been sacrificed to prevent them falling into enemy hands, and the idea of fire ships was almost as old as the sea itself. He had also been looking for a way to divide the enemy, and King's plan would seem to do exactly that. No, it was just the potential loss of men that worried Shepherd. He looked through the plan once more. Ingenious and quickly, if not thoroughly, thought out. Shepherd glanced across at King. The lad had done well; he had a future and it would be a shame to lose him. However, the Navy existed because men like this were prepared to take risks, and to deny him the chance because of the danger would be wrong.

The final and deciding factor was no more than a hunch, one that Shepherd had been harbouring for a while. The enemy were still making for them and had shown no sign of dividing to take the faster ships, which were steadily heading for safety. Clearly their commanding officer was cautious, either by nature, or due to orders. A shock like this might do more than simply divide his force; it could dissuade him from pursuing the rest of the convoy, and might even give him an excuse to break off altogether. It was a long shot, but one Shepherd felt worth the taking.

"You'll need volunteers; genuine ones mind—even from the marines." There was a slight pause as the captain caught his eye. "And I am sure you are aware of the laws of war? Any man captured in this type of venture can legally be put to death."

"Yes, sir."

"Then you had better see to it that your party does as well. Choose from your own division by all means; it is better the people know each other if they are to work together."

King nodded.

"And both cutters."

"Both, sir?" he had only asked for one.

"Yes, spread the men out. They'll have more space, and if one is sunk we might at least see half the force returned."

"Yes, sir."

"Ask Captain Carling and Mr Dyson to see me immediately, and arrange for cutlasses and pistols for the men. The gunner will advise you as to the rest of your requirements. Take who you want from the midshipmen as your second. You're sure of the cargo?"

"Dockyard stores: Petersburg hemp, coal, Stockholm and Archangel pitch, tar, candles, rope, blocks and powder. She was due to leave the convoy at twenty degrees, and make her own way across the Atlantic. I saw the manifest before we left Spithead."

"Powder?"

"Yes, sir. For small arms, but a considerable amount."

"Very well." An expensive cargo, worth a small fortune to whoever was financing it; this was one entrepreneurial venture that had failed at the first hurdle. They were also essential stores, ones that the French would find extremely useful; it might be considered his duty to deny access to them.

"Drogher she may be, but she is someone else's property, although considering the situation you shouldn't have much trouble clearing her crew; I'm sure you can cope with it if you do."

King nodded, conscious of the pulse in his neck that had begun to drive at an incredible rate.

"Better get on with it; the less the enemy expects the better."

Shepherd stood up and extended his hand. "I wish you luck, Thomas."

"Thank you, sir." The captain's unexpected use of his Christian name shocked him almost as much as his acceptance of the plan. He took the outstretched hand awkwardly, before turning and heading from the cabin and into the brightness of the quarterdeck. His head was filled with a jumble of tasks he had to complete in very little time, and there was a faint feeling of nausea that had just made itself known, deep in his stomach.

*****

Flint had finished his dinner and was relaxing in the maintop. After standing the forenoon watch he was technically off duty, although he had seen enough in the morning to realise there would be no time for leisure that afternoon. From his lofty position he watched as two signal mids attempted to coax the merchants into order. The ideal formation for ships pursued without the windward advantage was roughly V-shaped, with *Vigilant* at the head, and the others trailing to either side. So far two ships had been persuaded to their correct station, and a third seemed likely to follow shortly. They would have problems with the last; she had been slow for the entire voyage, and even the prospect of being the first to be overtaken by the French had not given her extra impetus.

The enemy were in clear sight: two liners sailing abreast, with a couple of heavy frigates ahead and to his right. Flint considered them without emotion. They were sailing with the wind six points large, or on the quarter, aiming for a point a good way ahead of *Vigilant* and her charges. Presumably they considered that the British would not alter course, and they might be right, although Flint had noticed signs of oncoming bad weather and felt a change was in the offing.

"You know we got the Irish with us." The voice of Dreaper, newly promoted from landsman to ordinary, cut into his thoughts. Flint glanced over to where he sat, fingering the end of his short, tarred queue as he stared back at the distant enemy.

"What was that?"

"Revolutionaries. The U.I.s. They're aboard."

Dreaper was several years younger, and far less experienced, than Flint. Normally a boisterous man with a ready wit, he seemed decidedly subdued as he watched the steady approach of the French.

Flint nodded. "Aye, they been with us for a while now."

The mainyard below gave a groan as the wind shifted slightly.

"Never sure who's with them, or with us," Dreaper continued. It was true, the membership of the United Irishmen was by no means confined to countrymen; at the same time, there were many sons of Cork or Dublin who were pleased to defend the British Crown, and would die doing so.

"They're no harm to us," Flint reassured him. "Their fight's elsewhere. It's the officers who have to watch theirselves."

Dreaper turned to Flint, his blank expression softening slightly. "Hear one of 'em planted a dead rat in t'wardroom fruit bowl?"

"Aye," Flint grinned. "I heard that."

The yard creaked again as the braces were tightened.

"Wonder how they'll measure up when this little lot comes to blows." Dreaper's voice was low and completely lacking in emotion, although Flint could tell the subject worried him.

"They'll fight," he replied, with utter certainty. "They'll fight, 'cause if they don't they're liable to be killed."

"French are supposed to be with them, though. You don' think they'll pox it for us?"

Flint shook his head. "How they gonna do that? Haul down the colours when no one's lookin'? French don' know they're U.I.s, an probably don' want to, neither. Meantime anythin' they do to wreck us is liable to snare them as much. Na, they'll fight for as long as they has to, an when it's all over, go back to rolling shot at officers."

"Rum lot," mused Dreaper, a note of relief sounding in his voice.

"Aye, rum lot, right enough," Flint agreed. He glanced down to the quarterdeck, where Dyson had appeared from the captain's quarters looking cold and severe; a sure sign that something was afoot. Carling then turned up with a corporal in tow. The boatswain joined them, followed by King, who began sorting through the watch bill with Dyson.

"Sommat going on down there," said Dreaper. "Be clearing for action afore we knows it."

Flint nodded, although he felt something other than striking down bulkheads was brewing. King was a popular officer, one with an eye for adventure, as Flint had discovered on at least one memorable occasion. If he was looking for men, as the watch bill indicated, then Flint wanted to be in on it.

"I fancy takin' a look for myself." He grinned briefly at Dreaper before transferring himself to a backstay and sliding down to the deck as easily as a bead on a string.

# CHAPTER FIFTEEN

IT would take several years and the influence of Admiral Sir John Jervis to allow the British Marines to be officially distinguished as "Royal", but long before then the elite band of sea soldiers had no doubt that they were special.

Corporal Jackson surveyed his men as they mustered for inspection on the upper gundeck. Contrary to the majority of the crew, and indeed a good proportion of the British Army, these men were true volunteers, and as such, were trusted above all others. A trained and businesslike force, more versatile than any foot soldier, as disciplined as a crack Guards regiment, and the main reason why the common seaman was still living in conditions and on wages that had not altered in a hundred and fifty years.

The idea of mutiny loiterd on the horizon of most men's minds, and, when circumstances became unbearable, it was the discipline and presence of the marines, standing sentry on every companionway and outside the captain's quarters, and even berthing between the officers and the men, that usually stemmed the revolt before it even began. It was the marines who deterred deserters by walking patrol on the channels, and the marines who would drag back any drunken seaman that, on the rare occasion when shore leave had been granted, abused the privilege. It was the marines who provided the main muscle power of the ship. The turning of the capstans and the pulling of the braces was mostly down to them: men who were in no way qualified as seamen, but who could stand and work on a deck in the worst of weathers.

But it was in action that the marines showed their true colours: standing firm in conditions that would horrify many professional soldiers, firing quickly and accurately with single-minded determination. So deeply was the discipline instilled that even in the thickest battle the idea that their NCO should hold a rod against their backs to ensure a straight line was considered completely normal.

Jackson walked along his squad, subconsciously checking the kit and clothing of each man, and grudgingly pleased to find no fault or variation. These were his men, he had trained them, he knew them totally and, although he would have instantly rejected the idea, he was fond of them.

"I'm going to ask you to a party," he said, in his customarily gruff manner. No man moved, but all were aware of the subtle change of atmosphere.

"We're goin' to meet up with some Frenchmen and have a high old time." The men remained still, as he expected them to be, as they would be if he'd openly insulted their god, mother, or anything else they might hold dear.

"There's not gonna be room for many: twelve is the number I've been told. Anyone interested in comin' along, make himself known. Anyone not, you know me; there'll be no 'criminations."

As a body the men advanced one pace, until the line, unbroken as before, lay eighteen inches further forward.

Jackson smiled grimly to himself, it was just as he had expected, and he was satisfied. There were exactly twelve men in the squad.

\*\*\*\*\*

"You looking for volunteers, sir?" Flint asked, as he approached King standing on the quarterdeck.

"Might be, Flint," King grinned. "You game?" The two eyed each other, conscious of the past experiences that bound them. Flint had been present when they had cut out the coaster off the West coast of France, and had been part of the prize crew that saw her back to England.

"I'll come along, sir."

"Right, go back to the poop," King made a small mark on the watch sheet. "We'll be using the cutters," he said, winking at Flint. "And it's small arms stuff: pistols and cutlasses."

Flint beamed and nodded, before making his way to where a group had already assembled. The master at arms was handing out weapons; Flint took his without comment. Fletcher was with them, as he had been on their previous adventures, and Copley, and Robson: it was the old team. He looked across at the French ships as Jackson marched his marines up to the quarterdeck and onto the poop. The sun vanished briefly behind a cloud, the air felt heavy with storm, and Flint was just in the mood for a scrap.

*****

Rogers was seated at the wardroom table, a half-finished bottle of port wine near at hand.

"Planning a little adventure, are you?" he asked. King's heart fell when he saw the lieutenant. It would take fifteen minutes to detail the rest of the crew, load the equipment, and rig the boats. He had nipped down to the wardroom to collect his own weapons and a boat cloak, and had no desire, or time, for conversation, especially as he sensed that Rogers was in a dangerous mood.

"Going to take the Frenchies on, are we?" Despite the proximity of the bottle Rogers hadn't drunk anything for over an hour. He was now at the stage where his head hurt, he needed sleep, and he hated everything associated with being alive.

King could not think of an answer, and tried to avoid the man's stare as he hurriedly gathered his things.

"God, hardly out of the cockpit and you're laying it down to the captain."

"The captain approved of my plan, if that's what you mean." He collected his dirk from the becket where it hung. It was shorter than the other officers' swords, a design usually only carried by midshipmen, but King had not been prepared for his promotion, and felt awkward about asking any of the lieutenants for the loan of a hanger.

"Think you can show us old 'uns a thing or two, do you?"

King berthed in the wardroom. Occasionally an acting lieutenant stayed with the midshipmen on the orlop deck. But Shepherd felt that a man should enjoy the privileges that went with his obligations, and King was granted the chance to mingle with his betters. There were times, as now, when he wished the captain had not been quite so thoughtful.

"Ask me, Shepherd's mad letting you take useful men, right when we need them most."

King winced and opened his mouth to reply, when another voice cut through with cold authority.

"I would think very carefully before questioning the captain's sanity, Mr Rogers."

Rogers blanched visibly as Dyson strode into the wardroom. The first lieutenant's expression was set in a rare half-smile; he was about to carry out a particularly unpleasant task that was absolutley unavoidable, and yet to all outward appearances he was enjoying himself. King saw the look and sensed danger. Without pausing he scurried past carrying his bundle of cloak, dirk and pistols. Dyson waited to hear the closing of the wardroom door before his next broadside.

"Your behaviour on board this ship is below the level of acceptability," he said.

Rogers stood up, facing Dyson, although he did not meet his eye.

"You have been aboard for less than a month, and yet in that time you have missed one divisional inspection, and on two occasions have absented yourself from the deck during watch."

The pain in his head was all but forgotten and Rogers became aware that sweat was breaking out on his forehead. Dyson waited for some reaction before selecting his next target.

"I do not have to say that the captain is also aware of your shortcomings; doubtless he will be reporting on them in due course."

That could mean the end of his appointment, and he would be lucky to get another. Even with his father's influence, the Admiralty board did not look kindly on officers who had earned a captain's disapproval. He met Dyson's eye just in time to receive the next salvo.

"Until that time, I expect you to make efforts to improve in every area." He walked around the man, looking him up and down in a critical, despising way.

"You are an apology for an officer. A drunkard, a lout, a fool. You are in command of men, and you do not deserve the right to breathe their air." His face was close to Rogers as he barely whispered the last words. Rogers tried to back away, but felt hypnotically drawn to the cold eyes so close to his.

That was all, his broadsides had been delivered on target, and now Dyson stepped back and briefly surveyed his work, before turning and walking out of the wardroom.

Rogers sank back down on the chair, his head finding support in his hands. Within a few hours they would be in the thick of a battle that might easily end his life. If not, there was more than an even chance that he would be a prisoner, with his career as a naval officer in ruins. And all because that intolerant machine of a man... A surge of emotion broke into his thoughts and he sobbed once loudly, before suppressing the tears into small jerks of his body until he felt the shameful spasms subside. Without being entirely conscious of the action, he reached for the bottle and held it gently by the neck before smashing it down hard on the wardroom table.

*****

The captain was clearly in no rush to clear for action, and Donaldson, the gunner, was not sorry. He was a warrant officer, originally promoted from the lower deck, who now had charge over the greatest number of men in any department, and a good few of them were at work now in the powder room of the grand magazine.

Both the grand and the forward magazine hung slightly below the level of the orlop deck, allowing them to be flooded with the minimum of delay should the need arise, and keeping them safe from enemy gunfire. Each room was lined with copper to keep its contents dry and prevent the ship's timbers from becoming impregnated with powder. The lining also ensured that the magazines were the only area of the orlop guaranteed to be free of vermin. When he wished to open either magazine Donaldson had to apply to the captain for the key. A note was made in the log, together with the reason for the request, and even then the precautions continued. To avoid any chance of a spark, the key, made of bronze, turned brass tumblers in the lock and, the felt-lined doors to the powder room moved on copper-butted hinges.

In the light room that stood to one side of the powder room Donaldson peered through the thick panes of glass to where several of his mates were opening casks. The barrels were distinguished with copper bands to prevent any chance of a spark were they to be inadvertently knocked together, and the tools the men used were also of brass or copper. On their feet they wore lint slippers, and all had emptied anything made of iron from their pockets before descending into the magazine.

The powder would be shovelled from the barrels into flannel cartridges which would then be sewn up. Flannel had only been adopted relatively recently, as it was found to incinerate totally when the charge was fired; paper, the previous choice, tended to leave small burning fragments that were liable to ignite the next charge as it was being inserted, if the gun was not thoroughly sponged. Donaldson kept cartridges ready for five rounds for each great gun, and waited until action was imminent before filling more. The mixture of charcoal, saltpetre and sulphur that made up the explosive was liable to separate, so he was always left with a last minute rush to make up cartridges before the ship went into battle.

A barrel was open now, and one of his mates inserted a wooden ladle and proceeded to stir the contents. Donaldson reached down to the lanthorn to trim it when a shock ran through him to his fingers. Someone in the powder room had sneezed, not an unpardonable offence in normal life, but bad enough when men were standing within touching distance of explosive death. He glanced around to see the youngest looking sheepish as his mates teased and chided him under their breath. The knock at the light room door was no less jarring to the nerves, and Donaldson all but whispered for whoever it was to come in.

The door opened, but the caller did not step inside.

"What is it you'd be wanting, man?" The gunner asked, testily.

"Mr King sent me, sir." Donaldson recognised the voice of Matthew Jameson, one of the ship's boys, although the lad had taken a step back from the light room.

"Come in, man, come in!" he shouted. "You'll na be safer back there as you would in here!"

Matthew entered the light room, blinking slightly.

"Now you were saying..."

The boy was clearly in awe of his surroundings, and glanced about before answering.

"Come on, man, I haven't the time to spare!"

"M-Mr King sent me. He needs two casks of powder, and lengths of slow and quick match." The room was very warm, and the smell of soot and burning oil was worryingly strong.

"Two casks, yer say. And was he wanting it for small arms or cannon?" Small arm powder was considerably weaker than the explosive used for the great guns.

"He didn't say, sir." Matthew swallowed dryly in the oppressive atmosphere.

"Och, away with yer. It'll be a blast he's awantin' I'll send a couple o' casks of cylinder powder with some match and incendiaries. Now get back on deck, yer makin' me nervous!"

The boy disappeared hurriedly, slamming the door shut with a noise that made them all jump.

*****

Dyson marched stiffly past the marine sentry and down the main companionway to the deck below. In a ship-of-the-line there were precious few places to be alone, and the only logical one, his cabin with its thin deal walls and door, was denied him by Rogers' presence in the wardroom. He continued to the orlop deck, a dark airless place, filled with junior officers' berths and assorted storerooms. King's party would be leaving the ship shortly, but he had enough time. At the bottom of the companionway he paused before making for the commissioned officers' storeroom. The small door was locked, and he fumbled for the key before collecting a lanthorn and stepping inside.

The low room contained all the dunnage not required in cabins, such as winter clothing and supplies, as well as any souvenirs that may have been purchased or looted. It was less than half full, and nothing it contained belonged to Dyson. He immediately noticed three large chests that carried Rogers' initials along with some absurd family crest. Dyson hung the lanthorn on the deckhead bracket, his face still giving nothing of the repressed emotion he was feeling inside. Then he closed the door so that he was quite alone.

His hands were shaking; he clasped them about his body before sitting down on one of Rogers' chests. Dyson was the product of a hard school. He had been in the Navy for most of his life and learned to survive, even prosper. Two years spent in a French prison had acted as a finishing academy for the strict, cold, silent character that evolved. He knew that his colleagues and other members of the crew thought him distant, and even despised him for his clinical manner. He knew, and he was glad, for that was the best defence he could want. If anyone so much as guessed at the sensitive, tender man beneath, he knew that his authority would be totally undermined, and all order and discipline destroyed.

Some men found comfort in drink, drugs or divinity; Dyson's need was more subtle and, as far as he knew, unique. He craved solitude. Only for a brief period; a few minutes alone, totally alone. A few minutes when he was certain not to be disturbed; a time that was his; a time to rest his body and mind totally. Afterwards he could return to work, and would be himself again. Or, if not himself, then at least the man that everyone expected him to be.

# CHAPTER SIXTEEN

THE two ship's cutters were proper sea-going boats: twenty-five feet in length, clinker built with twin masts and lug sails. They were handier than both the stately barge and the long boat, as well as easier and faster to launch, as they hung from davits at the poop.

King looked over the equipment already stashed in his boat before walking across to Pite, who would command the second.

"Have your people prepare the sails, but don't rig them or the masts. We'd rather Monsieur Crapaud remained ignorant of our plans."

Pite nodded. "Shall I hook on to the fore or main chains, sir?"

King swallowed, it was only a couple of weeks back that they had been equal rank and friends, sharing the same berth.

"Fore, I'll take the main. And starboard side, mind."

Only a fool would hook on to larboard, the windward side; it would be a more cumbersome manoeuvre, and likely to be spotted by the enemy.

"Starboard side, aye, sir."

There was just a trace of humour in Pite's voice which King chose to ignore. Pite had never been in command, and gave no allowance for King having to make sure of every detail.

Corporal Jackson had already split his marines into two sections of six and divided them between the boats. The seamen followed; and, after a nod from the captain, King also clambered aboard and ordered the boats down.

Now the full motion of the sea could be felt. There was no doubt that heavier weather was on the way, and the small boats rolled drunkenly in the swell. Flint cast off the fall tackle and clambered forward.

"Remember which boat you came in, and be sure to take the same one back." King had to shout above the noise of the sea. He looked across to where Pite's cutter was leaving the lee of the ship. Pite was gripping the side of his boat, looking very young and vulnerable in the tossing water.

Flint and another seaman were clearing away the masts, making them ready to step, while six more took oars and began guiding the boat towards the oncoming merchant ships. King felt his nausea returning; it was a sensation he had experienced before when going into action, only now his course was entirely self-inflicted. This was the first time he had instigated a plan. The first time he would see if an idea of his could be made to work. Men could be wounded, men might die; there was a strong likelihood of both. And were it not for him and his ideas, they would all be safe aboard *Vigilant*. He swallowed dryly and set his mouth firm as he watched the distance dwindle between him and the *Hampshire Lass*.

*****

Shepherd saw them go from the taffrail. The enemy were now about eight miles away and unlikely to spot the cutters. Besides, even if they did there could be a hundred reasons why a warship should be sending boats to a merchant in these circumstances. Some particularly valuable item of cargo might have been called for, or he could be arranging to transfer important passengers. King's plan was deviously simple; he didn't think the French would guess it. And if they did, there was very little he could do now to change things.

He turned to Dyson, who had returned to the deck some minutes before and was standing a respectful distance from him.

"Mr Dyson."

"Sir?"

"I think it is time to clear for action."

Dyson touched his hat and set the procedure in motion that turned *Vigilant* into a ship of war and gave it purpose.

The marine drummer raised his sticks before beating out the stirring rhythm of *Hearts of Oak*. The boatswains' pipes trilled as each man hurried to his allotted task.

Aloft topmen rigged chains to reinforce the slings that supported the yards, while others roused out rolls of *Sauve-Tete*, the splinter netting that would catch some of the debris, or men, that might be shot down from above. More net was rigged from the yard arms to deter boarders, and grappling irons were hauled up to the tops, where they could be used to lash the ship to any enemy who ventured too close.

Deal bulkheads were hinged up, and canvas screens broken down to free the gundecks of all obstructions. Wilson, the surgeon, donned his black smock and broke out fresh supplies of bandages, sutures, turpentine and tincture of laudanum. His loblolly boys pushed the midshipmen's sea chests together to make operating tables and covered them with canvas. Sand was liberally sprinkled about the deck to maintain a sure grip for the gun crews, and render any spilt powder safe.

The cook's mates shovelled the galley fire into metal buckets which were emptied over the side, while their master approached the pigs, sheep and chickens that were penned forward in the manger. He had a small sharp knife in his hand, and murder on his mind.

Dampened "Fearnought" felt was placed about hatchways to prevent fiery debris falling below, and buckets of water laced with vinegar laid out to quench the men's thirst. Cabin furniture was folded up and struck below, and ladders removed on certain hatchways to be replaced with scrambling nets.

Each gun captain lifted the lead apron that covered the breech of his gun and checked his powder horn, quill, priming tubes and wire. The darkness of the lower deck was broken as the ports opened, and the great guns, already loaded, were run out. Servers went to the shot lockers and assembled their load on the garlands that stood by each gun, while the boys checked the two charges of ready use powder that were kept in the salt box to the rear of each piece.

And all without a word or order. Only the rumbling drum and shrilling whistles gave them guidance, and no more than a nod or a shake of the head was needed to direct the well drilled routine. Even the fresh hands caught the tenor of the occasion, and fell to what work could be trusted to them with soundless efficiency. When it was finished, and the drumming ended with a stifled roll, the ship lay totally quiet, and heavy with expectation.

"Cleared for action, sir," Dyson reported, consulting his watch. "And beaten our best time by two minutes."

"Very good, Mr Dyson."

"Beat to quarters, sir?"

Shepherd looked back at the cutters, which had just reached the *Hampshire Lass* and were hooking on. The wind had risen slightly, and already some of the merchants had moved from their station. He shook his head. He could safely dismiss the watch below, although there was precious little comfort in a ship cleared for battle. Besides, waiting without activity could be demoralising. He decided it would be better to keep the ship active.

"No, I fancy a little sailing practice, Mr Dyson. And send the signal midshipman back to me; we can entertain our little fleet while Mr King does his work."

Matthew found he was missing Flint far more than he had expected. In the anti-climax that followed clearing for action he had time to consider his position. Soon there would be a battle, and he would be in the middle of it. Not something written down in a book or spoken about over the dying embers of a fire, but a proper fight; here, now, and happening to him. His mouth was very dry, and he looked to the men who were chatting nearby in the hope of distraction and reassurance.

They were officially the watch below, and until the order to beat to quarters came, none had any proper station. Lewis was sitting in between two guns, his back resting against the internal oak spirketting of the ship as he read from a small book. Jake and some of the other lads had been detailed to plucking hens in the galley. With Flint gone, and Crehan, O'Conner and Jenkins detailed elsewhere, Lewis was the only man present that Matthew knew, and he longed for a chance to catch his eye. Lewis seemed more interested in his book, however and Matthew fidgeted awkwardly, while the other men chatted and laughed amongst themselves.

The shrill blast of the boatswains' pipes filled the lower deck, backed up by cries from the mates.

"Topmen aloft, starboard afterguard to the braces!"

Men began rushing to the companionways, encouraged by starters: short lines, generously knotted and used without restraint. Within thirty seconds half the men had disappeared, leaving the others momentarily silent.

"We'll be changing course."

Matthew looked round to see that Lewis had emerged from his book and was addressing him. He gratefully wandered over and settled himself against a gun carriage.

"Where are we off to, then?" he asked.

"Not to anywhere," Lewis smiled. "Captain's just manoeuvring the ship. Probably getting into a better position."

"What would be a better position?"

"At the end of a fleet of liners!" A man with vivid tattoos and a toothless smile butted in, and there was general laughter.

"A lot depends on where a ship lies in relation to the wind," Lewis explained patiently, when the noise had died down. "Right now the enemy has the weather gauge, which means they are between us and the wind. That gives them control; we cannot escape without them running us down when they choose."

"But if we were the stronger fleet?" Matthew asked.

"Then they could use the wind to try an' lose us, but I can't see much chance of that today."

There was general silence as the other men around took this in.

"When we come to fight, they'll have the advantage again," Lewis continued, as a few hands began to shuffle nearer to hear. "A ship to windward can choose the moment to close with the enemy. Furthermore the wind will be bearing down on her masts, so that when she fires, the shot will tend to be low, and hit the other's hull. The leeward ship will be firing uphill as it were; unless she is careful to fire with the roll, her shots will mainly go high and hit the spars."

"Aye, an what about the smoke?" the tattooed man chipped in.

"That's another business," Lewis agreed. "Windward means your smoke rolls away. Might obscure the target for a while, but better that than fogging the decks and blinding your gunners, like on a leeward ship."

There was a series of groans from the ships timbers, and *Vigilant* began to lean onto the opposite tack.

"Mind, in strong wind a weather ship may be stuck with her lower ports half under, but it ain't blowing hard enough for that."

*Vigilant* completed her turn and settled on the new course. The tattooed man leant towards the gunport and looked back.

"Merchants are in a hell of a state," he said, without emotion.

"Is that what the captain's doing?" Matthew asked. "Getting us on to the weather gauge?"

Lewis smiled. "No, lad. Take more than a change of tack for that. We got to get past the French 'fore we can take the wind."

"Ain't much chance o' that, neither!" the tattooed man added, and there was more laughter.

Matthew began to grow more despondent. The men around him were quite clearly mad. They were to face a fight that they would almost certainly lose, and yet they still laughed about it; there must be something he was missing, something he didn't know about. Again he wished that Flint had stayed with them; nothing could seem so bad with him about.

"You a scholar, lad?" Lewis asked. Matthew looked up.

"I know my numbers," he said, hesitantly.

"Can you read?"

"Oh yes." He caught the book that Lewis threw at him.

"You can test me on my buoys, I al'ays get 'em muddled."

Matthew opened the book and studied the pages. There was no doubt that the atmosphere on the deck was lifting; from the stern came a sound of men humming "Tom Bowling" softly in unison, and the rattle of dice showed where some bold hands were chancing a game of Crown and Anchor. It all made very little sense, and yet he found the mood reassuring, and with a smile that was almost philosophical he settled down to test a man who might shortly be dead for an examination he would probably never take.

# HIS MAJESTY'S SHIP

\*\*\*\*\*

The crew of the *Hampshire Lass* stared openly at King as he clambered over the side and walked towards the small quarterdeck. A mate stood next to the wheel, and beyond him stood a man who appeared to be the captain. Both were dressed in blue coats with black collars, while the captain also sported a pair of knee britches. Clearly they intended to see the end of their ship properly dressed.

"Good afternoon, sir," the captain's greeting was equally formal. "Robert Newton, at your service. I don't believe I have had the pleasure." He was a mature man, with skin that was lighter than most seafarers'. King accepted the proffered hand. It was soft. He gave his name before taking a breath and continuing in a firm voice.

"Sir, I fear we have need of your vessel." It was the best way, straight to the point. "As you are aware, there are enemy ships in pursuit, and we believe we can delay them."

"You will do my ship harm, sir?"

King nodded. "That is inevitable." Behind him he could hear the noise of the marines forming up, and as he looked over the captain's shoulder at the French ships the urge for action became great.

"Your crew can remain here, or transfer to another merchant or my ship," he continued in a hurry. "They will be placed in safety, and not be pressed or asked to fight against their wishes."

The captain nodded, and turned aside. Despite the need for haste, King felt a certain sympathy for the man. He had already decided that Newton must also be the vessel's owner, and guessed that any insurance he had would not cover these circumstances. Compensation might be paid by the government, but that would be a long time in coming.

"So be it," he said finally. "Allow us to assemble a few belong-ings."

King nodded, and the captain left the mate to bellow at the crew, while he descended to his cabin for the last time.

The ship was armed with two four-pounder guns. Fletcher had spotted these and was inspecting one gingerly, clearly not trusting any piece that was not Royal Ordinance. The weapons had reasonable carriages, and were positioned on either side of the quarterdeck.

"Any use, Fletcher?" King asked.

He looked up at the young officer. "Can't say, sir. Neither's loaded, and this one's got rust up its barrel."

"See what you can do. Robson, Douglas, Determan and Barnard, help him. If you think they'll serve, shift them both to the larboard side." There was a port spare, and a four-pounder would be reasonably easy to move across the deck with enough man power. "Flint can captain the other gun when he's done with the cutters. The rest of you, to your stations."

Men clambered about the unfamiliar ship, occasionally knocking into the departing crew, who had assembled their dunnage and were trying to launch the small boat that hung from the taffrail. Jackson had his marines sit down beneath the cover of the forecastle where their vivid uniforms would best be hidden. King walked back to the cutters. A single powder cask lay in the bottom of each, and the four men detailed were in the process of attaching lines before parbuckling them up the side. Copley was standing near, a canvas bag containing slow match and flint swinging from his belt.

King turned to Pite, who appeared to have little to occupy him. "The cargo includes powder," he said. "See if you can identify the casks; they should make a good home for that lot."

"Aye, sir," Pite nodded, and flashed a look at Copley who followed him across to the main hatch.

King watched as each body of men undertook the tasks they had either been allotted or assumed. He looked about his command; the rising wind seemed to emphasise her frailty and size. *Vigilant*, thrashing through the water ahead of him, appeared safe, powerful, and all too far away.

\*\*\*\*\*

Flint was the last to leave the cutter. Both boats had to be left with the masts lying loose in their keepers so that the first men back could step and rig them in a matter of seconds. Once the trap was set they would need to leave in a hurry. He was still thinking of this as he climbed up over the side and found himself looking straight into the eyes of another seaman.

His feet touched the deck as the face registered in a distant part of his brain. Then, as the realisation came, he had to fight back the instinctive desire to embrace the older man. But there was no controlling the grin that spread across his mouth, nor the hand he thrust out in greeting.

"Dad, it's me, John."

The older man looked at him in horror, and did not extend his hand. "John? What you doin' here?"

Flint shrugged, "Same as you, I reckon. Gonna leave a nice surprise for the frogs."

"Come on, Charlie, we's off!" the mate shouted.

"Dad, it's fine to see you; maybe we can meet up, after this is over, like?"

The older man scoffed dismissively. "You mean in a French prison? I'd like that."

"Flint, if you don't get a move on we's goin' without you!" Both men turned, but it was the older who was being addressed, and he moved to join the departing merchant crew.

"Hey, wait; you can stay with me." Flint followed his father. "We're gonna be heading back to *Vigilant* in no time. I'll get you a berth, we can ship together."

His father turned back, a look of horror on his face that quickly gave way to something even more awful. It was an expression that Flint had never seen before, nor expected. His father appeared embarrassed, ashamed almost, and yes, there could be no denying it: he was afraid.

# CHAPTER SEVENTEEN

THE wind was rising; King could see the cat's paws increase as they spread across the ocean; the air was coming alive, blowing moist and strong. In the *Hampshire Lass* the deck heeled as a fresh gust hit them, thrusting her down as the sails grew taut and full. She was on the opposite tack to the other British ships, and had more canvas showing than was sensible. Still, they had wrung an extra two or three knots from the old tub, and King looked back at her wake with satisfaction. Beyond were the two French frigates that had broken off to pursue as soon as the merchant had left the main convoy. It was all going as he had anticipated, although the cold feeling in his stomach almost made him wish it were otherwise.

Pite stood next to him on the tiny quarterdeck, his hands firmly wedged behind his back as he closed his mind to the dangers about him. At any moment he expected a spar to snap or a stay to part, leaving them dead in the water, a rich treat for the French to enjoy at their leisure. And even if that did not happen, the frigates were gaining fast and would be up to them within the hour. At any time now there would be the opening shots, and King would put his idiotic plan into action.

A seaman approached, knuckling his forehead.

"Cutters secure, sir." It was Copley, the man King had entrust-ed with the incendiaries. "They're taking a bit of a pounding, but nothing a lick of paint won't sort out later."

"Very good." King remained unmoved, trying to assume the poise of an untroubled man, and fooling everyone but himself.

To his left Fletcher and the others had rigged both guns to fire to larboard; the side, King guessed, from which the French would approach. If he was wrong it would mean the effective waste of both weapons, although he had boarded the merchant unaware that she was in any way armed. He tried to justify his actions with the guns and in planning the adventure, while struggling to stop the nervous fidgeting that was so eager to take him over.

Both guns were loaded with round shot; there had been no canister to hand, although Corporal Jackson had produced a store of musket balls that had been added to the charges for good measure.

"Not long now."

Pite gave a tight smile. King could tell his nerves were stretched to breaking point. On two occasions he had noticed the midshipman staring at the French with an expression rich with fascination, and guessed he would have given anything for the action to begin. This was the same lad who had fought so well on the streets of Toulon, who ventured into the hold when the ship was thought to have sprung, who could be trusted to rouse his men to lead or fight off boarders, but whose raw courage could not stand the long drawn out wait for a superior enemy to attack.

"Better take a look at the cutters," King said, more out of sympathy than doubt. "Just to be sure."

Pite made his way forward, passing the groups of squatting seamen who were keeping out of sight as much as possible. From watching Pite, King's gaze naturally fell on *Vigilant*, now several miles away. For the past hour she had been leading the merchants a merry dance, changing course by a point or two every twenty minutes. The exercise must have caused no end of consternation to the civilian captains who, by nature, would tack or wear as infrequently as possible. Shepherd was discarding valuable time with each exercise as even small alterations allowed the enemy to close that much sooner. But then there was no doubt that the ships were responding with more speed and fluency, even after such a brief practice. If Shepherd had plans to manoeuvre the fleet later, the time would have been well spent.

King had ignored all the signals, being only intent on getting *Hampshire Lass* as far away from the convoy as possible. His behaviour would be accepted by the enemy; indeed it was quite common for ships to strike out alone when chased *en masse*. It might even have been a feasible bid for freedom, especially as a good proportion of the convoy had escaped only that morning. The French commander could well have considered a single merchant unworthy of a chase, instead of despatching his frigates to deal with them and any that might follow.

The shot passed overhead, missing him by a good twelve feet. Despite this, King instinctively ducked before looking back at the ship responsible.

A wisp of smoke was fast disappearing from the bows of the nearest frigate, and shortly afterwards a dull boom told him that he was not mistaken and the enemy had opened fire. It was the first shot of the battle, and it had passed overhead, not a cable or two short, showing that the captain was neither excitable, nor an amateur. King quickly assessed the calibre of his opponents, and hoped that Shepherd had also noticed.

"Splice that backstay there!" yelled Pite turning back to the quarterdeck.

"Belay that!" King waved a seaman away. The sight of a well trained crew repairing damage might be all the warning the French needed. "And take cover, all of you!"

The men who had risen instinctively to the clarion call of the shot slunk back, reluctantly taking shelter behind the brig's scant timbers as another shot pitched close alongside and short.

Pite rejoined King, "I beg your pardon. I didn't think."

King allowed him a reassuring look. "We're going to have to put up with it a while longer. Just pray we don't lose anything vital." Pite nodded stiffly, his face set with tension and anxiety.

"And don't worry," King continued in a softer tone. "It'll be over in no time."

\*\*\*\*\*

Flint was stationed next to Fletcher at one of the guns. The weapon appeared ludicrously small compared with the twenty-four pounders in *Vigilant*, and as he blew on the glowing end of the slow match, he wondered what use it would be. In the scupper beside him were his pistol and cutlass. The former was a clumsy affair, heavy and without sights. Sea service pistols were unreliable, the pan frequently needing re-priming, and even then the conditions they were used in meant that there was a likely chance of a misfire. Used properly they could be effective: fired in a volley at a boarding crowd the weapon even carried an element of terror that might knock the stuffing out of a hesitant opposition. It also made an excellent club afterwards. The cutlass was another matter, and a far more efficient killing tool. Well though crudely made, it would hold a good edge, while being heavy enough to take considerable punishment without breaking.

The severed backstay caused the mainmast to creak ominously, adding to the tension that Flint felt building about him. He glanced at Fletcher, who grinned nervously back. Normally that would have been enough to dissolve his own fear and boost him up above common men, with their natural and healthy dread of battle. Flint had always told himself he was different; built of sterner stuff: one with a pedigree of bravery that had to be lived up to.

But now the trick would not work. He had finally found his father; less than two hours ago they had even spoken together, before the older man turned away. Turned away because he was scared, either of the oncoming action or being spotted as the deserter he undoubtedly was. Whichever, the fact of his fear pierced the illusion that Flint had built about him. The brave young man who had inspired him in the past was suddenly revealed as old, vulnerable and frightened. Consequently Flint was now experiencing the various stages of fear, and finding the interminable pause before action as hard to take as any man on board.

The frigate fired once more, another of the shots that had been punctuating the time every ninety seconds or so for the last half hour. But this one caused more damage, hitting them somewhere low on the stern, making a loud splintering noise and sending a shockwave jarring throughout the small craft.

"Can't hold her, sir!" The helmsman spun the wheel helplessly as the ship fell away.

"God, they've taken the rudder," Pite yelled, his voice slightly higher than normal. King accepted the information without visible emotion, although inside his mind began to race. That was an end to it, an end to his bold plans of destroying a frigate. An end to the worry of how close he could go, and almost an end to the responsibility he held for endangering men's lives. He felt a mixture of relief and exasperation roll over him as he tried to clear his mind to think. "Stand by, but keep your cover until I tell you." They were losing speed fast and beginning to wallow on the choppy seas. There could be no point in closing further when the ship was unmanageable; indeed, they should think about leaving without delay.

Flint looked about and saw the other frigate coming up on their starboard counter. They would be bound to notice the cutters, and may well smell a rat. He looked across to the ship on the larboard side. She was heaving to, and lay about three cables off. It was good enough range for a considered broadside, although there was some other activity taking place. Then Flint noticed a boat being swung out. He lowered his head, leaning against the gun carriage beside him as he suppressed the desire to urinate. Fletcher was to his left, crouching by the breach of his piece; he had the quoin ready for when the order was given.

"You keep that alight, Flint!" he whispered under his breath. "Don't want no misfires now!"

Flint blew on the match, which had indeed died to no more than a glimmer. He was losing his grip; for the first time since the action with the revenue cutter his imagination was running free, and he knew his hands were shaking. He closed his eyes, willing the time to pass. In an effort to calm himself, he bobbed above the bulwark once more to see what was about. The boat, a cutter slightly smaller than their own, was in the water and setting off for them under oars alone.

"Depress your guns," King ordered. Whatever the need to run, there was no point in leaving just yet; especially as the French boat would be bound to give chase. Better string it out a little longer in the hope that they could at least disable the enemy cutter. "Hold fire until I tell you."

Fletcher pressed the wedge-shaped wooden quoin under the breach of the gun and easily lowered the muzzle to the maximum extent.

"Try doing that with a twenty-four," Flint said, determined to keep up an illusion of bravery in front of the other men, as he pressed his own quoin home. A couple laughed, but the rest were too nervous to notice. This would normally have bolstered him, but now he only felt a strange camaraderie.

The cutter was making good progress. It was crewed by twelve seamen, with four uniformed soldiers and what looked like an officer in the stern. More than enough to overwhelm the crew of a merchant, but nothing like what it would take to tackle them. The *Hampshire Lass* was wallowing in the swell, her sails flapping impudently in the strengthening wind, an open invitation.

"Marines form up." King spoke softly, as if frightened of being overheard. The line of red uniforms took position, kneeling along the side.

"Two groups," whispered Jackson. "One to six, take aim and fire on my one; seven to twelve, wait for my two." It was the best way of making sure that the same target was not chosen by too many. The second volley would be aimed at those left standing after the first.

The cutter was close now, less than forty yards; it was time.

"Fire as you will!" King's voice cracked as the order was given.

Flint jumped up and sighted along the gun's crude barrel. He held his hand out to the right, while clutching at his match. Two men eased the gun over until Flint's hand went down, then stepping to one side, he plunged the match into the powder at the touchhole.

The gun discharged almost simultaneously with Fletcher's, and one scored a direct hit, although it was impossible to say which. On the cutter three men fell from their oars and one screamed out in pain or surprise. For a moment the boat's crew stopped and stupidly looked about them, as if wondering where the shots had come from. Then the cutter began to settle as it took in water.

The marines stood up in a rigid line and levelled their muskets.

"One!" bellowed Jackson. The first six shots rang out in a single note, and threw the boat into total disarray. Two more slumped at their oars, and a soldier in the process of aiming his carbine rolled into the sea. The Frenchmen had begun turning the boat clumsily and were clearly attempting to pull out of danger when Jackson spoke again and the second volley hit them.

Flint swallowed dryly. He had hoped to feel better as soon as there was some action, although as he reached for his pistol his hand was still shaking. He fired once in the general direction of the boat. The gun cracked loudly and dropped from his hand, and he had an almost uncontrollable desire to run or hide.

Shots were coming from the frigate again now, and a heavy ball crashed through the light scantlings of the merchant.

"Time to go, lads!" King yelled. "Flint and Fletcher, rig the cutters, Pite, stand to your boat. I'm going below. Come on, Copley."

The order came just in time and, abandoning his cutlass, Flint ran headlong for the side and vaulted over. He tumbled clumsily into his cutter and lay in the relative safety of the boat for several seconds, taking fast and shallow gasps of air while he wondered if he would ever find the ability to move again.

Meanwhile King and Copley had dropped down the main hatch, as more shots swept across the deck. In the murky depths they picked out the powder charges that were lying in readiness. The explosion would not be as devastating as he had intended, indeed King doubted if it would do any good whatsoever. But he had come to destroy the ship, destroy her in the age old way; the way of Drake when he sent his *brûlots* to singe the King of Spain's beard, and there was still a chance he could take a few Frenchmen with him. The yard of slow match would burn at just over an hour to the foot, but King had no intention of allowing anything like that amount of time. Copley struck his flint and blew on the tinder to encourage a flame.

"There!" shouted King, pointing to a spot about three inches from the charge. Copley pressed the flame to the match and paused to see it burn.

"That'll do, come on!"

In the brief time they had been below much had happened. The French cutter was now filled with dead and injured, and barely afloat in between them and the larboard frigate. Its presence had prevented the ship from firing a broadside, but the frigate on the starboard quarter was coming up fast, and would have no such inhibitions.

"All right, Jackson, fall back!"

The red and white line broke as the men made for the boats, Copley and King followed them, joining Pite, who was by now the only other member of the deck party left.

The marines split into two groups and clambered into the boats. The masts were raised and ready with sails loose. King jumped, scrabbling amongst the confusion of the cutter. He looked up. Pite was safe in the other boat, and Copley was about to board his.

"Cast off!" King's voice was no more than a squeal as Copley loosened the painter and a seaman pressed the hull of the ship with his oar. The sails ran up the masts and were just filling when it happened.

With a rumble like rocks tumbling down a hillside the first shots of the broadside hit the hull of the merchant ship just above them. Every man dropped instinctively to the bottom of his boat as carnage and destruction rained about. King felt a splinter rip into his chest, followed by a stream of warmth that soaked his shirt. Pite's cutter was hit and one of the masts fell across them, adding to the confusion. Copley, who had been caught mid-flight as he jumped into the boat, was screaming and holding his leg, where his foot hung as if from a string. King could see Pite as he gazed up from the water, floating on his back with an amazed expression on his dead face. From somewhere above a loud crash told the end of the merchant's main topmast, and blocks, tackle and lengths of line rained about them in a murderous tangle as the yards fell to the ship's deck. King held a hand to his wound and glanced over at *Vigilant* sailing safe and strong and so far away.

\*\*\*\*\*

From his position at *Vigilant's* taffrail Shepherd could see it all quite clearly. The second French frigate had been several cable lengths off when she turned to present her broadside to King's party. Many of the shots went wild, as might be expected of a ship firing at long range, but enough had fallen amongst the cutters to do the business.

Dyson stood next to him, and both men surveyed the scene through their glasses. Pite's boat appeared to have sunk, and the water all about foamed with the arms of struggling men.

"Looks bad, sir," Dyson muttered. The scheme had been hazardous from the start, but that had in no way lessened the feasibility in his mind. If plans were rejected purely because they were dangerous, there would be little point in venturing out of harbour.

Then King appeared to have taken control and the small boat started to pull away.

"She's swimming low!" Shepherd commented. It was true; the cutter's gunwales were barely inches above the heavy waves as the sails filled and the men began to row.

"They may have holed her, or she could be carrying survivors." Shepherd nodded, although there would have been precious little time in which to collect any of Pite's men. The French frigate was staying hove to, clearly intending to send another broadside shortly. Shepherd brought out his watch, a crack British ship would be at least ninety seconds reloading; he hoped the French would take longer.

Tait was also surveying the scene. Standing near to the other two officers, he was not officially on watch and had no glass of his own. The night glass, which gave a clearer sight upon removing one of the lenses, was free; on an image that was upside down and back to front he watched his shipmates fight for their lives.

Crehan had no glass, but perched in the mizzen top he could see the general situation, and Mason, a midshipman of wealthy means, was giving a running commentary to the men who crowded the top as he gazed through his own handsome five element Dollond.

"They're pulling clear, and someone's hoisting another sail. Yes, it's taken; they'll make good speed now!"

"Any sign of Copley?" Pamplin's anxious voice this time. He thought he had caught a glimpse of his companion as he fell from the side of the merchant ship.

"Can you not stand to be apart from him for a moment?" Crehan had no time for such friendships.

"I can't see him particular," said the midshipman, as he peered through his glass. "But they're making better progress now."

"Only the Frenchie's gonna fire presently," Crehan muttered. For him the French held a special fascination. Morally they were his ally rather than enemy, and it was not lost on him that those very ships might be bound for the Americas.

Pamplin shifted his position. He had thought Copley a fool to volunteer; their parting had been distinctly cold on his side, and now he yearned for the chance to make up.

The smoke of the first shot billowed from the frigate's side, and the second broadside began to roll out in disciplined order. At that range it was almost possible to watch the flight of individual shots, as the ripple of fire ran along the warship's hull. A spread of individual splashes followed, all short and to the stern of the escaping boat, and a few seconds later the low guttural rumble of the broadside reached them.

"They've missed her!" screamed Mason above the thunder of the shots. A small cheer erupted amongst the crew of *Vigilant* as the cutter continued apparently unharmed.

"Piece of luck, that!" murmured Crehan. Clearly the gun layers in the French ship had not allowed for the increasing speed of the small boat. By the time the next shots were ready they should be at extreme range.

"The frigate's manoeuvring," the midshipman continued. "She's taking in her braces and coming back to her old course."

That meant she intended no more broadsides, although she could still continue to take pot shots with her bow chasers.

"Why doesn't the silly ol' fool of a captain drop back?" Pamplin's voice broke out with more than a hint of hysteria.

The midshipman turned away from his glass and surveyed the seaman, uncertain as to whether a breach of discipline had just occurred.

"The captain made it plain that we could not leave the convoy," he said, with as much authority as a fifteen year old could muster. "It was up to them to get back to us." He was quite right; Pite had said as much in the midshipman's berth, only a few hours ago.

"Aye," added another. "Them knew well enough what they was lettin' theirsel's in for."

\*\*\*\*\*

What they had let themselves in for was a nightmare. King was allowing his wound to bleed freely while desperately bailing water with his hat. Some of the marines were doing the same, their leather shakos holding almost a gallon at a time. Flint was pulling stroke, and setting a good fast pace, despite a somewhat strained look to his face. In fact, with the help from the sails, the boat was making good progress, but still it would be some while before they caught up with the nearest British ship. Copley moaned softly. He was packed up to the stern of the boat with a crude bandage over his foot and a rope tourniquet biting deep into his thigh. The cold water slopped over him, cooling and cleaning the wound, although King still doubted that he would make it back in time. Glancing behind he could see the second frigate draw level with the merchant ship, about a cable off to one side. She was clearly intending to launch another boat. The first frigate was nearer, less than fifty feet to the other side, abeam of her own shattered cutter, presumably rescuing what survivors she could. The explosion would not be enough to do great damage; maybe shake them up, nothing more.

But then he was assuming that the destruction caused by the first broadside hadn't dislodged the charge. He glanced at his watch, amazed at the passage of time. It should have happened by now, if it was going to happen at all. King composed himself, thinking of the reaction if the charge failed to explode. That would really be a waste; all his efforts would only have achieved the delivering of a fat merchant straight into the hands of the French. He swallowed dryly, wondering about the implications, and it was at that moment that the *Hampshire Lass* rose up and separated amid a ball of red flame.

# CHAPTER EIGHTEEN

A call from the masthead alerted Shepherd, and he looked back in time to see the tongue of flame and pillar of black smoke that marked the last position of the *Hampshire Lass*. Both the French ships were far enough away to escape serious damage, although the sheet of fire, presumably fuelled by the merchant's cargo, swept dangerously close. Specks of flame could be seen on the water, and then the larboard frigate's forecourse was alight. The sail flared briefly, before being totally consumed. Rousting out and setting a replacement would not take long, although the enemy was likely to be more cautious when approaching the remaining merchants.

Shepherd's gaze naturally fell to the small cutter, now nearer to the British ships, but by no means safe. The wind, which had backed further and was strengthening all the time, had forced them over, so that the leeward side was almost underwater. King was sailing the cutter as hard as he dared in order to close with the convoy; certainly the small boat was travelling appreciably faster than *Vigilant*, or the pursuing French. At their present course and rate, and assuming no further changes in the wind, Shepherd estimated that it would be slightly over an hour before they caught up. He smiled grimly to himself; if he was correct the cutter's crew would be boarding *Vigilant* just in time for the opening shots from the French.

He began to pace the deck, unconscious of the many eyes that followed him. King's ruse had separated the frigates from the line-of-battle-ships and created a chance for *Vigilant* to strike at either. If he maintained his present course for too long that advantage would be lost. Worse, the two pairs of ships would simply close on the convoy, still with the wind in their favour, in a classic pincer movement. Clearly he needed to act and act now.

To turn towards the line ships might be the best ploy; even with the odds so heavily against him, it was unlikely that the French could escape serious damage and still be able to cross the Atlantic. Of course it would be the end of his ship; more to the point, the end of any further influence he could exercise on the battle. The frigates would be free to round up the rest of the convoy, possibly give assistance to the liners, leaving *Vigilant* no more than a wreck and a memory.

The alternative? He looked again at the cutter battling towards him through the heavy sea, and the enemy behind it. The two powerful frigates would put up a hard fight; assuming that he was able to disable them both, what state would *Vigilant* be in to go on fighting? And there was an additional question that was almost as unpleasant: how would the Admiralty and his brother officers look on a man who chose to fight frigates in favour of line-of-battle ships?

Suddenly his attention was brought back to the cutter. An unlucky fluke of wind had laid it over, and the crew were striving to right the boat. He stood motionless as they fought for their lives, pulling back on the shrouds to drag the sodden sails clear of the water. All at once the cutter was upright again, although riding lower than ever, while a series of splashes indicated that bailing had resumed in earnest. Then the sails were pulled taught; their speed increased and the chase continued once more. Shepherd rubbed his eyes; his head ached dreadfully; the hours of relative inactivity were starting to tell on him. One of the merchants might easily wear round and collect the cutter, although he doubted if a signal to that effect would be understood, or acted upon. And all he could do was ponder and deliberate, while men he knew well were fighting for survival.

"Wear ship!" he said, convincing himself that he was doing this for the good of the entire convoy and not merely the crew of a small boat. The unexpected command caught his officers off guard, and it took several seconds for them to react.

"What course, sir?" asked Dyson, slightly ahead of Humble.

"Intercept the cutter," Shepherd almost snapped the order before turning away and starting to pace the deck once more.

Humble glanced down at the compass card and then up to the returning boat, hardly seeing the pursuing frigates. "Steer south, one 'undred an' ten." The course would mean abandoning the convoy, although they may still be close enough to witness its demise. It would also take them into the very teeth of the enemy.

"Let go an' haul!" the master's voice held steady, just as it would if the captain had ordered the colours down, the anchors dropped, or women to be allowed on the quarterdeck. The ship creaked as it was brought round to the new course, and Shepherd felt the pressure almost physically build up in his brain. Then they were free of the convoy and picking up speed with the wind two points abaft the beam and the bows, for the first time pointing towards the French ships.

Tait turned his glass on the merchants and studied their inverted image on the night glass. They would see *Vigilant* change course and know she was taking on the frigates, although what solace that would give them he could not guess when they were to be left for line-of-battle ships. He turned his glass back to the smaller warships, glad, not for the first time, to be free of his captain's responsibilities.

Dyson noted the course on the traverse board and looked towards the cutter. He estimated they would be with her in less than fifteen minutes. The wind had backed and increased further and *Vigilant* was fairly racing under her forecourse, jib and topsails, so the time might even be less. Shepherd was still pacing the deck, a sure sign of agitation, while he remained still and composed next to the binnacle. But despite the differences in activity, Dyson was at one with Shepherd. It was the right move, one that he would have chosen himself, although naturally there was no opportunity to reassure his captain without a distinct breach of etiquette.

If they were to take on the French line-of-battle ships, they must first silence the frigates; not to do so would open up any amount of chances for the more manoeuvrable vessels to position themselves inconveniently across their bow or stern while the liners pounded them on either side.

Of course to silence the frigates was no small task in itself. The French carried considerably heavier broadside metal than an equivalent British ship, and were also quicker and more agile. *Vigilant*, sailing alone against two, and rated as a mere sixty-four, was facing a significant force. Dyson smiled to himself; they could muse all day, but both sides of the sword remained as sharp. Whether they steered larboard or starboard they would eventually meet with the enemy. Perhaps they would do damage, maybe take some with them, but *Vigilant* was bound to be overpowered eventually, of that there could be no doubt.

And the odds were not lost on Gregory. He had left the quarterdeck and was standing in the waist looking over the upper larboard battery of twelve pounders. He too was calculating the pick up time of the cutter, although he also allowed for *Vigilant* to slow and take on the men, some of whom would be wounded. With the frigates close on behind he felt that they would be in action within thirty minutes, and was determined to see that everything in his section was correct.

Rooke, one of the master's mates, was of the same opinion, and had been checking through the weapons laid out for ready use: the pikes, cutlasses, pistols and axes, necessary for the hand to hand fighting that would follow were they to be boarded, or themselves attempt to board. Occasionally Rooke cast an envious eye over the twelve pounders that made up the armament of the upper gundeck. Each gun captain should have double-checked their equipment, and any discrepancy was the direct responsibility of them, the quarter gunners, the gunner's mates, and ultimately the gunner or the gunnery lieutenant; not something to concern a master's mate. Still, Rooke could hardly resist a twitch as he noted two swab pails only half filled, and an area of deck that was not sufficiently coated with sand.

"Sharp enough for you, Mr Rooke?" Gregory enquired.

"Aye, sir." Rooke self-consciously replaced the boarding pike in its bracket about the mast. "Reckon we'll be needin' them afore long!"

"Belike you're right!" Gregory grinned before turning and addressing the nearest quarter gunner. "Miller, that area needs more sand, and you're low in two swab kids!"

There was a scurry of movement and Rooke relaxed slightly, before turning his attention to the cutlasses.

Rogers stood at the break of the quarterdeck and stared forward at the two enemy ships. At any moment now they would beat to quarters, and he would take up his position on the lower gundeck. But here the air was fresh and clear, and he was taking consciously deep breaths before he had to descend to the suffocating atmosphere of battle. The dressing down from Dyson now appeared totally insignificant; in fact his whole life seemed to have taken on a subtle change of direction. Priorities altered; he had wanted to appear the seasoned officer, one whom his peers would hesitate to cross or offend. But now, in the eve of a true fight, his previous conflicts dwindled to inconsequence. So Dyson might degrade him in the eyes of his fellow officers and even the Admiralty; he would still prosper. Many before him had left the Navy to pursue careers in commerce, politics; even the Army if it came to it. The main thing was to see this out, stay alive; be captured if need be—his father would be sure to secure his release. Then say goodbye to all this nautical tomfoolery; there were better ways of spending a life.

Shepherd paused in his pacing and turned to Dyson. This was not the first time they had seen action together, but in all previous occasions they had sailed with the might of a fleet, or against a far inferior enemy. Now they would be together in defeat and, almost in a revelation, Shepherd realised quite how much he had come to rely on this queer, clinical man. He allowed him a half smile. "Beat to quarters if you please, Mr Dyson."

Dyson touched his hat, then gave the order that set boatswains' pipes squealing. The marine drummer beat out the *rafale* until the ship was alive with sound. Men primed for action jostled with each other as they took up their battle stations. Shepherd watched them as they joked foolishly amongst themselves, mocking an enemy that was about to put all their efforts into killing them. The majority of the crew were old hands, but the new had clearly integrated themselves well enough in the short time they had been aboard. He felt a pang of regret that the cruise had not lasted longer. Within hours many of these men would be dead or wounded, and the ship, if she survived at all, nothing more than a trophy for the French. But these were not thoughts to carry into battle, and once more he looked for his first lieutenant. "Ask the purser to organise a tot of rum for every man."

Some considered it wrong to send men into battle with spirit in their bellies, but Shepherd had found it made the uneasy that much more likely to hold together. Besides, rum before battle had become something of a tradition, and it would be the last favour he would be able to do for many of them.

In the waist the purser's stewards began passing amongst the men, handing out tots as they ticked names off their list. At every gun the gun captain was allowed to draw his ration neat, before carefully transferring it to a private bottle or jar. With an act of immense willpower it was then hidden away, to be enjoyed after the action. Gregory noted this, conscious not only of the pride that each man placed in his position, but also of his supreme confidence in the outcome of the battle. So certain were these men, not only of victory, but their own immortality that they were willing to postpone a precious drink to that end. He stopped a steward and, stepping in the cover of the gangway, helped himself to his first tot of rum since leaving the lower deck, nine years before. This was not his first time in action, and he had no such illusions.

*****

With Flint gone, much of the discipline of number three gun, lower battery, had departed as well. Matthew had positioned himself next to the open port and, resting against the gun barrel, was peering out at the approaching cutter.

"'Ow close's 'e now?" Jenkins asked. Matthew, who found judging distances hard, tried to be non-committal. "Not, far. Reckon they'll be up to us in a few minutes."

"What about the Frogs?"

That was more difficult. Once, when his father had taken them on a day's walk to Box Hill, he had pointed at the distant village of Brockham, and told him it was all of two miles away.

Matthew swallowed. "About two mile off," he said, with misplaced confidence.

"Two mile?" The men looked at each other doubtfully. Two miles meant they were almost within range; the enemy would be opening fire before long. Should Flint not be back in time Lieutenant Rogers would nominate one of them as gun captain. It was an honour they all seemed equally eager to avoid.

"I can see Flint!" shouted Matthew, dispelling their worries, and almost sending himself over the side in the excitement. Sure enough, the seaman was standing next to the foremast of the cutter, preparing to throw a line up to *Vigilant* as they moved into range. The sails came down, and for a moment or two the small boat lay wallowing in the water while shouts were exchanged with cronies from the upper deck as the big ship bore down on them. Then there came a succession of creaks as the wind was spilled, the mizzen topsail backed, and *Vigilant* slowed, sweeping round to shelter the boat in her lee with the last of her momentum.

"Stand away, there!" Rogers' voice was sudden and deadly. Matthew struggled back through the port while the others grouped themselves about the gun at attention. In the short time they had known him the lieutenant had not endeared himself to any of the crew.

"Peering out like washerwomen on a Sunday!" There was silence, then Jenkins allowed a nervous laugh to escape—one of the many things that was known to annoy Rogers and might easily lead to the entire gun crew being disciplined. Lewis nudged him firmly in the ribs. On this occasion, however, Rogers appeared not to notice.

"We are at quarters; that means silence, do you understand?" His tone was brittle, with a trace of urgency that was quite misplaced. For a moment he held them with a ghastly look. Then he too broke out in a laugh. It was high-pitched, and mad, and finished as suddenly at it had begun. Rogers stood in front of them for a second longer, as if uncertain of what to do, before turning away and continuing along the deck. Matthew breathed out in unison with the rest. There had been something in that laugh that had disturbed him far more than any reprimand.

But then everyone was behaving strangely; he supposed it was a symptom of nerves, although he for one had fewer worries. Flint was back; with him and his supreme confidence, Matthew knew he would be quite safe.

*****

On deck Tait watched as the boat grappled on to the main chains and the first fit men scrambled aboard. He saw Jackson and six, no, seven marines, and six seaman, including Flint and Fletcher. There was also what looked like Copley lying in the bottom of the boat, although he might well be dead. Within seconds slings were lowered and the body strapped and swayed up to the main deck. And then there was King standing beside him, his face creased with strain, carrying his left arm awkwardly.

"Nearly given you up for dead, Thomas." Tait's voice was harsh although there was no mistaking the relief in his eye, and his hand was readily accepted by the younger man.

"Cast off that boat, there!" They both started as Gregory erupted next to them. Clearly the cutter had been deemed unworthy of salvage. The mizzen yard creaked back and the boat was soon lost as *Vigilant* picked up speed.

"Are you wounded, Mr King?" Dyson enquired as he joined them.

"A scratch, sir." He opened his coat to show the dark patch of blood that stained his white shirt.

"Very well. Go below and let Mr Wilson attend to it. You can return to your station as soon as he thinks fit."

Tait walked with him as far as the main companionway. He paused before descending. "Seems you've joined us just in time."

King's serious eyes searched his face. "It was a mistake, Dick. A lot of men were killed, Matt Pite amongst them."

"I know," Tait nodded grimly. "And you're thinking, 'If it weren't for me...'"

King gulped. "Exactly."

"If it weren't for you *Hampshire Lass* would be in one piece, and probably about to be taken by the frogs."

Gregory's interruption caught them both unawares, and he continued. "The crew would all be prisoners; more important, the enemy wouldn't have split, and we'd not have had a cat in hell's chance against them." He looked King in the eyes before walking away with a slow, but solid, step.

Tait smiled. "Well, you've gained someone's approval at least!"

King paused before descending below. "Is it me," he asked, "or can you smell rum?" His face finally broke into a grin, and then a laugh that robbed his body of all the pent up tension of the last few hours.

"Mr King." It was Dyson's voice. He had turned round and was looking towards them. "You will be wanted shortly; kindly have yourself attended to."

King stifled the laughter and allowed Tait to all but push him towards the companionway, under the wooden gaze of the marine sentry.

# CHAPTER NINETEEN

"YOU'LL excuse me, Mr King, if I attend to Copley first."
After the strong daylight, the darkness of the orlop made
Wilson's features indistinct. "One of my men can have a look at
it, if y'like, else I'll be with you presently."

King nodded. Like every man on board he knew the protocol
in treating the injured; despite the nearness of the enemy, he
felt in need of rest and was in no rush to return to duty.

"Or, if you've a mind, you can watch my work." The
surgeon's teeth shone yellow in the gloom as he grinned.

Wilson stood hunched above a group of sea chests that
made up his operating table. His patient was lying ready for
him, his body naked except for a bundle of rags that covered the
wounded leg. Four lanthorns hung from the low deckhead, their
golden light casting soft shadows over the macabre scene and
giving the impression that Copley was already dead.

"How's he, Skirrow?" Wilson asked his assistant who was
wiping the body with a turpentine-soaked rag.

"Out cold, an' the shakin's stopped."

Wilson nodded. "Be ready if he wakes when I start." His
hands felt the bandages, still wet from the journey in the cutter.
"Cold salt water's the best he could have asked for," he said,
patiently loosening the dressing that one of the marines had
tied. "Reckon he'll have lost a deal of blood..." Then the wound
was exposed. Wilson looked at it for no more than a second
before reaching for a fresh leather tourniquet. "But he's a fit
man, an' stronger than most. Bone's badly splintered; I'm going

to cut a few inches back to give a decent stump, and leave a bit of flesh for padding. If he survives the next five minutes, we'll see him draw his pension."

King, usually sickened by any form of operation, stared in fascination. The cutting was over in what seemed like seconds, with the dead limb falling away like so much meat to be whipped out of sight by a loblolly boy. Now he watched as the surgeon's powerful fingers tied lengths of horsehair about the ends of Copley's arteries. The bloody stump was then cooled with turpentine, and a pledget bound into place with fresh bandages before the tourniquet was released. Wilson stood back from his work and reached for the bottle held ready by Skirrow. It was no more than three minutes since he had first picked up the saw.

"Will he be all right?" King asked, somewhat artlessly.

Wilson wiped his lips with the back of a blooded hand and gave him a smile. "If he's a mind, he'll be." He returned the bottle to Skirrow and reached for the fleam-toothed saw that had made such short work of Copley's leg. "It's a sharp saw," he explained. "Less chance of complications when you cut quick and clean. At the end of this action I'll have used this 'bout forty times. Them that gets cut last al'ays seem to come on with gangrene. I put it down to the blade dulling an' 'aving no time to sharpen it." King nodded. He'd heard a hundred different reasons for complications in surgery, and each sounded about as likely as another.

"Splinter, is it?" Wilson said, turning his attention to King's chest. He pressed the wound with fingers stained dark with Copley's blood. "Yes, just a small un," he muttered, standing back. "Well, no point in leaving it there. Get your shirt off and we'll have it from you." As an afterthought, he picked up the saw and wiped it on his already soiled smock before tossing it back on to the pile with the rest of his tools.

*****

Flint made his way down to the lower gundeck with little of his usual aplomb. The fact that they had returned, surviving several broadsides from a frigate and a nightmare journey in a leaking open boat, did little to ease the lingering terrors that still haunted him. His father would be on board one of the merchants, so there was no chance of running into him in the next few hours. Maybe they would meet up later; probably in some French gaol. Then, he supposed, he could get to know him, although the idea did not appeal. In the time that Flint had been at sea he had lived alongside many men and, of necessity, had learned to assess them accurately and with remarkable speed. In those brief seconds on the merchant's deck he had sensed his father's worth; the man might have appeared a hero when Flint was a lad, but with the maturity of age, he now saw him as anything but. His feet touched the warm smooth surface of the gundeck and he felt slightly better; this was his home after all, and he was once more amongst friends.

"Here he is, the wanderer returns!" The jovial greeting from O'Conner raised his spirits slightly, although it still took some effort to maintain a likeness of his old self.

"An' what have you all been up to, while I've been away?" Flint asked.

He rubbed a large hand through Matthew's hair as he smiled round at his mates.

"Ain't had much time to do nuthin'," Jenkins replied with his usual slow drawl. "Been too busy watchin' your lot racin' frog frigates!"

"How is it with Mr Pite?" Lewis asked.

"Right, did he really catch one?"

Flint's smile faded. 'fraid so. There were a few others as well, and Copley's with the surgeon now."

"What's his damage?"

237

Flint swallowed. "He was out cold last I saw of him. He'll lose a leg, that's certain; can't say more." Indeed he could not, and no one knew how near he came to trembling while he spoke of Copley's wounds.

Jenkins pulled a face. "He allay's was a rum one, that. Like as not young Pamplin will be all over 'im if he gets better, and cryin' like a toad if he don't."

Flint spurred himself back to the job in hand. Copley's place had to be filled, and with Pite gone they were without a divisional midshipman: someone else would have to appoint the new man. His eyes flicked around the men. "Klier, you'd better take Copley's station." It was a simple enough decision, but taking it raised Flint's spirits further.

The short-haired Dane was part of Copley's mess and knew the duty well. Flint turned away and began to check out the gun, his hands shaking only slightly as he inspected his priming equipment.

Since getting back to *Vigilant*, the normal routine and camaraderie from his mates had done much to restore his old trim. Even the smell of the ship, the familiar mixture of tar, bilge water and humanity, was enough to persuade him that the discovery of his father, along with the uncontrollable terror he had felt in action, were nothing more than temporary aberrations. It had to be that way: he knew for certain that if the fear did return he would be finished.

Men had turned soft during action before; it was not uncommon. He had seen it, even in those he had previously considered friends, and at the time thought himself justified in despising them. But now he knew their fears, knew and fully understood the horrors that could make a man run from battle. Understood and totally accepted how, even the threat of certain death by hanging was not enough to make some stand their ground.

"Thought you was dead meat," Matthew whispered, daringly using a phrase he had overheard only recently. Flint almost jumped, and took a grip on himself to appear natural as he turned from the gunlock. It was clear that the lad had been watching him for some time, and for a dreadful second he feared he had noticed the change: seen past the brash exterior of the old Flint, and through to the coward that was now trying to diminish him. But the boy had an odd look on his face, somewhere between concern and worship. Flint registered this, and with it came realisation.

"You don't want to worry," he said with a smile that was hardly forced at all. "It'd take more than a bunch of Frenchmen to shake me."

He might have lost the one person he had admired, but clearly there was still someone who looked up to him.

*****

The wind had backed still further and was now strong enough to raise white crests on the mounting waves. After pausing to collect the cutter's crew, Shepherd had ordered *Vigilant* round and she cut through the water with the wind still abaft the beam, heading for the oncoming frigates. These were rapidly approaching the mile and a half range that Shepherd would need to allow his twenty-four pounders, loaded as they were, to fire with any accuracy. The sun had moved down in the sky, but there would be more than enough daylight to see the job done. Over to the east the merchants were on the starboard tack, sailing for all they were worth, although the two line-of-battle ships were running down and would cut them off before long. Shepherd stood on the quarterdeck, watching the movements of each group of ships, and measuring in his mind the likely time they would take. If anything he wished the merchants would slow down, bringing the course of the liners nearer to *Vigilant*, although that would only be an advantage if he were successful in disabling the frigates. He turned his attention to these now.

They were modern affairs, with sleek lines and long hulls that were not yet a common sight in British fleets. One, the smaller of the two, was painted conventionally in dark brown, with lighter beige highlighting above the wales in a long, wide stripe. The other was clearly commanded by a dandy. Her hull was jet black, with no contrasting colour, making her appear even more swift and sinister. There was a flash of gold about the bows, and he guessed the stern would be equally ornate; clearly someone with money, or influence, captained her. Shepherd wondered if this gave him any clues to the capability of its commander, then dismissed the thought as useless speculation.

The two ships were about three cables apart, and sailing on variant courses to widen the distance between them. Clearly they intended to pass *Vigilant* to either side and hold her in their cross fire. It was a common enough move, and normally Shepherd would have been content to stake his ship's timbers against those of a frigate, even if it meant employing both batteries simultaneously. Today, however, he was not looking for a pitched battle; this had to be one strike, hard and fast; then leave, even if the job was only half done.

Dyson came and stood next to his captain. "We're making nigh on eight knots, sir." He muttered the words while looking straight ahead at the enemy, as if passing a tip to a fellow punter. Shepherd glanced up. *Vigilant* was a good ship to make eight knots under the fighting rig of topsails, jib and driver. There were plenty of seventy-fours that would need more sail to keep up the all important speed. More sail meant more men to tend it, and less to fight; that was ignoring the extra fire risk when courses were involved.

"Very good, Mr Dyson." Shepherd measured the distances once more. They would be within range in no time; at any moment he expected the bow chasers of the nearest frigate to open up.

"The guns are ready?" he asked.

"Yes, sir. Loaded with chain, and the people know their duty."

*Vigilant* carried five rounds of chain shot for every gun. Twin balls, joined with a length of chain, designed to wrap about shrouds and spars, bringing down rigging and damaging the enemy's sailing ability. Such a broadside would do little, if any, damage to the frigate's fighting power, but that was not the captain's intention.

"I wonder if I might mention a matter, sir?" Dyson still seemed intent upon the oncoming French, and Shepherd was mildly intrigued as to the subject his frosty second in command wanted to bring up at that moment.

"You have given no orders about Simpson."

Heavens, he was right. For the last few hours thoughts of their failed deserter, still presumably chained up on the punishment deck, had been far from his mind

"You would have every reason to release him, sir."

Shepherd glanced sideways, but his first lieutenant was apparently intent on the oncoming ships. The man continued: "It might be thought bad amongst the people if he were to remain under restraint, and Simpson is a trained hand who has fought well in the past." At last Dyson turned towards his captain. "Possibly you could accept his parole, sir?"

It was completely within Shepherd's powers to grant Simpson temporary release, but still he wondered how much the need for an extra hand had influenced his first lieutenant. It was almost conceivable that Dyson felt sorry for him; although it would take a cold heart indeed to send a man into battle without a chance to defend himself.

"Very good, Mr Dyson. As you say, we need every man."

"Of course, sir." Dyson threw a meaningful look at one of the midshipmen, who darted from the quarterdeck, evidently aware of his instructions without further prompting. There were captains who would be furious at such an example of his officers conspiring in secret; as it was, Shepherd was mildly amused. The rare insight into Dyson's character was also of interest, something that could be worth remembering for the future.

A shout from one of the lookouts drew their attention back to the enemy. Grey smoke was billowing from the forecastle, and a shot skipped less than half a cable from the British ship's bows.

"They've opened fire, sir!" Dyson said, unnecessarily, as the dull boom reached them.

"Yes, tell the men to take cover."

Dyson stepped forward and collected the speaking trumpet from the binnacle.

"Secure yourselves!"

The gun crews promptly stood down from their battle stations and sheltered in untidy heaps beneath the ship's stout bulwarks, while the marines folded themselves into crisp neat lines beneath the hammock stuffed netting. Someone muttered a comment, and there was a ripple of laughter, quickly cut short by a growl from a boatswain's mate. Shepherd was glad to note the spark of humour; it remained to be seen how long that would last when they stayed under fire without replying.

Another shot from the frigate, this time it hit them square on the starboard prow. Despite the fact that the bows and stern were her weakest areas, *Vigilant* was quite able to withstand a shot from that range. The wind was growing stronger, and they crept perceptibly closer, closer into the area the French had left for them, closer into the space that Shepherd had no intention of filling.

Another crash, this time followed by a scream that was quickly muffled. A shot had come over the starboard side and struck a hand who happened to look up at that moment. It was a lucky hit, and even as the man went spinning into the scuppers, Shepherd wondered if it was to be an omen.

There was a muttering amongst the men as the unfortunate was lowered down to the surgeon. Shepherd considered ordering the bow chasers to return fire. They might at least bolster morale, even if the chance of doing real damage was small. But no, he must conserve all his fire power for the time when it would do the most good. It would only be minutes now, perhaps even seconds.

*****

Below the waiting was starting to tell on some at number three gun. Most had used the pissdales at least once, and there was nervous muttering and crude comments that attracted no laughter. Matthew was sitting on the salt-box that held two ready-use charges of powder, Lewis was trying to read from a small book, and Jenkins stared aimlessly at a tobacco tin that was embossed with a horse's head. Rogers walked along the deck, cursing the absence of Pite and taking time to swear at Mintey, one of the remaining midshipmen, whenever the chance arose. Fletcher was spinning wild tales about his recent exploits to the men on his gun who, to a man, were not listening. King came up from the orlop, on his way to take position in charge of signals on the quarterdeck. His coat was draped over his shoulders and his open shirt revealed a bandage across his chest. He looked along the line of men, before acknowledging Rogers with a nod. Throughout the ship, all knew the time was very near.

The chaplain had now joined the purser and his stewards, and all stood ready to assist the surgeon, who was currently putting wide, strong stitches into the shoulder of the most recent casualty. The schoolmaster and five seamen were in the after powder room, while the cook, gunner and twelve men tended the grand magazine. Carpenter's mates had been stationed in the wings, the small corridors that ran level with the waterline and gave fast access to hull damage, and Crehan had returned to his post at the masthead.

The Navy held no grudges: a crime was considered cancelled out by punishment, as if it had never been committed. Now that his body was healing he could take up his previous rating and responsibilities. The Irishman could not forget as easily, however, and the episode with Matthew still sat heavily with him.

On one hand Crehan felt entirely justified in taking his revenge; there was no doubt that the lad had broken a cardinal, if unwritten, rule in peaching on him. But however deserved, Crehan's retaliation had all but killed the child, something that was equally against his principles. Throughout his time on the punishment deck, and in quiet moments ever since, he had tried to absolve his conscience with reasoned arguments and explanations. A good deal of unspoken regret still remained, however, and as he took up his station it was with all the solemnity of a repentant serving atonement. The French were not his enemy, and yet an inner voice told him that to fight this battle for the British would be one way of absolving the guilt that plagued him. He glanced across to Kapitan at the main and exchanged a wave with the forecastle lookout below. The sun was still quite warm. It shone on his back, which was mending well under the fresh bandages. He curled his leg about the fore topgallant mast and drew a deep sigh. Then, for the first time in ages, he began to whistle very softly.

Gregory and Tait paced the upper gundeck, ignoring the midshipmen, who whispered nervously, while Carling stood in cool contemplation, an example to his men and a credit to the bright red uniform that would make such a tempting target. On the forecastle the boatswain and two mates stood ready to protect their beloved rigging, while the quartermaster and four men were at the helm.

Also on the quarterdeck, the captain stood between Dyson and Humble, along with Sheperd's secretary Lindsay and a master's mate. Two midshipmen were positioned close by as *aides-de-camp*, ready to run messages or take the place of fallen men. And all of them, from the captain of the heads upwards, waited while the afternoon sun shone down, and the wind took them closer to the enemy.

# CHAPTER TWENTY

"MR Humble, we will tack in approximately one minute." Shepherd consulted his silver watch as if for confirmation. Dyson stood motionless beside the captain. They were hardly a mile from the frigates now, and he was surprised that the enemy had held back for so long. Clearly they were waiting for *Vigilant* to enter the crossfire area, but it was unlike the French to play such a cool hand. Both could turn and bring their broadsides to bear, and the temptation to do so must be great. Of course that would naturally force *Vigilant* round to meet the threat, and any hope of a simultaneous attack from both sides would then be forgotten.

"They appear to be saving their first broadside, Mr Dyson." The captain was mirroring his thoughts, although there was no longer any great surprise in that. "Belike they don't trust themselves to load quickly," he added. Yes, that was a point he had not considered. And a slow loading crew usually meant an inefficient one. Dyson drew private comfort from the thought, although his face remained cool and impassive.

Shepherd caught the master's eye. "Very good, Mr Humble." Humble leant back and bellowed.

"Hands to tack! Put the helm down! Let go and haul!"

The forecastle party let loose the headsail sheets and the afterguard began to pull back on the braces. There was a series of loud cracks as the sails flapped and the ship heeled slightly while the helmsmen spun the wheel, turning *Vigilant* through the wind and onto the starboard tack.

"You may open fire when you are ready, Mr Dyson."

The first lieutenant touched his hat with due solemnity before stepping forward and peering at the image of the frigate as it passed through the starboard shrouds. He raised the speaking trumpet.

"Starboard batteries, on my word!" *Vigilant* had finished the turn now and was running straight. He gave it a little longer. The gun captains would have to sight their target, and he wanted the ship to gain as much momentum as possible to give their next move a good chance of succeeding.

"Fire!"

On the lower starboard battery Flint plunged his right fist into his left hand, and after a barely perceivable delay, the gun spoke, simultaneously leaping back against the breaching line. Standing at his post mid-deck and almost behind the gun, Matthew felt a instant, savage pain in both ears, and heard little of the others as they fired.

On the upper deck the smoke was already rolling back into the eyes of the crew as each moved to service their piece as soon as it was still. Tait, standing at the starboard shrouds, climbed above the smoke to get a view of the enemy. His tall frame put him over the haze and he saw the broadside strike. The frigate almost staggered as the rain of iron peppered her masts, forcing her to roll back, even against the pressure of the wind. Then the fore topmast leaned suddenly and, as he held his breath in hope, he saw it fall away, taking spars and sails with it and dragging the main topgallant mast down to hang at a drunken angle. He turned round in excitement looking for someone with which to share the success but met only intense activity and a stream of orders from Gregory, Humble and Dyson.

"Starboard batteries, reload with chain!"

"All hands wear ship!"

"Larboard batteries prepare to open fire!"

It was asking a lot of *Vigilant* and her crew to loose off one broadside, reload those guns, take her on to the opposite tack, and stand ready to fire the guns on the other side of the ship. The men almost forgot the presence of the enemy in their haste to finish each job before the other began.

On the lower gundeck they had slightly more time, as men would only be taken from their guns if the ship needed to alter sail. Rogers stood in silence, apparently watching the work about him, while Timothy, his hand resting on the hilt of his hanger, bellowed to the men as they flew about the deck, securing the starboard guns and preparing the larboard.

*Vigilant* began to turn once more. On the quarterdeck Shepherd surveyed the damage he had caused. The sudden turn to larboard had fooled the French as he hoped it would, but what he had not anticipated was the fallen topmast. The wreckage from this was now acting as a sea anchor, holding the frigate's bows still and allowing her stern to swing round. The Frenchman's broadside would soon be pointing directly at *Vigilant* as he was forced to wear ship, exposing her vulnerable stern in the very teeth of it. In a well trained ship the enemy might even spot *Vigilant* begin to make her move, and delay firing until they could take full advantage. The broadside of a heavy frigate could cause serious damage to a line-of-battle ship if it raked her hull. Shepherd swallowed dryly as the ship swung onto the opposite tack.

From his position at the foretop masthead Crehan had the least of all to do. He stared down at the French ships while the rest of the crew were busy below him. The frigate was damaged and could be discounted as far as further voluntary movement was concerned until the wreckage was cut away. But she could still fight; indeed, apart from a couple of her forward broadside guns that were draped with debris, her fire power was unaffected. Crehan shuffled slightly, only too aware of his position should *Vigilant* suffer a similar fate to her own foremast.

Something drew his attention and brought him back to the matter in hand. Across the water there had been a change in the French line-of-battle ships. He looked up and over to Kapitan, at the main masthead. The man raised a hand in acknowledgement.

"Deck there! Enemy liners are altering course. Steering east to intercept!"

Shepherd smiled grimly to himself. He should have guessed that the French would not allow odds of two to one, when they could be raised still further in their favour. The other ships would not be on him for another twenty minutes, however; there was more than enough time to do what was necessary.

The rush of a shot took them all by surprise as it passed close amongst the command group. Dyson swore as he pitched headlong onto the deck and Shepherd staggered, for a moment completely disoriented, before falling also.

King ran over to Dyson. "The bow chasers!" he gasped as he helped the first lieutenant back to his feet. Despite the wreckage about her forecastle the frigate was able to pop at them with her forward mounted guns. Dyson brushed his coat down and looked back at the enemy, before turning to Shepherd, who lay on the deck, apparently shaken. The shot must have passed between them. It could as easily have killed most of the officers on the quarterdeck.

Shepherd mumbled something, and Dyson knelt down to him. The captain put a hand to his head, where a blue mark could be seen growing between his fingers.

"You've been hit, sir, better get below!"

Shepherd went to shake his head, and instantly closed his eyes from the pain that the movement caused. He bent forward and rested both palms on the deck for a moment, before forcing himself to his knees, and then upright, leaning heavily on Dyson. He was giddy and longed for a chance to sit down. Dyson placed a hand on his shoulder as the air began to rush back into his lungs.

"Just stunned." He explained with a slight slur to his words. He opened his eyes, smiling lopsidedly at the concerned look on Dyson's face. "Leave me a spell, if you please."

"You're certain, sir?"

"Leave me, Mr Dyson." The last words were all but shouted; Shepherd had a sudden feeling that he was about to be sick. Then the pressure in his head faded slightly and the nausea eased, although there was now a strange numbing sensation spreading down his left side.

*****

The crew of number three gun had reloaded the starboard and crossed the deck to the larboard piece. On the way they passed Lieutenant Timothy.

"We're wearing!" Jenkins informed him unnecessarily. "That'll mean showing our bum to the frogs!"

"Get to your station!" Timothy bellowed, conscious of the tension that almost made his voice crack. Still, the man was right; *Vigilant* would be in a dangerous position, especially as the enemy had yet to let loose its first broadside. He glanced across at Rogers, already hard to spot in the smoked filled gloom.

"Mr Rogers, we must secure the men!"

There was no reaction from the senior officer, and Timothy felt mildly annoyed that he was being forced into taking charge. He turned to the nearest gun crew. The guns were ready. "Lie down, shelter yourselves!" he shouted, as he took position behind the trunk of the mainmast. The men tumbled to the deck, sprawling alongside the cannon in untidy heaps. Within seconds the only sound was that of deep breathing; the entire lower gundeck was heavy with anticipation as *Vigilant* began to turn.

*****

She swung round in the last of the sunshine, a thing of beauty in a terrible world. Shepherd caught himself looking at the deep blue of the sky, and contrasting it with the green sea. Both colours were rich and luscious, with the occasional trace of white as the wind shaved a wave top, only emphasising their depth as salt does the flavour of a nut. Their stern was now fully towards the enemy, but he continued to watch the sea, the sea he had known for all his life, yet only at this point properly noticed. It was the green of her eyes, not his wife's but another. And he suddenly recalled her deep rich skin, unfashionably tanned, yet refreshing; refreshing and unspeakably attractive. Dyson was talking to him, but he had no time to waste; there were other, far more important things to think about.

*****

"For what we are about to receive..." Gregory muttered, as the ship continued to turn. Still the Frenchman was quiet, and it would only need another thirty seconds or so of peace for *Vigilant* to be safely on the opposite tack. He stared at the enemy's ports, unconscious of the fact that he had not drawn breath for some while. Then he saw a sudden stab of flame as the first gun spoke.

The broadside hit them as they were just over half way through the turn, so that only three shots actually raked the ship. Of these, two lodged into knees on the starboard side lower gundeck where buckets of water quickly cooled their latent heat. The other quenched itself in three men from number fifteen gun before smashing into the carriage and dismounting the weapon.

On deck there were more casualties. Four marines fell as the shots came over the quarter, and a master's mate lay wounded in the scuppers. A block falling from the main Burton pendant came clean through the netting and knocked out one of the afterguard, while splinters from the torn up deck and spirkettings flew amongst the men, causing a minor wound here and major one there. And still *Vigilant* turned; turned until, once more, her fighting side was facing the enemy.

"Got off lightly there, sir!" Dyson commented, although Shepherd appeared distant in thought.

"Larboard battery, prepare to fire!" It was natural that the second in command should take over now, as the captain had done everything necessary to take his ship into action.

"Fire!"

Once more the smoke rolled over the deck, as the guns erupted in a ripple of deafening crashes. On the lower gundeck Flint's hands still shook slightly as he pulled the trigger line, but as his gun barked and flew back, he pressed the vent closed with more control. This time the broadside finished off the main topgallant and took away the frigate's mizzen topmast, which fell down onto the hull like a spear, dragging the gaff of the driver with it. Now they could leave her in relative certainty that she could take no further part in the action, other than as a stationary gun platform. Dyson turned to Shepherd and gave a rare smile, his teeth unnaturally white against skin already blackened with smoke.

"One down, sir!"

Teeth unnaturally white, and her smile came so easily. He could almost taste the clear air of Surrey as they wandered through the dusk; the heavy, impotent red ball of the sun dipping below the fringe of trees that marked out their horizon. They would have too few evenings such as this before the sea called him back.

Crehan's horizon was filled with the second frigate, now turning slightly to fire her starboard guns into *Vigilant*. It would be a blow they could do little about, as their own larboard guns were still at least a minute away from being ready. Their first warning was smoke from the frigate's black hull, shortly followed by shot that began to fly amongst them.

"For'ard there, secure that larboard anchor!" Tait's voice came out in a high falsetto, but three men ran to replace the catting that had been struck by an eighteen pound ball. Another shot bit into the mainmast, nine feet above the deck. Gregory looked at it warily, but it had not penetrated past the centre line and the mast seemed sound.

"Two men down from number five, sir!" A midshipman appeared, eyes round with excitement.

"Take one from seven." Gregory looked along the deck to check for more casualties, but they were mercifully few. Amid the confusion gun captains began to signal their pieces ready; before long they would be able to return the compliment. Gregory looked towards the quarterdeck, and realised for the first time that the captain was injured.

*****

The chaplain held his Bible tightly in his left hand while his right rested on the forehead of Clarke, the boatswain's mate, who was wounded terribly in the groin. Bryant's eyes were closed in prayer as his lips moved silently.

"All right, parson, we're ready for him." Wilson's words were quietly spoken, but Bryant removed his hand immediately and opened his eyes.

"Plenty more for you over there," The surgeon nodded to an untidy line of men waiting for his services. Bryant left Clarke to the terrors that awaited him and approached the next casualty a little warily. It was Hunt, a heavily tattooed man of middle years; one of the many who had mocked and taunted him in the past. The man looked at him now, eyes filled with pain and hope; the chaplain laid a hand on his head and began to work.

"Take my arm, sir." Dyson caught his captain as he was about to fall once more. "We'll get you below." Shepherd registered the face of his second in command, but no more. The man was asking the impossible, and he had no time to waste on things that were beyond his control. There was now no sensation in the left side of his body, his vision was hazy, and his tongue felt far too large for his mouth.

Dyson swung round on a group of seamen watching in silence. Their captain, fit and well one moment, was now apparently wounded. The men appeared stunned and confused. "Help me, damn it!" Dyson roared. King, along with Lindsay, joined him and together they lowered Shepherd to the deck. King opened his captain's coat and felt about his chest for some sign of injury.

"There's no wound that I can find!" King almost shouted at Dyson.

The first lieutenant nodded briefly. "The head's badly bruised; it was probably that passing shot," he said quietly. King took in the news, ashen faced. The bruising suggested some impact, although with heavy round shot even the wind of passage could be enough. He had heard of such things causing everything from extreme physical shock to heart failure. "We'll get you below, sir," Dyson repeated, then instinctively looked forward along the upper gundeck. The guns were ready to fire, and must have been for several seconds. He moved away and stood up, momentarily forgetting Shepherd. The frigate was in clear sight, there was no time for further delay.

"You have control, Mr Gregory," he shouted, and paused to watch the shots as they pelted the masts of the frigate. An empty spar fell from the main, but nothing more. Apart from some severed lines, and possibly a few men taken from the tops, the broadside had been ineffectual. Something moved by his feet, and he looked down. Shepherd had raised himself slightly and was now resting back against Lindsay. Dyson knelt to join him.

"How is it with you, sir?"

Shepherd's eyes, open and strangely dark, seemed to be set on something far in the distance. "Time to go back now." His words were slurred and barely discernible. Dyson drew closer, trying to catch every syllable as blood began to trickle from the captain's ear. "Time to go back, else we'll be missed." He paused for a moment and a smile flickered crookedly about his face. "Out too late," he continued, apparently noticing Dyson for the first time and staring deep into his face. "We'll come again tomorrow, though, won't we?"

Dyson looked his captain straight in the eye and suddenly understood.

"Yes, yes of course we will," he said.

Then the smile twisted into a gasp, and with no further word, Shepherd died.

# CHAPTER TWENTY-ONE

DYSON pulled himself away from the fact of his captain's death with an effort that was very nearly physical. The men about him appeared in a trance, but the second frigate was still bearing down on them, and a further broadside could be expected at any moment.

"Mr Humble, take the ship round, I want her running south." This would give them more room, and take them further away from the oncoming battle ships. Next he stepped forward and shouted to the lieutenant standing in the waist. "Mr Gregory, we will be passing close to the enemy; we'll deliver one more broadside with chain, then it's round for the lower battery and canister for the top!" The time for hitting at spars had passed.

Dyson had taken up command instinctively, and the men responded in the same way. Now that he had time to think, however, the enormity of what lay ahead appalled him. To fight a battle as second in command carried nothing like the responsibility he now held, and he had to stop himself from pacing the deck like an excited child. Another thought occurred, and he swung round to single out a likely candidate. His eyes fell on the captain's secretary.

"Mr Lindsay, kindly deal with the captain." Lindsay's face was white with shock, but many years of discipline had instilled in him an automatic response to orders. With the help of two men from one of the quarterdeck carronades he picked up the body and carried it back under the poop. After clearing for action the captain's quarters were merely an extension to the quarterdeck, although the small chart locker was empty and relatively uncluttered. Without a word they deposited the body inside, closing the door on it with a sense of finality that was shared by all who had time to watch.

The frigate was keeping station with them now, and running very nearly parallel. She was weighty for her class, probably mounting at least forty eighteen pounders. Her timbers would be more fragile, however; and even allowing for the heavier classification of French gun, she was no match for *Vigilant*. Dyson watched without surprise as her hull came round, until she was on a converging course.

"She's trying to get in close to board!" It was King's voice, pitched higher than usual, although he clearly had a grip on the situation. Dyson glanced down at the gun crews, as they hurled themselves back on the tackle, hauling their guns into the firing position. It was what he would have done in the enemy captain's shoes. The French were known to carry large crews, often fortified with soldiers; the men of a big frigate would be quite capable of overwhelming a small line-of-battle ship, and there would be hardly time for more than one broadside to see them off.

Gregory had his sword clear of its scabbard, waiting for the chance to raise it. A shout came from the midshipman at the main companionway; the lower deck was ready, and the sword went up. Then, with a series of horrible crashes, the first shots of the French broadside began to strike them.

The range was less than half a mile, but despite this *Vigilant* took the broadside well; accepting the punishment on her heavy frame like a prize fighter might an unexpected blow. In two places bulwarks were pierced, but neither was important to the integrity of her hull. A man was cut down on the forecastle, and a boy on the quarterdeck fell, knocked senseless by a flying hammock. Ironically this had been struck clear from the netting where it had been placed to absorb small arms fire. A marine was hit by the blast of a shot and fell back, dropping his musket on the deck where it fired, the ball embedding itself in a bulwark, dangerously close to the boatswain. Immediately the line closed up to fill the gap, while Corporal Jackson turned and touched his hat to the bemused petty officer.

At the foretop masthead Crehan felt the timbers beneath him shudder. The enemy still had the windward gauge, and most of the broadside had fallen low. But one of the last shots, whether by accident or design, had hit the fore topmast, level with the topsail yard, and, more important to Crehan, below his perilous station. Again the mast trembled, and he grasped on to the shrouds for their doubtful support. He would have to make a dash for it; a back stay was the obvious choice, although that would mean being dependent on the topgallant mast holding until he reached the deck. The alternative was to throw himself down the ratlines and make for the fore top. That would give him relative safety, and he could continue to the deck by a stay if he wished. He glanced about him, strangely unwilling to give up his post, although there would be little use for a fore lookout in the next few hours. Kapitan was still at his station, and everything would be horribly plain from the deck. Cautiously he swung his body round, but the mast gave an alarming lurch. He froze, frightened to move. There were a series of loud groans as the shrouds and stays stretched. The deck below seemed far away and yet ridiculously close. He moved once more, and once more the mast quivered. Then, throwing caution to the wind, he began to scramble down the ratlines. He was less than a third of the way to safety when the shrouds slackened, and the mast gave way.

"Fore t'gallant's goin'!" The boatswain roared, pointing to the tangle of spars already crashing down towards the deck. They dragged with them the fore topsail, which draped over the forecastle like a shroud. "Damage party: axes!"

The waisters and forecastle men surged forward with a will, hacking at the limp shrouds and roughly throwing the tackle and torn canvas overboard. The fore topgallant mast, fore top yard and the remains of the crosstrees went the same way, and within ninety seconds there was little sign of any wreckage on the deck, and none whatsoever of Crehan.

Then they could reply. Gregory was ready, sword held high in the air. Dyson nodded, the blade came down, and *Vigilant* responded.

They were close enough to see the damage in detail. The chain shot reeked havoc amongst the delicately balanced rigging of the frigate, causing blocks, tackle and in two cases soldiers to hang for a moment, before crashing down to the deck, or the ocean beside it. The gaff of the driver sagged as its lift was shot away, and the jib fell down upon the bowsprit like so much laundry from a broken line.

The French ship slowed, the wind taken from her sails, then her yards began to creep round and the hull leant in response to a kick from the rudder. She was turning harder towards them and soon settled on a collision course.

Dyson swallowed, clearly his opposite number had planned this, as the evolution ran smoothly, despite the damage just inflicted. Now he was faced with the choice of continuing as he was and taking the frigate amidships, or altering heading or speed and having his stern or bows raked. There was a third option; he could turn towards the enemy and attempt to pass and capture the windward advantage. Then he could take her with the unfired starboard guns, and at that range the damage would be devastating. Dyson considered this for no more than a second; his men were unprepared and he doubted that they would be capable of such a manoeuvre at short notice, especially with the fore topsail missing. Besides, the advantage they would gain would be nothing to what might be lost, for to fail halfway would leave them in irons, the ship entirely at the mercy of the waves and current, with no steerage way to bring her back to the wind. She would be an open and easy target.

"Back mizzen tops!" The men responded to the command immediately, and *Vigilant* slowed up with groans of protest from her stays and shrouds.

The decrease in speed would bring the collision forward, giving his gunners the best possible opportunity of doing damage. The frigate should strike them in less than two minutes. Men sweated as the hot guns were run out once more. The angle had increased, they would be aiming almost straight at her bows; the two ships would hit and lock before a second shot was possible.

Gregory looked at the enemy forecastle, already filled with men: some soldiers, some seamen, variously armed with pikes, axes, swords and various fire arms, and all making ready to leap on to their deck. He glanced at Dyson. There was no time for a request; he would have to take the initiative.

"Fire when your guns bear, men, then make ready for boarders!" Broadsides were all very well, but they slowed the rate of fire to that of the slowest crew. This way their guns could be discharged with the least possible delay, allowing the men to prepare themselves for the oncoming assault.

On the lower larboard battery, number three gun was one of the fastest, and Flint was already sighting his piece. Timothy appeared next to him, staring through the port at the approaching enemy.

"That's your target!" He shouted to the entire battery. "Take her foremast out and we'll keep the buggers off!"

Timothy withdrew from the gunport as a small cheer ran through the waiting gunners. The feeling on the lower deck was good; the men had spirit and would fight well. His eyes fell on Rogers, standing motionless beside the trunk of their own foremast. Timothy grinned, his blood was up and he was spoiling for a fight, but the older man gave him a cold look and turned away.

Flint was concentrating; all thoughts of fear and disappointment had been postponed as aiming at the

Frenchman became a totally absorbing occupation. He had set the gun slightly ahead of the target, and was now watching as the mast slowly came into his field of vision. Silently he counted, measuring the speed of the ship, to anticipate the correct time to fire. Then, several seconds ahead of the ideal moment, he stood to one side and counted to three. He pulled the trigger line with a firm, even pressure and watched with satisfaction as the gun flew back.

\*\*\*\*\*

Carling was ready, sword and pistol drawn, beside the forecastle detachment of marines. Sergeant Bate had started them firing in volleys as soon as the frigate was within range, and now the men were busily reloading and shooting at a rate equal to that of a crack field unit. To his right seamen were assembling, armed with pikes, cutlasses and axes. *Vigilant's* main guns were firing spasmodically as each gun was ready and found its target. Carling imagined he could see splinters flying from the frigate's bows, although that could be merely imagination, or wishful thinking. The enemy's bowsprit glided closer, and shots from her marksmen began to thud into the netting about them. King joined him from the quarterdeck, his dirk drawn and young face set in an odd expression that might be eagerness or fear.

"Some will fall coming across," the marine officer told him in a steady, professional voice. "And some will be cut down by my men. Those that make it are all yours, but don't get carried away and follow them back." King turned to him and opened his mouth to speak. Then a shot cracked into the frigate's foremast, and it began to give way.

The British seamen waiting at the bulwarks cheered as the entire mast dropped in a tangle of line and sail. Those stationed in the tops fell as their platform was taken from them, their screams all but drowned by the crash of timber and tearing fabric.

"A fortunate shot!" Carling grinned at King. "About the first bit of luck we've had so far!"

The wreckage dropped about the frigate, almost stopping her in the water and forcing the stern round. Gregory yelled at his crews, who quickly returned to their guns and began to reload with a vengeance.

*****

On the quarterdeck Dyson allowed himself two seconds to consider the frigate before looking back to the battle ships that were running down on them. They would be in range within ten minutes; there was no time to finish the frigate off.

"Make sail!" he snapped at the master. The marines were still taking pot shots at the men on the wreckage, while the gun crews slaved at their pieces. "I want the forecourse on her, and rig a replacement jib!" The forecourse would correct some of the balance lost by the fore topsail, and the jib would be needed to carry out the manoeuvres that Dyson knew would be necessary.

There was a distinct pause after Humble bellowed his order. The men at the nearest quarterdeck carronade glared rebelliously back at him, and Dyson was conscious of a sudden atmosphere of disapproval that was almost tangible. Taking hands away from the upper deck guns to set more sail appeared a terrible waste when they had the enemy at their mercy. The extra speed would hardly justify the effort, and another two or three full broadsides would see the Frenchman wrecked. But only he was in command, and only he knew of the almost painful urge to put as much sea room as possible between them and the approaching liners.

"Get to it, you lubbers!" Gregory's voice cut through the squeal of pipes; clearly he had noticed the men's reluctance and was hitting back with true lower deck logic. "Plenty of time to finish her off when we've dealt with t'others!"

Some gave a cheer, and all went to their work with added will. Dyson caught Gregory's eye and nodded his thanks; Gregory nodded back, and through the smoke and confusion, touched his hat in a token salute.

*****

On the lower gundeck the guns were being swabbed and loaded with a will never found in exercise. Matthew dumped a charge with a loader before spinning round to start back to the main companionway. They had suffered a number of casualties, and the intricate loading chain had almost broken down as boys were being called to make up deficiencies in gun crews. Acting alone, Timothy had organised a different system, with a fewer number of lads running for the main hatch, where two men, under the direction of a midshipman, were handing out the charges passed up from below. Each took a double load, thus halving the number of journeys, and slightly easing the confusion. A small queue of panting boys lined waiting for their charges, stoically ignoring the screams of the wounded that came up from the orlop. Jake was at the end, and Matthew smacked his back as he took place behind him.

"How's it with you?" Matthew asked. Jake grinned, his face was blackened, he had a cut to his shoulder and blood was smudged on his shirt.

"Lost our loader!" he shouted, although Matthew could hardly make out the words. "An' number fifteen's out of action; carriage broke and men all smashed to pap!"

Matthew nodded. He too had seen sights that would have appalled him normally. Ever since the first gun had fired he had been largely deaf, and it was rather the same with his other senses. They were numb, paralysed, deadened; whatever atrocities were being committed, he only registered a fraction, and even then they seemed unable to affect him.

"Buzz is the cap'n's down," said another as he joined the queue.

"That right?"

"Stopped one early on," the boy confirmed.

It was their turn now, and a grizzled hand passed them the charges. Matthew snatched at his twenty pounds of high explosive and rushed back to his guns.

Flint was laying the gun when he arrived, and Matthew stood to one side, waiting for it to fire.

"Captain's dead!" he muttered to Lewis. "Does that mean we got to surrender?"

"Nay, lad." the man replied with a grin. "We goes on. It's not a game of chess!"

Then the gun spoke, and the process began again.

*****

The extra speed was taking them away from the frigate; in no time they would be unable to fire on her. Dyson looked up at the sails, now filled and pulling well, and back at the pursuing line-of-battle ships. The first part of the plan had worked moderately well; both frigates were temporarily disabled, whereas apart from the loss of the fore topyard and fore topgallant mast, *Vigilant* had suffered remarkably little structural damage. The French liners were in full pursuit, every yard they made taking them that much further away from the escaping merchants. A jet of smoke came from the bows of the nearest, and seconds later a splash erupted a cable's length off their stern.

A wardroom steward, carrying a pewter tray loaded with mugs, appeared on the quarterdeck and approached the group of officers. King took one and sipped cautiously. It was lemonade, sour and strong. Without another thought he drained the mug.

Humble caught Dyson's attention.

"Bosun's rigged the fore topmast stays'l," he said, his voice unnaturally loud. "It's slung lower than normal, but he reckons it'll serve well enough."

"Very good, take her on to the starboard tack," Dyson replied, also accepting a mug. "I want the wind well on our quarter." Their speed was all important, yet with the rigging already weakened, he dare not risk more sail.

Gregory had left his guns in the waist and now joined them on the quarterdeck. "What do you intend?" he asked Dyson, almost conversationally.

"Run for as long as I can," the first lieutenant replied. "But when they come into range I will have to turn and fight."

Gregory nodded, and accepted a mug of lemonade from the steward. "Will you strike?"

It was the question Dyson had asked himself a dozen times since the captain's death. "Yes, when it comes to it," he said simply, before sipping at his drink. British line-of-battle ships were not known for surrendering. Dyson would always be remembered as the man who yielded to the French, and in later years there would be few who would give any consideration to the odds he now faced.

Gregory nodded, and handed his mug back with a grim smile. "We'll take a few with us though, eh?"

*****

On the orlop, the chaplain was closer to God than he had ever come in his life. The line of wounded now consisted of twenty-two, with twelve still waiting to meet the surgeon. Bryant, who had long since abandoned his Bible, was administering neat rum with the care and devotion he had previously given to communion wine.

The man in front of him had a splinter in his leg. It stuck out, bold and black, through the torn white duck trousers. The least he could do was make the wound ready for the surgeon; he began to carefully cut away the bloody material with a pair of scissors. Skirrow appeared from out of the gloom and knelt down next to him. Both knew that most of the waiting men needed attention without delay.

"Surgeon says he'll be a while, an' I'm to do what I can for the rest."

"I understand," Bryant said, and he did, all too clearly. "Can you operate?"

Skirrow's teeth gleamed in half light. "No, sir. Mister Wilson don't trust me to cut toenails."

It was exactly what Bryant had been expecting. He had been placed on board *Vigilant* for a reason; that had never been in doubt. Now his purpose had been revealed he was almost relieved, however ghastly the calling might be.

"If you clean the wounds and assist, I'll see what can be done." His father's estate included several farms, and in his youth he had regularly helped, both during the lambing season, and whenever an animal injured itself and needed stitching. Though no expert, he knew a little of wounds, and he didn't suppose a human body would be so very different from that of a sheep.

"You're sure, sir?"

Bryant nodded.

"We'll need tools, and more light."

"Aye, sir; there's free space next to t'surgeon."

"Very well," he said, before continuing with rare authority. "Get a move on!"

Skirrow was right; four sea chests were set out next to Wilson, presumably for just such an emergency. Bryant moved the lanthorns until the light was more or less on the place, then Skirrow and another appeared with the wounded seaman hung between them.

They lowered him down on to the operating area. Bryant looked at the black splinter for a second or so, before picking up a small knife. On wooden ships splinters accounted for a large number of casualties. The natural barbs of the grain meant that they could rarely be removed the same way they had entered, and this one was no exception. It ran down the length of the leg, deep into the muscle; Bryant would need to cut it out sideways. He looked up and for a second caught the eye of Wilson, the surgeon, literally up to his arms in his current patient.

"Do what you can, they won't get better on their own." the surgeon's voice was strained, and his manner almost brusque. "You can call me if you have a real problem," he added, before returning to his work.

Bryant glanced down at the leg once more. He was strangely confident, and yet knew little of what was expected of him. Skirrow understood the procedure, and began to pour spirit on to the wound. The patient tensed, gave a low moan, and Bryant began to cut.

\*\*\*\*\*

"Five minutes should do it!" Gregory told Tait, as they looked back at the French liners. Already shots from the enemy's bow chasers were straddling the ship, and it was just a question of time before the broadside guns would be able to reach them. "Dyson'll be taking us round to starboard, so we'll only have the one to fight for a while."

The manoeuvre would mean a long wear round, then holding *Vigilant* as close to the wind as possible.

"What if they turn with us?"

Gregory snorted; the stress of battle had awakened his seaman roots, and he spoke with the guttural parlance of the lower deck. "Like as much they will, then we gets both broadsides to our one. Mind, they'll needs to be right spry to follow, an' careful not to bunk the other when they does."

"How are you loaded, Mr Gregory?" Dyson's voice came from the quarterdeck.

"Round on the lower deck, sir. Though I took the liberty of switching back to chain, seeing as how we are losing the range for canister."

"Very good." Dyson looked over to the binnacle. It was reassuring to be able to leave details such as the shotting of the guns to competent men. Close hauled, they should be able to manage 300 degrees, with the wind as it was. That would take them across the starboard bows of the leading ship. If they were to mask the other, it would mean holding their current course for a while longer and suffering a few broadsides in the meantime. The sun was falling lower in the sky; he glanced at his watch: well past four o'clock. Another shot passed close overhead, knocking off the galley chimney with a loud metallic clang. A murmur of laughter rose from the men. They were still in good spirits; just how long their morale would last was difficult to say, but he had a suspicion he would find out before the day was done.

# CHAPTER TWENTY-TWO

CAPTAINE *de vaisseau* Duboir was also looking at his watch. They had wasted time and made mistakes; he wondered vaguely how much longer it would take to capture the English warship.

"You have an appointment, maybe, Captain?" Lafluer asked. He was equally aware of the situation, although in his mind their lack of success was entirely due to bad luck.

A bow chaser cracked briefly, the shot eventually falling alongside the English ship. Lafluer grunted at yet more proof of his ill fortune. "Cannot we show more speed?" he asked, of no one in particular.

Duboir looked up to where topsails and topgallants were pulled tight. He could order courses to be reset, but the cordage supplied at Brest had not proved reliable, and he also had doubts about the strength of the spars. There seemed little sense in taking risks which might prove disastrous when they were overhauling the enemy with the canvas they were already showing.

"Rouault is falling back." It was a change for someone else to be the target of Lafluer's anger. "Signal to him to keep better station!"

Duboir nodded to the *enseigne*, who consulted his signal book. The other ship, sailing several cables from them was certainly well on their quarter, but that was by no means poor station keeping. Rouault was an experienced officer who had commanded a warship for longer than either of them. He knew the danger of sailing line abreast, when they might need to manoeuvre at any moment. In addition, to keep slightly behind would be an advantage when they closed with the enemy. There would be less chance of shots passing through the English hull and hitting their own.

They were level with the second of the damaged frigates now. Her crew had managed to clear away most of the wreckage and were in the process of rigging a spare main yard in place of their missing foremast. Duboir took the opportunity to cast an astute eye on the admiral as he inspected the damage. His face was red with anger, and he brusquely brushed aside the waves of the frigate's crew like so many annoying insects.

"Imbeciles! Two powerful ships and together they could knock away only a single spar!"

"The enemy is damaged, Admiral." Duboir felt obliged to defend the frigate's crew. "She has taken punishment, and even now she runs!"

"Pah!" Lafluer turned away in impatience.

Duboir walked over to the side rail to look at the maimed frigate. She would be able to sail again, possibly even by nightfall, but not cross the Atlantic. The other was in no better state, and now both line-of-battle ships were heading on a course that may well place them in the same position.

The convoy had proved anything but the easy capture Lafluer had predicted; consequently he had lost an important part of his force, and was all set to risk the rest, just because he allowed his anger to get the better of him. Even now they could turn back, collect the merchant ships, and head off to join Canard. The frigates could fight the English, stay at sea, or attempt to make their way to port, dodging the blockading squadrons. He did not care greatly for the small craft; it was proper warships like his own *Lozere* that won battles. It was these that Canard wanted, and these that Lafluer would be risking in his quest to sink one small English vessel.

The frigate was now some way behind, and Duboir turned from the sight. It would not be so bad if they were to tackle the English sensibly. He had no practical experience in these matters of course, but the books he had read on strategy had taught him a good deal. With the advantages they had of wind and power it should be a simple matter to force the English to concede. As it was, Lafluer seemed determined to keep up a stern chase. Admittedly they were edging closer; soon their broadsides would reach, then presumably they would turn and open fire, only to continue the chase when the English crept out of range once more. In the meantime both ships were being pulled further from their frigates, and deeper into Biscay. He may have little experience of battle, but as a seaman the area was well known to him. The wind was moist, another storm could come at any time, and with the ships scattered and the crews untrained, it may easily see the entire enterprise wrecked.

"Captain, do you not think we can hit her with our broadside guns yet?"

The question Duboir had been waiting for had finally arrived. Yes, they could; both ships could wear and open fire without any trouble. He hesitated before he spoke, knowing that what he said would not be approved of.

"We can turn whenever you wish, Admiral, but it would be a mistake." The look that Lafluer directed at him was eloquent enough to dispense with words. Duboir was committed however, and continued with no more than a pause. "There are better ways to take the English ship."

Lafluer's eyebrows rose. "Better ways?"

"Yes, Admiral. I have one in mind which will account for it with little loss or risk to ourselves."

There was a moment's pause while Lafluer digested this rare piece of insubordination. Watching, Duboir was confident of his position. Were this conversation to be taking place in private, Lafluer would have had little hesitation in demolishing him along with his suggestions. But on the quarterdeck, in plain sight and hearing of several officers, the admiral could not resort to such bullying tactics. Besides, he was only offering advice; and as senior captain of the squadron he had a right to voice an opinion on the situation. Something of this must have occurred to Lafluer, for he continued in a conciliatory tone, although his face was raw with indignation.

"If you have a suggestion, Captain, I would be only too glad to hear of it."

Duboir's mouth was now quite dry, but he had started something he was determined to finish, if not for the good of the squadron, then for his own self esteem. He forced a smile on to his face.

"I shall be pleased to explain."

*****

"They're altering course!" King turned to the group of officers on the quarterdeck, before looking back, to be certain of what he had seen. Sure enough, one of the liners had turned several points to larboard, while the flagship continued the stern chase. No, the flagship was shedding sail; her topgallants were being gathered in even as they watched.

"Flagship's slowing, sir," Humble uttered the words without emotion. "Looks like they're trying to keep station with us."

Dyson regarded the flagship for some time before nodding gravely. There was no doubt about it, the reduction in canvas had taken the advantage from the French ship, which was now just keeping pace with them. He turned his attention to the other: still gaining, even though her course took her further away. Dyson measured the distance carefully. By the time she was level she would be just out of range of their lower twenty-four pounders. The French mounted heavier guns, however; thirty-six pounders which, due to their continental ways of measurement, actually threw a shot that weighed in at nearer forty. *Vigilant* would certainly be in range of those heavy pieces, and with little chance of replying, unless he was rash enough to attempt a close action.

He took a turn up and down the deck. There were a number of options. He could steer towards the other line-of-battle ship, thus keeping the range tight, although that would only allow the flagship to close on the other side. He could attempt to out run them both, risk further damage by showing more canvas, in an effort to at least keep pace until bad light rescued them. Or he could alter course, wear about and turn on the flagship, like a terrier rounding on a charging bull.

His legs ached; he realised that he had been on deck for almost the whole day, and must have paced several miles since the captain died. He paused, bending his knees to ease them, inadvertently catching the master's eye as he looked about the deck. Humble clearly took the eye contact as an invitation to share his thoughts, and strode towards him. Dyson cleared his throat, unsure of his exact position. Certainly, with the captain's death, he had charge of the ship, but considering the circumstances which gave him command, he would probably be wise to consult with the master.

No. A wave of determination broke over him and he began to pace once more, apparently unconscious of Humble, who had almost reached him. The master may be a more experienced sailor, but he could not fight battles; that was Dyson's job. And it was a job that he was going to do alone.

*****

"Frenchie's comin' up on our larboard counter." Jenkins could see the seventy-four clearly through the gunport. "Reckons they're 'tending to close on us like a clam!"

Lewis nodded. "Not much we can do about that. I heard the fore topmast's weakened, so we can't put no more canvas up."

"An' if we alter course to starboard it will only slow us more!" This was Simpson, the man who had struck Critchley, and was now rated to number three gun to make up their numbers. Matthew eyed him in awe, his red pigtail and bold tattoos were impressive enough, but to a youngster the fact that he would surely hang as soon as they touched port gave the man a strange aura; it was as if he were already dead.

Simpson noticed Matthew's eyes on him and smiled at the lad. A few days back Matthew would have been embarrassed, but now he grew bold. "Where d'ja get them tattoos?" he asked.

"Same place you sees 'em now." Jenkins answered in a level tone. He was finding Simpson's presence hard to take, and reacted by keeping his old friend at a distance.

Simpson grinned readily, and pointed to the mermaid that trailed decorously down his right arm. "Young Gloria here, she joined me at Cadiz. An' her sister"—her sister was draped about his left—"she came along at New York, back when we owned it."

"Better make sure they never meet!" warned Jenkins, although no one seemed to hear him.

"Did it hurt?" Matthew was round-eyed with awe.

"Nah. I got some badness in the one at New York, but it righted itself 'ventually."

Jenkins was starting to feel left out. He opened his shirt to reveal a large eagle etched in blue across his chest, wings spread out to reach his armpits. "If you want to see tattoos, this is a real un!"

Matthew was impressed. "Wow! How long you had that?"

"Since it were an egg!" The laughter spread to the gun crews on either side, and for a moment, none were thinking about French flagships, or the prospect of being killed. Other men began baring various pieces of their bodies and yarning about the time they got theirs, until Lieutenant Timothy, drawn to the larboard side by the disturbance, felt bound to intercede.

"All right, that's enough of the flesh show," but he found himself grinning despite himself. "When y're all properly dressed, we got an action to fight!"

The men returned to their stations in a good humour, and Timothy withdrew once more.

Matthew squatted down on the deck, next to his powder carriers. Lewis was near him and he caught his eye.

"Why do they have tattoos?" he asked, in a soft voice.

Lewis shrugged. "Comes from the Polynesian Islands, mark of manhood or somthin'. Never cared for the idea much myself. Navy allows them 'cause it's a way of telling one body from another. Most men don't want to go to the bottom unknown, even though there'll be precious few who'll care about them afterwards. An' some," he looked pointedly at Simpson who was now talking with Jenkins, "some won't need no 'dentifying when they gets to take their trip."

\*\*\*\*\*

On the quarterdeck Humble had turned back from Dyson, conscious of the snub and yet unoffended. He had known the first lieutenant for two years and was impressed with his strength of character. With the captain gone, he had thought Dyson might want advice, although the fact that he did not was more a source of relief to him than resentment. The French seventy-four was coming up fast, and he suspected that they were close to being within range of her great guns. They would need to close a good three cables more before their own lower deck battery could reply. Behind them the flagship was keeping station, watching for any change of direction on their part. She was content, it seemed, to shadow the English ship, and allow her consort to do the business. Dyson was still pacing, his face totally void of expression.

A steward appeared, this time laden with mugs of coffee. The man had taken advantage of the relative lull to heat a pot on the pantry spirit stove. Humble took his and sipped it gratefully, noticing how the servant diplomatically ignored the absorbed Dyson, even though he was barely feet away. A shout from the masthead drew their attention, and Humble was just in time to see threads of smoke carrying away by the wind. Seconds later a ball ricocheted off the water just in front of *Vigilant* and about half a cable short. The faint boom that followed barely reached them. It would be a sighting shot to see if they had their range. The French ship seemed to creep closer as he watched. They could expect one, maybe two more; then the broadsides would begin in earnest.

\*\*\*\*\*

On board the *Lozere*, Duboir was relieved to the point of feeling faintly smug. The plan that he had all but forced on Lafluer was panning out nicely. The English ship was now locked between the wind and the guns of the *Savarez*, Rouault's ship, while they stood behind as back stop and interested spectators. Lafluer had left the deck as soon as it appeared the English were doomed, and for the first time since leaving Brest, Duboir felt properly in command of his *Lozere*. He watched the shot from the *Savarez* as it skipped willingly towards the enemy. They would be close enough in no time. If he commanded *Savarez*, he would have no hesitation in turning a point to starboard and opening fire almost straight away.

He pulled up short as he remembered that this was the first time he had been in command of a ship in action. Possibly his recent success was going to his head. It was a fault; one he must beware of in the future.

An *aspirant* began to make notes in a small book. Probably this was just for his personal journal, though Duboir wondered if Lafluer had ordered minutes taken of the action in an attempt to discredit him. Duboir began to walk across the quarterdeck with an attitude of unconcern on his face. He had presented his plan in such a public way because he wanted to ensure it would be acted upon. There was still the very real possibility that Lafluer would take the credit for himself, however; and in a cruise that should last several months, the admiral would have plenty more occasions to criticize his conduct. France was still effectively under martial law, and Duboir knew the penalties a poor report from Lafluer might attract.

The gun rang out again, although this time he did not catch the shot. Possibly it had even hit. The *aspirant* began to scribble once more and he was about to question the boy when something caught his eye.

It was the English ship: no longer was she heading with the wind one point large; her yards were moving, and she was coming round. Yes, he could see the hull lengthening as she turned from Rouault's fire. The ship began to wear when the ripple of Rouault's first broadside burst from *Savarez*, and was almost fully about as the shots fell. Clearly the manoeuvre had been well timed, as most fell half a cable short and behind her moving hull. Now the enemy was bearing down on them, heading for his own *Lozere*. Duboir drew breath. His ship, with nearly a hundred guns, many far larger than anything the English had to offer, was more than a match for a mere sixty-four. Still, the Royal Navy had a reputation for hard fighting, and there was something about the way this particular ship had been handled that revealed her commander to be a man of determination and skill.

"Send for the admiral!" He almost spat at the young *aspirant*. "Say the enemy is turning towards us, and ask him, no, tell him that his presence is required on deck!" Duboir had no intention of engaging a line-of-battle ship without his superior by his side. Despite her damaged foremast the English were making excellent speed, and the acute angle meant that he would not be able to open fire until they were less than two cables apart.

Lafluer appeared and glared at Duboir, his face a mixture of anger and fear.

"Order Rouault to intercept!" he bellowed. Duboir turned to the *enseigne de vaisseau* in charge of signals, and nodded.

Lafluer was breathing heavily as he stood next to him.

"We must turn!" Duboir all but shouted at his superior. "If we do so now we can fire two, maybe three broadsides into her before she reaches us!".

Lafluer watched the enemy ship bearing down. Despite the damage, she carried herself well, as with most English ships. But three broadsides from his guns would make a difference to that solid hull.

"Do it!" he shouted back. "Let her feel the weight of our metal! Tell the *lieutenants* to open fire as soon as their guns bear!"

# CHAPTER TWENTY-THREE

TIMOTHY looked hard at the midshipman.

"You're sure?" he asked.

"Yes sir, that's what Mr Dyson said." A creak from the mainmast seemed to confirm it: they were going about. Timothy turned from the youth and brought his hands up to his mouth to bellow.

"D'you hear there? Starboard battery! Man your guns and train them for'ard!"

The midshipman who had delivered the message watched as men sprang into action and began crossing the deck to clear the starboard guns for action. The gun layers were just beginning to insert their hand spikes to heave the heavy carriages over as the boy made his way back to the quarterdeck, amazed at the activity his message had created, and terrified in case he had made some dreadful mistake in its delivery.

"We's goin' about!" Jenkins muttered as he kicked a splinter of oak into the scuppers. "Takin' on a three-decker, now there's a thing!"

Sure enough the ship began to heel as the yards and rudder pulled her over onto the reciprocal course.

Lewis was peering though the gunport. "We're heading for the Frenchie all right!"

"How's she bearing?" It was Flint this time, all trace of humour absent from his voice.

"No change, still comin' right for us!"

"Not going to wear?"

"Not yet."

"But why should she?" Matthew asked, of no one in particular.

"If she keeps as she is we meet her that much quicker." Lewis had turned back from the port. "An' neither of us can fire broadsides 'til we're almost on top of one another."

Simpson nodded "But if she turns we gets the benefits of her three decks pointin' at us while we run down on her." He gave Matthew a brief smile. "The closer we comes the better, then we're left with at least the prospect of reply!"

Matthew smiled back, and naturally turned to Flint for further reassurance. He was surprised to note that his friend's face remained deadly serious and there was a far away look in his eye that neither Matthew nor any of the others had noticed before.

*****

On deck the men were quiet. *Vigilant* steadied onto her new course and began to take up speed. In the waist Gregory was watching the flagship so intently that the bark of their own bow chaser took him by surprise.

"Level and short!"

Gregory made his way to the forecastle, where Tait had both guns under his command.

"Fire!"

The second eighteen pounder went off, and they watched in silence as the shot fell, barely feet from the flagship's bows.

The two officers exchanged glances. "Extreme range but we might reach them with the great guns," Gregory commented.

Tait nodded. His fair hair made an odd contrast to his face, which was now quite blackened. He pointed forward suddenly. "Hold there, she's coming round!"

Sure enough the hull of the French ship was lengthening, and her yards swung as she began to present her broadside.

"Now we's for it!" Gregory said grimly, as the triple line of gunports turned to greet them.

The first bow chaser was ready again, and at a word from Tait spat once more at the slowing ship. There was no sight or sound of a splash.

"A hit!" Tait hissed. The shot must have stuck the French ship, or passed over. Then her unused sprit yard sagged in confirmation.

"An' not quite maximum 'levation!" The gun captain added, grinning toothlessly at the officers.

Gregory nodded. "We can reach her now!" He looked back to the quarterdeck, although Dyson could not be seen. "You carry on, I'll go tell the senior!"

*****


Dyson was on the quarter deck, although hidden by the trunk of.the mizzenmast. He was well aware of the situation. For some while the officers and men had been keeping him under covert surveillance, clearly expecting a change of course.

"Steady as she goes," he said in a quiet voice. The quartermaster repeated the instruction, and King was exchanging looks with Humble when Gregory bounded up to the binnacle.

"We got her range!" he shouted. "She's steering into the wind and coming round, but we can reach her with our lower deck!"

Dyson eyed him coolly. There was no private way to prick his bubble. "Thank you, Mr Gregory, I am aware of that."

Gregory faltered for a moment. "Well, why don't we turn? We can fire on her!"

"We can," Dyson confirmed, "but I feel it better that we do not."

The look of incredulity on Gregory's face would have been comical, were it not for the circumstances. "But she'll be opening up on us directly!" he persisted.

"Yes, I expect you're right, Mr Gregory. But we will hold this course a while longer." Dyson turned away, discouraging further comment while his stomach heaved against what he was about to do.

Gregory was right; they could bear round to larboard now and open with their lower deck guns. Pound for pound they might be out-gunned, but that could be balanced to some extent with their firing speed, which was almost certain to be faster. The two ships were not equal in timbers, however; the three-decker, possibly Toulon built and from Adriatic oak, would boast scantlings that could withstand their fire well: certainly better than *Vigilant* might handle shot from the heavier French guns. By maintaining his present course he was gambling against losing any vital equipment aloft, so that they could close with the three-decker. If they made it that far, he had a chance to play his next card. This, he knew, was bold, bordering on the reckless in fact; so much so that he hesitated even to think of it.

"Enemy's opened fire!"

The call from the masthead alerted them to the ripple of flame that was now spreading along all three decks of the flagship. Dyson waited, resisting the temptation to order a hasty turn of the wheel. After a second or two the salvo passed, peppering where they would have been if he had ordered them round. He glanced at his watch. The French were unlikely to fire again for a good three minutes; that meant there would be two more broadsides before he intended to reply, and he could expect no further confusion as to his course. Two broadsides and, with the range closing, each would be more accurate and devastating than the one before.

Dyson's plan soon became clear as *Vigilant* clawed her way towards the French flagship. She approached with her bow slanted towards the enemy's stern, the oblique angle giving extra protection from the murderous broadsides. Her bowlines drew the canvas tight, catching the strengthening wind and forcing her over until Timothy decided to order the larboard ports closed, to avoid any danger of the lower gundeck flooding.

Rogers watched this without comment. Certainly he was the senior officer, but Timothy was handling things well enough. Besides, at that moment he didn't trust himself to speak, much less give orders. He pressed his hand under his collar and eased the stock. They had been in action for a long time, far too long for him, and he was feeling the pressure. Pacing the deck in that crowded space was all but impossible, and with the larboard ports closed he began to dream of fresh air and open spaces. A hand-spike, dropped at a nearby gun, caused his feet to almost leave the deck in fright. A sailor caught his eye, looking at him with interest, curiosity almost. Rogers turned away, ashamed, taking refuge in the bulk of the mast trunk that seemed so solid and safe. The guns were ready now, although as long as they held this course, there was no chance of using them. He watched as some of the men began to whisper and joke amongst themselves. Stupid fools, had they no idea what they were about? Didn't they care that every second brought the next broadside closer? Didn't they know that they could die shortly, die horribly? Die without ever seeing the sky or the sun again? He pressed his hands deep into his pockets in an effort to control the shaking, and leaned his body against the warm wood of the mast.

The broadside came late, approximately five minutes after the first, and still took everyone by surprise. A shout from above, then the familiar sweep of fire from the triple striped side of the flagship. This time the range was shorter, and the guns better laid. *Vigilant* was neatly straddled, with the majority of the shots hitting or passing over her forecastle.

Half the crew of the starboard bow chaser were all but wiped out in front of Tait. The young man watched in dreadful fascination as their gun took a lucky hit to the side of the muzzle. The barrel reared up and was sent spinning round, sweeping them aside as if they were nothing more than pot house skittles. The dolphin striker was neatly separated from the bowsprit, and the improvised jib fell slack, robbed of the lower tension. Both round houses crumbled as the heavy shots passed through them, and the figurehead exploded in a mass of plaster, paint and wood.

But apart from the crew of the bow chaser and the boatswain, who took a splinter in his side, there were no other serious casualties. The work to rectify the damage could begin, with men heartened by the prospect of at least five more minutes to live. Five more minutes before the next salvo would land amongst them.

As the work was being done, Dyson summoned King.

"The men have three minutes to clear what wreckage they can, and splice the important shrouds. After that I intend to steer three points to larboard, and reply with our starboard broadside. The turn will be signalled by the striking of the ships bell. As soon as the guns are fired I will turn back to my original course. Do you understand?"

King gave a quick nod and was gone; there was no time for comment. Dyson watched as he summoned a group of midshipmen and began speaking earnestly to them. Thirty seconds for that, then the news could spread about the ship. Most would get the message in time; some would not, but he could delay no longer.

After the loss of power from the jib, *Vigilant* had slowed slightly, and the quartermaster had been forced to let her drop off a point. Still, she was making good way; and if the next broadside could be weathered, his plan may yet be put into action.

The bell rang before anyone bar Dyson and the quartermaster were completely ready, and the hull levelled slightly as she came round. Seconds ticked by slowly. All waited, eager for the gun captains to be certain of their target, whilst dreading the answering salvo from the French, which could also be expected at any moment. It was a race the British won. Their guns fired erratically as each captain made sure of his mark. The broadside may have lacked the disciplined ripple of the French, but the job was done, and almost every shot told.

From the quarterdeck Dyson surveyed the damage, while the ship creaked back to her original course. He glanced at his watch. Six and a half minutes since the last broadside, extra time that must have been bought by his own shots. But the range was closing rapidly now, and it was just conceivable that the enemy were holding their fire, intending to deal a devastating blow later.

The second French ship was still a good distance off, and unlikely to be a problem to them for at least five minutes. He found no difficulty in ignoring her. In that time *Vigilant* should have closed with the flagship, or be a total wreck.

Seven minutes. Surely their broadside had not caused so much confusion? Already most of their own upper battery gun captains were signalling readiness; the enemy must be holding their fire. Then, again when the men in *Vigilant* least expected it, the French guns replied.

The shots came in a slow ripple, were better aimed, and hit harder than any the British had endured so far. A splintering crash told the end of the mizzen topmast, which fell back over the taffrail and slowed the ship considerably. On the lower deck a shot knocked two gunports into one, and accounted for six men from the crew of number five gun, barely feet from where Matthew was returning with two fresh charges. A twelve pounder was hit on the upper gundeck, the barrel torn free of its carriage to fall across two unfortunate members of its crew, and the starboard main channel was struck in two places, causing the main shrouds and backstays to slacken. Blocks and other debris clattered from the top hamper, and shouted orders and obscenities mixed seamlessly with the screams and pleadings of the wounded.

King dropped to the deck, the wind of a round shot taking most of the breath from his body. He lay on the warm burnished planking, stunned and disorientated, and it was only when the air began to trickle back into his lungs that he realised he had forgotten to breathe.

"Axes there!" Dyson bellowed, pointing at the tangle of rigging and sail that was now draped over the stern of the ship. The wreckage acted like a sea anchor; the ship was slowing and would soon be a sitting duck for the French gunners.

A master's mate led a team of men who began hacking at the lines. King, who was still shaken, staggered forward to help, but was stopped by a hand from Dyson.

"They have their job, and you yours," he said, roughly. "Boatswain's wounded; find a team and rig the mizzen staysail."

King slumped off towards the waist, his hand to his head as he tried to think. The mizzen staysail would be a blasted nuisance hanging as it did over the quarterdeck, but it was clear they needed to equalise the pressure lost by the topsail. He saw George, the negro, a topman who also worked one of the quarterdeck carronades. There would be precious little use for guns until the ship could sail again. He summoned him and three more hands and directed them to the sail loft. They knuckled their foreheads and moved quickly through the chaos, ignoring the cries of wounded shipmates as if they were nothing more than birdsong.

\*\*\*\*\*

Timothy guessed that they had lost part of a mast from the way the ship settled. His guns were ready to fire once more, but their position prevented any from bearing on the flagship. The other French liner was coming up fast, and he hesitated about selecting that as a fresh target. He peered through an open port. Yes, she was heading to pass behind her companion, and would be in range in five minutes, possibly less. He glanced about and saw Rogers, standing in the gloom and looking vaguely lost. For a moment he considered consulting him before tossing the idea aside like so much rubbish. As far as responsibility went, he was on his own, and had been for a while.

Young Davis was near by. Timothy caught his attention and pointed to the companionway.

"Go up on deck!" he shouted, roughly. "Tell Mr Dyson I can't reach the flag at this angle!"

The lad looked at him blankly. His face was white and his eyes were round and staring. Clearly the events of the past few hours had taken their toll, and he was fast approaching a state of extreme shock. Timothy looked for another messenger.

"Get out of my way!" Rogers voice was thick and his face unusually white. He brushed past the shaken lad carelessly without waiting for answer or comment.

"We need a target," Timothy began, but Rogers was already making for the main companionway and the upper deck.

As soon as he appeared in the waist Rogers was horrified by the sight. With the loss of two major spars *Vigilant* was a confusion of trailing lines and fallen blocks. He picked his way through groups of men desperately trying to make order of the jumble. A party pushed past him carrying a heavy, unmanageable grey lump that was the mizzen staysail and began to bend it on to the mizzen stay. King was in charge, and the men worked with a focused determination that Rogers vaguely envied. He moved on without comment.

On the quarterdeck he found Dyson surrounded by trails of line that had been cut to free the mizzen topmast, now floating a few yards off their counter. Men moved about him with white shocked expressions; most were cut or bruised, few spoke. The stained decking and strong smell of effluence told its own story.

"Mr Rogers, what brings you here?" Dyson alone appeared normal, his manner crisp and businesslike even if his jacket was stained and had a torn facing.

Rogers drew breath and collected himself. It would not do to show fear in front of the first lieutenant.

"A target, sir. Shall we train for the flag, or yonder?" he pointed to the warship bearing down on them, and now horribly close.

"Round shot, and for the flag." Dyson's voice was slightly louder than usual. "We will be underway directly. As soon as we gather speed I will turn as before: the signal will be the same."

Rogers nodded and opened his mouth to say more. A sudden wave of fear gripped him, conjuring up a madness that threatened to take over. For a moment he considered begging Dyson to surrender, or making a run for it, jumping over the side, anything that would stop the terror and see him safe. His mouth hung slack while the panic held him. Tears welled up behind his eyes and he had to take a conscious grip lest he disgrace himself on the quarterdeck. Fortunately Dyson's attention was taken by the setting of the mizzen staysail, currently flapping like a distended sheet above their heads. Then the sensation passed; Rogers closed his mouth and retreated. Passing down to the upper gundeck, he continued, unnoticed, to the lower gundeck and then down further to the orlop. The surgeon and his mates were at work in the cockpit, and charges were coming up from the magazines, but now he was below the waterline, the safest place in the ship, and there were still some secret areas that beckoned, dark and forgiving, where he could hide.

*****

When the flagship came into their field of view Timothy had received no instructions from Rogers. Instead he made up his own mind, anticipating Dyson's moves as those he would have taken in the same situation. The enemy was closer this time, and for a moment appeared impregnable, the tiered sides towering up, with numerous spaces where large black-faced muzzles were even now peering out to grin at him.

"Fire as you bear!" Timothy bellowed, and the first gun went off a few seconds later. Nash, one of the youngest midshipmen, approached him, waiting until the last had fired before attempting to speak, and even when he did it was in a yell that Timothy barely heard.

"Mr Dyson sent me, sir. Said we must be short of juniors if Mr Rogers 'ad to come up."

Timothy nodded. He had seen no sign of Rogers and thought him still on the upper deck.

"What's the position?"

"Bad, sir. We've lost mizzen top and fore t'gallant masts."

Timothy digested this. "Will he take us much closer?"

The lad shook his head with all the experience of his fourteen years. "Shouldn't think so, sir. We've done all we can." The pause was dramatic, even in the circumstances. "Reckon he'll strike 'fore the next broadside."

\*\*\*\*\*

But Dyson did not strike, and the broadside hit them, causing untold damage to the ship and her crew. And still she came on, closer to the flagship, and closer to the position that the first lieutenant had seen in his mind's eye over thirty minutes before. The seventy-four was still heading for them, while *Vigilant* was now so close to the flagship that the marines were exchanging pot shots with French marksmen. The next broadside from the three-decker was due in less than two minutes, and the other liner would be on them straight after, if he didn't wear away. But still Dyson held his course.

"Message to Mr Rogers!" he shouted to one of the midshipmen, standing by the binnacle. "Tell him to double shot his guns, and hold fire until we round her stern. Round her stern, that's important, have you got it?" The lad nodded and ran off; Dyson walked to the break of the quarterdeck to bellow at Gregory in the waist.

"Round shot on canister, Mr Gregory. And await my word!"

Gregory waved a hand in acknowledgement, while Dyson returned to his place by the mizzenmast.

There, he had said it: there was no going back now. Everything depended on their surviving the next broadside, and being able to press on, to pass the line of waiting guns and steer round the stern of the flagship. It was a move so bold, so outrageous, that it hardly deserved to succeed, but he had given the orders and revealed what was in his mind.

It was a strategy he had used before in other situations: volunteering for an operation, starting an argument; things that once said could not be unsaid, and the very act took much of the worry from the task. Now all knew what he intended. Not to board her, not to fight it out gun for gun, not to surrender, but to move away from conventional fighting tactics and attempt to tack a damaged ship about the stern of an enemy nearly twice his size. The thought terrified him almost as much as it would the men, when the truth dawned on them.

He could still countermand the order; still opt for the more conventional course. He even had adequate grounds to surrender, at that very moment, if it were in his nature. But no, he would see it through. Besides, he had given the order; he'd started a train of action in motion and was committed.

# CHAPTER TWENTY-FOUR

THEY had almost drawn level with the flagship; her three rows of cannon were much less than a cable away and pointing straight for them. Dyson could see the French gun crews on the upper decks as they went about the final stages of loading; an officer dressed in a splendid uniform rushed between them, epaulettes flashing in the late afternoon light. He also noticed the yards move as they began hauling on the braces. Clearly the French had guessed his plan, and were working to move their ship out of danger. Regular sharp cracks told where enemy marksmen were firing from the tops, while further intermittent volleys came from muskets and swivel guns manned by soldiers who lined the enemy's bulwarks.

Dyson collected the speaking trumpet from the binnacle and raised it to his lips. He wanted no uncertainty, no confusion; nothing must go wrong, least of all because an order had been misheard.

"Lower battery will hold their fire." He looked once more at the French ship and drew breath. "Now, Mr Gregory!"

The upper deck guns went off in a tight ripple, ending with the carronades on the quarterdeck. He saw men in the French ship fall, swept down by the rush of shot and musket balls. Guns stood unmanned, and the line of soldiers had all but vanished, although there was still the regular pop of musket balls raining down from above.

"And again, lads!" Gregory bellowed for the men to reload, although Dyson was quite content. Their broadside had done its business; by the time the enemy's upper deck artillery was fit to fight again, *Vigilant* should be safely positioned off their counter, or a derelict. It was just the heavy guns on the lower two decks that could do them real damage.

The French broadside came over their starboard bow just as Dyson was about to order *Vigilant* round. Now the range was so close that the noise of the shots fired coincided with them striking the ship, and *Vigilant* was pressed physically sideways and sternwards by the force. Men fell at every station, and a cloud of splinters and dust rose like smoke above the decks as they were ripped, pounded and mauled by the hot iron. With a crack like an axe striking a log the weakened starboard channels were taken out, ripping back the main topmast as they went. The spar fell slowly, reluctantly, as individual lines parted, until it finally crashed diagonally across the deck. Gregory was at the spot almost immediately, and with a party of seamen took to hacking at the remaining shrouds in a desperate attempt to clear the wreckage before they lost all speed.

A gun fired unexpectedly from their lower gundeck. It was too early; Dyson held his breath, but none followed. Possibly a chance shot had struck the gunlock, or a captain had panicked. Rogers must be keeping good order down there to stop the entire broadside from discharging prematurely. He turned his attention back to the activity on deck.

With an effort that can only be summoned in battle, the bulk of the mast was gradually eased over the side, until it finally hit the ocean and was set free, while *Vigilant,* powered by her last ribbons of canvas, continued.

"Take her round!" Dyson yelled at the quartermaster, now manning the wheel himself with only one helmsman to assist. The ship turned, and was reluctantly guided into the teeth of the wind. For a moment momentum carried her, then she began to slow, with what sails that were left, flapping in protest. The flagship's stern drew steadily nearer as the British ship's bows came round and her speed decreased further. She was yards, feet, away from the optimum position, although now, with nearly all impetus spent, *Vigilant* barely moved across the water. With agonising lassitude her forecastle inched past the stern of the flagship, moving slowly, so slowly, away from those murderous guns, and into a position of relative safety.

Gregory's sword was raised once more; the upper deck guns were ready. Dyson found time to marvel at the resilience of men who could continue to load while an enemy broadside swept over them. A group of officers were plainly visible on the Frenchman's deck, and even at that distance Dyson fancied he could detect an air of panic about them as *Vigilant* took up position.

\*\*\*\*\*

King was out of station when she turned; after helping to clear away the mess of what once had been their main topmast, he had moved forward and now stood at the end of the waist, watching the gilded stern of the flagship as they rounded on her. Two heavy guns were run out just above the rudder, but that was all the fire they would face as *Vigilant* crept closer. Then something caught his attention, and he looked forward, past the ship and the smoke that surrounded her.

The French seventy-four could just be seen coming round from behind the three-decker. King guessed that she must have turned some minutes ago, probably when Dyson's plans had been revealed. Her guns were run out, and she would start to cross their bows shortly. He swung round and put his hands to his mouth as an improvised speaking trumpet.

"T'other ship's on our starboard bow!" He panted, summoning more breath to bellow again. "She's passing the flagship an' crossin' us!"

Dyson heard the cry and assumed it had come from aloft. He looked to see who had spoken, but with the mizzen staysail flapping and the smoke and confusion of action he could not tell.

"Tell Mr Rogers to fire the starboard battery, then man the larboard!" he shouted at the nearest man, no midshipman being at hand. "He is to train the larboard guns for'ard. For'ard —do you understand?"

The man, Kelly, who had once claimed to be a tailor, nodded, touched his forehead and was gone. Dyson watched him as he explained himself to the marine sentry, before continuing down the companionway. It would take a good thirty seconds for the message to be relayed. The upper gundeck sent a further cascade of iron across the short distance that separated the two ships. Dyson watched as enemy officers on the poop and quarterdeck were swept to one side, and could actually hear the screams of the men as they fell. Almost without thinking he drew his sword from its scabbard and rested the blade comfortably over his right shoulder. At any moment they would rake the stern of a three-decker, and yet Dyson's mind was on the seventy-four. A broadside could be expected from that quarter; then they really would be for it.

\*\*\*\*\*

On the lower gundeck there was still no sign of Rogers. When the gun captain on number seven had fired early, it had been Timothy who acted so promptly, and stemmed the premature broadside. With the confusion of the last few minutes the second lieutenant could be dead or wounded; Timothy cared not which. He received Kelly's message without comment before bracing himself to issue the order that would devastate a French three-decker.

"Starboard battery fire when you bear!"

The first gun spoke almost immediately, and the entire broadside was spent within twelve seconds.

"Starboard battery continue at will!" Timothy yelled as soon as the cacophony died. "Number two crew, clear larboard battery!" Only the nearest gun crew heard him. Davis began repeating the order in a strained falsetto as he moved stiffly down the deck, and before long the gun crews had divided and were manning both batteries. Timothy crossed the deck and waited while a larboard port was opened, then poked his head into the fresh damp air to look. It was a horrible sight: the jib boom of the seventy-four was in plain view; in no time she would be in the ideal firing position across their bows.

\*\*\*\*\*

On the quarterdeck Humble watched as the stern windows of the flagship disappeared under the bombardment. To rake a ship at close range is to rip the very heart from her; the damage that their broadside caused to the three-decker was devastating. Those shots would continue through the hull until they hit fabric or flesh enough to absorb their tremendous momentum. The elderly man trembled slightly, trying not to imagine the scene: the low decks packed with men; the noise and confusion; the panic. Two or three more broadsides like that would do serious damage to the structure of the ship, and probably kill or disable more than half her crew. He looked away and saw the other liner passing across their bows, and in an instant knew that the same was about to happen to them.

\*\*\*\*\*

Dyson also watched the seventy-four. For all his preparations, there was little he could do. *Vigilant* had lost all speed and was now totally unmanageable.

"Keep her hard over, quartermaster!" Dyson grunted. The gnarled face hardly nodded back in reply; he knew his duty, and also knew it was hopeless.

More shots were striking the deck all about him as the marksmen on the flagship's mizzen top took aim, but Dyson was strangely tolerant of them. They were no more than raindrops, compared to the tidal wave that was due at any moment.

It came, appropriately enough, like a sea breaking over their bows. The shots smacked into *Vigilant's* dry timbers in a succession of tearing crashes, taking the bowsprit and foremast with them. Humble watched the wave of destruction as it thundered on, wiping the decks clear of men and fittings as it went. The master, who had been in action on several occasions, now felt a strange apathy take over. Seeing their previous broadside rake the flagship had altered him in a fundamental way; he felt listless and tired. The energy that had kept his fighting soul alive was suddenly missing. He was an old man, a grandfather thrice over; his war was done and as death flowed towards him in a mighty rush he almost greeted it with relief.

*****

Below deck the men at the forward great guns were smashed into one with their equipment. Matthew stared in horror as Klier fell lifeless across his own weapon, only to be pulled roughly aside and tossed into the scuppers by Lewis and O'Conner.

"Bring her round!" Simpson was shouting, despite the carnage. Lewis and another began to haul the gun to train her forward. Matthew had one powder charge left, with both guns in action he must get more without delay.

"Load the charge!" Simpson shouted. With the loss of men and having to man both guns, everyone had to work twice as hard. Matthew ripped the cover off the carrier and placed the cartridge into the waiting feeder, before setting off once more for the main hatch.

Flint stood at the breach of the gun, apparently content to watch the men as they worked. Lewis caught sight of his face and paused for a moment; Simpson also noticed the difference.

"Set your priming!" he bellowed into Flint's face, but there was little response. The shock of knowing his father for a coward had shaken Flint deeply. His eyes were set somewhere in the distance, and his mouth hung slightly open. Lewis was inserting the charge, and looking to his captain to announce it placed. Simpson grabbed the priming wire from Flint's limp fingers and set it in the touch hole.

"Home!" he shouted. The words seemed to jerk Flint from his apathy, and he looked about him.

"Get with it, man!" Simpson bellowed. Flint considered him. He turned, his face now filling with panic, to see Matthew coming back with two fresh charges slung over his shoulders.

Simpson pushed Flint to one side, inserted the firing tube, wrenched back the hammer and frizzen, and emptied a measure of priming powder into the pan. "Stand clear!" he bellowed before pulling the lanyard and sending a twenty-four pound ball in the general direction of the French ship.

Matthew watched the gun fire and paused, suddenly uncertain. A shot passed in front of him, just where he would have been if he had not stopped. Instead the shot hit O'Conner and wounded him horribly. The lad dropped his charges and looked up to Flint, while his mouth opened in a scream that was totally without sound.

"Come on lad, move it!" Flint's voice was no more than a screech, and he spoke as much to himself as the boy. "Don't mind the noise, the one you hear has gone past—noise can't hurt you." It was the instructions his father had given him that night, during the action with the revenue cutter. Neither watched as Lewis dragged the screaming O'Conner to the middle of the deck where he could die without getting in anyone's way. "Come on," Flint continued. "We're dependin' on you!"

Matthew blinked and picked up his charges once more. Lewis returned from his work and reached for a cartridge, before turning and hurriedly inserting it and the feeder into the warm muzzle of the gun.

"Home!" shouted Flint, now back in his correct position, and feeling with his wire down the touch hole. The routine re-established, Matthew crossed the deck and handed the other charge to the feeder of the starboard gun before returning once more to the main hatch.

He had reached the short line of waiting boys at the companionway when he noticed someone else, an officer no less, coming up from the safety of the orlop. Despite the carnage and confusion that reined all about, it was a sight so strange as to cause him to pause, before standing to one side and allowing the man to pass. Then he was called back to duty, and after accepting two more charges Matthew began the dangerous journey back to his guns.

*****

The seventy-four had turned and was now creeping along their larboard side; less than fifty yards away and closing. King looked back to the quarterdeck which was all but invisible in the smoke and debris.

"She's comin' 'long side!" his voice sounded weak and ineffectual amid the roar of battle. He paused for a moment, uncertain as to the next move. Gregory could not be seen, and the starboard upper deck gun crews were still firing at the flagship. He shook as a wave of cold fear flowed over his body, and for a moment felt the need to hide. Hide and be safe; let the others do the fighting.

"Boarders to larboard!" he screamed, pushing the idea aside as he did. Men working a starboard gun looked back at him. He repeated the call, pointing desperately towards the impending seventy-four. They came across, almost inquisitively at first; then, seeing the danger, at a run. The upper larboard battery had been left loaded, but with round shot. There was no time to reload with canister. "Fire the guns, then prepare for boarders!" King gasped, in a voice all but hoarse. Rooke, the master's mate, appeared, and began passing out boarding pikes and cutlasses. King had left his pistol on the deck of the *Hampshire Lass*. He considered taking another but instantly rejected the idea; he would only have to worry about loading the thing, and at that stage he knew himself unequal to the task. From below irregular crashes told that their lower larboard battery was firing, and as he watched the French hull appear from out of the smoke he felt his pulse begin to race. Then the upper battery exploded in a ripple of shots. At that range it was no effort to see the bulwarks buckle and disintegrate as the twelve pound balls struck. For seconds afterwards there was silence, then heads began to appear once more, and a roar of defiance erupted from the French.

King turned to see Rooke joining him, cutlass in hand.

"Fend off there!" His voice was almost gone, but the men about him caught the idea. A shattered end of a main yard lay on the deck, and eager hands manoeuvred it lengthways over the side.

"That's it, lads. Keep them back!"

Another spar was found and used in a similar manner, and another after that. The enemy ship was being held at bay, but only for so long. If they could man some of the guns as well it might make a difference. Marksmen from the Frenchman's tops began to pick off men; King felt the breeze of a shot pass by him as he looked about desperately for help. But there were none left to assist; in a ship still crowded with men, he seemed totally alone.

\*\*\*\*\*

Dyson had heard King's shout, and saw the seventy-four coming round on them. He also noticed how the flagship was turning about and would soon be presenting her broadside, possibly against their stern. He had done enough, in fact he had done more than he had ever intended, although now, when surrender seemed the next logical step, he felt unable to take it. The quarterdeck carronades were still being worked, and he could hear guns from the lower batteries as they barked intermittently. But they were totally outnumbered, men were falling all the time, and he doubted if anything could be gained by continuing further. Then he saw Rogers.

He was clambering up what was left of the quarterdeck ladder and staring about wildly. His face was slightly blackened and his uniform awry, although compared with others who manned the deck he seemed peculiarly well dressed. What drew Dyson's attention were the eyes glowing white and round above a mouth that appeared altogether too large for his face. The whole apparition reminded him of a shrunken head he had seen once when a junior officer. But this was no vile souvenir; this was real; real, alive and making for him.

"Strike, sir, why do you not strike?" Rogers' voice was also distorted, but the words came through as clearly as the fear that fed them. A hand reached out and grabbed at his uniform coat, the face pressed close into his, and screamed straight at him.

"Strike, you bastard! Strike!"

Dyson took a step back; Rogers drew his sword, holding it up in front of him.

"You damned fool!" Dyson spat the words with contempt. There was no time for this.

The sword was raised menacingly, and Dyson took another step backwards, holding his own blade at the parry.

"Strike, curse you!"

Their swords touched once; then Rogers was gone, disappeared as if he had never been. At Dyson's feet all that was left was a crumpled form wearing a lieutenant's uniform. He looked up and into the eyes of Gregory, who was standing opposite, rubbing the knuckles of his right hand with his left.

"'Scuse me, sir," he said, with an odd formality. "But he never was much good, that one."

\*\*\*\*\*

King had been joined by Tait, who brought with him seven men.

"Good work, Thomas. Try and keep them at bay, I'll get a gun or two on them!"

King nodded; a sweep of canister would make a difference, even if it would not reach the enemy marksmen aloft who, despite being the targets of Jackson's marines, were steadily eroding their small force. Beneath him the deck vibrated as shot form the French heavy guns bit into the hull, and on the upper deck men stood ready to board.

An unlucky hit from one of their own twenty-four pounders smashed a fend-off, and the enemy's hull crept closer. A second crack; this time a spar had proved too weak to hold the force of the ship and broke in two. Another followed, then there was a brief pause before the two hulls met and ground together with a moan that might have come from the very soul of the ship herself.

The first wave of boarders landed almost simultaneously. King, his dirk already in hand, found himself facing the pointed end of a pike that was being propelled towards his belly by a seaman with a fat moustache. Instinctively he side-stepped the charge and hacked sideways at the man, feeling the blow strike deep as it cut into his body. Another was coming towards him, this time armed with a cutlass. King hesitated for less than a second before diving under the blow. Then Dyson, appearing from nowhere, stepped over his prone body and laid in with brief economical sweeps of his hanger. More came; one was armed with a wide mouthed carbine. King collected himself and sprang up, grabbing at the barrel and pressing the piece back in its owner's face. The blow knocked the Frenchman into the scuppers, where King kicked him in the face with his boot.

Already the sweat was starting to pour from his face, but there was no time for rest. Carling came from the forecastle at the head of a fresh band of marines who advanced into the *melée* with fixed bayonets and began to chisel a clear channel into the confusion. King followed them, cutting this way or that as the opportunity arose. This was not the place for fine fighting or gentlemanly tactics. To one side he saw Rooke being overwhelmed by a vividly dressed officer, and broke off to charge at the man, barging into his side and slashing at the body as it fell. Rooke looked his thanks, before retrieving his cutlass and heading back into the fray with a wild scream. One of the Frenchmen had a change of heart; King chased him back over the side and he fell into the water below. It was then King realised the two ships had drawn apart once more. He looked back to see the battle on the deck almost over, and Carling causally wiping his blade with a white pocket handkerchief.

"Lower deck guns must have driven them off!" Tait shouted in his ear. "That or they're frightened of taking fire from us."

King nodded. His body felt incredibly tired, and yet there was still much to do. More shots began falling from the French marksmen. Tait opened his mouth to say more when suddenly he was sent spinning to the deck, a red wound opening below his right shoulder. King knelt down to him immediately, but the lieutenant was clambering to his feet.

"Got my arm!" he said, unnecessarily, as he leant against King. "Can't move my fingers!" King squeezed at the wound, and felt the bone crumble beneath his grip.

"Better stay down," he said. "You've done all you can."

Tait looked him in the eye and smiled slightly. "You're right there. Reckon we're about finished."

*****

The same thought was in Dyson's mind. The ship was nearly a wreck, and he dared not guess at the number killed or wounded. He looked about him before tossing his sword into the scuppers and searching for some means to surrender. The ensign had been shot away some while ago; he would just have to order the men to cease fire, and trust the French to do likewise.

He noticed that his uniform jacket was moist; it was raining heavily and must have been for several minutes. The deck was wet; blood, sand and unspeakable filth mingled to create strange patterns on the strakes. It was almost a shame the boarding attempt had been beaten back; nothing had been gained by it. He looked up and saw Carling. He spread his hands wide in a gesture of despair. The marine officer smiled and nodded. The rain now fell in torrents about them. They had fared well; few could have done better, but now it was over.

# CHAPTER TWENTY-FIVE

THE sensation of defeat passed through the ship like an evil wind, and for a moment no one appeared able to move. It was as if the British had come to the end of their stamina and had nothing left with which to fight. Dyson stepped down to the half deck, and spotted Gregory coming towards him, his face a mask of exhaustion. As if by mutual agreement all great guns had ceased to fire and the air held a dull ringing sound, nothing more. The rain fell noiselessly. There were no shots from the enemy marksmen, no bellowing of orders from petty officers, even the wounded had ceased to cry. Dyson turned towards the French seventy-four and noticed how the ship was now some distance off. He supposed they were frightened of *Vigilant* exploding; maybe the incident with the *Hampshire Lass* was still fresh in their minds. In the enemy flagship they were also making preparations to move; the topgallants dropped and filled even as he looked. Gregory was next to him now and between them they watched as the French ships drew back.

"Reckon they've had enough of us?" Gregory asked hopefully. Dyson shook his head.

"No, there's more to it," he said. "We're no danger to them; they can take us whenever they have a mind."

But shortly the men at the upper deck began to grow more confident and stood up, staring at the enemy as they gathered way. There were the faint murmurings of conversation, and from somewhere Dyson was certain he heard a laugh. He looked up to the mizzen top, the only lookout position left, although it stood barely a third as high as a main masthead.

"What do you see there?" he bellowed, his voice unnaturally loud. The rain turned to drizzle then died; a shaft of early evening sun appeared signalling the end of the squall.

"Clear horizon, sir."

So they had left the two French frigates behind, and presumably the four remaining merchants had made good their escape. Considering that, and the sizeable damage caused to the French ships, Dyson supposed he had been successful; certainly all of Shepherd's original objectives had been met. It was just strange that now, now they were finally beaten, the enemy seemed content to quietly take their leave. A pigtailed gunner on the quarterdeck shouted something obscene at the departing flagship, but only received a derisory wave in return. Dyson looked at Gregory; both were equally bemused.

"Deck there!" the call from the mizzen top took them by surprise. "Sail to windward! Two, no three, comin' down on us!"

The officers spun round and foolishly tried to make out the sighting, but the mizzen top was still that much higher, and nothing was visible from the deck.

"Frenchie's got mastheads!" Gregory shouted as realisation dawned. It was true: both the enemy ships were badly damaged, but each had at least one lookout set far higher than any on *Vigilant*; their horizon would be correspondingly wider, and the strange sails must have been made out some while before.

"Two more, sir!" the lookout continued. "An' I think the first three are frigates."

Frigates! That could mean another escaping squadron, or the scouts of a larger body. Both were possible, but the chances were heavily in favour of a British fleet lying just over the horizon. More than that, a sizeable portion of it was bearing down on them. Dyson found himself grinning foolishly at Gregory, the latter beaming heartily in return.

Timothy came up from the lower gundeck and raised a blackened hand to shield his eyes from the soft evening light. He looked at the departing ships, clearly as bewildered as they had been. King stumbled over; both wore uniforms that were stained and torn, a testimony to their part in the battle; neither noticed nor cared.

"What goes, Thomas?" Timothy asked, placing his hand on King's shoulder.

"We got supplements, that's what!" Gregory beamed as he joined them, clapping both heartily on the back and all but knocking each into the other. "We been rescued at the eighth bell!" His massive arms enveloped them both in an embrace as reassuring as any father's.

The buzz slowly circulated about the deck and down into the very bowels of the ship. Some began to cheer, some to sob and some to almost scream with relief. And as the cries grew stronger three frigates came into plain view, followed by the reassuring bulk of two British line-of-battle ships.

Matthew and Jake watched the frigates as they passed. With not a mark of action and all plain sail set they looked powerful and dashing as they cut through the dark crested seas, a direct contrast to *Vigilant*, whose lack of masts and spars gave her an ungainly and lopsided appearance. But these were the badges of valour, and as the two lads waved they did so without envy; already to have been in *Vigilant* that day was honour enough.

*****

The British ships caught the French on the horizon, just as dusk was turning to night. Dyson, who had set the crew to work cobbling the ship, stood them down to watch and cheer afresh. It was the least he could do; he felt he owed them that. That and so much more.

The seventy-four struck as soon as it was clear the British would overtake them. The flagship fired one broadside before doing the same. By night the British had returned with their trophies, leaving a frigate to stand watch over *Vigilant* until dawn. It was then that she was taken under tow, to join the might of a homeward bound convoy that would see them safely to England.

*****

The next morning Dyson stood on the quarterdeck once more. He had changed his shirt and wore a fresh uniform coat over his number one pair of britches. During the night they had all worked like demons to secure the ship, clearing away debris and fixing what damage they could. A draft from the frigate had given them fresh blood, but even these men now looked exhausted as they were stood down to breakfast. A team of topmen had rigged an improvised spanker to give them a degree of stability; apart from that there was no need for intricate repairs aloft, as they would undoubtedly be towed all the way back to harbour. Dyson supposed he was pleased with the efforts they had made, although his mind was numb with fatigue. The regular mournful clatter of a chain pump told how the hull was leaking badly, and they still had many miles to travel before they could really call the battle over.

From the state of the ship, his mind naturally ran on to the condition of his people. Wilson, the surgeon, had made his report just before daybreak. Twenty-seven men had died in the cockpit, and another ten were expected to go that day. This probably accounted for less than a third of the fatalities; the others would have been thrown over the side in the heat of action. Another ninety-eight were wounded, so *Vigilant* was left with over a third of her men as casualties. It was a colossal toll, and one that filled Dyson with doubts that were more than tinged with guilt.

Tait was one. Dyson had spoken to him less than an hour before, when he had carried out his inspection. The ball in his arm had gone deep and done a deal of damage to the bone. Still, Bryant had retrieved the spent shot efficiently enough, before closing the wound and setting the arm against a splint. If all stayed healthy there was a good chance that Tait would get through with nothing worse than a scar and a memory. The fact that Bryant had performed the operation did not greatly surprise the first lieutenant. Battle did much to bring out extremes in men; with Bryant it had revealed a natural talent for surgery. As far as his record in ministry was concerned, Dyson felt their chaplain had found his true vocation.

In Rogers something far more sinister had been uncovered. Currently he was below, seeking shelter and comfort in the remnants of the wardroom and a bottle of port wine. Dyson would have to make a full report, and it would be unfair to the other officers if the man's conduct went unremarked. He would be finished, as far as future service was concerned; he should be set ashore to follow another course. If he was lucky they would not waste a court martial on him; if he was not, he might even be shot. Dyson found he cared little either way; he would be quite content just to be rid of bad rubbish; there was no room in his ordered world for revenge.

Gregory joined him. He was dressed in a watch coat that gave a welcome shelter from the stiff morning breeze, as well as hiding the remnants of his uniform that he had not seen fit to change.

"Flagship's *Aurora*: ninety-eight, sir." He rubbed his red raw hands together as he continued. "Captain Michael Morris in command, carrying Vice Admiral Nichols. They've nigh on a hundred ships, most back from the India station."

Nichols: Dyson had met him once when he'd captained a seventy-four stationed in the Americas. He remembered him as a solid, dependable man, which would explain his action the previous afternoon. The word had come from a master's mate sent across from the frigate. It seemed that *Taymar* and *Badger* had run into the British fleet early in the afternoon. To denude a convoy of a fair proportion of her escorts on nothing more than a vague estimation of their position marked the commander as both bold and spirited. Especially when the nearest land was France, and for all a homebound convoy would know, the entire Brest fleet was at sea and hunting for them.

King appeared and touched his hat to the first lieutenant. He had also spent the night awake and working, and his face betrayed his exhaustion.

"Carpenter's almost done on number two pump, sir. Says once it's in use we should be able to gain on the level in the well."

"Very good." Dyson gave the lad a brief smile. "Have you eaten?"

"I took some biscuit and a bite of cheese earlier. The cook wants to get the galley open in time for dinner. I said he could, providing he don't take men from their duties. I also told him to cancel the banyan day; reckon they'll need some beef inside them."

It was Friday; a day when the British Navy did not normally serve meat. That was good thinking on King's part. The hands would work better with stomachs full, and it was a sign of initiative and confidence that King had gone ahead without referring to him.

"I wonder what they'll make of this in England!" Gregory mused. What indeed? Dyson had known of similar engagements, and was conscious that public opinion was not always predictable. Some may find fault in his actions; the butcher's bill may offend others; and it only needed a bad press to taint his future career forever. Fortunately King interrupted his thoughts before they became morbid.

"You'll be goin' aboard the flagship to report, sir?" It was not a question he would normally have asked, although they had been through so much together that now it seemed perfectly natural.

"Yes, if I am asked."

All three smiled; it seemed likely.

Then they were closing with the convoy. A fleet of merchants sailed in tight formation in a central block, with frigates and line-of-battle ships to either side. In the van was the flagship, a fifth rate on her windward side. Slightly ahead of them were the two French frigates, now under jury rigs. Ahead were the enemy flagship and the seventy-four, sailing with the British ensign flying proudly over the flag of France.

"Familiar lookin' craft," Gregory commented. "Sure I've seen a cut like theirs afore!" They laughed easily, although in Dyson's case it was partly out of relief. The frigates had been at the back of his mind ever since they had disappeared over the horizon. Had they managed to effect repairs and avoid capture, they would have played a merry dance with shipping in the North Atlantic. Skilfully handled, they could have tied down three or four times their own force in vessels sent out to find them. He made little allowance for his own actions in disabling the ships and making their capture inevitable.

"Make the private signal and our number, Mr King." Dyson's voice was formal now; the bonds of discipline had tightened with the joining of the fleet.

"Flagship acknowledges," King replied after a time. "She's signalling to *Puma* to take station two cables to leeward of her."

The towing frigate took them boldly past a stately two-decker, whose people lined the sides to stare at them. Dyson felt stupidly self conscious under the gaze of his peers. It was probably the most public moment of his life, and not one he particularly enjoyed. Then they were safely stationed, almost within hailing distance of *Aurora*.

"Our number, sir," King said, as another signal broke from the flagship. "Flag to *Vigilant*," he consulted his signal book hurriedly, and looked up before he spoke. "Just one word, sir: Welcome."

# CHAPTER TWENTY-SIX

ON the lower gundeck some semblance of order was becoming apparent. Those guns which had lost carriages were now cleaned and resting on the deck in their rightful place, awaiting the time when the carpenter and his crew could remount them. Neat lead patches marked the small round entry holes where shots had come in, while larger pieces of wood covered the ragged square exit wounds. The decks were all but free of debris, and there were several parties working with dry holystones, smoothing down areas where deck strakes had been ripped up.

Matthew was set to work with a kid and swab, clearing the scuppers. Normally washing out the accumulated muck of battle would have turned his stomach, but now he found the exercise positively therapeutic. The mixture of vinegar and water ran out through the dales, leaving clean painted wood behind, and as he worked the sharp smell of hygiene began to overpower that of spent powder, sweat, and things far worse. He met up with Jake as they queued to refill their buckets at the deck pump.

"They say we'll be home in no time," Jake told him with his customary air of authority. "Convoy's Pompey bound, so it's back to where we started."

Matthew leaned forward to fill his kid. Portsmouth might be where they'd begun, but he felt he had made a considerable personal journey since then.

"Found this," he said, straightening up and thrusting a gully at Jake. The boy took the long, thin-bladed knife and examined it with ill concealed awe.

"French, you reckon?"

Matthew nodded. "'Less one of our lot dropped it."

It was Jake's turn to dip into his pocket. He brought out a small metal tobacco box with a horse's head embossed on the lid. Matthew inspected it thoughtfully.

"Where did you find it?" he asked.

"In the fore scuppers, why?"

Matthew was not sure. He thought he had seen one like it but could not say where. "Anything inside?" he asked.

Jake shook his head. "Just a bit of paper with some writing on, an' a funny sort of brooch. No baccy. You know who it belonged to?"

Matthew shook his head. The box was familiar, but he could not put a name to the owner. He comforted himself that whoever it was would probably be long past caring about tobacco tins now.

*****

Captain Morris met Dyson at the entry port with due ceremony. He was a broad, fair-haired man of middle age, and showed some surprise when a lieutenant appeared from the gig, rather than the fellow senior captain he had been expecting. Dyson caught sight of side boys, assembled to pay compliment, being hurried away as he shook hands with Morris. Clearly the news of Shepherd's death had not reached the convoy. After nearly thirty hours without sleep he realised that he would now have to explain everything to a vice admiral, and probably most of his staff. Dyson found his teeth were tightly clenched as he followed Morris to the admiral's quarters.

But Nichols received him alone, apart from Morris, who took a seat to one side of the huge state room. Dyson was directed to an upright but comfortable chair and for the first time in ages was able to rest his back. He was mildly conscious that his hair still held the bonfire smell of battle as he looked up to meet the kindly eyes of the admiral.

"Your captain is wounded, lieutenant?"

"No, sir. I regret Captain Shepherd died during the early stages of the action. A passing shot caused concussion that brought on a seizure."

"I see." Nichols looked genuinely sorry. "He was a fine man; we served together in *Monarch*."

A servant entered the room and, after a nod from Nichols, placed a small table beside Dyson.

"Wine, sir?"

Dyson watched as the red liquid filled the crystal glass. The admiral smiled sympathetically.

"I am sure you are tired, lieutenant, but you have no idea of the rumours that are circulating about your actions. Perhaps we could persuade you to give us a verbal report, in advance of your written journal?"

*****

Dyson finished speaking about half an hour later. It was not the end of the story, and he was conscious that some aspects had been missed, or not given sufficient emphasis. But his head swam with the combined effects of wine and exhaustion, and he knew he could not say more. For a moment no one spoke, then Morris moved forward and poured a fresh measure of wine from the decanter. Dyson was taken aback at being waited on by a senior captain, although his tired mind interpreted the action as positive.

Nichols cleared his throat. "Well, it seems you have been busy. We learned a little from Douglas of the *Taymar*. And *Vibrant*, our leeward lookout, spotted one of the frigates shortly afterwards." He cleared his throat again. "Of course I cannot comment on your late captain's actions, nor your own, come to that," the smile came readily. "But I do feel it would be fitting if you remained in nominal command of *Vigilant* until we reach England."

A cough was rising in Dyson's throat; he took a hasty sip of wine. To remain in command showed a good measure of approval, possibly one that would help him on the next important step to Commander.

"We are currently transporting several battalions of foot soldiers, as well as the outgoing consular staff from Bombay. I am sure your surgeon would welcome assistance from their medical service?"

"Yes, sir; that would be appreciated."

"And you will call on us for any materials, provisions or man power your ship needs, as well as any personal requirements that you or your officers may have, is that understood?"

Dyson said it was, although later he would have doubts as to whether the admiral had actually made the offer.

"There is one, rather awkward point..."

A faint alarm bell rang in Dyson's muddled mind as the admiral continued.

"The capture of the two frigates was undertaken while *Vigilant* was out of sight." That was quite true, although Dyson's tired mind failed to grasp the significance of the point. "That means you cannot benefit from the prize money. However, the two liners are certainly down to you, and as *Vigilant* was sailing under Admiralty Orders, there will be no eighth for a Commander in Chief." He smiled again. "I think you will find your share will be adequate enough."

There was irony in the fact that at no time during the action had Dyson considered prize money, and as soon as he did, he found that a good proportion was to be taken from him. But then, even allowing for sharing with the other ships, the commissioned officer's portion would be substantial.

"Well, I am sure you have many things to occupy you. I hope I can count on your presence at dinner at least once during our journey home." The admiral smiled, "Lieutenant?"

Dyson realised that he had lapsed into a trance, and had been staring into space for several seconds. With an effort he stood up and allowed himself to be led from the great cabin. Morris saw him off at the entry port.

"The admiral was impressed, I could tell," he said softly as they shook hands. "With his influence you should go far; indeed you deserve to."

"I had exceptional support from my officers, sir," Dyson managed to reply.

"So you have said, and that is also to your credit." Morris suddenly grew serious. "You made no mention of your second. Was he injured?

"No, sir." Dyson eyed the captain guardedly. "Lieutenant Rogers survived the battle."

"Anthony Rogers?"

Dyson grew more wary. "You know him, sir?"

"I know of him," the look was unmistakable, "and I know the kind of man he is. You made no mention of his conduct."

That was true; Dyson had not trusted himself to give a neutral account. "Mr Rogers did not impress me with his actions," he said simply. "I considered the subject more suited to a written report, sir."

"Probably very wise, and you may wish to be a trifle circumspect. He is a known rogue, but does have important friends." The words registered even in Dyson's weary brain. "A bad report from you may affect more than one man's naval career; you might consider that."

The thought remained with him as he was ferried back to *Vigilant*. It was true; Rogers did have important friends, whereas he, in contrast, had very few. He also knew of men who had risen to be admirals who by rights should never have been commissioned. Men such as Rogers, men who achieved rank through connections, rather than capabilities. Was he to allow another to go that way when it was in his power to expose him? Dyson swallowed as a thought occurred. In a service where promotion relied so heavily on influence, he had finally been given one small chance to exert his, albeit at a personal cost. He smiled grimly as he prepared to clamber up the wounded side of *Vigilant*, knowing himself well enough to predict the outcome, even before he had properly thought things through.

\*\*\*\*\*

It was a different group of men that now sat at Flint's mess table. Matthew, perched on the bread box at the end, looked down the line of faces. Some were new, fresh hands drafted from the convoy, while others were his friends of several weeks, although already it seemed that he had known them for ever. Some, for various reasons, were no longer present. O'Conner had left the ship only that morning. Together with many others, and under a union flag that was yet to carry the colours of Ireland, his body had been bound in a weighted hammock and sent over the side to take his final journey to the bottom of the sea.

Others were there in body only; on Matthew's left Flint was eating intently, his eyes fixed on the table, his thoughts kept entirely to himself. It was more than the recent burial service that had subdued him; his attitude had been different since the battle. He remained friendly, but now was detached, as if he were considering matters from a different angle. Simpson sat opposite; by rights he should have been back in bilboes on the punishment deck. But Critchley, the master at arms, had died early the previous day, and with so much still out of kilter since the action, no one had seen the necessity of placing his assailant back under arrest. Matthew watched as the red-haired man cut a chunk of the cheese with his clasp knife and sat back on the bench, his eyes finally resting on Flint.

"Out bound convoy was sighted 'smorning," he informed him. Flint looked up as Simpson continued. "Gib. bound. Came into signalling range jus' 'fore six bells."

"'Sright," a man from the frigate confirmed. "*Taymar* and *Badger* been sent across to join, 'long with the merchants you was escortin'."

For the first time since the battle Flint's eyes showed a flicker of interest.

"All of 'em?" he asked.

"Reckon," Simpson had noticed the change and was eyeing Flint with curiosity. "'cludin' the las' four." He took a generous bite of his cheese.

Flint nodded, while his mind began to race. That would mean his father would be leaving the convoy; probably had done so already. So there would be no embarrassing meeting in Portsmouth, no fear of running into him in a dockside pot house, no need to explain to what was left of his family the terrible truth he had discovered. The British Navy, larger now than it had ever been, was still small when viewed against the area it covered. One meeting in ten years was probably more than he could normally expect, especially when his father now knew where he was likely to be and would doubtless take even greater precautions to avoid an RN vessel.

The idea brushed some of the despondent thoughts from his mind; he straightened his back and felt his shoulders relax. Simpson was still eyeing him quizzically, although he could not know the importance of the news. No one knew what he had discovered on the deck of the *Hampshire Lass,* and no one was aware just how deeply it had affected him.

To his right Matthew was munching his cheese with hardly a care. The boy had been afraid, that was natural. And he had even allowed his fear to show; the cardinal sin of which Flint was equally guilty. But what might be excused in a lad was liable for punishment in a man, especially one so old and experienced. He had expected repercussions from the other men, certainly Simpson and Lewis: both had noticed. To his knowledge there had never been a time when cowardice had been ignored, and yet he was still being treated like any other member of the crew. It might mean that the men had not realised, thought the terrible moment when he had stopped and all but ran from the deck was not due to fear. The memories of the battle were already starting to fade in his mind, and he could recall little in exact detail, apart from Simpson bellowing into his face, and Matthew standing rigid on the deck. But then for all he knew others experienced similar moments; it might even be considered common, and not worthy of comment later.

He saw then, with rare insight, that this had been his first time in action alone; the first time he had not depended on someone else, however distant, to give him strength. And it was only when he had realised just how weak that person was that he had discovered his true self; the one he had hidden ever since that night when the revenue cutter closed with them.

Now he had changed; the battle had seen to that. Now he was no longer dependent on a memory, an image that had grown in his mind with the years. He had himself to live up to, and himself to live for. Should action come his way again he knew he would cope with it; possibly not with the devil may care attitude of the past, but sufficiently well: certainly with more maturity. He glanced at Matthew, eating in childlike innocence, with all memories and doubts consigned to the cag bucket, and told himself that there were still some examples that were worth following.

*****

"You realise, of course, that you could be shot?"

Rogers showed no surprise, only a slight sneer of disdain marked his face. "You may think so, but I fear you will meet with others who have my interests at heart."

"That's quite possible, and yet somehow I feel I will be believed." Dyson paused, timing his stroke as accurately as any he had used to fend off boarders. "Few are willing to befriend a coward."

At this Rogers stood to face him, as Dyson had known he would. "Say that in front of witnesses, and I shall..."

"Demand a meeting?" he scoffed. "No, I think not. I have witnesses of my own. Men who saw your conduct, and know you for what you are; I think a court martial would soon decide your fate."

The words seemed to sap some of the fight from Rogers, and he sat down once more, helping himself liberally from the black bottle on the wardroom table. It was early evening, and just starting to grow dark. The stewards should have been in to light the candles by now, but for some reason they were holding back and giving the two officers unheard of privacy.

"You'd do that?" Rogers asked, after drinking deeply.

"I would."

Rogers smiled, a generous *bon homie* smile, and reached out with his hand. "But I could do you so much good. I know people, my father knows people. I could get you promoted to commander; surely you'd like that?"

"I want nothing from you."

The smile vanished, and Dyson could all but see the workings of the man's mind. It took almost five seconds for him to think of his next gambit.

"What about Gregory?" he said, the snarl now firmly back in his voice. "Striking a superior officer; that's one for the court room." He warmed to his subject. "And I'd wager there'd be one or two things we could dig up about you, given the opportunity."

"It was you who attacked a senior officer; Gregory only hit you following direct instruction from myself." He hardly drew breath as he continued. "You drew your weapon and made to strike me; I ordered that you should be restrained."

The cold lie hung in the air, and Rogers seemed unable to comprehend what was being done to him.

"You wouldn't swear to that," he said, the smile momentarily returning.

"I would. And I will also state as much in my report." That was another lie, but Dyson was long past caring.

Their eyes met and the tension increased with each breath. Finally Rogers broke.

"What do you want?" his voice was tired, almost resigned, and Dyson knew that he had won.

"I require your journal; a written account of the battle, and your conduct in it. No fudging or licence; the bare facts."

"And?"

"And you will sign it, and pass it to me before we enter harbour."

"The court martial?"

"There will be no court martial, providing you decide to resign your commission immediately."

Rogers shrugged. "Anything else?"

"No, that will be sufficient."

Dyson walked quietly from the room, leaving Rogers to consider the matter. Slowly the sun began to dip below the horizon, and soon the wardroom, and Rogers, was left in darkness.

# ALARIC BOND

*****

In the early morning of the fifteenth of June, HMS *Vigilant* waited at the entrance to Number Three Dock, a little over seven weeks since she had first set sail. Her few remaining yards were set cock-a-bill signalling the death of her captain, and the patched sides bore witness to the recent battle. News of her exploits had travelled before her and there were a good few onlookers gathered to shake their heads and stare at the damage. Dyson stood on the quarterdeck surveying the scene. Despite the fact that the journey back had been as uneventful as any undertaken when a leaking ship is under tow, he felt a strange mixture of emotions. He was tired; he longed to be free of the ship and his responsibilities, and yet he also felt a wrench, as if a part was about to be taken from him and left in the hands of strangers.

*Vigilant* had been due for a minor refit even before the battle, and it was likely that a year or more would pass before she saw open seas again. She may even have her upper deck removed, and be turned into a heavy frigate, like her sister, *Indefatigable* that Pellew was now making his own. Dyson hoped not; the sixty-four might be considered an antiquated type, but it was one that could still carry itself well in action, as *Vigilant* herself had shown.

The hands were assembling in the waist wearing their tiddley suits: the smart shore going clothes that each kept stowed away. Their ditty bags were slung over their shoulders, and they stood next to a block of sea chests, piled high and ready to be swung ashore. Dyson examined the faces as they jostled with each other, eager to be free of the ship. The commissioners had arrived early yesterday morning and initiated a ceremony that was taken every bit as seriously as 'Up Spirits'. Each hand had been called in turn, and his allowance doled into his hat. In every case six month's pay was kept back as an incentive against desertion. Some noticed, and some did not, but most now had money in their pockets. Money they had earned like horses, which now was certain to be spent by asses. A good few would find themselves back in the Navy within a month, although none would ever know how close they came to being transferred straight into a receiving ship, without a chance of tasting the pleasures of the shore. Some Dyson would meet again, as he had with former shipmates, while others were doomed to disappear into obscurity.

One had gone already; while they had waited at anchor at Spithead a small splash and the sight of a red pigtail vanishing beneath the waves was the last they had seen of Simpson. Dyson supposed he should feel bad about the loss of a known deserter who had compounded his crime by striking a superior officer, although curiously he could not summon the emotion.

King appeared on deck, and touched his hat. Dyson had commended the lad in his report, and hoped he would be given a chance to attend an examination board without delay. Men like him, Timothy, and Tait (who was recovering well from his wound), these were the future of the service; the captains and admirals of tomorrow. Gregory was forward, looking to the warp that would carry them in. He was not so much the Navy's future as its foundation, although Dyson knew that whatever praise he might receive, Gregory would be unlikely to rise any further than his present rank.

Flint was at the head of his mess. He stood by the young lad who had fallen from the masthead. Next to him, and no longer a part of the mess, stood Lewis. Dyson had noted changes in all three. Flint was certainly less cocksure. The journey back had shown him to be far more dependable and mature, yet still with the ability to command respect. Were they to continue to sail together, Dyson would consider him for promotion; just as an experiment to see how he would take to it.

Lewis had already got his, and not before time. In addition to his skill with numbers it was clear that the men looked up to him. Such natural ability was not to be wasted, and Dyson's report had favoured him well. The recent action had accounted for a good number of petty officers, and the admiral had agreed to rate him as quartermaster's mate, with a recommendation that he should be considered for further promotion.

And the lad, Jameson; he hardly seemed to have been on board ten minutes, but had grown tremendously. The adolescent stammer had gone, and the boy looked likely to make a solid and reliable hand, even a potential warrant officer. England would need men like him if the war were to continue any longer.

There was a commotion on the wharf; a group of women, doxies or wives, were shouting out to the men. Dyson was glad to see the boatswain's mates rear up to keep order. As he looked he caught sight of a pair of ladies standing apart from the mob. Both were dressed in black, and one he recognised as Shepherd's wife. Presumably she was here to see her late husband's ship home. Dyson inwardly nerved himself for the meeting that he already knew would be awkward. He was far from good when it came to speaking with women, and this would not be the easiest of circumstances.

"Rosie! Rosie!" His attention was called back to the waist by an outburst. Jenkins had broken free of his division, and was leaning over the bulwark, waving like a child at a woman who returned his greetings. A grinning boatswain's mate stepped forward to pull him back, but Jenkins brushed him aside.

"I lost your brooch!" he shouted, as the mate grabbed him once more, and began to drag him away.

"'Sall right," the girl shouted. "I knows where you are, an' I'll wait!"

The men in the waist were all smiling now, and Dyson found that he was doing the same. Admiral Nichols had spoken about the importance of stopping the French, how a fleet was rumoured to be building in the West Indies, and the ships they had captured would have strengthened it, possibly to the point where another invasion of England could have been attempted.

He didn't know about that, in the same way that he didn't know what his next posting would be, or when this war would end. But they were back, and there was at least one on the quay who was glad about it.

# THE JACKASS FRIGATE:

The afternoon was dark and cold, with a thin, but persistent, drizzle that had been constant since first light. Lewis stood next to the quartermaster, his woollen coat gaining weight as it steadily soaked up the rain while allowing just enough past the collar to make him thoroughly miserable. Beneath his feet *Pandora* moved with a steady, rhythmic motion, pressing through the leaden waves with little show of effort. The light, fitful wind came on her larboard quarter, and with topsails, forecourse and topgallants set, she was making reasonable progress; nothing more. Only occasionally would she hint at her true potential when a sudden blast of cold wet air pressed her hull down, chilling the men who had to stand her decks, and changing the regular hum of her lines to a scream that grated the nerves like a baby's cry. There were still several hours of supposed daylight left, yet the low blanket sky gave the impression of dusk. Lewis suppressed an involuntary shiver and rubbed his hands together while he told himself there had been plenty worse watches when he had been a lower deck man.

King strode aft, hands clasped behind his back in an effort to break the lifelong habit of thrusting them into his pockets. The toothache that had been bothering him on and off for the past day or so had gone for the moment, and he felt reasonably at ease. Lewis caught his eye, and the two exchanged a smile; it might be cold and wet, but to be on deck was a pleasant contrast to the oppressive, quarrelsome atmosphere that had become common below.

"We must be well clear of Ushant b'now," King said.

Lewis pointed back over his shoulder with his thumb.

"A few leagues astern. Plenty of room if the wind shifts."

"You think it will?"

"That or die completely. Glass is playin' strange japes."

*Pandora* had been making steady progress for the last few days, although all on board sensed she could have done better; certainly she had shown little of the dash expected of a frigate fresh from the dockyard. No single reason could be found for this; no fluke of wind had carried away a vital piece of equipment, no error of navigation set them dramatically off course. Any delay was subtle, and possibly more a question of not being fully up to scratch; the men, though experienced in the main, had yet to shake down together and learn to work as a team. The officers were equally uncertain how to get the best from her rig, and even the master was still deciding on the optimum layout of stores; one that allowed everything to be within reach, yet left a tidy ship with a serviceable trim. Pigot made his way on deck, barely acknowledging the pair. Of course there may have been other reasons for *Pandora's* lacklustre performance.

"Deck there! Sail ho! Sail on the starboard bow!"

All eyes turned aloft to where the masthead lookout was peering out across a dark heaving sea.

"What do you make there?" Pigot's voice, loud and demanding.

"Lost it now, sir. It were no more'n a glimpse."

The first lieutenant snorted with annoyance.

"Foremast, what have you?" There was a pause before the apologetic tones of the second lookout reported a clear sea. Pigot glared about the deck, his eyes naturally falling on the most able midshipman.

"You, King—get aloft to the main with a glass. Tell me what you see."

There was only one response acceptable when Pigot gave an order. King moved quickly, collecting the deck glass from the binnacle and strapping it across his back as he made for the main shrouds. He swung himself out with barely a thought, rapidly climbing the sodden ratlines, letting the tight weather shrouds run through his hands as he went. Up to the main top, hang back for the futtocks, then on to the main crosstrees. Here the ship's motion could be felt more readily, with every movement magnified by the height of the frigate's main mast. The lookout was from King's own division and he knew him to be trustworthy.

"What did you make, Wright?" he asked, as they clung to the mast.

"Nothing to be certain of, Mr King. Looked like a ship, a warship or a big Indiaman; mebbe a liner or frigate, couldn't be sure."

"Where away?"

Wright stretched out a hand. "Two points off the starboard bow. Headin' west nor-west, or so it seemed." He stopped, then added more guardedly, "Might have got a sight of sommat afore, sir; a few points off the larboard beam, but I couldn't be certain, like."

King nodded and peered out. The horizon to starboard was indistinct; small patches of fog were rolling with the wind, and there was a band of heavy weather slightly behind the point that Wright indicated.

"Reckon it's closing in," Wright said, as the midshipman swept the glass along the horizon. It was true, even in the brief time he had been aloft *Pandora's* motion had lessened; the main topgallant was just beginning to loosen, although the air still felt as cold.

"Nothing to see now." King tried hard to mask his feelings. It was the worst sighting possible, no more than a peep, and that just by one man. Wright's report might easily change the ship's course. An enemy warship—perhaps a squadron, maybe even a fleet—could be heading up towards the Channel. At that very moment *Pandora* might be the first line of defence against an invasion.

But then, of course, he could be mistaken; with the best of intentions Wright might have taken the combination of fast moving cloud and poor visibility and made it into a ship. Instances had been known of two or three men making the same certain sighting, only to find their supposed squadron was no more than scud and spindrift. *Pandora* might be off course for days investigating the mirage. Then the wind could shift; they could waste more time fighting to regain their original course, and all the while her mail would be delayed, and Jervis deprived of a valuable frigate.

Topgallant and topsails were flapping now as the wind died further, and King felt the pain in his tooth return. Wright pointed out to windward. "There's a fog comin' for us. An' a thick un, by the looks o' it." The midshipman glanced back across their quarter: sure enough the individual patches had spread into a dark grey wash that was rolling forward, eating up the horizon by the second.

He looked again, while Wright reported the fog to the deck below. Now there was something; a shape, nothing more, several points behind that which Wright had reported and almost abeam of *Pandora*. King felt the blood drain from his body as he raised his glass. Yes, that was definite. He nudged Wright, pointing at the break in the cloud. As he watched, the image detailed into a ship: a warship, hull up and a Frenchman, judging by her bow. There was also a trace, no more than that, of other sails. Not merely another vessel; two, maybe three, further forward. He held his breath, straining to make the misty shapes more distinct.

"Maintop, there—what d'ya see?"

It could have been his imagination, or did Wright stiffen slightly at the sound of Pigot's voice? The seaman's eyes were more accustomed to the work. He handed the glass across without a word; Wright took it and focused on the spot.

"What do you make of that?" King asked, after several seconds had dragged by. The seaman passed the glass back and shook his head sadly.

"Nuthin' I can see, sir."

King took the glass and raised it again; no, the cloud had thickened and now sat like a rug over his sighting. There was no ship in sight, certainly no squadron; that was assuming there ever had been to begin with.

"What do you see there?" Pigot's voice was edged with anger as it drifted up to them. King swallowed; here was a quandary. He could say nothing, he could stay safe; or he could report exactly what he had, or thought he had, seen. Report it and accept the consequences. If Banks believed him and altered course only to find him wrong he could kiss goodbye any hopes he might have of his commission being confirmed.

"Masthead, make your report!"

"Ship sighted to windward, sir; mebbe two or more," he shouted back, with barely a shake in his voice. "Headin' west nor-west."

King gave Wright a grim smile, while the seaman looked at him with renewed respect. Now he had really started something.

*****

The air in the great cabin could never have been called warm, and yet King's coat steamed liberally, while his damp nankin trousers (breeches were only for ceremony) cloyed about his legs making him long for a hot, dry towel, and his sore tooth ached like it was five times the size. Banks wore a heavy dressing coat over a baggy shirt and his feet were wrapped in old flannel carpet slippers, although his manner and poise remained very much that of a captain.

"For how long did you see this ship?"

King swallowed and repeated his story once more. Banks nodded. "What do you think, Mr Pigot?"

The first lieutenant appeared composed and thoughtful, very different from the man King had met on returning to the deck. "I've been in the same position m'self, sir. I know what it's like, expectin' to see somethin', and only half certain. Still, what Mr King says hardly constitutes a sightin'. I don't think we should take any action at present." Pigot smiled benignly at the midshipman, every bit the well meaning and supportive executive officer; King wondered how much Banks really knew about his second in command.

"Thank you, Mr Pigot. I feel Mr King is reasonably experienced, and there is also the matter of the lookout's earlier report."

Pigot stiffened. "May I remind you sir, that convoys from Lisbon and Quebec are at sea? Both are due about now, and both could be hereabouts."

"They could be in the area, certainly, but not heading west nor-west."

Pigot said nothing, although King could almost sense him begin to prickle as Banks continued.

"I had not intended to alter course, but I think this puts a different perspective on matters." He looked across to the tell-tale compass. "Take her two points to starboard, if you please; that way we should run into whatever it is Mr King has spotted. I could wish for a little more wind, but so be it."

King was prepared to go, but Pigot, it seemed, had other ideas.

"Forgive me, sir, but that will delay our arrival at Gibraltar, as well as our meeting with Admiral Jervis."

Bank's expression did not change, although his voice became marginally cooler. "That is so, Mr Pigot."

The first lieutenant opened his mouth, then closed it again. A late rendezvous would reflect as badly on him as the captain. "I was just concerned, sir," he said, eventually. "Concerned that we would be wasting our time."

King closed his eyes. Pigot was talking himself into a hole, and the midshipman already knew how any displeasure encountered from the captain would be paid back many times over on those whom Pigot would consider rightly to blame.

"Mr Pigot, I have made my decision, and I do not wish to discuss matters further." The atmosphere in the cabin had suddenly become distinctly unpleasant. "If there is nothing else, I will not keep you from your duties." There was nothing else, and the two turned to go. "Not you, Mr King, I'd like a word. Thank you, Mr Pigot."

King felt a pain in his breast that almost overtook that in his jaw. In one action he had caused the ship to alter course and fallen foul of Pigot. The latter would be seething from the interview with Banks, and the fact that King had been witness to the captain cutting him down to size and present when he was dismissed from the cabin would not make him any more popular. The door closed, and they both could hear Pigot's boots as he stamped out along the upper deck.

"Mr King, I recollect that you have passed your board but not been made, is that right?"

King said that it was.

"I have no need for another lieutenant in this ship, but I am aware of the risk you ran this afternoon. Many would have chosen the easier path and not reported the sighting. If you are proved in any way correct, I will be happy to speak for you."

"Thank you, sir." Banks was clearly influential; a word from him, or his supporters, would secure King's commission.

"Very good, you had better return to the deck now. I am sure the first lieutenant will appreciate every sharp eye." Was there just the flicker of humour in that face? It could be that Banks was not totally ignorant about Pigot, although King could not be sure. "And I do hope you are right," the captain added, as King left the cabin.

*****

The fog had reached the ship by the second dogwatch, a dense, evil mist that coated her every fibre. At times it was so thick as to hide the forecastle from the quarterdeck, with only the occasional break when an area of fifty, maybe a hundred feet would show clear, and the black night was allowed in to fill the temporary void.

As the watch wore on Caulfield stared vainly at the traverse board. There had been no change of course since that ordered by the captain, but the wind had also shifted several points, and their speed had altered, dropping to barely three knots despite the addition of jib and staysails. They could increase sail further, although creeping through the fog as they were, without any audible warning, was the very edge of folly. Caulfield looked up to where the main lookout would be settling in. The previous man had reported dense cover, and Caulfield guessed it was likely to remain so for the rest of the night. King appeared, compelled by the inescapable urge to be where the news would come first: to stand on deck, smell the fog, pace up and down, to hope; only to return below, as he had done for every half hour or so since Caulfield had taken the watch.

"You'll be on in no time," the lieutenant informed him, approaching out of the gloom. "Better get some rest while you can."

King shook his head. "I'd be happier out here, if that's agreeable, sir. The waitin's far worse below."

"Very well." Caulfield turned away; it was not the night for conversation, even if there had been anything to say. King might have been right in his sighting. Even now, an enemy force could be crossing their path, heading for the Channel and invasion. Colpoys' offshore squadron would miss them in this fog, as would the main force of Bridport's Channel fleet, currently sheltering in Spithead. They might be there, they could be within a mile of them at that very moment, but there was nothing he, nothing anyone on board *Pandora*, could do while this darned fog persisted.

Flint was on watch, along with Lawlor and Jameson. The three were sheltering in the lee of the larboard gangway. No action had been called for from them for several hours and they were cold, their kerseymere jackets wrapped tight about them and woollen caps pulled down over their ears.

In the cockpit Lewis was looking at his glass, peering at the gauge in the dubious light. The reading was low, very low, with barely a flicker of movement since that afternoon. The tension had eased slightly since King went on deck, but there was still an aura of hushed expectancy that filled the entire ship. Lewis shivered suddenly, rubbing his hands against his forearms to warm himself as he moved back and sat down at the table. In front of him was the cold and fast congealing portion of lobscouse that Collins had served over an hour ago. He looked at it with surprise, then picked up his fork to annoy it for a moment or two, before sitting back in his chair. There was a Guernsey on top of his chest, fine knitted from heavy wool, and just waiting to be put on. He leaned forward, still shivering, grasped it and pulled it over his head, stretching the tight garment around his body. The rich smell of lanolin came out to greet him, and he gratefully pressed his arms into the sleeves. He knew that in a few moments he would start to grow warm, even though it now seemed the Guernsey was merely trapping his damp shirt against him. He shivered again, considered turning back to his food, dismissed the notion, and pulled off the Guernsey, before getting up to study his glass.

In the great cabin, Banks had supped sparsely and alone, and now lay, fully clothed but without his jacket, on the upholstered stern lockers. His eyes were closed, his breathing deep and regular, although he remained wide awake and ready to move at a moment's notice. On a clear night it would have been relatively easy to miss another ship, even a whole squadron, if they were properly darkened. With this fog it would be strange, no, a miracle, if anything was spotted, and yet still he remained alert, still ready for the call.

Stuart, the surgeon, had heard of the supposed sighting but gave it little consideration. The ship, so recently fresh from port, was healthy, and until anything came along to cause him a nuisance he was content to allow illness and injuries to appear in the normal way. Certainly there was little enough for him to do; the amount of preventative medicine available to him was too small to consider. He had the standing orders from the physician of the fleet, and his medicine chest and tools were in order; Manning, his mate, had seen to that. Some might spend this time of relative leisure in reading, but Stuart had no intention of improving or even changing his mind. New techniques might have been developed, but in the end the human body remained the same. In his youth he had attempted several surgical operations, some with reasonable success, but now he had no desire to open a body that had not already been penetrated by injury. He could remove a man's leg in four minutes, far less if it was a lad and the saw sharp. He could tell a case of scurvy, and identify most of the more common types of shipboard ailment. He was especially good with venereal disease; few were novel to him, and most could be, if not cured, then at least slowed long enough to allow the sufferer to pay the regulation fifteen shillings for his trouble.

He walked into the cubical partitioned off from the gunroom that was his berth. On the spirketing next to his head the carpenter had erected a small shelf for him to keep a few personal possessions. It was to this shelf that he reached now, and removed a large blue bottle. Laudanum, the alcoholic tincture of opium, was one of his more powerful tools, one of the few drugs that actually made an impression on his patients, although Stuart was in no way deceived by its healing powers. Still, for a bored and indolent man it was exactly the right prescription, and he added a generous measure to the half-filled wine glass that he had taken from the gunroom. This would give him just the right amount of comfort to see him through a cold night. He drained the glass, feeling the warmth of the drug run pleasantly throughout his body, before filling it once more. From somewhere far, far away he heard the tolling of *Pandora's* bell as it marked the half hour; but Stuart was no longer concerned with the ship's routine, or even time itself. He drank the neat dose, and fell heavily against his cot, gripping the sides and swinging himself in with practiced ease. Within seconds he was snoring heavily, lost to the ship, the world, and anyone who might need him.

Back on the quarterdeck the tension persisted.

"No ships yet, Mr King?"

It was Pigot. Presumably the waiting had affected him as well, and he was reacting in the only way he knew. "No fleet of invading Frenchmen, ready to burn our homes and cut up our wives and sweethearts?"

"No, sir." It was the safest reply.

"I suppose you'll ask the captain for a change of course shortly?" Say, we must 'ave missed 'em on our first pass, time to go back for another?"

"No, sir." King swallowed. He was on duty shortly, and Pigot would be the officer of the watch. Just his luck to run into him now, a good hour before he was officially due on deck.

"I'd send you aloft, young man," Pigot continued in a conversational tone. "Send you aloft; masthead you for the rest of the night, but I fear for what we might run in to. Mebbe a school of fightin' whales, hell bent on takin' the ship an' sailin' her to China? Who can tell?"

He was going to evoke the first lieutenant's wrath whatever happened; so when the next glass was turned, and Pigot became distracted by the casting of the log, King did go aloft.

He took a slow passage; the ratlines were thoroughly soaked and slipped beneath his feet, and he was in no rush to reach the masthead. Once there, however, he found the situation was starting to change.

"Mist's fadin', Mr King," Lawlor, the Welshman, informed him. "Not clear 'nuff to report, but I gets a proper view everso often. Give it a couple of moments and we'll be fair."

King nodded, and together they stood looking out into the blank mist.

Then, as Lawlor had predicted, it lifted. Lifted, but only for them, only for those many feet above the soft waves. The light from the half moon began to break through, and then they were in clear air. Clear air, over a bed of cloud, a bed that sat barely eight feet below their position. They could look out for several miles in every direction. It was a strange experience to be many feet above the deck, and yet apparently safe over a dense floor of solid mist. King looked about as Lawlor reported the situation to the expectant deck below. No sign of topmasts, no break in the solid rind of cloud. There was an empty ocean, and *Pandora* was in the middle of it.

"Bad luck, sir," Lawlor muttered.

King smiled grimly as his toothache returned to pester him once more. Now he really would be for it.

\*\*\*\*\*

The boy Rose tapped at the door, and Banks' eyes opened instantly.

"Mr Caulfield's duty, sir, an' the masthead's clear of the fog."

"Anything in sight?" It was an obvious question, but one he had to ask.

"No, sir."

"Very good." He closed his eyes again as Rose left. So that was it, a wild goose chase. King had either been wrong, mistaken, or just plain unlucky; whatever, they had ventured off course and far deeper into the fog than was necessary. They should turn back right away. Now that the threat was gone he realised just how tense he had been. For a moment he considered staying as he was, maybe dozing for a moment. It was a feeling that had become rather common of late; possibly the onset of old age. That was the exactly the right thought to stir him into action, and he sprang to his feet and made for the quarterdeck, the very essence of youth and vitality.

*****

"A fleet, he says. An invasion fleet!" Pigot's voice was low, but dangerous. "Saw a bunch of liners, did yer?" The face was barely inches from King's and his breath warred horribly with the clean, cold night air. "Took us on a right little rainbow hunt, didn't you, my lad? Well, I'll tell you what! I'll tell you what you can look forward to once the watch is called." He turned away and caught the eye of Rose, who was acting as the midshipman of the watch and sheltering unhappily by the binnacle.

"Pass the word for Mr Smith," he said loudly. Smith, the gunner, was the officer traditionally responsible for discipline amongst the midshipmen; although King, with his age and experience, had not had to face such a situation in years. Pigot turned to King, an evil expression on his face. "I'll show you the correct punishment for barefaced cheek."

Smith made his appearance fully dressed; only his eyes, still bleary with sleep, showed that he had been roused from his hammock.

"Mr Smith, Mr King here wishes to become intimate with your daughter." To kiss the gunner's daughter was the euphemism given to that particularly humiliating punishment which Rose had experienced so recently.

"Mr King, sir?" Smith was not so wide awake as to accept Pigot's suggestion without question. "But 'e's a lieutenant, sir, near as can be!"

"Mr Smith, you will do your duty!" Pigot's voice rose unnaturally in the still night. Smith stood uncertainly for a second, before his eyes became fixed on someone approaching from behind.

"One moment, Mr Pigot, if you please." King drew a breath, hearing the captain's voice. "I think we will discuss this matter in my cabin." It would be wrong to countermand Pigot's order in public, although Banks had no intention of allowing King to suffer any form of punishment, simply for doing his duty.

For several seconds the lieutenant remained staring at King before the spell broke.

"Yes, sir." Pigot's voice was sulky, and he turned toå follow Banks toward the companionway with a look of thunder on his face.

"Very good, Mr Smith, you may go below." Caulfield, this time. He gave King a sympathetic smile. "It might have been better for you if the captain hadn't turned up," he said, softly. "When that bastard gets back he'll want more than just blood."

King's eyes fell. Caulfield was right; he could not rely on the captain's protection forever. In his elevated position Banks would always be unaware of the subtle unpleasantries that Pigot could inflict at will. And Pigot was no fool; he had eyes, and knew exactly when it was safe to use a rope's end on the men, unheard of for a commissioned officer. He knew just how many beatings and mastheadings he could inflict on the midshipmen, without arousing comment; how often he could have the same man flogged and it be ignored. There were many stories of one unpopular officer wrecked the lives of many. King had even known an oldster midshipman who swore he had been passed over for treading on the port admiral's dog. But this was real, and happening to him. The captain's words about having his commission confirmed came back to mock; there would be little likelihood of that once Pigot got his teeth into him. Any lieutenant had the power to make a mere midshipman appear incompetent; a first lieutenant could do it without leaving his cot.

"You'll be on duty in less than half a glass; get something hot inside you." Caulfield again, speaking sense and giving more than advice, although there was little he could actually do to ease the situation. King turned to go below, when a voice cut into his thoughts.

"Sail ho! Two points off the larboard bow!"

Caulfield waited while the report was repeated, then, "What do you see there?"

"Topmasts; two ships, no, three. Tops'ls set. One looks to be a liner, headin' west nor-west."

Topsails, in this weather, hardly likely to be Indiamen. Caulfield smiled at the midshipman. "Mr King," he said, as the ship erupted to the call of all hands, "I think we might have found your squadron."

# CONTINUED IN
# THE JACKASS FRIGATE

# GLOSSARY

Able Seaman—One who can hand, reef and steer and is well acquainted with the duties of a seaman.

Back—Wind change; anti-clockwise.

Backed sail—One set in the direction for the opposite tack to slow a ship.

Backstays—Similar to shrouds in function, except that they run from the hounds of the topmast, or topgallant, all the way to the deck. Serve to support the mast against any forces forward; for example, when the ship is tacking. (Also a useful/spectacular way to return to deck for a topman.)

Backstays, running—A less permanent backstay, rigged with a tackle to allow it to be slacked to clear a gaff or boom.

Barkie—*(Slang)* Seamen's affectionate name for their vessel.

Belaying pins—Pins set into racks at the side of a ship. Lines are secured to these, allowing instant release by their removal.

Becket—A hook or loop of rope for securing items.

Bilboes—Leg irons used to confine prisoners.

Binnacle—Cabinet on the quarterdeck that houses compasses, the deck log, traverse board, lead lines, telescope, speaking trumpet, *etc.*

Bitts—Stout horizontal pieces of timber, supported by strong verticals, that extend deep into the ship. These hold the anchor cable when the ship is at anchor.

Blab—*(Slang)* A gossip.

Block—Article of rigging that allows pressure to be diverted or, when used with others, increased. Consists of a pulley wheel, made of *lignum vitae*, encased in a wooden shell. Blocks can be single, double (fiddle block), triple or quadruple. The main suppliers were Taylors, of Southampton.

Board—Before being promoted to lieutenant, midshipmen would be tested for competence by a board of post captains. Should they prove able they will be known as passed midshipmen, but not assume the rank of lieutenant until they are appointed as such.

Boat fall—Line that raises or lowers a ship's boat.

Boatswain—*(Pronounced Bosun)* The warrant officer superintending sails, rigging, canvas, colours, anchors, cables and cordage *etc.*, committed to his charge.

Boom—Lower spar to which the bottom of a gaff sail is attached.

Braces—Lines used to adjust the angle between the yards, and the fore and aft line of the ship. Mizzen braces, and braces of a brig lead forward.

Brig—Two-masted vessel, square-rigged on both masts.

Broach—When running down-wind, to round up into the wind, out of control, usually due to carrying too much canvas.

Bulkhead—A wall or partition within the hull of a ship.

Bulwark—The planking or wood-work about a vessel above her deck.

Canister—Type of shot, also known as case. Small iron balls packed into a cylindrical case.

Carronade—Short cannon firing a heavy shot. Invented by Melville, Gascoigne and Miller in late 1770's and adopted in 1779. Often used on the upper deck of larger ships, or as the main armament of smaller.

Cascabel—Part of the breach of a cannon.

Cat's Paws—*(Slang)* Regular ripples on water that indicate a wind or breeze.

Caulk—*(Slang)* To sleep. Also caulking, a process to seal the seams between strakes.

Chamber lye—Urine, used, often with ashes, to wash clothes.

Channel—Projecting ledge that holds deadeyes from shrouds and backstays, originally chain-whales.

Chit—*(Slang)* An infant or baby.

Cleat—A retaining piece for lines attached to yards, *etc.*

Cock a Bill—Describes the intentionally tilted yards of a ship in mourning.

Close hauled—Sailing as near as possible into the wind.

Coaming—A ridged frame about hatches to prevent water on deck from getting below.

Cock-a-bill— or cock bill, or scandalised—The setting of yards intentionally askew to signify the ship in mourning

Companionway—A staircase or passageway.

Counter—The lower part of a vessel's stern.

Course—A large square lower sail, hung from a yard, with sheets controlling and securing it.

Crimp—*(Slang)* One who sells a man to the impressment service.

Crown and Anchor—Naval board game.

Crows of iron—Crow bars used to move a gun or heavy object.

Cutter—Fast, small, single-masted vessel with a sloop rig. Also a seaworthy ship's boat.

Deadeyes—A round, flattish wooden block with three holes through which a lanyard is reeved. Used to tension shrouds and backstays.

Ditty bag—*(Slang)* A seaman's bag. Derives its name from the dittis or 'Manchester stuff' of which it was once made.

Dollond—Premier makers of optical instruments, telescopes, sextants, etc.

Driver—Large sail set on the mizzen in light winds. The foot is extended by means of a boom.

Dunnage—Officially the packaging around cargo. Also *(slang)* seaman's baggage or possessions.

Diachylon plaster—An early form of sticking plaster.

Fall—The free end of a lifting tackle on which the men haul.

Fetch—To arrive at, or reach a destination. Also the distance the wind blows across the water. The longer the fetch the bigger the waves.

Fleet (Prison)—Notable prison in London, first built in 1197. Note, civil prisons were normally used to house those awaiting trial, the repayment of debt, transportation, or execution, not as a punishment in themselves.

Forereach—To gain upon, or pass by another ship when sailing in a similar direction.

Forestay—Stay supporting the masts running forward, serving the opposite function of the backstay. Runs from each mast at an angle of about 45 degrees to meet another mast, the deck or the bowsprit.

Free trader—Popular euphemism for a smuggler.

Glass—Telescope. Also, hourglass: an instrument for measuring time (and hence, as slang, a period of time). Also a barometer.

Guffies—*(Slang)* Marine (one term of many).

Go-about—To alter course, changing from one tack to the other.

Grappling-iron—Small anchor, fitted with four or five flukes or claws, often used to hold two ships together for boarding.

Halyards—Lines which raise yards, sails, signals *etc.*

Hanger—A fighting sword, similar to a cutlass.

Hawse—Area in bows where holes are cut to allow the anchor cables to pass through. Also used as general term for bows.

Hawser—Heavy cable used for hauling, towing or mooring.

Headway—The amount a vessel is moved forward (rather than leeway: the amount a vessel is moved sideways) when the wind is not directly behind.

Heave to—Keeping a ship relatively stationary by backing certain sails in a seaway.

HEIC—Honourable East India Company.

Holystone—*(Slang)* Block of sandstone roughly the size and shape of a family Bible. Used to clean and smooth decks. Originally salvaged from the ruins of a church on the Isle of Wright.

Hoxton—The Royal Navy's own mental hospital. Men were seven times more likely to go mad in the RN than on land.

Hulled—Said of a ship that, when fired upon, the shot passes through the hull.

Interest—Backing from a superior officer or one in authority, useful when looking for promotion.

Jape—*(Slang)* Joke.

Jib-boom—Boom run out from the extremity of the bowsprit, braced by means of a martingale stay, which passes through the dolphin striker.

Jibe—To change tack with the wind coming from astern. Also to wear, a term more commonly used in square-rigged vessels.

Jigger—*(Slang)* Mizzen mast.

John Company—*(Slang)* The East India Company.

Junk—Old line used to make wads, etc.

Jury mast/rig—Temporary measure used to restore a vessel's sailing ability.

Kerseymere—Woolen cloth.

Landsman—The rating of one who has no experience at sea.

Lanthorn—Lantern.

Larboard—Left side of the ship when facing forward. Later replaced by 'port', which had previously been used for helm orders.

Leeward—The downwind side of a vessel.

Leeway—The amount a vessel is pushed sideways by the wind (as opposed to headway, the forward movement, when the wind is directly behind).

Linstock—The holder of slow match which the gun captain uses to fire his piece when the gunlock is not working/present.

Lubberly/lubber—*(Slang)* Unseamanlike behaviour; as a landsman.

Luff—Intentionally sail closer to the wind, perhaps to allow work aloft. Also the flapping of sails when brought too close to the wind. The side of a fore and aft sail laced to the mast.

Main tack—Line leading forward from a sheave in the hull, allowing the clew of the main course to be held forward when the ship is sailing close to the wind.

Martingale stay—Line that braces the jib-boom, passing from the end through the dolphin striker to the ship.

Peach—*(Slang)* To betray or reveal; from impeach.

Pipe—Cask holding 105 gallons.

Pipeclay—Compound used by marines to polish and whiten their leatherwork.

Pledget—A wad of tow, or cotton waste, used to seal a wound.

Pox—*(Slang)* Venereal disease.

Prigger—*(Slang)* A criminal, usually a thief.

Pin—Cask holding four and a half gallons.

Privateer—Privately owned vessel fitted out as a warship, and licensed to capture enemy vessels. The licence allows a greater number of guns to be fitted than would be allowed in a civilian vessel..

Protection—A legal document that gives the owner protection against impressment.

Quarterdeck—In larger ships the deck forward of the poop, but at a lower level. The preserve of officers.

Queue—A pigtail. Often tied by a seaman's best friend (his tie mate).

Ratlines—Lighter lines, untarred and tied horizontally across the shrouds at regular intervals, to act as rungs and allow men to climb aloft.

Reef—A portion of sail that can be taken in to reduce the size of the whole.

Reefing points—Light line on large sails, which can be tied up to reduce the sail area in heavy weather.

Reefing tackle—Line that leads from the end of the yard to the reefing cringles set in the edges of the sail. It is used to haul up the upper part of the sail when reefing.

Rigging—Tophamper; made up of standing (static) and running (moveable) rigging, blocks etc. Also *(slang)* Clothes.

Rondey—*(Slang)* The *Rendezvous*: where a press is based and organised.

Running—Sailing before the wind.

Schooner—Small craft with two masts.

Scran—(Slang) Food.

Scupper—Waterway that allows deck drainage.

Sheet—A line that controls the foot of a sail.

Shrouds—Lines supporting the masts athwart ship (from side to side) which run from the hounds (just below the top) to the channels on the side of the hull.

Snow—Type of brig, with an extra trysail mast stepped behind the main.

Spring—Hawser attached to a fixed object that can be tensioned to move the position of a ship fore and aft along a dock, often when setting out to sea. Breast lines control position perpendicular to the dock.

Sprit sail—A square sail hung from the bowsprit yards, less used by 1793 as the function had been taken over by the jibs although the rigging of their yards helps to brace the bowsprit against sideways pressure.

Squealer—*(Slang)* Youngster.

Stay sail—A quadrilateral or triangular sail with parallel lines, usually hung from under a stay.

Stern sheets—Part of a ship's boat between the stern and the first rowing thwart, used for passengers.

Stingo—*(Slang)* Beer.

Strake—A plank.

Tack—To turn a ship, moving her bows through the wind. Also a leg of a journey relating to the direction of the wind. If from starboard, a ship is on the starboard tack. Also the part of a fore and aft loose-footed sail where the sheet is attached, or a line leading forward on a square course to hold the lower part of the sail forward.

Taffrail—Rail around the stern of a vessel.

Tattletale—*(Slang)* Gossip.

Tight ship—In good order: watertight.

Tophamper—Literally any weight either on a ship's decks or about her tops and rigging, but often used loosely to refer to spars and rigging.

Trick—*(Slang)* Period of duty.

Turnpike—A toll road; the user pays for the upkeep. Usually major roads.

Veer—Wind change, clockwise.

Waist—Area of main deck between the quarterdeck and forecastle.

Watch—Period of four (or in case of dog watch, two) hour duty. Also describes the two or three divisions of a crew.

Watch list—List of men and stations, usually carried by lieutenants and divisional officers.

# HIS MAJESTY'S SHIP

Wearing—To change the direction of a square rigged ship
across the wind by putting its stern through the eye of the
wind. Also jibe—more common in a fore and aft rig.

Windward—The side of a ship exposed to the wind.

# ABOUT THE AUTHOR
## ALARIC BOND

THE FIGHTING SAILS:

HIS MAJESTY'S SHIP
THE JACKASS FRIGATE
TRUE COLOURS
CUT AND RUN
THE PATRIOT'S FATE

Alaric Bond was born in Surrey, and now lives in Herstmonceux, East Sussex. Bond has been writing professionally for over twenty years with work covering broadcast comedy (commissioned to BBC Light Entertainment for 3 years), periodicals, children's stories, television and the stage.

Bond now divides his time between writing and helping his wife run "Scolfe's", a traditional English Restaurant and Tea Room, housed in their 14th century Wealden Hall House home.

Other interests include the British Navy 1793-1815 and the RNVR during WW2. Bond regularly gives talks to groups and organizations, and is a member of various historical societies. He is a keen collector of old or unusual musical instruments, and of 78 rpm records. Bond also enjoys sailing, classic cars, Jazz, swing and big-band music, and badgers.

# THE PATRIOT'S FATE
## BY
### ALARIC BOND

"In his new novel, The Patriot's Fate, Alaric Bond joins the ranks of well-known Age of Sail authors C.S. Forester and Patrick O'Brien in his skillful combining of historical fact with compelling fiction to produce another gripping novel in his Fighting Sail series.

It is 1798 and Ireland rises up against years of repression and injustice. Rebels, supported by a mighty French invasion fleet, prepare to claim their land but find themselves countered by a powerful British battle squadron. Two friends and former allies, separated by chance and circumstance, witness developments from opposing sides while storms, political intrigue and personal dynamics abound. In The Patriot's Fate Bond maintains a relentless pace that climaxes in thrilling naval action and noble sacrifice."

*Fireship Press*
www.FireshipPress.com

WWW.FIRESHIPPRESS.COM
HISTORICAL FICTION AND NONFICTION
PAPERBACK AVAILABLE FOR ORDER ON
LINE
AND AS EBOOK WITH ALL MAJOR
DISTRIBUTERS

# Other fine Napoleonic Era books from FIRESHIP PRESS

# IF YOU WANT TO LEARN MORE ABOUT THIS FASCINATING PERIOD IN BRITISH HISTORY

# *DON'T MISS...*

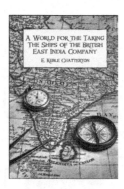

## *A WORLD FOR THE TAKING:*
### *The Ships of the Honourable East India Company*
### *by E. Keble Chatterton*

It was a time when one of the most powerful rulers in the world wasn't a government—it was a corporation.

It's official name was "The Company of Merchants of London Trading into the East Indies." Some simply called it "John Company," others "Company Bahadur." But most people knew it as the Honourable East India Company.

It was the first major shareholder-owned business enterprise. At its height it ruled more than a fifth of the world's population, and generated a revenue greater than the rest of Britain combined— including the government. To hold all this together it had it's own private army and navy consisting of over a quarter million men.

But at it's heart, it was still a "company of merchants" and it was her merchant ships that made everything else possible.

This is E. Keble Chatterton's authoritative account of those ships and the men who helped forge the history of two continents.

### With 32 ILLUSTRATIONS

# The Perfect Wreck
## Steven E. Maffeo

## "OLD IRONSIDES" AND HMS JAVA
## A STORY OF 1812

*A highly recommended must-read for every naval enthusiast—indeed, for every American!*

**Stephen Coonts**
*NY Times* best-selling author

HMS *Java* and the USS *Constitution* (the famous "Old Ironsides") face off in the War of 1812's most spectacular blue-water frigate action. Their separate stories begin in August 1812—one in England and the other in New England. Then, the tension and suspense rise, week-by-week, as the ships cruise the Atlantic, slowly and inevitably coming together for the final life-and-death climax.

*The Perfect Wreck* is not only the first full-length book ever written about the battle between the USS *Constitution* and HMS *Java*, it is a gem of Creative Nonfiction. It has the exhaustive research of a scholarly history book; but it is beautifully presented in the form of a novel.

## WWW.FIRESHIPPRESS.COM
## *Interesting • Informative • Authoritative*

## For the Finest in Nautical and Historical Fiction and Nonfiction

# WWW.FIRESHIPPRESS.COM

## Interesting • Informative • Authoritative

CPSIA information can be obtained at www.ICGtesting.com
Printed in the USA
BVOW11s0250171115

427022BV00008B/145/P